Select Praise for

Jerome Charyn

"Jerome Charyn, like Nabokov, is that most fiendish sort of writer—so seductive as to beg imitation, so singular as to make imitation impossible." —**Tom Bissell**

"Charyn is one of the most important writers in American literature." —**Michael Chabon**

"Charyn is a one off: no other living American writer crafts novels with his vibrancy of historical imagination." —**William Giraldi**

"One of our most rewarding novelists."
—**Larry McMurtry**

"No one writes historical fiction better than Jerome Charyn." —**Brenda Wineapple**

"Charyn skillfully breathes life into historical icons." —***New Yorker***

"One of our most intriguing fiction writers."
—***O, The Oprah Magazine***

"Charyn's blunt, brilliantly crafted prose bubbles with the pleasure of nailing life to the page in just the right words." —***Washington Post***

"[Charyn's] storytelling is off-the-chart wonderful." —***Jerusalem Post***

"Absolutely unique among American writers." —***Los Angeles Times***

"A contemporary American Balzac." —***Newsday***

"[Charyn] writes with the sort of whirlwind energy that turns the seediest story into a breakneck adventure." —***Wall Street Journal***

"Charyn has a gift for the unexpected, both linguistically and narratively. . . . The result is at once surprising and very entertaining." —***BookPage***

"For half a century, [Charyn] has been an unpredictable, unclassifiable, and above all exactingly smart author." —***Open Letters Review***

"Charyn is an institution. . . . His skill is such that it's difficult to separate the real-world figures and entities from the characters and places the author is inventing." —***Washington Independent Review of Books***

"Wherever he takes us, Charyn's mind is always agile, and his prose is stunningly electric." —**Jewish Book Council**

Maria La Divina

Also by

Jerome Charyn

from Bellevue Literary Press

Ravage & Son

Sergeant Salinger: A Novel

Cesare: A Novel of War-Torn Berlin

In the Shadow of King Saul: Essays on Silence and Song

Jerzy: A Novel

A Loaded Gun: Emily Dickinson for the 21st Century

Maria La Divina

JEROME CHARYN

Bellevue Literary Press
New York

First published in the United States in 2025
by Bellevue Literary Press, New York

For information, contact:
Bellevue Literary Press
90 Broad Street
Suite 2100
New York, NY 10004
www.blpress.org

This is a work of fiction. Characters, organizations, events, and places (even those that are actual) are either products of the author's imagination or are used fictitiously.

Library of Congress Cataloging-in-Publication Data
Names: Charyn, Jerome, author.
Title: Maria La Divina / Jerome Charyn.
Description: First edition. | New York : Bellevue Literary Press, 2025.
Identifiers: LCCN 2025006990 | ISBN 9781954276482 (paperback ; acid-free paper) | ISBN 9781954276499 (ebook)
Subjects: LCSH: Callas, Maria, 1923-1977--Fiction. | Sopranos (Singers)--Fiction. | LCGFT: Biographical fiction. | Novels.
Classification: LCC PS3553.H33 M36 2025 | DDC 813/.54--dc23/eng/20250214
LC record available at https://lccn.loc.gov/2025006990

Bellevue Literary Press would like to thank all its generous donors—individuals and foundations—for their support.

Book design and composition by Mulberry Tree Press, Inc.

Bellevue Literary Press is committed to ecological stewardship in our book production practices, working to reduce our impact on the natural environment.

NEW YORK STATE OF OPPORTUNITY. | Council on the Arts

This publication is made possible by the New York State Council on the Arts with the support of the Office of the Governor and the New York State Legislature.

∞ This book is printed on acid-free paper.

Manufactured in the United States of America.

First Edition

10 9 8 7 6 5 4 3 2 1

paperback ISBN: 978-1-954276-48-2

ebook ISBN: 978-1-954276-49-9

Our songs will all be silenced, but what of it?
Go on singing.

—Orson Welles

Contents

CHAPTER ONE: The Lone Canary 13

CHAPTER TWO: The King of Verona 83

CHAPTER THREE: A Dangerous Diva 125

CHAPTER FOUR: Dumpy and Anna Bolena 182

CHAPTER FIVE: Enter Aristotle 194

CHAPTER SIX: The Second Soprano 231

CHAPTER SEVEN: La Divina 291

Maria La Divina

ONE

The Lone Canary

-1-

Profesora, Profesora, Profesora!"

Elvira de Hidalgo was bored to death. It was stifling in the audition room; the porter had forgotten to close the shutters, and the room was flooded with bitter, blinding sunlight and hot wind from the mountains. Elvira had to remove the summer cape she'd once worn in *Il barbiere di Siviglia*. This stranded diva, who had sung with Chaliapin and Caruso, was stuck at the Athens Conservatory, a teacher of students without a crisp of talent. The intruders sat on a long bench with their mothers and aunts, jabbering and calling out to her like a flock of sick canaries, *"Profesora, Profesora!"*

She cursed under her breath and then assumed her stage mask. "Please," she said. "A little patience. I do not have a dozen ears. I can only deal with one student at a time." And the canaries stopped their horrid chirp. Elvira was practically fluent in Greek. She'd arrived in Athens several years ago, with a traveling troupe from Bilbao, but the troupe disbanded within weeks. And this veteran of La Scala, a coloratura soprano, who began losing the upper registers of her voice by the time she was thirty, decided to remain right where she was.

Elvira stood next to the accompanist's piano and noticed a stout girl sitting all by herself on the bench, removed from the other applicants, as if she wanted to hide. The girl had no discernible shape other than a pair of slouching shoulders, and she wore thick glasses and battered sandals. She had a long nose, a large mouth, and a barrage of pimples that seemed to scar her face. It was laughable, ridiculous, that this pasty, half-blind girl in an ill-fitting smock should waste Elvira's precious time with the fantasy of becoming a fledgling soprano. The girl kept biting her nails as she sat there, revealing a glimpse of her swollen ankles.

Elvira went through the canaries, one by one, dismissing them all and sending them home with their mothers and aunts, who kissed her hand, curtsied, and said, "Thank you, *Profesora*" in a very musical Greek. And then Elvira came to the stout girl in the corner, who took off her thick glasses and wiped the sweat from her forehead with a handkerchief that had as many furrows as the Greek flag. She had the deepest eyes Elvira had ever seen—dark and dead—while her mother had flaring blue eyes and bleached blond hair. These poor, listless girls always seemed to have mothers with the manic energy of a firecracker.

"Child," Elvira said, "stop biting your nails. . . . What is your name?"

"Maria," her mother said, "Maria Kalogeropoulos."

Elvira looked at the girl's application form. She was born in America, had come to Athens at the age of thirteen, and had studied these past two years at the National Conservatory with Madame Trivella—an amateur, with her precious prodigies. Madame Trivella had never sung at La Scala, had never sung anywhere. And yet she taught the half-forgotten art of bel canto—the art of embellishment coupled with the finest phrasing—to these prodigies who graduated from Madame Trivella's séances, got married within a month, and practiced arpeggios while they shopped at Plaka Market. That was the beginning and end of their careers.

"Child," Elvira said in the slightly mannered English she had picked up while performing at Covent Garden, "did Trivella invite you here?"

"No," Maria said without looking at Elvira. "She cannot teach me bel canto, and I cannot master it on my own."

Elvira smiled beneath her stage mask. "Bel canto was lost a long time ago. But why did you ever leave New York? You could have had some of the best teachers in the world."

"*Profesora,*" the girl's mother said, wiping her brow with the back of her hand, "my Maria wanted to study with you."

Elvira ignored this blue-eyed pest. "Madame, I cannot audition her with people in the room."

The haughty blonde rebelled. "But you did not banish the other mothers, *Profesora.*"

"Still, you will distract your daughter, throw her off-key. You must go."

Elvira had the porter escort Maria's mother out of the audition room, while Maria rose off the bench with a furtive look as she handed the accompanist the aria she intended to sing from *Oberon,* an opera about a mischievous company of elves and the bedlam they bring to Baghdad. Now Elvira smiled with a bit of malice. She knew the girl would fall flat. The aria was too complex for a fifteen-year-old girl. It is sung by Rezia, the luscious daughter of the caliph of Baghdad, and this duckling from the "Bronx" could hardly inherit a princess's voice or aristocratic manner. She stood there in her sandals and swayed like some molten creature.

Maria's eyes widened as she broke into song, while the soprano from Bilbao suddenly started to shiver at the melody this strange girl could summon from the very first notes. The voice was rich, deep with emotion that a fifteen-year-old shouldn't have been able to capture. Elvira was shaken, enthralled. She lost control, started to cry. This duckling with the bad eyes and botched skin moved her arms like a princess, and her once vacant eyes flashed with fury. The bitten nails meant nothing. Elvira saw a startling, beautiful girl.

She wouldn't let Maria finish the aria. She could not bear the rough enchantment of her roulades, the way Maria could stretch and magnify a note.

"Stop, please. I beg you."

Now it was Maria who started to cry. "*Profesora,* did I disappoint you?"

"Child, you'll ruin your voice with such roulades. You're much too young."

Fifteen or not, she accepted Maria on a full scholarship. "Classes start in a week, and please don't have your mother pester me."

"But *Profesora,*" Maria said in that "Bronx" accent—an accent that utterly vanished when she sang. Maria understood with the clarity of a witch what syllables to emphasize and what syllables to drop in each musical phrase. "It was my mother who sent me to your conservatory. I wouldn't have had the courage without her."

"But she is not my pupil, child. You are. You will be here every morning at ten when the term starts. And you are not to practice roulades until I tell you."

Elvira couldn't say why, but she kissed this magnificent brute of a child on the cheek as she would have kissed a comrade of hers, another soprano at La Scala, when she, Elvira, still had a voice and was adored; she would promenade in the tunnels under La Scala after her final aria as the rich young beauty Rosina in *Il barbiere*; she'd enter a private door of Biffi Scala with her painted cheeks and sit at the center table of La Scala's own bistro as opera buffs knelt at her table and asked her to sign their autograph books . . .

Maria looked down and kneaded her fine, expressive hands, alive with sweat. "*Profesora,* my mother will want to come with me to every class."

"No," the diva said. "I cannot teach under such conditions. You will have to tell her, child. Mothers are forbidden." They were the wreckers of a girl's career, ruinous and willful.

Maria bit her nails. "She will not believe me, *Profesora.* She will insist."

"Then I will have the rector write her a letter with the conservatory's seal. . . . And I told you. Stop biting your nails."

The girl hesitated for a moment. Elvira began to notice little things. Maria had a feistiness under her mulish look. "Mother will convince the rector. She knows how to seduce."

Elvira removed her stage mask. "Child, she will not win. Now go home. And don't practice your roulades without me."

Maria left, like a hulking ghost. Elvira could not console her. She would train this girl, teach her how to dance, how to move, how to sing. Elvira's sojourn in Athens began to make sense. She'd arrived like a fugitive, a member of a company that unraveled so fast, it could have been a figment of her imagination. She found a maid's room in a firetrap not far from Constitution Square. She had to grovel for a living, with a student here, a student there, until the rector at the Athens Conservatory realized that Elvira de Hidalgo had almost plummeted into his lap. He'd seen her at La Scala, had been one of her admirers, had left a bouquet of roses outside her dressing room, and now he invited her to join the faculty.

She moved into a stone building near the Royal Garden and the Little Royal Palace, where George II, the puppet king, lived in his own internal exile. King George was always coming into power and was always being forced out. He'd lived in London for many years at Brown's Hotel in Mayfair. And he now lived in the shadow of General Metaxas, the prime minister who declared himself military dictator. Greece had a parliament that never met. Metaxas prowled the Old Royal Palace with all his colonels in purple riding boots. Elvira had stayed at Brown's whenever she sang at Covent Garden. It was famous for its cucumber sandwiches. She never missed an afternoon tea at Brown's. But that was before King George's time in London, and she never had the pleasure of introducing herself to the deposed king. Now she often saw him on the ramparts of the Little Royal Palace, wearing his medals and military cap, and she would wave to him. The king waved back, a prisoner inside his palace.

George's plight softened her own exile. Elvira could see the Parthenon and the Acropolis from her balcony. And on the days she didn't teach, Elvira would often climb the Acropolis and stand within the ruins of the Parthenon—it was here that all human measurement began. And opera itself had emerged from the Greek chorus on this hill. The birth of song began here, long before *Carmen* and *Il barbiere de Seviglia.* She giggled like a schoolgirl. She wouldn't have been surprised if bel canto had been discovered by the Greeks.

–2–

MARIA WAS BORN IN THE MIDST of a snowstorm. Her mother, Litsa, expecting a boy, had been knitting little blue caps for months. Maria was a giant at twelve and a half pounds. None of the blue caps would fit. Maria's blond, blue-eyed three-year-old brother, Vasili, had succumbed to typhoid fever earlier that year, and Litsa wanted another Vasili. She wouldn't even look at Maria for several days, wouldn't hold her, wouldn't fondle her. Litsa was despondent, the luster gone from her blue eyes, as she mourned the lost boy who never arrived. This child had dark eyes, and a crown of black hair.

She cursed her husband. "I had to marry a pharmacist. I had other suitors, distinguished men. Why did you bring us here?" They had landed in "Little Athens," a modest Greek enclave in the outback of Astoria, across the East River from the glow of Manhattan. Litsa came from a background of military officers and physicians to the king. Her own uncle was known as the "Singing Commander," because of the natural beauty of his voice. And she had married a handsome rogue, George Kalogeropoulos, a "peasant" from the tiny town of Meligalas, in the Peloponnese. His people were poor, and George had labored for years at the single chemist's shop in Meligalas, preparing potions that could "cure" a myriad of diseases. Somehow he managed to get his degree at Athens University, and inherited the chemist's shop from its owner, a crotchety man who keeled over right in the store on a rainy afternoon.

George prospered. He married Litsa, provided her with a cook and two maids and the finest house in Meligalas, almost a mansion. But she continued to deride her peasant husband. She wanted to act on the stage.

George had a wandering eye. He might have gotten the mayor's daughter pregnant. He had a daughter, Jacinta, a dead son, and a wife who was pregnant with yet a third child. And without warning, he sold the shop and sailed off to America with Jacinta and his blond wife, who still dreamt of a stage career . . .

George got a job at a pharmacy in Little Athens and had his name shortened from Kalogeropoulos to Callas at the courthouse in Astoria. He still had a wandering eye, even while Litsa gave birth at a Manhattan hospital. She couldn't bear to name the baby girl, obsessed as she was by the ghost of Vasili. She called the little creature Sophie, or Maria, or Mary Anne, according to her mood and her whim. Litsa took more interest in blue-eyed Jacinta, now called Jackie, who was six years older than Maria and was Litsa's only comfort.

George managed to buy his own drugstore in a rough-and-tumble neighborhood of Manhattan known as Hell's Kitchen. He moved his family into a labyrinth of tiny rooms above the shop, which he dubbed Splendid Pharmacy.

Litsa badgered George until he brought a player piano into the house, a magical gift. Litsa found piano rolls perforated with pieces of operatic scores by Verdi and Bellini; while George was with his potions, Litsa would hover over the player piano and pump at the pedals. Jackie was bored by Litsa's incessant pedaling, but the music enchanted Maria. Soon she hummed the scores by heart; she couldn't work the pedals the way her mother did. Maria was much too small. But she could perch between her mother's thighs and push at the pedals with her own hands. This was the way she found Bellini.

Maria was myopic. She began to wear thick lenses before she was five. And the world, without her glasses, was a barrage of discordant colors. Once, when Maria was six, Litsa discovered George flirting with a customer in the shop; while he flirted, Litsa scoured his mysterious jars—jars that looked like swirls of flaming color to Maria from her father's apothecary shelves—and drank a portion of belladonna. She was driven to Bellevue in an ambulance and spent a month locked away in a rear ward of Manhattan's legendary madhouse.

Litsa's only friend in America, Alexandra Papajohn, another Greek lost in Manhattan, served as a maid and a cook for the children in their mother's absence. Myopic as she was, Maria noticed something strange between George and her mother's friend. They kept touching all the time. Maria tried to step between them, so they couldn't touch each other as often as they did.

"Papa," Maria said, "you must fire the maid."

"Why?" George asked, his gray mustache crinkling right under his nose.

"Because she is standing where Mama used to stand, taking Mama's place."

Alexandra Papajohn was sturdy as a rowboat, with a chest that seemed to rise and fall under her apron. "Sweetheart," she said with a puzzling smile, "I am only looking after you and your sister until your mother is well enough to return. Litsa swallowed a bottle of poison—by mistake."

Maria knew she had an enemy for life.

"It wasn't a mistake. Mama is unhappy—on account of you."

"Maria," George said, "you mustn't say that. Apologize."

"Yes," Jackie said. "Apologize. Alexandra has worked like a dog."

"Sister," Maria said, "please don't mix in. This is an argument between Papa, me, and Big Chest."

"Apologize," George said, "or I'll spank you."

"Spank," Maria said. "See if I care." She loved her father, but she wasn't going to share him with Alexandra Papajohn even if it meant missing an Eskimo Pie from the ice-cream truck near Central Park.

Papa and Alexandra didn't touch so much in Maria's presence, but she was always around when Maria woke and after Maria went to bed. And then one day she was gone.

Mama had come home from the madhouse. She wore dark glasses and seemed very somber, like an undertaker's daughter rather than a pharmacist's wife. She didn't have fights with Papa. They had made a pact, a truce between themselves. Litsa was determined now. She insisted that Jackie have music lessons. She envisioned her elder daughter as a prodigy at the piano, a child star.

"How can you be so sure?" George asked. "She's never played."

"I'm sure."

But the stock market crashed and George had to vacate the Splendid Pharmacy in Hell's Kitchen. It stood there, with row upon row of empty vials. George moved his family uptown to an apartment in West Harlem, a few blocks from the Hudson River. It was the same apartment house where Alexandra lived with her own father. George worked for a cosmetics company, traveled from town to town with a suitcase full of products. He paid for Jackie's lessons and for a piano, too. Litsa wasn't cautious. She entered Jackie in contest after contest, though her daughter never won a prize.

"Culture," Litsa said. "We need culture. Your father isn't refined, isn't refined at all." Litsa traveled down to the New York Public Library on Forty-second Street, where she borrowed the records of Verdi and Puccini operas and played them at home in Harlem on the Victrola that Litsa had bought with the shopping coupons she'd been saving for years. And they all listened to the *Metropolitan Hour* on the radio every Saturday when an opera was performed from the Met's majestic repertoire. Maria heard *Tosca* once, and the music continued to swirl inside her head—sounds had more color for her than the sights she could barely see in the streets; sounds had shape and substance, could almost be rubbed in her hand.

And then one afternoon, Maria suddenly burst into song. The lamps trembled in the wake of her voice. She performed "La Paloma," an old Spanish tune that had become popular on the radio. Maria didn't have to bother memorizing the words or the melody. She knew the song, word for word, after she listened to it once.

"My daughter is a genius," Litsa said from behind her dark glasses. And suddenly she woke from the dead. She removed her dark glasses, powdered the deep ridges under her eyes, and shifted all her attention and manic energy from her older daughter to Maria.

She found a voice teacher who lived across the street, but this so-called teacher was a charlatan, and Maria recognized it in a moment.

"Mama, Mr. Luria can teach me nothing. He doesn't even know the scales. He ought to pay me for helping him."

Maria sang at school, was the star of all the little playlets and operettas that the school put on. Her teachers couldn't contain her.

"I know better," she said, "I know better." And her teachers had to give in. They'd never had such a rich voice at their command, even if they couldn't command her.

Maria was tall for her age. The other students didn't like her. She was aggressive and sullen. The girls kept away from her, and she had fistfights with the boys. She always won, even if she often came home with a bloody nose.

The family moved from West Harlem to Washington Heights. George was more successful in America as a salesman of cosmetics than he'd ever been as a pharmacist with his potions. Maria could feel the estrangement between her mother and father. Litsa flinched whenever George came near her.

"Mama, is it because of Big Chest?"

"What are you talking about?" Litsa demanded.

"You know. Big Chest. Is Papa still seeing her?"

"Don't talk of such things. You're a child."

Maria missed her father. Whenever he returned from a road trip, he would take her to Fort Washington Park and they would share an Eskimo Pie from one of the ice-cream vendors. Maria loved the chocolate skin that covered the vanilla bar. George would let her crack the frozen skin with her teeth and devour the chocolate. Then the two of them would take turns biting into the bar.

"Papa, will you take me with you on one of your trips?"

"And have my little Maria miss school?"

"Papa, are you blind?" she asked from beneath her thick glasses. "I'm not so little."

Besides, Litsa had other plans. It was the era of child prodigies and stars, like Shirley Temple and Winifred the Wonder Girl, who passed Stanford University's entrance exam at the age of nine, or Hollywood's lead juvenile songstress, Deanna Durbin; Litsa hoped to cash in on this phenomenon.

"Maria, stand straight when you walk, like a Russian princess. And you can't wear glasses while you sing—never. They'll think you're a blind girl, selling pencils."

"But Mama, how will I see the stage?"

"Memorize it!"

Maria couldn't even tell if the ambition she had was her mother's or her own. She sang at local contests, winning one prize after another. The prize she cherished the most was a Bulova watch with silver dials and a golden crown. It was much too precious to wear in public. Her father housed it in a blue velvet box. The Bulova had a patent leather strap, and Maria would wear her watch at home from time to time, parade around with it on her wrist.

–3–

LITSA RETURNED ONE AFTERNOON with three canaries, whom she dubbed David, Elmina, and Stephanakos, while they sat in their separate cages. "Here, my beloved," she said to Maria, with a touch of iron and ice in her voice, "what better tutor than a songbird? Elmina and her brothers will help teach you how to sing."

Elmina wasn't much of a tutor. She could barely sing

at all; she would make a stuttering sound from time to time, but David and Stephanakos could sing like Caruso; they warbled from morning to midnight unless Litsa covered the cages with a piece of cloth. Elmina and Stephanakos were a glistening yellow, while David had a greenish touch to his coat of feathers. David was the outsider, jealous of any attention that Stephanakos paid to Elmina. Maria couldn't keep the two males in close quarters, or they would peck at each other ferociously and leave spots of blood on the wall.

But Maria was their muse; she would serenade David and Stephanakos with that stuttering sound of hers, and they would warble back at her, matching pitch for pitch. Thus Maria had her own opera house in Washington Heights, with a pair of male sopranos.

Litsa sensed that Maria would never make her mark as a diva in the United States, where it was far too expensive to hire a legitimate opera coach.

Litsa would have to return to Greece, where, she convinced herself, her own family would support Maria, help her rise as an opera star once she had the right training. She cornered George, home from one of his frequent trips across the country, and insisted that he pay the fare for her own voyage and the voyage of their two children across the Atlantic. George wasn't startled at all.

He hadn't fondled Litsa in years. He was in love with Alexandra Papajohn. He promised to send Maria and the children the sum of $125 a month.

Maria wouldn't graduate from the eighth grade until January, so Jackie left first, that December. And then Litsa and Maria boarded an Italian ocean liner, the *Saturnia,* in March 1937, with Maria's Bulova in its blue box, while a porter clutched the three canary cages and George stood dockside, weeping into a soiled handkerchief. Litsa and Jackie were already lost to him—they mocked him, whispered in his presence—but he couldn't bear to lose Maria.

"Papa, Papa," Maria shouted, "no more Eskimo Pies."

The canaries were making a terrible racket, singing their plaintive song.

"But when I have one, Maria," George shouted back, "I will think only of you."

"No, Papa, it is forbidden. You cannot have an Eskimo Pie without me."

"I promise, I promise," her father said.

Maria rose higher and higher on the gangway with Litsa, the porter carrying the three canaries, and George watched them as they disappeared onto the *Saturnia*'s deck . . .

The first two days at sea remained turbulent, and both Maria and her mother were nauseous the whole time, as their tiny tourist class cabin rocked relentlessly, and the canaries screeched in their cages. The sea was much calmer on the third day, and Stephanakos woke Maria with his own love song to Elmina, while Litsa toured the main deck in a muskrat collar that she had sewn for herself and told the first-class passengers about the prodigy she had on board with her, who would one day sing at the Met. It reached the ear of the ship's captain, and he invited Maria to perform at a party he was giving for his officers and two Italian contessas in the first-class lounge. Maria had nothing to wear but her blue cotton dress with a rumpled white collar.

Litsa was better prepared. Long before this voyage, she had taken a peach-colored satin bedcover and sewn it into a tea gown. Mother and daughter arrived in the first-class lounge with its rococo furniture and fittings. The captain, whose name was Stefano, had bushy eyebrows, a bent back, and a gray beard. He saw how nervous Maria was and he sat her down at the piano and offered her lemonade. Maria took one sip and removed her thick glasses. Suddenly, her eyes shone, and accompanying herself on the piano, she sang the Habanera from *Carmen*, transporting the entire lounge to a square in Seville outside a cigarette factory, where cigarette girls and soldiers congregate.

The captain was astounded. He didn't care about the two contessas. How could this weak-eyed girl who had arrived from her cabin in the bowels of the ship sing with such force while she sat at the piano in her dress with the rumpled collar?

Maria had never been to the Met, but she memorized the broadcasts with all their commentaries. And after she finished singing, she plucked a rose from a vase on the piano and tossed it at the captain, exactly as Carmen does to the defiant Spanish corporal, Don José.

Maria and her mother dined at the captain's table for the rest of the voyage. Maria danced with the captain, despite her myopia. She had become a sensation on board the captain's boat, with all the privileges of a diva, despite her cramped quarters and the three witless birds that warbled and coughed incessantly. Passengers stared at her and didn't know what to make of myopic Maria, who talked like a tough girl from the Bronx and sang like an angel with a rich, deep voice, never slurring over a single note.

-4-

THE MASTER OF THE *SATURNIA* DIDN'T ABANDON Maria when they arrived at the port of Patras, in the Peloponnese. He stood on the quay with Maria and her mother, and the three canaries in their cages, parked on a mountain of luggage. Captain Stefano realized now where some of the diva's gifts had come from. Maria was an actress, like her mother, who never stopped performing, not even for a moment.

"You have been so kind," Litsa said, waiting like a grand duchess for the captain to kiss her hand. He wouldn't disappoint this half-crazed woman. But he felt the strife that would soon tear mother and daughter apart. He helped them into the ancient military vehicle converted into a cab with a huge luggage rack that would take them and their canaries to the train station.

Maria and her mother rode across the peninsula in a train with wooden carriages and wooden seats. Maria had never seen houses made of mud. The tiny villages that passed in front of her eyes had dirt lanes rather than streets. She sat with the canaries and their cages on her lap. Stephanakos was nervous about this new terrain. And Maria answered every one of the songbird's calls with a call of her own. The other passengers were amazed. They crossed themselves as they stared at this canary girl and her mother with a black feather in her hat . . .

Litsa's brothers and sisters met them at the station in Athens. Frosso, Litsa's widowed mother, the matriarch of the Dimitriadis family, had not come. She was as willful and cunning as her "American" daughter. Once a landowner of considerable means, she had lost most of her properties during the Great Depression, and now presided over the family from a house that was little more than a bungalow north of the Acropolis.

Maria was allowed to audition in front of the family. Litsa's brothers and sisters weren't used to the deep metallic tones of Maria's voice. "Mama," Frosso's eldest son whispered in her ear, "we cannot sponsor this girl. She sings like a man."

But it wasn't really a question of money, or the harshness of Maria's voice. Litsa and Frosso didn't get along. Litsa had imagined a warmth that wasn't there. She quarreled with Frosso within a month and moved out. They had no furniture and had to sleep on the floor of a rented apartment near the Royal Garden.

It was Jackie who rescued her mother and sister. The son of a prominent Greek shipbuilder, Milton Embirikos, grew infatuated with her—she was blond and delicate, like an American movie star. Milton had met Jackie at Zonar's, a popular café and patisserie near Syntagma Square, in the heart of Athens; politicians often had fistfights in front of other patrons at Zonar's, which was right across from the Old Royal Palace, parliament's new home; poets gave readings at the tables; gangsters plotted; lovers had breakfast under the awnings in the late afternoon; novelists worked in some isolated corner over a double espresso. And Milton stared into Jackie's blue eyes, after his third encounter with her at Zonar's, wondering why she wouldn't allow him to accompany her home. He liked her veil of mystery.

He was in his thirties and was looking for a wife, although he could not marry until his younger sisters found husbands for themselves. And Milton floated from woman to woman until he found Jackie. But she made the mistake of her life. She told Litsa about her rich suitor, the shipbuilder's son.

Litsa plotted. "Bring him home."

"Mama," Jackie said, "we're sleeping on the floor."

"Bring him home," Litsa said, with ice in her eyes.

Maria met him first at the front door. He was short, with an unruly crown of black hair.

Litsa made him coffee in the empty flat and bargained with him like a horse trader, while Jackie wasn't allowed to utter a word.

"Mr. Embirikos—may I call you Milton? I cannot give my daughter away. We come from a noble line. My father was a general. We must meet your parents first."

"Madame," Milton said with all the elegance of his caste. "I do not think that is a good idea. My father is not in the mood to have me marry."

"We shall see," Litsa said.

They could not all fit into Milton's roadster. So he borrowed one of his father's company cars, a well-waxed Cadillac, and they rode to the Embirikos estate in Kolonaki, east of Syntagma Square. Maria saw the rows of mansions, with their iron gates and complicated rooftops, near Lycabettus Hill.

Milton's father, a stern little man in a frock coat, did not take kindly to Litsa and her tribe. She talked of her father, the general.

"I knew him—slightly," Mr. Embirikos said. And the interview was over. He would not grant his son permission to marry. But Milton wasn't helpless. He ran his father's empire and was flush with cash. And so he bargained with

Litsa on the ride back to the family's empty flat near the Royal Garden. He agreed to furnish the flat.

Litsa growled at him. "Furniture? We want a better home."

"Granted," Milton said while he spun the wheel. "You will have it."

"With a cook and a maid—and a cash allowance."

"Yes, yes," Milton said. "You will have it all."

He moved Litsa and her family into an apartment near the Olympia Theatre and the green trolley cars that ran along Ippokratous Street; most of the streets in the area were unpaved. The apartment had a balcony and three small rooms, with a kitchen and a bathroom.

Milton would not allow Litsa to have a telephone in the apartment. He didn't want Jackie's other admirers to call her. He was very jealous and very kind, also resilient in his own stubborn way. He took Jackie to parties where his father was present. And he stood firm when his father shouted, "Why do you bring that woman here? I will never consent to a marriage."

"I know, Papa. But I love her anyway."

"And still you defy me?"

"No, Papa. She will remain my fiancée—forever."

Milton waited six months before he slept with Jackie. He never once called her his mistress, though mistress she was. The family had a maid and a cook, as promised, and the flat was stocked with food. Maria couldn't stop stuffing herself. She particularly adored *tyrópita,* a cheese pie that the cook prepared for her. Her thighs thickened. But she continued to eat.

In the autumn of 1939, Milton moved Litsa and her two daughters into a much larger flat on the fifth floor of

61 Patission Street, an Art Deco building with ornamental ironwork. The flat had two bathrooms and a separate room for the canaries. The walls were painted blue, according to Litsa's instructions; the furniture was blue, as well as the kitchen cabinets. Litsa had become a fanatic about her favorite color.

Maria had to wear her mother's and sister's castoffs, dresses and smocks that Litsa stitched together. She studied day and night when she wasn't at the Athens Conservatory, a decrepit building near Omonia Square, with a well and a mulberry tree in the courtyard.

Elvira de Hidalgo ruled from classroom 25, a monk's closet with a grand piano, eight chairs, a tiny window that looked out upon the mulberry tree, and an even tinier stage. She taught her students the dying art of bel canto, a strict art, where each student tenor and soprano had to sing and move with an infinite grace, and embellish only where embellishments were allowed. She began with Bellini's *Norma,* an opera about a Druid high priestess who has broken her vow of chastity and conceived two children in secret with the Roman proconsul of Gaul. *Norma* takes place during a planned uprising of the Druids against Roman rule. But the real "uprising" is within Norma herself. She is still in love with the proconsul, who has cast her aside and is now in love with another Druid priestess.

Madame Elvira brought an accompanist into the room, while she climbed onto the tiny stage and performed the entire opera in pantomime. The other students giggled to themselves, watching this handsome heavyset woman do a kind of ballet on the sunken boards of the stage. But there was not one exaggerated gesture, not one false move. Maria had an advantage over the others. She had memorized the music and the libretto of *Norma* and grasped the force of Madame Elvira's exercise, how she could reveal the severity of the opera, its stark, majestic sounds in the utter silence of her moves, except for the creaking boards.

–5–

WHATEVER CASH MILTON GAVE TO LITSA, none of it fell into Maria's hands. She did not even have the trolley fare—two drachmas—that would take her to the conservatory on Pireos Street. And so she had to walk to school and walk home. The other students laughed at her and made snide remarks about the heavy tread of the shoes she sometimes wore, which looked like the battle-torn boots of a defeated soldier. Maria did not have the mettle to ignore these remarks. She had fistfights in the halls of the conservatory. The other students learned to ignore her and keep away from the "Battling Bulldog," as they called Maria.

But when they heard the rich, stentorian notes that escaped through the walls of classroom 25, they began to look at Madame Elvira's wild "American" with a certain alarm and awe. None of them had the range of Maria's voice—nearly three octaves—as if the Battling Bulldog were three separate creatures in one, with a very different upper, lower, and middle register. None of these students, no matter how gifted, could compete with Maria's virtuosity, or her ability to act out a part, to move her hands like a conductor's baton, as if every part of her could enliven the music.

That February of 1940, as there were rumblings of war between Italy and Greece, and Athens had its first snowfall of the year, Maria had been picked by Madame Elvira to take part in a benefit concert for needy students at the conservatory's Great Hall. Maria was the very last to sing, with another student soprano from Madame Elvira's opera class. Maria played Norma in a simple white dress. She was sixteen years old, and she performed the duet, "Mira, o Norma," with her fellow student playing the young priestess, Adalgisa, the proconsul's new favorite . . .

The audience at the conservatory was amazed by Maria. Norma rent the hearts of everyone in the upper and lower tiers with the quicksilver of fire and destruction in her enormous brown eyes and the terrifying stillness of her body under that simple white dress. It was not the performance of a sixteen-year-old novice. Maria had *become* Norma that evening, under the slanting fall of the snow.

Even Madame Elvira, who recognized Maria's brilliance and had nurtured it, was startled. No performance of *Norma* at La Scala had touched her as deeply as this duet sung by two amateurs, two unknowns.

Maria was voracious—like a wolf in a tattered coat. She attended every class that Madame Elvira gave at the conservatory. "Even the poorest voice can teach you *something,*" she would later remark. But it was pure bravura on Maria's part. The conservatory had become her home and her survival kit. She did not feel comfortable among her mother's blue walls on Patission Street, except in the canary room, where she could serenade Stephanakos and the other two, and in the pantry, where she stuffed herself with chocolate and cheese.

She was now the star pupil at the conservatory, Madame Elvira's "pet," who appeared on Athens Radio, replicating her role in the duet "Mira, o Norma," stunning opera lovers with the volume and colors of her voice. It was hard to believe that *this* Norma was so young, that she could encapsulate the suffering, rage, and despair of a Druid high priestess.

She often accompanied Madame home to her new ornate fifth-floor flat at 79 Patission, a few doors from where Maria consoled herself with the canaries when she wasn't at the conservatory. Maria looked after Madame Elvira's spoiled terrier, Gigi, who ripped apart the furniture and often peed on Madame Elvira's plants.

It was an enormous flat, with a signed portrait of Mussolini sitting on Madame's grand piano. The Italian dictator was the enemy of Greece, but Madame didn't seem to care. She was a foreigner who loved furs and French perfume, and she loved Maria. Using her influence as a former prima donna at La Scala and the Met, she was able to find Maria a position in the chorus of the National Opera, founded a year earlier, in 1939. It was an opera company that had to maneuver like a wanderer in a storm, without a permanent opera house of its own. Still, Maria earned fifteen hundred drachmas a month—she had signed a contract for a year. She was the one student at the conservatory who had landed at the opera.

Just prior to her audition, Madame went with this pugnacious nail biter of a girl to have her nails trimmed and her unruly shock of black hair washed at Madame's favorite beauty salon in Athens, right near Zonar's. They sat under the café's awning afterward and both had a dish of butterscotch ice cream, then a second dish to calm their nerves and soothe Maria's rapacious appetite. And then they visited Madame's tailor on Solomou Street.

"Martin," the Spanish soprano said in her most musical voice, "you will make my Maria trim and vivacious."

"Madame, I cannot work miracles. This girl—"

"Martin," Madame Elvira said in a much less musical tone, "you will not refer to my protégée as 'this girl.' She has a name. And it is Maria. You are a magician, are you not?"

"Yes, Madame, if you say so."

"You will make her positively svelte."

"In green, Madame?"

"No, the darkest blue."

Martin took Maria's measurements, crouching under her armpits. And then Madame Elvira picked the material, the purest silk, from the tailor's shelves.

"Martin," she said, "we will be back in three hours."

"Madame," the tailor said with a sunken look, "that is impossible. I cannot—"

"Did I not call you a magician?" Madame asked, as if she were delivering a recitative at La Scala as she pointed to Martin's little team of tailors. "It would not be wise to disappoint my Maria. She might return in a year as Athens' most glorified prima donna. Five hours, then."

Madame Elvira had time to kill, and she was in a frivolous mood. She went with her protégée to the movie palace at Omonia Square, watched the newsreels, saw General Metaxas strut across the Old Royal Palace in his plum-colored riding boots, denouncing Il Duce, while the press followed him from room to room. The king had become Metaxas' pawn, yet the general spoke of himself as the savior of the crown and Greece's "royal" government.

Madame shouted at the screen. "Liar! Imbecile!"

A bit embarrassed, Maria shook her patron's sleeve in the dark.

"Madame, they will throw us out if you keep making a fuss."

"Then we will go elsewhere."

But Madame didn't move. She'd come to Omonia Square to watch Greta Garbo in *Ninotchka.*

Madame whispered in Maria's ear. "She is funnier than funny because she is always serious, and it's her seriousness that charms us and makes us laugh. Learn a lesson. Always do the opposite of what the audience expects."

"But that is impossible."

"No, it is bel canto. Garbo sings to us in her own inimitable way."

Next they ate souvlaki on the sly from a vendor near Solomou Street and returned to the tailor. Maria's dress was incomplete, of course.

"Martin," Madame said with a yawn, "you disappoint me."

"Time," the tailor said, "is an ax, Madame, that delivers what it wants to deliver. We are doing the best we can."

Martin and his team scrambled across the shop with pins in their mouths and they swaddled Maria in silk, as if she were a tailor's dummy in soft armor. The tailors marked Maria with pieces of white chalk and then withdrew to a table with their strips of silk, where they sewed and sewed.

Madame waited with Maria for another hour, tapping her left foot on a floor strewn with swaths of material and knots of thread that looked like hair balls.

"Martin," the ex-diva said, "I will pluck your eyes out if you are not finished soon."

"A pity, that," Martin mumbled, with pins in his mouth. "A blind tailor would not be of much use."

"Ah, you're a philosopher now," Madame said.

The tailor returned with Maria's dark blue dress in his arms. Maria stared at the blue silk. She marched into the tailor's closet with the dress in her arms while the entire shop waited with all the suspense of some great adventure. Martin had never worked this way before. And he would have declined the invitation if it had been anyone but Madame Elvira. He was a fanatical opera fan. He had purchased one of the robes she wore at La Scala from a dealer in stolen costumes, purchased it at a phenomenal price . . .

Maria walked out of the tailor's closet in the dark blue dress that did mask her full figure and make her look like a tigress with a pouncing step.

Even Martin was mystified. "Madame," he said with a stutter in his voice, "this girl—she is a different woman."

"No, she is my Maria," Madame Elvira replied, and marched out of the tailor's shop with her tall tigress in the blue dress.

–6–

The other students at the conservatory didn't recognize Maria. At first they thought she was another one of Madame Elvira's protégées they would have to compete against. Then they heard her sing and their hearts sank. She was even more dangerous now that she had a kind of pedigree. They felt a little more comfortable when her veneer faded and she had fistfights with male students in the courtyard.

"The Battling Bulldog is back."

Maria didn't do much better at the National Opera. The new female members of the chorus resented her and feared she might pounce on them and seize their place in the chorus.

"She's a child," they said, "and she isn't really Greek—let her go back to America, where she belongs."

So Maria had little solace among her sisters in the chorus.

It wasn't much better on Patission Street. Her mother resented Maria's sudden makeover.

"That witch at the conservatory has no right to dress you up like a doll. And blue isn't *your* color; it's mine."

"Mama," Maria said, "at least I'm not biting my nails. And you're not the queen, Mama. You can't own a color."

She went into the canary room and played with Stephanakos for a while, sang a duet with him, while David and Elmina remained silent in their cages. But after a month or so, Maria stopped wearing her blue dress. She began biting her nails again. She clomped around in her soldier's boots, the same slovenly Maria.

Madame Elvira was furious. "Look at you! Didn't we go and see Garbo together? Idiot that I am, I devoted an entire afternoon and evening to your welfare. I besieged poor Martin. I made him perform a miracle, and he did—for my sake. And how do you reward me? Ungrateful girl! You will never, never sing at La Scala."

Madame raised her arm, not to strike Maria, but to emphasize her disappointment and disgust.

Maria flinched and began to sob. The sound frightened Madame. It was like the bellowing of a sick cow.

Madame was overwhelmed with remorse. She knew the

circumstances that Maria had to overcome—a mother who dyed her hair blond and paraded around in dark glasses, scheming to turn Maria into another Deanna Durbin, a nightingale sitting on a gold mine.

Maria was as close to a daughter as Madame would ever have, she a prima donna who had landed in Athens for the duration, with talentless pupils except for this child, who did have Deanna Durbin's gold in her voice, more than gold.

She hugged Maria, hugged her for the sake of her own life.

–7–

MUSSOLINI DECLARED WAR ON GREECE that October. Air-raid sirens wailed the very first morning of the war. The incessant noise frightened the canaries, and their cages filled with feathers. But Stephanakos was not to be outdone. He answered the sirens' wails with shrieks of his own. Not even the hood on his cage could silence his screams. Stephanakos was in the middle of his own war.

Litsa and the girls had to cover every window of their flat with blue blackout paper. The lights of the trolley cars were painted blue, so that there was an eerie shimmer after dark, as if the dead were riding the boulevards and the living had disappeared. Not one bullet was fired the first two days, and then the butchery began. The Italian invaders were soon repelled and pushed back into Albania. Victory flags flew over the Acropolis.

Italian prisoners of war with gaunt faces and bedraggled uniforms were marched bootless across Patission

Street with their bloody toes bared. Litsa hissed and spat at them, but Maria could hardly look into their bewildered, rabbity eyes. They seemed both comical and tragic to her, like characters in an opera playing out right on Patission Street. One prisoner in particular appealed to Maria. He seemed to be doing a pantomime for her, singing a silent aria, as he pretended to tip a hat he wasn't even wearing. This prisoner belonged to Maria in some secret way, talked to her with the slope of his shoulders, as if he was telling her, her alone, that Mussolini and his war were insane—in fact, the whole world was insane. He shaped a kiss with his crooked mouth and rolled his bloodshot eyes.

Maria tossed a chunk of chocolate at him, but other prisoners swatted it away, and clambered for it among themselves, until the chocolate splintered into impossible pieces, creating a riot, as Greek wardens in rumpled uniforms beat the prisoners back with their batons into the semblance of order, a doubtful double line.

One of the wardens reprimanded Maria. "You mustn't do that, miss. They're no better than animals."

"I like animals," Maria said.

Litsa chided her. "Imbecile, do you want us to be arrested for aiding the enemy?"

"Mama, I tried to give a starving soldier some chocolate."

"That's close to treason," Litsa said.

Still, Maria had to conspire with Madame Elvira after the war began—Madame feared that Metaxas, the military dictator, might deport her because of her devotion to that other dictator, Il Duce. So she and Maria hid Mussolini's signed portrait in the cellar at 79 Patission. A bit shaken now, she also hid her jewelry and furs, worried that the

Greek government might descend upon her and confiscate whatever she had. She stopped going to visit the diplomats and secret agents at the Casa d'Italia, which had its headquarters a few doors down, at 47 Patission Street.

She worried that Greek agents were following her. She gave fewer classes at the conservatory and began seeing more and more of her pupils at home. She had a locksmith provide her with two extra locks and an armor-plated door. She kept a revolver in the house.

Maria had met one of the consuls from the Casa d'Italia at Madame's flat—Maj. Attilio De Stasio, who had a military title but not a uniform to go with it. De Stasio didn't wear plum-colored riding boots like General Metaxas. He didn't wear boots at all. He was a bit shorter than Maria. He had a boyish face, though he must have been forty. He also had a wife and two children in Ravenna. But he'd been sent into exile in Athens, Maria heard him say. She knew it was a lie. He was gathering intelligence, spying on the Greeks. But Maria couldn't inform on Tilio, as everyone called him at the Casa. He was Madame's confidant, one of her dearest friends.

He had a gray mustache and piercing green eyes that embarrassed Maria, made her feel that Tilio was undressing her with every regard. He didn't chase after Maria, though he did dance the fox-trot with her at one of the parties in Madame's flat—before the war. The lights blinked and went out for a moment. He brushed his lips against her in the dark—it felt like a salamander's kiss. But after the lights went on, he pretended that nothing had happened.

"Maria," he said in a deep baritone, "I heard your *Norma* on the radio. You were magnificent."

That salamander's kiss had disoriented her. "I did one duet, Major, only one."

"Call me Tilio," he said with a note of alarm. "You mustn't use military titles in a foreign country. People might get suspicious. But I am not wrong about your *Norma.* It gave me the shivers. How could you summon up such sadness—a girl like you."

"I am not a girl, Signor Tilio. Soon I will be eighteen."

He smiled. "*Signor* is much too polite," he said. "Tilio is enough."

That was the last conversation they had had. But she dreamt about this major who wasn't a major, with his green eyes and gray mustache. And he chased Maria in her dreams with Madame's pistol. He shot her many times. But she never screamed.

–8–

THE GERMANS INVADED GREECE IN APRIL 1941 and arrived in Athens with their tanks and trucks as darkness descended upon the streets. Athenians stayed at home while the swastika flew rampant above the Acropolis. There was no food, none at all in the shops.

The Greek headquarters occupying the Hotel Grande Bretagne on Syntagma Square vanished overnight. King George had fled to Crete, abandoning the capital and its entire population. From her window in the canary room, Maria watched the German motorcycle troops ride down Patission Street on their way to Omonia Square. She went up to the roof with Stephanakos on her shoulder, with the wind in her eyes. Stephanakos would not sing. The motorcycle troops had polished leather jackets that blazed like black diamonds in the sunlight.

But there was little magic after that. The wealthy lost whatever they had—their homes, their cars, their jewels—as the Germans grabbed whatever they could. Black marketeers and gangsters operated with full German consent. They sat at Zonar's café and bartered like potentates and grand masters. No one could defy them, not even the German generals, who flourished from all the loot, while everyone else began to starve.

In Maria's mind, it was *Norma* all over again. She was the Druid high priestess with her three canaries as a chorus, but without a lover, without two sons, without a role to sing. Athens was suddenly Gaul. The Germans were the Roman invaders, with generals in long leather coats rather than a proconsul, rather than Pollione. They seized the Grande Bretagne for themselves, occupied Syntagma Square as a kind of parade grounds, and sent the Athenians tumbling into utter submission with an elaborate, orchestrated show of force.

The flamboyance of the motorcycle troops left most people in a daze. They had an aura of invincibility. No Druid high priestess could combat them, yet the young soprano with her three canaries was still Norma, a lonely Druid without an aria that could console anyone, not even herself.

Yes, there were Greek Communists in the mountains, and a scattering of British soldiers who had been left behind as guerillas, but a good number were flushed out of the hills and hanged from the lampposts on Syntagma Square, in full view of the Grande Bretagne and black marketeers at Zonar's café. Soon these dead resistance fighters were hanged from lampposts on random streets as a lesson to all of Athens. A corpse in the blue jacket of a British commando dangled from a lamppost beneath Maria's window; the dead man's face was the color of hard white clay—he'd been tortured; he had no fingernails and two of his toes were missing. Yet he seemed to have a defiant grin as he twisted about.

Maria felt more and more like Norma in an invaded land; she couldn't sing to a corpse of white clay. The populace had to survive on artichokes and black beans, while German officers feasted on fresh fish and honey cake in the salons of the Grande Bretagne. The Greek government and the king, chased by the Germans out of Crete, ran to Cairo. Meanwhile, Maria went back to the conservatory, which had reopened in May. The students in Maria's class all had sunken faces, and she shared with them whatever scraps of food Milton had managed to barter on the black market. Maria watched with an overwhelming pity in her dark eyes as they gobbled the figs and gnawed at the black bread like wild animals, fighting with each other over the very last morsel. Soon she couldn't bear to watch, and she turned to Madame Elvira, who sat so benumbed in her chair that she could no longer teach the class.

Most of the male students had been drafted into the Greek army—half were dead—and many of the females had lost their desire to sing during the occupation of Athens. Maria continued her studies at Madame's apartment. The Italian prisoners of war Maria had seen marching like mummies on Patission Street were back in uniform, their roles reversed. They were now Maria's jailors. The Germans had them watch over the Greeks while their own generals still dined at the Grande Bretagne, still had honey cake and ice cream.

Madame Elvira plotted endlessly on Maria's behalf at

the National Opera. She had Maria made a soloist that summer. The other soloists rebelled, riled by the attention that the prima donna from La Scala and Patission Street paid to this plump girl with pimples on her face who had the sound of hot tin in her voice. But Maria fought off their cabal with curses and sometimes with her fists, myopic as she was. The soloists complained to the governor-general of the company, baritone Ulysses Karapanou, who had once been prominent in local productions of Puccini, having played Scarpia, the Roman police chief in *Tosca*. He'd been Scarpia ever since.

"Honorable Governor-General," said Marguerita Nikolaou, a mezzo-soprano, who was the leader of the cabal, "your Maria is a cow and a pig. She stuffs herself with chocolate, while we have nothing to eat. You must put her back in the chorus, where she belongs."

"My darlings," the governor-general said, "if you are not satisfied with your situation, you can always quit. We will find other soloists—not as talented as you, but talented enough. Besides, we are under the German heel, and you should be grateful to have a salary in such hard times."

It wasn't the Germans whom the governor-general feared; it was the Italians, who had come back to Athens with a vengeance and gained control of all the arts. Ulysses was like a puppet in their hands, a politician who had to juggle his wares to survive. And he juggled well. He avoided the German generals at the Grande Bretagne, and pleaded his case to the cultural magnates at the Casa d'Italia, with Madame Elvira at his side. He knew that half these magnates were secret agents of some kind, but the Greek National Opera couldn't survive without their patronage and their passion for whatever bric-a-brac of a performance he could conjure up. He had little cash in his coffers. He could not mount a full production of *any* opera or operetta. And here he was, the commander of Greece's national opera company.

"*Comandanti,*" he said to these jackals, all military officers in disguise, "we have the finest soloists. We can offer you a selection of arias and Italian folk songs, a medley that will delight your audiences and make them forget their temporary exile from their homeland."

"Karapanou," said the chief magnate at the Casa, a balding man whose name was Bonavista, "Athens is our homeland, and it will be for a very long time."

"But surely you will want to return to Italy at the end of the war," Ulysses said with a wan smile.

"Maestro," said another one of the magnates, "we are in Italy right now. Or I should say, we are about to annex your pathetic little country. Soon Greek will be a forgotten language in Greece."

Ulysses wanted to slap Bonavista's face. They were a band of adventurers at the Casa d'Italia, adventurers and pirates. But he did not contradict such fascist gangsters.

"*Comandanti,* what would you like to see on our program for the next season?"

They did not hesitate.

"*Tosca.*"

Ulysses began to perspire. "But that is impossible. We don't have the funds for the costumes or the sets. We cannot mount a full production, *Comandanti.* We do not even have an opera house."

"*Tosca,*" Bonavista said, gritting his teeth. "We must have our Puccini. *Tosca,* Maestro. A full production, or I will have you shot." Then his mood changed. "Ah, I almost forgot.

You didn't come unarmed, Maestro. What does the *profesora* think?" And he kissed Madame Elvira's hand.

"*Tosca*," she spat, signaling to Karapanou with a swipe of her head, and marched out of the Casa with him, abandoning the *comandanti*, who dreamt of swallowing up the National Theatre and all of Athens for themselves.

-9-

One thing was certain, Greece's most celebrated tenor, Antonis Delendas, would assume the role of the painter, Mario Cavaradossi. And Ulysses would play Scarpia. But how the devil were they to cast Floria Tosca, the Roman diva who's in love with Cavaradossi? Should they audition every soprano in Greece, right out of the cradle?

And that's where Madame Elvira leapt in. "There's no need for an audition, Scarpia. We already have our Tosca."

Ulysses was intrigued. "But who is this mysterious woman?"

"Maria."

Ulysses groaned. "Madame, she's a child—seventeen."

"She will be eighteen, Maestro, when she plays the title role of Floria Tosca."

"But the other girls will scratch our eyes out—they hate Maria."

"That's no reason to shun her."

Ulysses had Madame in his grip now. "But she has a tremolo, Elvira, a wobble that can't be fixed."

"Then I will fix it," Madame said. "She is the only bel canto singer you have. You cannot find another Floria Tosca."

Ulysses' eyebrows wandered, like Scarpia's. "But the

Casa is behind us. We can import a soprano from Italy, a slew of sopranos."

Madame Elvira stared at him without mercy, and his resistance melted away.

"Scarpia, we need one, only one. And we have her. Leave the Casa d'Italia out of our affairs."

"But you sing there all the time, Madame. How many concertos have you had in its halls?"

Madame pondered for a moment, gathering her thoughts like salvos of ammunition. "Scarpia, they may profit from us, and give us the funds we need. But if the Casa picks our cast, then there is no such thing as a Greek National Opera."

Madame didn't tell Maria, didn't utter a word about *Tosca.* She knew all the variables, all the heartbreak of a role given and then ripped away and given to another. The cultural wars in Athens were a kind of quicksand, as the German generals had forbidden all public performances and displays—no theater, no opera, no clowns at the circus, no circus at all. Winter arrived with a bone-shattering chill. Thirty thousand Athenians died of starvation. But some families plotted among themselves, took the corpses of a father, a mother, an uncle, or an unwelcome aunt, tossed them over the cemetery walls, and kept their ration cards.

Spring brought torrential rains that sent trolley cars floating along their tracks, while entire streets shifted about in mudslides, and half the air-raid shelters went underwater. Summer brought little relief. Old men keeled over and died of sunstroke without warning. Locks and gates began to melt, and shoemakers and grocers had to hack their way into their own shops. The buses to the beaches were half empty.

And in the middle of the heat wave that June, the Germans lifted the ban on live performances. The National

Opera, with the help of a bank draft from the gangsters at the Casa d'Italia, could suddenly afford to mount their production of *Tosca.*

Maria found a mysterious note in her mailbox at the National Theatre, a palatial building on Agiou Konstaninou Street—she had been selected to play the title role in the upcoming production of *Tosca.* The note was unsigned. But rehearsals had already been scheduled at the theater's main auditorium. And Maria was informed that she would be fined three hundred drachmas for every rehearsal missed.

Maria ran to Madame Elvira's flat. She was still clutching the note as she climbed up the stairs.

"*Maîtresse,* I don't understand. There are so many other sopranos at the National, with much more experience."

"Liar," Madame said with a mischievous smile. "You have been training for that role ever since you were in your mother's belly."

"Oh," Maria said, with all the élan of Madame Elvira's favorite pupil, "long before that."

And both of them laughed like little girls.

"How did you convince Ulysses?" Maria asked. "He has no fondness for me."

"But he's not a fool. You're the only soprano in the company who has enough timbre in her voice to rise above the stone seats of the amphitheater. Yes, I bullied him a bit. But he didn't need that much convincing. Ulysses will be your Scarpia."

And Maria lifted her head, gallantly, royally, like the Roman diva Floria Tosca. "Then I will have my pleasure stabbing Scarpia to death."

Maria panicked the moment she left Madame Elvira's flat. How could she play Tosca when she was so nearsighted that she couldn't see the conductor's baton and would barrel into every prop on the stage? She had to be as sly and adventurous as Tosca herself. There was no room for an orchestra in the auditorium on Konstaninou Street. The company would have to rehearse with a piano. So there was one less thing for Maria to worry about. She memorized the placement of every bit of furniture in every scene—at the church with Cavaradossi, in Scarpia's rooms, and on the battlements. And she blocked out with a piece of yellow chalk on the roof of her mother's apartment the movements she would have to make in every scene—Tosca's little dance. She'd memorized the libretto and every note of the score, knew every role by heart, so she didn't require a prompter, whose directions she wouldn't have been able to see.

But it was hard to deal with the wickedness of the company's other soprano soloists. Their derision was absolute. They left a jar of cow shit in her locker at the theater. They hissed at her on the stairs. And after Maria shoved Margarita Nikolaou, the leader of the cabal, Margarita's husband, a brawny fellow who hauled furniture for a living, grappled with Maria, who arrived at the next rehearsal with a black eye that was as swollen as a small balloon.

The moment she had mastered every pitfall of the stage inside the auditorium, the rehearsals were moved to the open-air theater at Klafthmonos Square with its three thousand seats. How could any human voice reach that far? And there were other traps. The stage was much larger here, with hidden corners. Again, she had to block out every prop in every scene. Again, she climbed up to the roof of her mother's flat and made her own riddle of chalk marks.

They all sweltered at Klafthmonos Square. It was the hottest sun in half a century. Maria had to drink a gallon of water and run to the toilets underground. She wasn't like the other singers, who rehearsed as little as they could. Antonis was adamant. "Maestro," he said to the conductor, "will you have me die of sunstroke? Is that what you want?"

And he strode out of the amphitheater with his barrel chest after a single run-through. No one, not even Ulysses, dared punish him. He was Antonis Delendas, tenor of tenors, whose presence would double the receipts at every performance, while Maria was utterly unknown. She attended every rehearsal of the orchestra, blocked out her own exits and entrances. She had no other choice. She was the blind soprano, myopic enough that she could barely see a few feet in front of her. She would have stumbled into Cavaradossi, missed stabbing the hateful Scarpia if she hadn't had a picture-perfect image of every portion of the stage in her head.

The theater was packed on opening night—that is, afternoon, since *Tosca* had to start at 5:00 P.M. because of the German curfew. The August sun had settled a bit at that hour, and the German and Italian superior officers who occupied the front rows of the amphitheater all wore their military tunics and caps. Lesser officers occupied the tiers just above them. It seemed that the entire arsenal of both enemy camps had come to see *Tosca* performed. And whatever Greeks there were in the audience had to be content with the uppermost tiers of Klafthmonos "mountain," as it was called.

Ulysses Karapanou would have played Scarpia with a marvelous evil allure, but he caught laryngitis on the eve of the opening and had to be replaced by Tiros Xirellis, a member of the old guard, who had little affection for Maria. In fact, he harbored a grudge. As a member of the governing board, he had petitioned to have a more experienced soprano put in Maria's place. He called Maria Madame Elvira's "*chouchou.*" And he didn't even have a chance to rehearse with the girl. So the half-blind Maria would have to act and sing blindly with *this* Scarpia, who had little faith in her gifts.

It thrust Maria into the darkest of moods.

The opera opens in the church where Cavaradossi is painting a portrait of Mary Magdalene. Suddenly, we hear Tosca call, "Mario, Mario, Mario!" from offstage. The audience inside the amphitheater is stunned. It is a harrowing cry they never heard before in previous performances of *Tosca,* or in any other opera. It is the love cry of a wounded animal, a wild, enchanted series of sobs.

The diva arrives onstage . . .

Maria was barely recognizable in the role. She wasn't unkempt. All the pimples on her face were covered with powder. She wore a ruby red dress pinched at the waist, pleated skirts hiding her thick ankles. Her hat was also red, and she carried a long staff. Her voice was strange, harsh at moments, almost guttural, then rich and much more varied than Cavaradossi's familiar baritone. Within a minute or two, she had eclipsed him. She was beautiful onstage, with her big black eyes that seemed to illuminate the amphitheater.

The audience hadn't expected a novice in ruby red to capture them to such a degree that they noticed nothing but Maria. Cavaradossi might as well have been an altar boy.

Scarpia interests us more than Cavaradossi does—at least his evil, rapacious side. He arrests Cavaradossi for hiding an escaped Roman consul. To protect her artist lover, Tosca visits Scarpia, Rome's police chief, in his palace apartment.

Scarpia is obsessed with the diva, has been for quite a while. If she gives herself to him on the spot, he will write out a safe-conduct pass for Tosca and Cavaradossi.

She agrees to Scarpia's wishes. He approaches Tosca, trembling with desire. "*Tosca, finialemente mia!*" he cries as she grabs a sharp knife off Scarpia's dinner table and stabs him in the chest. It's a trick knife, of course, with a retractable blade. But the force of Tosca's blow unsettles Scarpia, who grimaces as he totters to the floor.

She recites the most celebrated line of the opera with a maddened fury in her big black eyes. "*Questo é il bacio di Tosca!*"

Here, she says, here is Tosca's kiss!

She lets the dagger drop in one slow move and watches Scarpia struggle on the floor to find his last breath. She's a tigress now, and the audience is bewitched. This is a Tosca they could never have imagined, a Tosca with such venom inside her that it could fill the entire amphitheater . . .

There was utter silence as the curtain fell. The audience had fallen in love with Maria's wild grace. Bewitched by her wildness as they were, they wanted to protect her.

Meanwhile, Maria ran to her dressing room, a tiny closet under the stage. She had to remove her bodice; she was soaking wet. Litsa was in the dressing room with Madame Elvira. Maria was wet through and through from the terrifying concentration of her performance. Litsa had to wipe her with a towel. But it was Madame Elvira who mattered now.

"*Maîtresse,*" Maria whimpered, "did I fail you?"

"How, child?"

"I should have stabbed Scarpia harder. My hatred wasn't convincing enough."

Madame tried as best she could to suppress a laugh. “Maria, you nearly broke the man’s chest.”

“Still,” Maria brooded, “it wasn’t enough.”

And the two women prepared Tosca for the third act. But nothing could compare to the intense poetry of Tosca’s own war with Baron Scarpia.

“Vissi d’arte, vissi d’amore.”

That was Tosca’s credo and her battle cry. “I lived for art, I lived for love.”

It had also been Madame Elvira’s song throughout her career as a prima donna. And she sensed that it would soon be Maria’s. Floria Tosca was the diva that Maria longed to become. That’s why the role was so tantalizing, as if Floria and Maria had melded into one, and Maria was singing to the future ghost of herself.

The audience didn’t want to let go of Maria—it was as if she had ravished these foreign invaders in their seats, these officers in their drenched tunics.

And saddest of all was that Maria couldn’t *see* their excitement. All she ever saw of the audience was an enormous blur—waves of movement, a sea of inchoate faces. But it was Madame alone who understood the ticket of Maria’s success—her utter isolation. She was trapped in a cage like the three canaries, and she sang from her cage with the force and coloratura of Stephanakos. She was a lone canary, after all.

–10–

NOTHING WAS EVER THE SAME after that first performance in the August heat. Maria had become the prima donna of the National Opera overnight, the diva of Athens, just as Tosca had been the diva of Rome. People ran up to her on the street, kissed her hand, muttered, "Tosca, Tosca, Tosca," like lunatics. Of course, several of the Greek opera critics had attacked her, those who were undying fans of Delendas and Xirellis. But these critics soon turned to tin, as they were swallowed up by Maria's growing fans, who reveled in her glory.

German generals invited her to Zonar's. She had to sign a hundred autographs between every bite of cake. The generals didn't force themselves upon her, though they did woo her with the rarest roses they could find. It was Madame who told her how to escape the generals.

"You must give them a parachute, child, so they won't flop on their asses when you refuse all their proposals."

"What kind of parachute, Madame?"

Madame's eyes were like lightning bolts. "You must tell them that you cannot disappoint your fiancé."

"But I do not have a fiancé, Madame. I've never even been kissed by a man."

Madame was harsh with her now. "And why is that? You refuse to dress properly. You are a diva now, the only diva we have in this poor crippled country."

"*Maîtresse,* I cannot bear to dress like an icon, a golden doll. I have to feel free—like Stephanakos."

Madame smiled. "Yes, yes, my dear, keep to your cage like that yellow bird of yours. You will never find a man."

"What about Tilio?"

Madame was cross with her now. "Major De Stasio has a wife and two children."

Now it was Maria who smiled. "I thought we were not

allowed to call the major 'Major.' It's supposed to be a big secret. Was he at the amphitheater?"

"Of course," Madame said.

Maria's dark eyes shone with a wickedness she had previously reserved for the stage. "And what did he think of my Tosca?"

Madame retreated a little as she realized that she couldn't match wits with this girl. "He adored it. He keeps insisting that I arrange a meeting with you."

"Well?" she asked, more Tosca than Maria.

"I don't run a bordello, my dear."

"He's not a child," Maria said. "He could pursue me on his own."

"I asked him not to," Madame said. "I insisted."

Maria was confused. "Why not?"

"Because he is what the French call a *tombeur*—a lady-killer. And I do not want to be a party to his schemes. Let him seduce some countess at the Casa, not a soprano who's still seventeen."

"*Maîtresse*," Maria said, "Tosca can decide for herself."

-11-

MARIA HAD DREAMT OF THE LADY-KILLER'S green eyes and gray mustache even while she was onstage—he was her Cavaradossi, not that tenor Delendas, so taken by his own small talent. She wouldn't have leapt off a battlement for him. Men had run after her, at least a dozen or so, including the generals who presided at Zonar's, but she preferred this *tombeur*, who was more than twice her age. She remembered the softness of his touch, how he had brushed against her lips while they danced at one of the parties Madame liked to give for her Italian benefactors. Yet he had never once pursued her.

She didn't depend on Madame. She phoned the Casa d'Italia, asked the receptionist for Signor De Stasio.

"Who is calling, please?"

"Tosca."

He came to the phone. He was smiling, right through the wires. That much she could tell. It was her canary's intuition.

"You're naughty, you know. I'm a busy man."

"Not naughty enough," she said.

He had one of the Casa's limousines pick Maria up and deliver her to a seafood restaurant on a side street near the port of Piraeus, a street where only sailors dwelled. Tilio had reserved a table in the rear, away from the windows and the tumult of the port. He arrived a few moments after Maria, with a gorgeously cut jacket draped over one shoulder, and he was wearing trousers with the same fine cut. The material was light blue velvet. He did not attempt to cover his bald patch. He hadn't come with a hat.

"Tosca," he said, saluting her before he sat down. "Elvira said she would murder me with her own hands if I ever went near you."

"And that was enough to discourage you?" Maria asked in Tosca's devilish tone. "Shame on you, Tilio. She is my teacher. She can command me in the classroom. But she does not control my desires. And I desire you."

Maria was startled by her boldness. But she was Tosca, after all. And even if she wasn't Tosca in this dark taverna of splintered wood, what did it matter? She had never been with a man. She could do whatever she liked.

"Ah," Tilio said, "Elvira is right to keep you from me. You are a special case. I froze, I swear to God, froze in that terrible heat, when you stabbed Scarpia. My darling Tosca, it was not an ordinary blow. You put your entire soul into the path of that blade—remarkable."

"I'm not your darling," Maria said, "not yet."

Tilio laughed so hard that his blue velvet jacket slipped from his shoulder. He left it in the sawdust.

"You really are a diva. You really, really are."

Tilio leaned over as valiantly as a leopard in the wild and kissed her on the mouth. Maria was amazed. She could feel a tingling that rushed to her toes.

"Tilio, do it again," she whispered hoarsely, shutting her eyes.

No one recognized her in this sailors' dive. Perhaps she could sign her name on a sailor's brow before she left.

"Tosca," he said, "behave yourself. We aren't in Elvira's flat. The sailors here are prudes."

"That's *their* problem," Maria said, and she climbed onto Tilio's lap. She could barely recognize her own brazenness. She hadn't even had a glass of retsina yet. She fed him cheese and spinach pies with her own hands. The waiter pretended not to notice. Perhaps he didn't care, or else Tilio had all his assignations at this particular taverna.

While Maria was curled up in Tilio's lap, the waiter arrived with a platter of grilled octopus. They devoured this platter like greedy children and asked for another. Both of them kept gulping retsina, almost biting into their little glasses.

"Forgive me, Tosca," he said, slurring every other syllable. "I'm at a cultural institution, and I have watched prima donnas come and go. I have seen *Tosca* more times than you can ever imagine. But they were children's fare, with dull, mechanical moves—dolls on display. When you did 'Vissi d'arte,' I wept, Maria. I could not sit on the stones of the arena. I had never heard that aria sung *this* way."

"You're drunk, monsieur. You don't make sense. How different could it have been?"

Tilio's eyelids began to flutter. He swayed in his chair. "Different? For the first time I heard—and saw—Tosca as Puccini had created her, not some musical whim, not the refinements and interpretations of a soprano sitting in a master class."

Maria was confused. "Tilio, don't torture me. I am that same soprano from a master class—Madame's."

"No," Tilio said, scooping up his velvet jacket and draping it over his shoulder again, leaving sawdust on his neck. "No, no, no."

Maria brushed the sawdust away with her fingers. "I studied the libretto and the score. I slept with the pages on my nightgown. I . . ."

"No," Tilio said. "You burned them into your heart. Maria, I was there—a witness. You were on fire."

"Then I'm nothing but a flame in your lap," she said, licking his ear.

He was pleading with her, Maria's spy in a velvet jacket, her own secret agent. "You mustn't mock me. You were not mortal on that stage. You were—something else."

He took Maria's hand and led her into another room. It had a simple cot and a crucifix on the wall.

"Tilio," she said, her tongue slightly warped from the retsina she had drunk, "is this your home away from home?"

"Quiet."

And he had an artistry beyond that of all the seducers she had read about in Madame Elvira's library of librettos. The only love Maria knew was opera love.

She was allergic to deodorants and perfumes, and so she could not wear one or the other, though she had bathed before this rendezvous with Signor Tilio. He seemed to find pleasure in her ampleness. He was not brutal as Scarpia would have been. His hands and mouth had their own magical gifts. He did not stifle her love cries or his own.

"Tilio," she whispered, "the sailors are playing billiards in the next room, near the bar. What will they think of us?"

"That I am on one of their own cots with a goddess."

"You must not call me that, or I will begin to believe you."

"But you were on fire and you're still alive. That's my definition of a goddess."

He smiled and smoked a Greek cigarette that stank worse than a broken toilet.

His mind was elsewhere while they got dressed, perhaps on the spies he controlled from his office at the Casa d'Italia as a master spy himself. Madame had told her about his adventures. Tilio had met with Mussolini, had received a medal of some secret order. He'd been wounded more than once. A British agent had nearly slit his throat in Crete.

Tilio brought his moodiness with him. Suddenly, he seemed more like an assassin than a lover. Perhaps it was all the same. He did not even kiss her good-bye or caress the least part of her with those lively hands of his.

They took separate limousines from Piraeus, though Tilio's headquarters at the Casa was only a few doors down on Patission Street from the flat that Maria shared with her mother. Jackie had moved out to a hotel in Kolonaki, east of Syntagma Square; it was close to Milton's office. She could have lunch with him every afternoon, and he stayed with her most nights at the hotel in Kolonaki. It had a French name: *avenir*—future. Jackie was staying at the Hotel de l'Avenir, in a town that seemed to have no future at all as it filled up with German and Italian troops.

Litsa was having a tryst with an Italian officer, Col. Mario Bonalti, who was passionate about opera and came from Palermo. He arrived at the apartment every evening in a ragged uniform. It wasn't clear what division or corps the colonel was affiliated with, or what his military obligations were. Maria had yet to see an Italian motorcycle patrol. The Italian troops were much better at reciting their favorite aria over a jug of retsina at some hole-in-the-wall than they were at policing Athens. They slept in their barracks or chased after Greek girls.

Bonalti often came to Patission Street with several other officers. Jackie couldn't bear to be around them. Milton might get into trouble, since he had rented the flat in his name, and it would hurt his father's shipbuilding business if he was ever called a collaborator. So he moved Jackie into the Avenir, away from Litsa and her rogue colonel.

Litsa liked to compare herself with Maria. "Who's prettier, eh?" she would ask the colonel in Greek. Litsa wasn't plagued with pimples or thick ankles. She didn't bite her nails, and she assembled a wardrobe from the bargain shelves in the enormous caverns of Attica department store on Panepistimiou Street, while Maria was as slovenly as ever.

But the colonel was wise enough not to get into a feud between mother and daughter. Besides, he was selling signed photographs of Maria as Tosca to his comrades for five hundred drachmas, sometimes six, because of Greece's rapid-fire inflation.

He tried to kiss Maria once while Litsa was taking a nap. It was halfhearted, like everything the colonel did. Still,

Maria slapped him so hard, he tumbled right over the couch in his rumpled tunic. Bonalti rose off the floor in several disjointed moves and apologized to Maria in Italian, Greek, and the few English words that Litsa had taught him. He didn't want to lose the revenue that Maria's autographs brought in.

Meanwhile, Maria didn't know what to do about Tilio. She could still taste the sweetness of his tongue. She called the Casa d'Italia, but the magic of Tosca's name no longer worked with Tilio. He didn't come to the phone. She had to call him from Madame's flat, because Milton still wouldn't allow a phone at Patission Street, whether Jackie was living there or not. Her admirers might call, and a message could get through.

Maria's unhappiness gave her more and more of an appetite. She gobbled the bars of chocolate and the sesame cakes that Bonalti brought. She ballooned to two hundred pounds.

"Maria," Madame Elvira said, "you'll need a fitter for every new performance."

But there were no new performances.

A coup had been staged at the National Opera. Ulysses Karapanou was ousted, and Tiros Xirellis, who had played Scarpia and didn't forget how he'd been manhandled by Maria at Klafthmonos Square, was elected the new governor-general of the company. He canceled Maria's contract as a soloist and put her back in the chorus. There was an immediate uproar. "A scandal," several journalists called it. But soon the diva of Athens disappeared. It was odd, Maria thought. Fame flew into the wildlands somewhere. A face not seen was forgotten. A voice not heard fell into the tundra of a winter afternoon. Bonalti's signed portraits of Tosca were worthless in a matter of months.

Madame Elvira caught Maria moping after a voice class in her apartment.

"Maria, didn't I warn to you to keep away from that *tombeur*? It wasn't out of jealousy, my dear. Yes, Tilio and I had been lovers when he first came to Athens with that velvet jacket of his. It didn't last more than a week. That devil is looking for recruits, some poor secretary who will give him a detail here and there about the German armaments in Athens. You must promise to keep away from Tilio."

Maria did promise, only what did promises mean to an eighteen-year-old girl who lived like a monk with her librettos and had never been in love before, had never tasted the salt in a man's spittle in her life until now? So she waited outside the Casa d'Italia like some huntress on the prowl. His eyes narrowed when he noticed her. It was winter. And he was wearing a cashmere coat and a Borsalino over one eye. He was her Caravadossi and would always be.

He didn't scowl at her. He saw Maria's threadbare winter coat.

"Wait here," he said without a kiss.

He marched back inside, came out with his chauffeur, who fetched one of the Casa's limousines, and drove them to the same dark street near the port where they had met the first time. Tilio leapt out of the car, went into a building, and returned with a winter coat made of the finest wool.

"Here you are, *ma belle*."

Maria remained bewildered by the major's clandestine movements. Where had he gone? Was it a warehouse for secret agents?

There was a bit of warmth in his green eyes, but that silvery touch of passion he'd had at the taverna was all gone. She had a sudden flash of feeding him grilled octopus.

"I see you have suffered a demotion," Tilio said. "Xirellis has sent you back to the coal mines of the chorus. It's pure spite. You overpowered him in the second act. He was *invisible* as Scarpia. He couldn't survive on the same stage with your voice."

And Tilio sent her back to Patission Street in the limousine, while he remained in the midst of some vigil in his cashmere coat. Maria couldn't tell if he was having a liaison—with a lover or another spy.

-12-

SUDDENLY, THE MAJOR DECIDED TO BECOME an impresario. He hired the forgotten diva of Athens to appear at the Casa d'Italia, in the *grande salle.* He could not pay her in drachmas—he had none at his disposal. But he could pay her in quantities of cheese and olives, black bread and provolone. He was her director, too. He had her perform moments from the second act of *Tosca* in front of Italian diplomats and embassy officials, and German generals whom Tilio had handpicked. And with Madame Elvira to coach him, he also decided to play Scarpia. Maria was baffled at first, and then she realized that Scarpia and De Stasio were both secret agents—killers of a kind. But that wasn't what drew him to Scarpia. It was the display of hidden desire. Perhaps she was wrong. Tilio could reveal his emotion—and his venom—in the role of Scarpia. And when they began their performance, Maria realized she wasn't wrong at all. He looked at Tosca with love—and with hate. He couldn't sing, but he could recite, and she sensed the blood and the bile in his voice.

Maria was confused as she sang. She could feel the pain

and remorse in Cavalier Tilio's green eyes. He did love her. She was certain of that. But he could only reveal that love in the guise of Scarpia, performing at an Italian cultural center in the middle of Athens. It was the one language Tilio knew, the language of a spy, always ambiguous, always open to a test. His entire life was an opera, and Maria could appear in it, but nothing more than that.

He wouldn't allow her to use a stage knife in the stabbing scene. He offered her one of his stilettos. She couldn't help but imagine the history of that blade.

She caressed the blade and nearly drew blood. That's how sharp it was.

She pleaded with her Scarpia. "I will hurt you, Tilio, with the simplest slash. Let me use a stage knife."

"No, no," he insisted. He would wear a padded vest, like some gladiator or ancient Greek warrior.

"I cannot stab you," she cried. "I cannot."

"Maria," he said with a smile, "you must, or else I will look foolish."

She rehearsed the scene in front of Madame.

"Harder," he said.

And so she stabbed Tilio in front of the diplomats and German generals in the *grande salle.* It was a great success.

She was able to feed half the chorus at the National Opera with rations of provolone and olives. The German generals demanded a second performance and a third. The *grande salle* was packed. She stabbed Tilio again—and again. It pleased Maria to hurt this Scarpia, whom she adored. He would take notice of her now. Specks of blood appeared on Scarpia's vest. She nearly swooned in the middle of the performance.

And then Titos Xirellis arrived with a battery of lawyers from the opera company. "Cavalier De Stasio," he said, "you cannot kidnap a member of the national company and stage your own opera."

"Governor," Tilio said, "this is a private gala. And you have not been invited."

The German generals glared at Xirellis, who stood his ground. "This is an insult, Cavalier. You do not have the right to steal from us."

Maria could see a trickle of blood on Tilio's calfskin shoe. She had dug too hard into the stuffing of his vest with the stiletto.

"You will desist," Titos Xirellis said. "I demand it."

His rage was hardly a match for Tilio, who grabbed the governor-general by the scruff of his neck and tossed him out of the Casa. His battery of lawyers followed right behind him.

Tilio had to quiet the audience in the *grande salle.* "Ladies and gentlemen, we have not finished the scene."

"You're bleeding," Maria whispered in his ear.

"It's nothing," he said. "A little scratch."

The rage had gone out of him. And he stroked her arm with a tenderness that he had not revealed until now, not even in that dank room near Piraeus with the crucifix on the wall.

-13-

MARIA WAS REMOVED FROM THE ROLLS of the National Opera.

The ex-diva's belongings were stripped from her locker and stuffed into a paper bag. She no longer had a mailbox. She still studied with Madame, still sang at the Casa d'Italia. But Maria's landscape shifted once Mussolini fell from power in '43 and the Italians surrendered. There was a curious vacuum for a week or two before the Germans struck. They drove the Italians out of Greece that September with abrupt and brutal efficiency. Soldiers stationed in Athens were tossed out of their barracks in the middle of the night and thrown onto buses with boarded windows.

Even Litsa's Italian colonel disappeared without a trace. His spare uniform, rumpled as ever, remained in Litsa's armoire.

Tilio was spared, it seems. The programs at the Casa d'Italia were untouched. Maria's moments from *Tosca* had almost become a monthly ritual. And then a fleet of sedans arrived one warm October afternoon in front of the Casa's neoclassical building with its Renaissance façade. Maria happened to be downstairs at the time, having come from a lesson at Madame Elvira's. She watched the parade of sedans with a feeling of dread. Several German soldiers entered the Casa in their pristine gray uniforms and escorted Tilio out to the sidewalk. Then one of the generals Maria recalled from Zonar's stepped out of a sedan in horseman's boots and kidskin gloves and began to slash at Tilio with his riding crop.

Maria wanted to approach the general and make him stop. He'd been to several of her recitals at the Casa and had sat in the front row at the outdoor arena when she had performed *Tosca* more than a year ago. But she lacked Tosca's courage, Tosca's power of seduction. She knew that she could not sway this general, who kicked Tilio to the ground.

Tilio did not grovel. His green eyes seemed on another planet as the blows landed.

Then, for a moment, he caught Maria's eye. He was never more beautiful to her than in his fallen state, his mouth bleeding and his favorite velvet jacket ripped to shreds.

No matter how hard the general slashed, he could not

break Tilio's will, could not rob him of his role as a secret agent. Tilio began to recite Scarpia's lines, as if he were right in the middle of a gala.

"Sei troppo bella, Tosca . . ."

The general held his riding crop in midair. "This is not a comedy, Herr Major, I assure you."

Then he noticed Maria standing in the street. He bowed to her with flecks of blood on his face—Tilio's blood.

"*Meine geliebte Diva,* you must not trust Herr Tilio. He is a wicked man. He has spied on our installations. He has seduced our secretaries, has dug his dagger into our best agents, has stolen documents from the safe at the Grande Bretagne. And he was considered an ally of ours, a friend of Herr Hitler. I am not a monster, I assure you. Tell her, Herr Tilio, or I will break every bone in your body."

Tilio recited to Maria from the ground, with half his teeth missing.

"Sei troppo bella, Tosca . . ."

The general kicked Tilio again and thrust him into the limousine, while Maria drew closer and closer.

The general touched the leather visor of his cap. "*Auf Wiedersehen,* Fräulein Diva. Perhaps we will meet again—in Berlin. And you will sing to us without this criminal, this Italian scum."

He rapped on the roof of the limousine and drove off with the entire fleet.

–14–

MARIA TUMBLED INTO A MELANCHOLY that deepened day by day. She stopped studying with Madame Elvira. She would not leave her room, except to visit her canaries in the middle of the night; not even Stephanakos, with his lustrous yellow coat and constant serenade, could heal her wounded spirit. Perhaps it was an idiocy, this notion of first love, but she reveled in it, would not abandon her feelings for Tilio. She mourned those monthly recitals at the Casa d'Italia with that secret agent who could not sing but was adept at reciting his lines. It was the only way that Tilio could make love to her, this *tombeur* who must have had mistresses in hiding everywhere—and nowhere at the same time. Tilio's entire existence was a secret. The only tangible part of him was that velvet jacket, and it was ruined by the German general.

Litsa left Maria a tray near her door, with the remnants of the pasta Colonel Bonalti had brought, his final gift to his Greek American fiancée.

"Maria, you cannot mope and mope, not over that despicable spy. You have no income, no income at all. I have found work for you at a cabaret, a German officers' club. You can sing your heart out."

"Mother," Maria shouted through the door. "Go away."

"Not until you come out. I have a daughter who's as big a stranger as any stranger in the street."

Maria opened the door. Litsa wore an elaborate mask of powders, mascara, and creams. Maria could barely see the blue of her mother's eyes under that mask. No wonder Jackie had moved into a hotel. It wasn't only Milton's fear of a Greek reprisal over Litsa's flirtations with Italian officers. It was Litsa's rampant insanity, her need to perform with every gesture, as if she moved across some palpable stage every moment of her existence.

I learned to act from her, Maria mused. She'd become the disciple of this madwoman. That's why her own gestures were so alert. But she had no idea how to free herself, to break away.

"Mother, I will not sing for German officers at any of their clubs."

Litsa remained behind her mask of powders and lotions. "And what of your concerts down the street? You sang for German officers at the Casa d'Italia. They fed you, didn't they? You sang with that rotten major. You were his whore."

Maria bristled.

"Yes, Mother. I was his whore. And I'd still be his whore if some Nazi general hadn't ripped him from me. Now go!"

Maria scooped up the tray and slammed the door shut. She stuffed herself with pasta, gobbled every last noodle. She was still ravenous, but she wouldn't raid the pantry with her mother around. Maria waited until Litsa went to bed. Then she ventured out of her room, tiptoed to the pantry, and devoured whatever she could find—figs, nuts, ricotta, black bread. It only deepened her appetite. She felt like a wolf from the hills with an insatiable hunger.

She returned to her room, famished as ever.

Maria found a note under her door in the morning. The scent was unmistakable. The note was marked with Madame Elvira's perfume.

Cara, I cannot come to you.
The Germans are on every corner.
You saw what they did to Tilio.
I'm next.

And so Maria went out in the winter coat Tilio had given her. There was a German sentry stationed in a hut right outside 61 Patission Street. The sentry was asleep. Maria ran to

Madame's building in her slippers, rang the bell. She had to ring again.

Madame unlocked the chain guards and let Maria in.

"Quick, who knows who's lurking in the halls. You haven't done your scales in weeks. I can tell."

"I'm in mourning, *Maîtresse.*"

"You're a singer in mourning. Don't ever forget that."

Madame sat at the piano and warmed Maria up, lingering over every note, torturing her for an hour. She wouldn't let her prize pupil sing the simplest aria.

"You've regressed," she told Maria. "Can you not hear the ripples, like a diva drowning in a tub?"

"An ex-diva," Maria said. "I'm banned from the National Opera. Xirellis won't even let me near the building."

"I'm still on the board of governors," Madame said. "I will squeeze that little man. I will whisper in his ear, if the generals don't arrest me first for my ties to Tilio. I was one of his couriers, you know. It is only a matter of time."

The Germans set up roadblocks, ringed entire boulevards with barbed wire. There were clashes between civil servants and the Greek puppet government, with its puppet parliament, its puppet police. A general strike was called. Athens became a nightmare—nothing moved. The trolleys remained idle on their tracks, without conductors, or a single rider.

Then the SS captured five resistance fighters in a mountain retreat and had them shot in full view of Syntagma Square. They left the corpses to rot. The electrical power was cut off in the hospitals and old-age homes. And still the strike continued. The famine grew worse. A member of parliament hanged himself from a chandelier in his vast apartment overlooking the Acropolis. Finally the trolleys began to move again.

The Krauts had canceled the 1943–1944 season of the National Opera, but Air Marshal Wilhelm Speidel, the military governor of Athens, was a rabid opera fan. He had a *lust* for Bellini. He defied his superiors and picked *Norma* to celebrate the reopening of the National Opera. He intended it to coincide with a vast parade, though the parade was finally canceled out of fear of the Brits and their Spitfires. The National Opera now had a home—the Olympia—at 59 Akadimias Street, which was still being renovated but would open in time for *Norma*'s dress rehearsals. Meanwhile, the cast had to rehearse in various rooms of the National Theatre.

Every soprano soloist at the company petitioned for the part of the Druid high priestess. But Speidel visited Xirellis' office at the theater one afternoon and said, while rubbing his nose with his kid gloves, "Herr Governor-General, do you recall that tall soprano who played Tosca at the open arena a few years ago? Well, she is *my* Norma."

"A pity," Xirellis said. "She is no longer with the National."

"Ah," the air marshal said in a voice that was menacing because it was so soft, "I beg you, Mein Herr, bring her back."

–15–

SHE WAS MUCH MORE CLEVER this time around.

She sang with Stephanakos, David, and Elmina, sang with her canaries for a week, pampered them as they pampered her. She could feel that familiar warble in her throat. She had memorized Bellini's score after a glance and returned to Madame Elvira with that pulsating sob in her voice, the profound sadness of a Druid priestess who had betrayed her people.

Madame turned away for a moment.

"*Maîtresse,* what is wrong?"

"Nothing," Madame said, a silk handkerchief balled in her fist. "I will never forgive you, Maria. This is the *second* time you have made me cry. Do you not remember the first? You were a little savage in that smock of yours, auditioning for a place at the conservatory. I was prepared to send you home. And then you sang—like a nightingale with a pebble in her throat."

"Well, Madame," Maria said, "is that pebble still there?"

"Sometimes."

And this is the agony that Maria had to live with—her voice might wobble in the middle of an aria as it moved to a higher note. Madame could lessen the "accident" of this wobble with hours of practice, but she couldn't erase it. It was Maria. It defined her as much as her versatility, her infinite embellishments. She hadn't mastered the art of bel canto—no one could—but she had become the devoted servant and the mistress of that art.

Maria went to the first rehearsal. She was the only one in the cast without a libretto or musical score. She knew every note of *Norma* and could have sung every role by heart. Meanwhile, the Allies bombed the port of Piraeus that January in raid after raid, smashing the entire port and its docks to pieces, with mounting civilian casualties. Not a ship could enter or leave the disappearing docks. And there was such a heavy snowfall that many of the Germans had to abandon their posts. They looked like helmeted ghosts. The electrical power was whimsical at best, and Maria and the others had to rehearse under flickering kerosene lamps. There was no running water several days a week.

The entire cast moved to the remodeled and revamped

Olympia Theatre, the new and permanent home of the National Opera. The air marshal sat with Xirellis in the royal box, in golden chairs that had been reserved for the king and his entourage, but the king was in Cairo with all the Greek generals, who'd been shunted aside like pawns on a mock battlefield. So Speidel occupied the king's golden chair during the final dress rehearsal of *Norma* and sat with his boots on the balcony rail.

Myopic as she was, Maria didn't catch the least blur of him in the royal box above her. She sang without a glance at the conductor's baton. As usual, she was alone on that stage.

Maria couldn't even run home to her canaries. She was obliged to have dinner with the air marshal and his men at the Grande Bretagne. No one else from the National had been invited, not even Xirellis. Speidel wasn't seeking romance. He was enchanted with Maria, wanted to bask in her presence, remain with Bellini as long as he could. He had triumphed with an Italian opera in a town under German control.

Speidel seemed in a trance.

"My dear, I will build you your own opera house, across from the Grande Bretagne. The Greeks can marvel about their civilization, but meanwhile our flag flies over the Parthenon and it will remain there for the next thousand years."

Maria didn't even taste her food. She sat, she listened, she nodded, and she made promises she never meant to keep. The air marshal's private chauffeur returned her to Patission Street as the uncrowned princess of Athens. She did not feel like a princess. Soiled is what she felt.

Litsa had waited up for her in the blue crepe dress she'd worn at the opera, her face still covered in her own concoction of powders and creams. "Well, what did he promise you? Money or food?"

"He promised me my own opera house."

Litsa began to cackle. "It would take a magician to turn an opera house into souvlaki, and we are not magicians."

Maria didn't bother to undress. She trod into the canary room and slept under the cages, while Stephanakos stared at her and didn't bother to announce himself with a single chirp.

-16-

Maria never had her opera house on a hill. Speidel received a telephone call in the middle of the night; two SS officers suddenly appeared in brilliant leather jackets and dragged him back to Berlin. *Norma* never opened. The entire production was shut down. Posters were ripped from the walls. Athens had an opera house with unlit chandeliers . . .

The Allies landed in Normandy that June.

The Germans marched out of Athens in October with dust on their uniforms and without much of a motorcycle brigade. The provisional military governor abandoned his quarters in the Grande Bretagne and emptied the safe. His officers also seized whatever cash they could—soldiers had turned into bank robbers at the end of their stay in Athens. A new Greek government was formed, as unstable as the last. The partisans came down from the mountains and clashed with the government. By December, Athens was in the midst of a civil war.

There were nests of barbed wire everywhere. Buildings burned. Entire streets were reduced to rubble. Trolley cars were caught in the crossfire. There was no electricity or running water, except during some random magic moments when the water did run and lamps flickered on and off, as if they were signaling their own disrepair.

Athens was divided into a White Zone and a Red Zone. The British ruled one; the Reds ruled the other. Patission Street was in the Red Zone, with snipers on every roof. The Reds, it seemed, were all sharpshooters and fired at anyone who flitted across a window.

Meanwhile, Maria and Litsa lived like hostages on a handful of beans. Maria had saved a bit of dried fig for the birds. She rambled about in the dark and went into the canary room, but her shadow must have crept across the window blinds. Suddenly, a burst of gunfire tore through the blinds and shattered the windows of the canary room. Maria had wanted to grasp the cages and hide the birds in the closet. But she would have needed a moment more. The snipers' bullets ripped into the cages and mangled the birds. Their feathers flew. Maria sat on the floor, staring at Stephanakos. His chest had exploded. Only one eye remained—he was a canary without any claws. David and Elmina were no longer recognizable. Their remains splattered the walls.

Maria did not even have the strength in her to cry. She sat there, the silent soprano.

–17–

No one seemed able to dislodge her. She lived with the remains of the dead birds, without a crumb to eat, while she dreamt about Stephanakos, who caressed her lips with his beak; then the beak splintered and grew bloody, and she woke with a jolt. British troops had smashed through the Red Zone with their tanks, commanding the boulevards and Syntagma Square.

The trolley cars were running again.

Maria spent an entire day scrubbing the walls of the canary room. She still had Stephanakos' love songs in her head, still sang arias with that bird. It was an opera that she and the bird had composed. It didn't have a name, and its only language was pure song.

She received a letter from the opera company, requesting her to sit down with the board of governors at the National Theatre on Konstaninou Street. The letter was quite cordial—it didn't have a menacing tone. Maria assumed that the National was preparing to offer her a new contract, with better terms than the last. She did not feel so confident once she arrived on Konstaninou Street. The National seemed like another casualty of the civil war; there were bullet holes surrounding every window on the lower floors of the building.

She climbed upstairs to the room where the governors met. Male and female soloists sat in the gallery behind the governors. Tiros Xirellis was no longer governor-general. He'd been ousted in some kind of a coup. The new governor, a tenor named Nikos Doxas, had helped arrange the truce with the Reds. Maria could imagine his political leanings.

"My dear," Doxas said, "we did not have much choice. Our budget has been reduced—radically. We had to make cuts, like a surgeon. And it seems that you were a little too close to the occupational forces."

Maria searched the gallery with one sweeping glance. It seems that Madame Elvira had been locked out of this inquisition, or else no one had bothered to invite her.

"And it wasn't only the Germans, my dear. You sang frequently, quite frequently, at the Casa d'Italia."

"Yes," Maria said, refusing to genuflect to the governor-general, "and brought back food for the entire company after every one of my concerts. You yourself did not reject the bread—and the ricotta, Governor. You gobbled it down with all the other soloists."

Doxas had a very crooked smile on his face. "And we appreciated that gesture of kindness. But it still does not excuse your closeness to the enemy. After all, you had dinner *alone* with Air Marshal Speidel at the Grande Bretagne."

"And should I have refused him, Governor? He would have hanged you from a lamppost outside the Olympia—by your balls."

Maria ran out of the pockmarked building and into a city of ruins.

The streetcar line to Patission Street was still out of service. And so Maria walked under the dim lamps with the stink of petrol in her nostrils. The partisans had destroyed all the stations, all the pumps, and so petrol ran in the gutters like liquid mud.

Maria marched across the mud to Madame Elvira's flat.

"They fired me," Maria said.

"I know. That little bastard Nikos clipped my wings. He wouldn't even allow me to vote."

"I can't stay here, *Maîtresse.* I'm going back to America."

Madame trembled under her silken gown. "And what will you find there? The Met will not even audition a Greek soprano."

"I'm American," Maria had to insist.

"But you sang in Greece and studied in Greece—with a soprano who sang at La Scala. You must go to Italy, child."

Maria did not answer. She kissed Madame Elvira goodbye. She'd always been an outsider in Greece. Could she be any less of one in New York?

She went to the American consulate across from Syntagma Square. Her U.S. citizenship had lapsed in 1942; she'd spent too much time abroad. The vice-consul approved her application to renew her registration as a U.S. citizen, and also approved a loan of eleven hundred dollars for the return trip.

None of this might ever have happened if the vice-consul hadn't seen her in *Tosca.*

"Miss Callas, I was surrounded by German officers, but I noticed nothing, nothing but you. Every movement, I swear, was like a little poem."

"But the Royal Opera didn't agree. I was demoted, and then dismissed."

"Then I will shun them," he said, "and they should shut their doors."

He kissed her hand like some count. "Bon voyage, Miss Callas. They must be fools at the Royal Opera, to let one of their own divas slip out of reach."

And so Maria had her eleven hundred dollars and the good fortune of a vice-consul who had come out of hiding to see her in *Tosca,* or she would have remained a diva without a country.

Litsa wanted to accompany her to America. She felt abandoned, and a madwoman's tic suddenly appeared under her left eye and wouldn't go away.

"What will happen to you when you perform? Who will attend to you between acts?"

"Mama, I might never perform again."

She went to Piraeus alone.

Less than half the port had been rebuilt after all the Allied bombings. Piraeus had gaping holes along its waterfront, like a gigantic mouth with most of its teeth missing. The vice-consul had found a berth for her on a local ship, the *Juno,* that would take her on a roundabout route to Le Havre, where she would board a steamboat to New York Harbor. She did have a tiny cabin of her own, thanks to the vice-consul. The captain and the crew left Maria to herself. She was the lone passenger. But the sailors loved to hear Maria practice her scales. They crossed themselves and considered her some kind of a mermaid.

She'd kept a few of Stephanakos' torn feathers in a handkerchief. She missed her three dead canaries, Madame Elvira, and no one else. Tilio had become a ghost with a gray mustache. She had stopped mourning him. But she couldn't break the habit of singing to Stephanakos, even if that bird couldn't answer her calls.

She had nightmares onboard the *Juno,* dreamt of the mangled cages, the snipers' bullets that tore through the blinds and ripped the birds apart. She couldn't calm herself until the boatswain brought her a pot of Earl Grey. She took out the one treasure she had from Greece, her trove of librettos. She read. She sang. She sipped her tea.

Two

The King of Verona

-1-

Battista Meneghini was a maker of bricks.

After his father died, Battista abandoned his studies to oversee twelve brick factories. All the Meneghini bricks were made by hand and required consummate craft—but the Germans had kidnapped the Meneghini craftsmen and left half the factories in ruin.

His enemies called him the "king of Verona" because he was ruthless in his bargaining and was the richest man in town. And he was known as Titta among his few close friends. Because he'd had to support the Meneghini tribe—his mother, his two sisters, and his ten brothers—he never had the chance to have children of his own. He'd had a luxurious apartment above the restaurant Pedavena on the Piazza Brà, but the German commandant of Verona had appropriated it during the war and Battista had to sleep on a cot in one of the restaurant's tiny attic rooms.

A plump, balding man in his early fifties, he was a passionate member of the town's Opera Association. Nineteen forty-seven would soon become the first full summer season of opera in Verona since the war, and Battista had volunteered to take charge of the new young soprano from the States who had been hired to do six performances of *La Gioconda* at the ancient Arena di Verona—damaged by constant Allied assaults, its pillars pocked and chipped, it could still seat an army of 25,000 opera fanatics. This American, Maria Callas, must have had a fool of a manager, since she had signed a "hangman's contract." She would be paid forty thousand lire a performance (the equivalent of sixty dollars), and she had to pay out of her own pocket all her travel expenses to Verona and most expenses during a month of rehearsals. Even worse, she would get very little profit out of her six *Giocondas*; the lyric soprano Renata Tebaldi was the star of this summer season, as Marguerite in Gounod's *Faust.* Tebaldi had performed at La Scala, where she sang under Arturo Toscanini's baton, and the maestro of maestros had declared that she had "the voice of an angel."

Battle-scarred, half its bridges in disrepair, Verona waited for the arrival of Tebaldi. No one awaited Maria Callas. Battista found her at the train station. She wore a winter coat in June and was carrying a cardboard suitcase held together by knots of string. That didn't bother Battista. She was nearly as tall as Tebaldi, but with intense dark eyes that hid such a hunger, they could have eaten up half the world.

Maria seemed lost in the station. Battista introduced himself.

"Signorina Callas, I am your chaperone from the Opera Association. Battista Meneghini. But my friends call me Titta. And I have a feeling that we will soon be friends."

Battista had his Alfa Romeo and could have squired Maria to the Hotel Accademia on the Via Scala, where she was staying at her own expense. He had just about enough petrol to accomplish that trip. But he decided to walk through the winding, half-broken medieval streets that had the marvelous stench of history, a stench that seemed to warm his bones. So he accompanied Maria to the Accademia, an eighteenth-century palazzo with its Venetian arches and balustrades. He carried the soprano's suitcase. She was much taller than Battista, and must have weighed two hundred pounds, but he liked women who had a lot of flesh. She wasn't a beauty like Renata. Her beak was too long, her ankles much too thick, but her smile was warm and welcoming enough for Battista.

They stopped at a caffè near the riverbank. The Adige flowed across Verona like a wily serpent; its soft purl always managed to soothe Battista. He understood Maria's plight. The Opera Association had managed to hook her in. She was Tebaldi's foil, brought here to help bolster Toscanini's angel with auburn streaks in her hair.

Maria and Battista both drank black coffee with daubs of hot milk and had little pies topped with almond paste.

Maria devoured the pies like a starving wolf. Battista placed a packet on the table. It was flush with cash. He carried these packets around in his pockets to entice contractors who supplied the materials he needed for his twelve factories.

"Titta," she asked, "what's this?"

"Nothing, Signorina Callas. Consider it a loan. It comes with no obligation. I'm afraid my compatriots at the Opera Association lured you here. They lied to you. You will not find much of a reception in Verona."

"But they hired me," Maria said.

"Yes, they could not find a decent Italian soprano who

would warm up the Arena for Tebaldi. No one would share the summer season with her."

Maria devoured him with those dark eyes. "But why are you telling me this if you are part of the Association?"

Battista wasn't even sure why. Perhaps the simplicity of her suitcase, with its cantata of knotted string, had moved him.

Battista loved to gamble. He would gamble on this girl who dressed like a vagabond in a winter coat, Battista's plump Cinderella in disguise.

"Romeo," she said.

He was slightly deaf in one ear. He'd been a field artillery officer in World War I.

"Signorina, I don't understand."

"Titta, my mother dragged me out of school when I was thirteen and took me with her to Greece. But I remembered studying about Romeo and Juliet, and all the battles between the Montagues and the Capulets. Didn't it happen in Verona?"

Battista laughed, and his double chin began to quake. "I could escort you to Juliet's tomb. It's in a crypt at one of our finest churches. There's also her garden to see. And the great palaces of the Montagues, now divided into tiny flats on darkened streets, where the poor live. Yes, we had our Capulets, our warring factions, and perhaps half a dozen Juliets. All of them real and invented at the same time. Romeo, I'm afraid, wasn't born in Verona, but in a nearby town. We have appropriated him, *cara*."

He said all this in a Veronese dialect. Maria understood every word. Madame Elvira and the Casa d'Italia had taught her Italian. And she had to study German, Spanish, and French on her own, if she meant to become a diva. It was her English that was flawed. She could intone her native tongue perfectly whenever she had to sing. But otherwise, she spoke it with a Bronx accent, though she wasn't from the Bronx. And she could curse with all the coloratura of a truck driver.

"Titta," she said, with that cunning smile of hers, crafted in the streets of Washington Heights. "I'm disappointed."

"*Cara,*" he said, "you shouldn't be. Verona has its jewels. But they are hidden."

"Then you must find them for me."

"But they are everywhere, darling," he said with a flourish, and pointed to the remnants of a Roman tomb right under her feet.

"Come," he said, "come," clasping her hand. Maria liked the firmness of his grip, though his hands were smaller than hers. He led her through narrow streets that had gaps between houses, revealing buildings that had been bombed but never rebuilt and that contained sand piles and mounds of rubbish.

He would not permit her to keep the tiny room at the Accademia that the Opera Association had reserved for her; it looked out on the hotel's tiny slaughterhouse in the backyard, with a chicken coop and a live cow.

Battista was very firm with the hotel manager. "I will want the very best rooms for Signorina Callas. She will be our Gioconda."

"*Commendatore,*" the manager said with a miserable mien. "Those rooms are reserved for La Tebaldi. The Opera Association booked them for our diva months ago."

"*Cavaliere,*" Battista said, "you are staring at the only diva in your hotel at the moment. You can find other accommodations for La Tebaldi—give her adjoining suites. I couldn't care less. The Association will pay for them, signor, I assure you."

Battista plucked the key out of the manager's hand and rode up to the Accademia's top floor with Maria, clutching the cardboard suitcase as if it contained gold.

Maria's rooms looked out on the breathing little metropolis that Battista adored, a provincial town that could not compare to the panoply of Florence. But Battista did not like museum cities. They did not have a reliable stench of their own.

"Are you tired, little one?"

She laughed the full-throated laugh of a diva. "Titta, you must be blind. I'm hardly little, but I will be *your* little one, if you like. And yes, I'm very tired."

He kissed Maria's hand and said, "A *domani,* little one."

But Battista couldn't get that Greek American *ragazza* out of his mind. *Ah,* he muttered to himself, *Titta, you imbecile, you're stuck with another protégée. And what a hotel bill you will have to pay when she is laughed out of Verona.*

–2–

SHE DID NOT REHEARSE IN THE ARENA. The Association had found a room for her in a building behind the Accademia and its live cow. This rehearsal room had a half-decent piano and an accompanist from the music school in Padua, but there were no backdrops, nothing to remind you of Venice in the seventeenth century.

Maria was preparing the death scene in *La Gioconda* with a local baritone as that evil snake, Barnaba, a spy for the Venetian Inquisition. The baritone's name was Roberto, and he was the understudy of the festival's own Barnaba, who was too busy to bother about Maria.

And it was the rehearsal of this scene that Battista happened upon. So much of the opera depended on the venomous charm of Barnaba. And this student Barnaba had none. But Maria bestrode all his frailties and lack of nuance. She held each phrase with a great gulp of air, as if she were biting every syllable, until Battista's heart pounded.

"You wanted my body, you devil?" she cried, taunting Barnaba. "And my body I give you."

And she stabbed herself in the heart with a hand-carved prop.

There was no glaze in Barnaba's eyes, nothing to reveal his pain or his anger. And Battista went after the young baritone.

"You're Barnaba, spy of spies, the most feared man in Venice, in love with a street singer, and you stand like a plucked chicken after she's promised you her body and leaves you with her corpse."

"Titta," Maria said, "you must not be so harsh with Roberto."

"You're right," Battista said. "I'm sorry."

Barnaba left, while Battista and Maria went out of this strange chicken coop together and sat at a corner caffè near the Accademia. Both of them saw the poster of Tebaldi attached to the front of a kiosk, calling attention to *Faust, Faust, Faust.*

Battista took Maria by the hand. "We must be cunning, more cunning than they are. I have a proposition."

Maria didn't even pretend to blush.

"I will pay all your expenses in Verona," he said. "I will provide a proper wardrobe. We will shop together, *cara.* I will serve as your manager. I can see that you have no one to fight for you. We will be ruthless and more cunning than they are. After a year, we will calibrate."

"Calibrate?" she asked. "Titta, I am not an accountant. What does that mean?"

"Measure our success."

"But how can you have such faith in me, Titta?"

"Maria," he said, "you were like no Gioconda I have ever seen. You sang poor Barnaba right into the riverbank."

–3–

HE SHOPPED WITH HER ON THE VIA MAZZINI, at all the little stylish holes-in-the-wall that had sprung out of nowhere after the war, selling the latest local fashions and a variety of secondhand goods, since nothing vital had yet to come from Milan. It was Battista who selected her wardrobe—her scarves, her shoes, her blouses, her capes. He had his checkbook. He didn't concern himself with the expenses. He had to create the aura of a diva.

He fought with members of the Association, who had invested so little in this unknown soprano and its production of *La Gioconda.* The costumes were shoddy and threadbare. Battista hired his own seamstress. He had all the backdrops redone. He didn't have the authority to tamper with the cast. But he hired voice coaches whenever he could. He had to build up the voices around Maria, or else her own voice would float into the wind. The Arena had fifty tiers, and he sat in that fiftieth tier, on a pockmarked bench, in the shifty "land of the gods" that could ruin a soprano if she couldn't project her voice, no matter where the amplifiers were placed. Maria's voice would have to fly with a scorching melody into the upper reaches of the Arena. And so he paid for extra rehearsals, defying the Association whenever he could.

The king went out onto the quay and approached the building behind the Accademia. Battista halted for a moment. He could hear the entire cast rehearse *La Gioconda.* The singing was exquisite. Barnaba had a richness in his voice all of a sudden, a profound melancholy. Battista stood in the doorway and peeked inside. He was baffled. Maria was alone. And then Battista realized that she was singing all the parts, male and female—tenor, baritone, contralto, mezzo, Maria hit all the stops. That's how she meant to perform *La Gioconda.* Maria would sing back to herself, create whatever echo it was that she needed in order to survive.

–4–

IT WAS DURING THE DRESS REHEARSAL. The sun had beaten down on the stones of the Arena all day, and it felt like a furnace. Maria was backstage with the wardrobe mistress. She must have gained ten pounds in Verona; she was on a strict regime whenever she ate with Battista at the Pedavena, but eating alone on the restaurant's balcony when he was off visiting one of his factories, she would stuff herself with macaroni and cheese. The wardrobe mistress had to rip apart the waistlines of Maria's costumes and sew them together again at the last moment, like a sorceress with a needle.

Maria wouldn't allow Battista to watch her from the audience. "I'll be nervous, Titta. I might forget a whole aria."

She was adamant and had Titta wait in the wings.

Maria kissed him and went out onto the stage, as myopic as ever. Battista was miserable.

He couldn't follow her in her glory, step by step. The Arena was utterly silent as she sang. The audience had never heard a Gioconda so vital, so sure of herself, though she did have a heavy tread. She was like a magnet that held the other singers in place.

But she couldn't remain a magnet forever, at least not that night. The stagehands hadn't completely "dressed" the stage. They'd left open one of the chutes that led to the underground labyrinth where wild animals must have been caged during the Roman era of gladiators. Maria had memorized the terrain but hadn't counted on the workmen's folly. She tripped against the chute and nearly tumbled into the labyrinth. She finished the second act. Her right ankle began to swell like a sick flower. The Arena's own doctor insisted that the dress rehearsal be canceled, or that one of the other sopranos read Maria's lines.

"No," Maria said while the doctor taped her right ankle. She limped into the third and fourth acts, using her left leg as a fulcrum. The pain whipped right through her words as she sang. She howled at poor Barnaba and nearly drove him off the stage, into the open chute. He could have landed with all those vestigial tigers in that underground labyrinth.

Battista didn't hear one sob from the audience after Gioconda stabbed herself. The curtain fell. The audience seemed more interested in the local singers who had surrounded Maria than in Maria herself. She took her curtain calls with the others on her one good leg, having to jab with her elbows to position herself, or she would have been entirely blocked from view, a lost Gioconda left in the shadows by the rest of the cast.

Journalists took little notice of the soprano who limped around on one leg. They were all waiting for Tebaldi.

Maria limped across the stage five more times. Battista had expected to field new offers for Maria's services, but none ever came. It was as if she'd had no Italian *prima,* and her voice had never reached the "gods" in the Arena's fiftieth tier. It troubled Battista, because the amphitheater was filled with opera fanatics, but they could not bring themselves to welcome a Gioconda who had come to Verona from another land. And so he would have to use all his cunning to construct her career in Italy, like a craftsman at one of his factories, brick by brick.

He decided to strike at the heart of the problem—La Scala. Even the king of Verona, with his attachment to the Opera Association, didn't have a fool's chance to meet with Antonio Ghiringhelli, the lord and master of La Scala, with his leonine mane of white hair and perfect aquiline profile; he had the aura of a movie star. He also had an air of mystery about him. It was impossible to find him in the halls of La Scala. He seemed to rule from within a private inner sanctum, surrounded by assistants with their own offices that somehow led to his. Battista had never been near his domain. But he was able to land an audition with Mario Labroca, who was Ghiringhelli's artistic director and general factotum. A busy little man in a rumpled suit and eyeglasses with one broken lens, he offered to devote himself to Maria if she and Battista could arrive the very next day at four in the afternoon. He could spare fifteen minutes.

The king rejoiced with Maria. "Tomorrow we will scale the walls of La Scala and who can tell what we will find?"

He kissed her, standing in front of the Accademia, felt the full moist flower of her body. He wouldn't give her up. She quieted the gnawing restlessness in him. She still had a bandage on her ankle. "Tomorrow," he said. "I'll pick you up at nine."

The diva seemed tense. "What should I wear, Titta?"

The king thought for a moment. "Ah," he finally pronounced, "the blue sweater we bought on the Via Mazzini."

"And heels?"

"No," he said. "I wouldn't want you to tower over Maestro Labroca. He is a nervous man. We must play him like a musical instrument, ease him into liking you."

The diva smiled, crinkling one eye. "Ah, you're a strategist, Titta."

She hugged him and went inside the hotel.

–5–

THEY ARRIVED AT CENTRAL STATION before two. The main gallery was filled with beggars and flooded with light. Maria admired the steel canopies that enveloped the entire terminal. It was the largest railroad station in all of Europe, another one of Mussolini's mad adventures. She felt like she was standing in a cathedral with a limitless roof. They had traveled to Milan in grand style, the only two passengers in the first-class carriage. The dining car had been closed for years on account of the war and never reopened. The porter himself had brought them the remnants of his own lunch, lemonade and slices of mozzarella on rustic bread.

But Central Station was filthy, its seats ripped out of their sockets, and the beggars who surrounded them did a mischievous dance, fondling Battista's pockets, reaching into Maria's purse, until Battista tossed a little sack of coins at them.

"Maria," he said, "it's warfare. I can't come to Milan without several sacks of coins. These beggar bands live in the station and feast on whatever voyagers they can find."

"Titta, can't the police drive them away?"

He laughed, and the echo of his laughter seemed to ride up to the roof. "Police? It's the police who give them a permit to operate with impunity."

"Then, I'm sorry," Maria said. "Titta, you live in a nation of thieves."

Battista couldn't stop laughing. "That's why we are here, *carina*. Opera is also a kind of thievery, artful though it may be. You do not exist unless you have performed at La Scala. And we can't meet the prince of thieves, Ghiringhelli. But we're here to see his first lieutenant."

They walked out onto the piazza in front of the station. There was a long, impossible line of stragglers waiting for taxis and buses. Battista didn't wait in line. He wore his finest summer coat. He waved down a police car.

"*Commendatore*," the driver said, saluting Battista, who handed him a tiny packet of cash. While Maria and Battista sat in the backseat, the driver turned on his siren and whisked them across boulevards with bomb craters in them and streets that contained palazzi without roofs, until they arrived at La Scala, a neoclassical building that looked like a great big box with balustrades.

Maria couldn't understand why such an ugly box should determine her future.

They didn't enter the main portal. They went to a side entrance, crossed a preamble of rear rooms, and arrived at a studio with a grand piano, an accompanist, and a pudgy man in a rumpled suit—Maestro Labroca.

The maestro looked at his pocket watch. "Meneghini, you are two minutes late."

"Maestro," Battista said with a slight bow, "it couldn't be helped. We had to navigate the den of thieves at Central Station."

The maestro stared at Maria. It wasn't a kind stare. "I'm told you walk with a pronounced limp. That is not ideal for a prima donna."

Battista was petrified. He could tell that Maria was prepared to maul Ghiringhelli's lieutenant, who could determine her fate in an instant and end her entire career as an opera singer. And so he stepped in.

"It was an imbecile, Maestro, a stagehand who failed to finish his job before the dress rehearsal. Maria tripped, and she had a sore ankle. I can guarantee that it will heal within a week."

"Good," the maestro said. "I cannot spare the time for lame sopranos." Then he turned to Maria, still glancing at his pocket watch. "Now what will you sing for us?"

"'Casta Diva' from *Norma*," Maria said.

The maestro had a wickedly wan smile. "Bravo. But, signorina, that is one of the most difficult arias in the entire Italian repertoire. It is not for novices. It's the height of bel canto. Norma is a high priestess with two children and a Roman lover. And she is prepared to sacrifice *all.* Are *you* a mother, signorina?" he asked like the head of some inquisition at La Scala.

"No, Maestro, I am not."

"Then how can you feel what Norma feels? A pain that's

akin to madness. Come to your senses and sing another aria. . . . Meneghini, can you not convince this child?"

"I'm not a child," Maria said.

"Then decapitate yourself, signorina," the maestro said.

Maria handed the accompanist several sheets of music, but he gave her a scornful look. He knew "Casta Diva." He sat slightly crouched and played the opening measures, and Maria sang the entire aria with such melancholy in her voice, such variations in timbre and tone, Battista was convinced that the maestro would break down and welcome her to La Scala. But the maestro wore an implacable mask and pretended not to be moved at all. Battista soon realized that the audition itself was a fraud. La Scala's own white-haired prince, Ghiringhelli, must have been in league with the Verona Opera Association in its attempt to discourage foreign sopranos from singing on Italian shores.

"Meneghini," the maestro said, "you must send this girl back to America, where she might be welcomed. We have nothing for her at La Scala. Who knows? She might ripen in a year or two."

"But she sang 'Casta Diva' perfectly," Battista said. "She did not miss a note."

"Ah," the maestro said, "it was too perfect for my measure—pure mimicry. She is a ventriloquist, not a diva. No one her age could command the depths of Norma. Impossible. As I said, we might find her something in a year or two."

"Maestro," Maria said, "I am not a ventriloquist," and walked out of the studio.

-6-

BATTISTA HAD NOT BEEN ABLE TO PROTECT her from vultures like Labroca, who did their masters' bidding. He couldn't protect her at all. It was becoming difficult for her to stay at the Accademia, a diva without a license to sing. But Battista hired craftsmen to reconstruct the maze of rooms above his office into a flat for Maria and himself, though Maria was reluctant to move in.

"Titta, you are an aristocrat among aristocrats. They will call me your whore."

"They wouldn't dare."

She was shunned the moment she left the Accademia and moved in with Battista at 21 San Fermo, near the Roman amphitheater. The two of them ate at the Pedavena, but not a single member of the Opera Association stopped at his table to greet him or Maria, who was the most gifted Gioconda the summer festival had ever had, even with a hobbled leg.

She gazed at Battista with her big brown eyes. "Titta, I must go back to America, or the very men who honored you will drive you away from the town you adore."

Suddenly, he felt a kind of panic he hadn't experienced in years, the possible loss of this gigantic girl.

"No," he said, "I will not permit it to happen."

But Maria was as stubborn as the king of Verona. "You know it yourself. I have not had a single offer since I sang at the festival, not one."

The king clasped her hands. "It is my fault, *carina*. I am not familiar with the world of theatrical agents. And the summer festival does not want you here—a foreigner."

"Like that maestro at La Scala," Maria said. "It wouldn't have mattered how many times I did 'Casta Diva.' He wouldn't have listened. I did not exist for him."

"We will make him listen," Battista said. "I promise."

Battista went back to Milan, almost like a beggar. None of the prominent theatrical agents would see him. But he was able to make an appointment with one particular renegade, Liduino Bonardi, who was considered a misfit by most other agents, and was not welcomed into their little club. Liduino wasn't located in a fashionable district near the Duomo. He had a tiny office behind a sewing factory, and he booked mostly magicians and jugglers and opera singers well past their prime. But this man in a sweater with ripped elbows and one unraveled sleeve, who had nothing but pencils on his desk and a telephone, seemed to have an uncanny grasp of the desires and needs of every opera company in existence. Liduino was a one-man rescue squad. An audition with Maria would have had no consequence for this renegade. He knew nothing about the quality of a diva's voice. He didn't even ask about Maria.

"*Commendatore*, can she sing Isolde, this angel of yours?"

Battista was suspicious. "Why do you ask?"

"Because Venice is in desperate need of an Isolde."

"La Fenice?"

Liduino tossed his pencils about with the palm of his hand. "Of course, La Fenice. Where else?"

La Fenice was one of the oldest and most beloved opera houses in Italy. It was where bel canto thrived, and where the castrati sang with unimaginable flourishes never seen or heard again, until they were banned from opera houses and church choirs by the Pope himself.

"Well," Liduino said, scratching himself with a pencil

stub as he grew more and more impatient, "*Commendatore*, can she sing Isolde or not?"

"Yes," Battista said, though he didn't have a clue. He wasn't ignorant of the magnitude of Wagner's four-hour extravaganza, an opera that was often crippling to mount. But, as Liduino told him, La Fenice was determined to begin its winter season with a major production of *Tristan and Isolde,* in Italian, of course. Not even La Fenice would have dared perform Wagner in German so soon after the war. It had counted on its very own dramatic soprano, Alida Rampani, who had performed Isolde more than once with a heartbreaking verve, both in Italian and German. But Alida's husband had died in one of Hitler's prisoner of war camps, and she had neglected to tell La Fenice's artistic director that she would never sing Isolde again. Suddenly, other divas of any repute became scarce. They didn't want to risk La Rampani's wrath—Isolde was *her* role, La Fenice *her* opera house. Besides, they were as temperamental and stubborn as the castrati, like Farinelli, the greatest of them all, who never sang unless he was in the mood and canceled almost as many contracts as he signed.

The divas ran off to Naples or Palermo, where they didn't have to study the nuances of Wagner's music, or deal with the crescendos of the "Liebestod," Isolde's love-death song, which had ruined many a novice's voice because of the deep emotion it demanded and its variations in tempi. So La Fenice had come to Liduino, the maverick in Milan, to find their Isolde. And Battista had volunteered Maria, without ever discussing the range of her repertoire. *Isolde,* he muttered to himself, like a mantra.

Liduino rang up La Fenice. "Giovanni, stop crying. I found your Isolde. . . . Name, what do you care about her name? She was the hit of Verona." Liduino clapped his hand over the speaker of his ancient telephone and whispered, "*Commendatore,* who conducted your angel in Verona? Quick, quick, who was it?"

"Tullio Serafin."

The renegade smiled, exposing his yellow teeth for an instant. He removed his hand from the speaker. "Giovanni, it was Tullio himself. . . . Yes, yes, I will ask the maestro, and I will have an answer for you as soon as I can. Stay near the phone, *per favore*!"

Battista was not pleased.

Now in his late sixties, Serafin was one of the most prominent musicians in the world, having been the chief conductor at La Scala for several seasons. But he had done nothing for Maria, hadn't recommended her to a single opera company, had even remarked that her voice was "*meravigliose vociaccia*"–had a *marvelous* ugliness. And Battista was convinced that Serafin would not consider her a suitable Isolde at La Fenice.

But Liduino had the local operator place a call to Serafin's rented villa in Rome. It was Serafin's wife, retired Polish soprano Elena Rakowska, who took the call. Rakowska was not eager to hear from Liduino. She considered him a gangster who swindled opera houses whenever they were desperate for a diva. She informed him that Tullio was indisposed. But Rakowska was still curious. "Why have you disturbed him, Signore Bonardi?"

"Ah," Liduino said, "it's on account of La Fenice. They are in dire need of a soprano to play Isolde."

"And why would that be of any interest to my husband?" Rakowska asked.

"Well, I believe a certain signorina sang for him this summer in Verona. Her name is Maria—"

"Callas," Rakowska said, her voice suddenly softening. "Wait. I will find the maestro."

Maestro Serafin did come to the phone. He kept Liduino occupied for a full fifteen minutes, grilling him like a sergeant major.

"No, Maestro, the signorina is not here with me now. . . . Yes, Maestro, she would be available. . . . I will relate all this to her manager."

Liduino hung up the phone, winked at Battista, and danced around his minuscule office—it did not have a single image of an opera singer on its walls.

"Liduino," Battista growled, "are you a lunatic? What transpired during that call to Rome?"

"*Commendatore,* we are completely out of the picture. The maestro will handle it himself. He will be in touch with La Fenice. It seems that La Rakowska is your little songbird's biggest fan. I heard her scold the maestro. But you must tell this Maria of yours that she will have to spend a month with the maestro at his rented villa in Rome to prepare for her role in Wagner's four-hour madness. A month, you hear? Not a day less. The maestro insisted on that. He does not want her, no matter what his wife says, if she cannot give him a month."

"And what is your commission, Liduino, your fee?" Battista asked, removing several packets from his pocket.

"None," the renegade said. "I made a fortune with one telephone call, and I never even met your diva. She is the maestro's responsibility now, not mine. La Fenice will blame him, not me, if she faints in the middle of the first act."

-7-

MARIA GONE FOR A MONTH.

Battista was prepared to rebel against Maestro Serafin and his witch of a wife, Elena Rakowska. He himself was busy with his own brickworks, and he knew that the maestro would see him as a distraction if he suddenly arrived in Rome and interfered with the hours Maria had to spend *becoming* Isolde under the maestro's wand as she learned the rituals of bel canto—magical singing. The castrati were masters of that art until they ruined it all with flourishes that were not in a composer's score. The worst offender, Farinelli, could not deliver a note without an extra frill. And so Serafin had to "tame" Maria and teach her at the same time.

"*Amore*," she wrote, "Tullio will kill both of us if you come within a mile of Rome. And he works me to death."

Often she wrote Battista twice a day. "Mornings without you, darling, hurt the most. Sitting with our coffee cups, chattering away . . ." But he could not write her as frequently. The maestro scrutinized every envelope handed to him by his maid. The maestro would frown, Maria told him, when he discovered Battista's scrawl on an envelope.

She was not Serafin's pupil, but his prisoner. And Battista raged.

Sometimes she called him in the middle of the night.

"*Amore*, I do not know anymore who I am. Maria? Isolde? Or both."

"One word, Maria, one word, and I will free you forever from that tyrant."

"No, no," she said. "Tullio is sweet to me. And so is his

wife. Rakowska believes in my talent. But it's lesson after lesson after lesson. . . . Darling, someone's here."

And she hung up.

One morning, Beppo, his least favorite nephew, appeared. Battista had hired him to work as his mother's chauffeur. But Beppo had exploited his position and become Mama Meneghini's ambassador. He moved into the Villa Meneghini in Zevio, a little town near Verona, and nothing Battista did could dislodge him from there. Battista had him fired several times, but his mother would come crying. "Titta, I cannot live without the boy."

She dictated her letters to Beppo; he did her finances, though she could have used Battista's own accountant. And here he was, dressed like Farinelli, in a red cape.

"*Commendatore*, the signora is waiting for you downstairs."

Battista had bought her an Isotta Fraschini that had once belonged to the silent film star Pola Negri, the rage of Italy during Mussolini's rise to power. The vintage car had a cockpit for the driver and an enormous rear cabin, which now served as Mama Meneghini's traveling parlor. She kept a little table in the cabin, with pastries and sandwiches, a variety of cups, and a thermos of coffee the size of a cannon shell. Battista had to scout for petrol, and it cost him a fortune on the black market. Still, he would have stolen for his mother. He had been her darling as a little boy, her favorite, her firstborn, her cavalier. She would not leave this traveling parlor of hers, and so Battista had to get dressed and go downstairs if he wanted to greet his mother. But he wouldn't allow Beppo to accompany him.

"*Commendatore*," Beppo whined, "La Signora Giuseppina depends on me. Who will serve the coffee and cake?"

"I will," Battista said. "Stay here."

And downstairs he traipsed in his velvet slippers. His mother revealed her disappointment beneath a face slathered in rouge. "Where's Beppo?"

"Indisposed," Battista said. "Surely, Mother, you can talk to your own son without that boy holding your hand."

"But he comforts me," Giuseppina said. "And I'm afraid that you cannot. You sponsor stray American singers, while I have to suffer the rebuke of strangers."

Titta adored his mother, but that imperial reign of hers was hard to live with.

"Mother, she will be singing Isolde at La Fenice. It's your favorite opera."

She squinted at Battista while he served them both coffee from that cannon shell. Then she tossed her head back like a diva. But all that rouge distorted whatever expression she might have had.

"Titta, you cannot cause a scandal and keep that girl. And should you be *pazzo* enough to marry her, you will complicate the family trust. We will all end up in the poorhouse."

He had to plead with her in that ocean liner of a car.

"Mother, I have given the Meneghinis thirty years of my life. I have nieces, nephews, but no daughters, and not a single son."

Giuseppina sipped her coffee, holding the cup in both hands. She was the matriarch of an entire clan, and she guarded its belongings like a ravenous hawk. It did not matter how much rouge she wore. "You took your father's place," she said, "and you must hold that place. But I am not without feelings, Titta. You have taken a fancy to this *ragazza*, fallen in love perhaps. That is your privilege. But we cannot afford a scandal among the Meneghinis."

She clutched Battista's hands with her claws. "You are our commander in chief. You cannot waver. But you mustn't worry. We will find a spot for her at the Villa Meneghini. She can be as lazy as she wants. She will beat the carpets from time to time."

"Mama," Battista muttered, his head whirling, "she has been picked by the maestro himself—Tullio, Tullio—as his Isolde."

Giuseppina began to crumble a piece of cake in her fist. "She will falter; they always do, these kittens you find."

Battista was helpless. How could his mother have realized that Maria's will was as fierce as her own?

"But I won't abandon you," she declaimed like a member of the chorus. "We will go together to hear her sing. I have never missed a revival of *Tristan and Isolde* at La Fenice. I'm not a barbarian, Titta. I wouldn't trade in our season tickets."

"And will Beppo come along?" Battista asked with a groan.

"Of course. Who else will drive us?"

–8–

THERE WAS A CAZZATA—A FUCKUP—at La Fenice. The soprano who was meant to portray the ice-cold Peking princess—with hot blood hidden under that crust of ice—in Puccini's *Turandot* had developed a bad case of bronchitis and had completely lost her voice. And so, while Maria was preparing for Isolde, the entire board of the opera company descended upon her with a proposition that sounded more and more like a demand. These gentlemen wanted her to step into the role of Princess Turandot right after *Tristan and Isolde.*

"*Cavalieri,* I have never sung the part."

"You are our Turandot," said the president of the board. "That has been decided. You signed the contract, Signorina Callas."

She ran to Serafin. "Maestro, I will only have eight days to learn the princess's arias and recitatives, *eight days.*"

Serafin was silent for a moment. Then he stared at her with his owlish eyes. "Maria, eight days is a lifetime. I have watched you. You can sight-read faster and better than any other diva I have ever known. You will learn *Turandot,* and you will sing it, but not under my baton. I have other commitments after *Tristan.*"

"Maestro," Maria said in a wavering voice, "you are abandoning me."

"Nonsense." And Serafin walked out of the room in his rented villa.

She cried on the phone to Titta.

"We will break the contract," Battista said. "The terms are barbaric. La Fenice cannot expect you to replace every singer who has a sore throat."

"No," Maria said. "We will never have another chance if I walk away from La Fenice."

Battista was miserable. He could not even stand beside Maria and comfort her at the *prima* of *Tristan and Isolde.* He had to ride with his mother in Pola Negri's Isotta Fraschini, with Beppo at the wheel, and all the half-grown grandchildren that his mother could round up, but not one of his precious brothers would even consider accompanying Battista, who had sacrificed his dreams so that they could grow up in splendor at the Villa Meneghini, while he breathed red dust in one factory after another.

"Titta," his mother said, like a queen in a blue satin gown, "why do you have such a forlorn face?"

"It's nothing, Mama," Battista said. No matter how magisterial, Venice was not a city that he adored, as it rose out of the mist of its lagoon like a pastel paradise that had begun to sink since the Middle Ages, when its doges and their disciplined horde of sailors ruled the seas.

–9–

IT WAS CONSIDERED THE "LITTLE JEWEL" of Venice—La Fenice. The opera house didn't hold much more than a thousand seats. It had been burned to the ground several times, except for the façade, but artisans, almost out of memory, rebuilt La Fenice—"the Phoenix"—with much the same splendor it had before. These artisans imagined La Fenice as an arbor, and decorated its five tiers of boxes with leaves and boughs made of gold filigree.

But Mama Meneghini preferred the orchestra. She could feel the vibrations of Tristan's voice, see the ridges in his armor plates, could almost reach out and touch *everyone* in the opera if she shut her eyes. The theater was packed, except for the three rows behind her, which were utterly vacant. The first and second bells had already rung. And then as Maestro Serafin arrived in the orchestra pit, a little band of trolls appeared, men and women—boys and girls, really, in outlandish costumes, with Alida Rampani beside them, dressed in modest blue. These were her acolytes, her die-hard fans, who never went anywhere without her.

The entire theater stood up—except for the Meneghinis—and chanted, "La Rampani! La Rampani!"

She acknowledged this overture with the simplest wave of her hand, as if she were mimicking the flight of a sparrow. La Rampani had never shown up at the performance of a rival in one of her signature roles. But Maria wasn't a rival, and could never have touched La Rampani's brilliance as Isolde. No one could. Maria was filling in for La Fenice's own diva, who had sworn never to sing Isolde again.

Still, it was curious that La Rampani had come to see a novice. She wore the coal black eye shadow and white paint of Isolde in her seat. And now Battista understood. La Rampani hadn't come to observe Maria, but to harm her, as if there were one and only one Isolde at La Fenice tonight, and this Isolde was sitting in the audience.

Battista recognized the stuffed leather balls and other "bombs" that La Rampani's mischievous acolytes carried under their cloaks. They were here to ruin Maria's performance. And Battista realized that he would have to stop La Rampani somehow. But before he could compose a sensible strategy to strangle La Rampani in her seat, the third bell rang; the maestro raised his baton and the prelude began. Wagner's music caught Battista unprepared; its lush sound of inexorable sadness washed over him and he was held in the opera's sway.

The dark green velvet curtain rose and the audience could see Isolde, the Irish princess, traveling to Cornwall on Tristan's ship, meant to marry King Mark at Tristan's command. Battista wasn't caught up in the magnificence of Maria's gold-braided costume, but in the "music" of her stance. This was a different Maria. Maestro Serafin had molded her somehow during that month of isolation in

Rome. Her entire body danced, even as she stood still, raging at Tristan. She sang with a full-throated melody, without the least hint of vibrato as her voice leapt to the uppermost range. She wasn't like the castrati, who loved to embellish an entire opera. The flourishes she sang were wedded to Wagner's score.

The audience clapped and whistled and stamped their feet whenever Tristan and King Mark made their entrances, but Isolde was greeted with utter silence. She was a foreigner who had invaded La Fenice, while *their* Isolde was sitting in the orchestra, her cheeks covered with white paint. Tristan took nine curtain calls. He was La Fenice's favorite tenor. Maria had to shove her way in front of the dark green curtain. There wasn't a whisper as Alida Rampani stood up and shouted, "Brava! Brava!" But the audience remained silent, even in the gallery, where many of her devotees sat with bags of rotten vegetables to fling at some baritone or soprano they didn't admire.

Suddenly, they shouted, "Alida, Alida!"

Amid all the pandemonium, La Rampani and her trolls abandoned their seats and galloped to the front of the auditorium, Alida with a purple rose in her fist. She climbed onto the stage and offered the rose to Maria. She waved her hand at the audience and shouted, "*Silencio! Silencio!*"

A hush fell upon La Fenice. And Alida bowed in front of Maria.

"*Piccolina*, it's no easy matter to make La Rampani cry. You accomplished a miracle."

And she turned upon the audience in the fullness of her fury.

"You ingrates! You must celebrate this girl. She sang with her soul. She revealed an Isolde you have never seen on this stage. She took you with her into the Night. Welcome her."

Then someone shouted from the gallery. "But Alida, darling, she could never be you."

The diva was not ruffled by any sense of rivalry.

"*Basta!*" she shouted. "No, she is not your Alida. But welcome her anyway."

-10-

MARIA WASN'T PERMITTED TO USE La Rampani's dressing room. It was kept locked whenever the diva wasn't in residence at La Fenice. And Maria had to share a much smaller room with her own maid in the opera, Brangäne. It didn't matter. No one greeted her but the Meneghinis. Maria was in a trance. She was still the Irish princess. Otherwise, she might have scolded Titta for not waiting for her in the wings. He always waited there whenever she performed—except tonight at La Fenice.

But she came out of her trance the moment Mama Meneghini gripped her arm. Mama had all the power, and Maria had none. She was no longer Isolde, a creature of the Night. She was the novice at La Fenice, in a medieval gown.

Mama Meneghini began to weep. Her shoulders throbbed.

"Mama," Battista asked, "what is wrong?"

"It was like dying," she said. "I was in the dark as I sat there, surrounded by golden things. It was . . . as if Isolde took me by the hand . . . and led me down into the dark."

"But Mama," Titta said, alarmed.

And Mama Meneghini kissed Maria on the cheek.

"You were magnificent, my dear. . . . Come, Titta, we have to go. I'll never forgive myself if Beppo falls asleep at the wheel."

Battista was like a wounded child. "But Mama, I planned to stay *here* in Venice, with Maria."

"Impossible," Mama Meneghini said. "I will not ride back to Zevio all alone."

"But you have your own grandchildren to keep you company. They can amuse you with card tricks."

"No," she said. "Say good-bye to your singer."

Battista was ashamed, a man in his fifties, ruled by his mother, the consequence of being her lifelong pet, her little doll, as she called him, her *pupatella.* Perhaps it was the reason why he had never married. Perhaps it had nothing to do with bricks.

Maria did not turn away and cry. "Go," she said, "go with your mother. She needs you now. Come back to me—when you can."

She whipped her head around in deep anger that she then attempted to hide. He thought she might strike Mama, or Beppo, or one of his grandnephews and grandnieces, who chattered away, enthralled by Maria's makeup bag, her costumes, and the wigs on their stands. She shivered once and regained her control.

"Go, my Titta, go!"

He kissed her on the lips in front of his mother and disappeared with his tribe of Meneghinis, while Maria stared into the slightly slanted mirror of her dressing table and saw her own shadow gaze back at her from that night world she had just inhabited. She stifled a scream just as Brangäne, at the next table, removed her wig and revealed a bald patch at the back of her skull.

-11-

TITTA DID RETURN. HE DID WAIT in the wings. The stagehands moved at a furious pace, lugging massive pieces of scenery that depicted mountains, the contours of Tristan's ship, and the sea. And this time Maria didn't have to sit in a closet between acts. La Rampani had insisted that the stage manager unlock her own dressing room for Maria. And so she stood in front of the diva's own mirror with her makeup bag, as Cecilia, La Rampani's seamstress, helped her change her costume; for the third act, she would wear a dark gown with gold on her sleeves—her "Liebestod" dress.

Maria did nothing more than darken her eyes; they seemed luminous in the soft light of La Rampani's dressing room.

Titta stood there, transfixed, like a *pupatella*. Maria had no time for him. And she was furious; he'd allowed Mama Meneghini to whisk him away after the *prima*. Still, the king of Verona kissed her for good luck.

The stage manager ducked his head into the room. "Two minutes," he shouted, which meant that she had a minute to "repair" herself, a minute to rush down one flight to the stage, and perhaps another thirty seconds to make her entrance, while people in and out of costume whirled around her.

Battista accompanied Maria to the wings. He could hear that leitmotif—Wagner's death cry—from the orchestra pit. *Tristan* was an opera of the Night, whether it was situated on land or sea.

Finally, Maria looked into Titta's eyes. "*Amore*, wait for

me!" And she went through the curtain with that sudden lightness she had developed under Serafin.

No one in the cast could match the deep melodic wound of Isolde's love song to Tristan, her dead prince—she would soon join him as a creature of the Night. Yet Battista's applauding in the wings had a silent echo. It never reached the other side of the curtain. The audience loved *their* tenor, Tristan, but Maria's mourning seemed too violent, too harsh, too metallic. Titta accompanied her to the dressing room without a word . . .

They stayed at the Hotel Fenice, which was right behind the theater. Maria slept late and had her breakfast in the room. She didn't want to see any of the sights, the half-hidden secrets of Venice that Titta could have revealed to her—a palace where a doge had been strangled, a bridge where a sailors' rebellion began some six hundred years ago. Nor did she want to read any of the reviews from the papers that Titta had fetched right off a vaporetto. She had *Turandot* to learn and Isolde's lines to repeat in front of the mirror.

She panicked, called Maestro Serafin at La Fenice, begged a half hour of his rehearsal time.

"Maria, dear, the orchestra has gone sightseeing. I cannot summon my first and second fiddles—even for a princess like Isolde."

–12–

SHE PLAYED ANOTHER PRINCESS, Turandot, in Puccini's last opera. And the difference was striking between the tumultuous, warm-blooded Isolde and Turandot, the ice princess of Peking, who has all her suitors beheaded when they cannot answer her three riddles. Yet the suitors continue to arrive at the palace gate.

A mysterious prince, the son of a deposed king, answers her three riddles and claims Turandot. She is lost, bewildered at her undoing, as he removes the princess's veil. Prince Calaf kisses Turandot, and we can almost hear the crack of her ice. Suddenly, all the "scars" of her coldness and cruelty are gone. We can sense her sudden delight. Her moves are graceful now. Maria was able to accomplish this with the hypnotic power of her eyes, the ballet of her beautiful hands, and the lightness of her glide in Turandot's royal slippers.

Standing in the wings, Battista was stunned by the miraculous shift in Maria's performance. He couldn't stop shaking and had to gasp for air. Yet the audience was blind to Maria. She did not have one curtain call.

Battista and Maria didn't return to the hotel. Their bags were already packed. They took the night train to Verona. Battista was despondent. Maria had occupied Venice like a foreign army of one, had "owned" the winter season at La Fenice as the prima donna of two major productions; no Italian soprano could have leapt from Isolde to Turandot with such facility—and remained brilliant in both.

Dreamer that he was, Battista had expected a call from Ghiringhelli himself with an invitation to La Scala, but no such call came. It didn't seem to matter that Maria had rattled La Fenice—Milan had its own imperial citadel, like Peking, and that citadel was La Scala. But he did get calls from artistic directors in the provinces. They understood the magnitude of what Maria had done.

Still, Maria was stubborn. She didn't want to perform

Turandot at some tiny playhouse in Udine after having sung the same role at La Fenice. It was Maestro Serafin who shouted at her.

"Maria, you can't remain invisible."

Maria chafed. "Maestro, was I *invisible* in Venice?"

"Yes," he said. "You performed in La Rampani's shadow. La Fenice is her house."

"But I will always be in someone's shadow, Maestro. I am the little foreigner—no, the big fat foreigner. That's who I am."

Serafin turned away. "Maria, you must impose yourself. The stalls and galleries are filled with fanatics. You must win them over."

"How?" she asked.

"By seducing them with your eyes, your hands. Some you will never win over. But the others . . . they will follow you from performance to performance, from town to town and country to country. And to do that, you must sing, sing, no matter where."

So she went to Udine and Genoa, from Genoa to Trieste, where she did *Turandot.* Then, with a nod from Serafin, she went on to play the mythic princess of Peking inside the fortresslike ruins at the Baths of Caracalla in Rome.

And Maestro Serafin invited her back to Verona for the next summer season to do four *Turandot*s at the Roman Arena. Maria was startled by the audience's immediate reception. These opera fanatics clapped the moment she arrived onstage. They did not see her as some stranger returning to Verona; rather, she served as *their* soprano now. The audience seemed wired to Maria. They followed her every move with a primitive hunger.

After the *prima,* there was a furor to find available

tickets. Turandot herself doesn't appear in the opera until well into the second act. And the fanatics began to chant "Maria, Maria." But all this excitement over her didn't seem to ignite her once she shed her wig and eye shadow and marched across the road to 21 San Fermo, where she lived with Battista in an apartment furnished with antiques—two tables with oval mirrors, a prie-dieu, a wooden settle that was six hundred years old—and bric-a-brac from the Villa Meneghini, including sconces made of bronze, cups with a golden lip, and plates with a silver trim.

She took out of her bag a tiny portrait of the Madonna painted in wood that she carried with her to every performance; she would kiss the Madonna, put it on her dressing table wherever she was, and it sat there while she sang.

Titta had given it to her as a kind of magical token during her very first performance at the Arena last summer, and Maria believed that the Madonna kept the wobble out of her high notes and placated "the Voice," a creature inside herself that was beyond Maria's control. But tonight it was not the Madonna or the fanatics in the upper tiers of the Arena that troubled Maria. It was Battista himself.

"Titta, your mother considers me a gold digger."

"She does not," Battista groaned. "You haunted her. Isolde appears in her dreams."

"But she has not invited me once to the Villa Meneghini."

The king of Verona had to humble himself, watch his words. "*Carina,* I cannot marry you—not right now."

Opera had molded Maria. She stared at him with all the intransigence of a high priestess, or a princess from Peking.

"Why not?"

"There are legal matters. Mother worries that her sons

will lose their rightful share of the family inheritance . . . if I should ever become entangled."

"Entangled? Entangled with me?"

Maria tossed a plate at him—one of Mama Meneghini's treasures with the silver trim. He ducked and it whipped past his head, a ceramic missile that shattered against the wall.

"*Mama!*" the king cried and crossed his fingers, as if he were an altar boy at church. "Maria, that was priceless—a Meneghini heirloom."

She tossed another plate. He had to duck again.

"I am going back to America—tonight."

She had learned the power of high dramatic art from the princesses she had played.

Battista pleaded with her. "We have to honor our contract. You have three more performances of *Turandot.* And then there's your engagement at the Comunale in Florence. Tullio arranged it all."

"Don't you dare mention the maestro's name."

But the king had managed to calm her down and spare most of his mother's precious china. Maria would be singing *Norma* for the first time in Italy. Again, she had to go to Rome for a month to study with the maestro at his rented villa. Serafin wouldn't even allow her to sing. He told her to study the words of the libretto, to speak them out loud in her room at the villa, and not to worry about the duration of a note, its *value.*

"Don't think of notes, my dear; think of words, words. Speak Norma's arias, feel their meaning, the depth of her emotion, and the notes will come to you, as if you were in a dream."

"Then I must *dream* Norma before I can sing a note."

"Exactly," the maestro said with the excited look of a gremlin. "The pitch and the value of each note, my dear, will rise out of that same dream."

And that's how she intended to sing Norma at the Teatro Comunale in Florence come November. The artistic director, Francesco Siciliani, was clever enough to limit her to two performances. He knew how taxing the role of Norma could be to a novice. That's why *Norma* had fallen out of the repertoire at the Comunale. None of the current crop of Italian coloratura sopranos had the stamina or the dramatic gift to deliver that role. It was Serafin who convinced Siciliani to revive the opera with Maria in the Druid high priestess's Titian red wig that Titta had to secure for her from a wigmaker in Milan.

But Siciliani was as cautious as ever. "Tullio, are you sure that this young American is ready for Norma? It is like running a marathon race. Tell me, Tullio, will she embarrass us?"

"Never," the maestro said. "The Comunale will fall in love with her."

And it did. The spectators were entranced. They followed the high priestess's every gesture. They had never seen an *actress* in the role, someone who could inhabit the depths of Norma's despair with a simple turn of her wrist. Her silences were as powerful as her songs.

Her Roman lover had betrayed her, and she had betrayed her entire Celtic clan. She moved about the stage with an unbearable sadness on her shoulders. The fanatics at the Comunale wept as she sang the most punishing of all arias, "Casta Diva," because it demanded more than any soprano could ever give, even Maria. Yet she seized every note, captured it. At the very end of the aria, she held a certain high note for twelve beats, like a magnificent bird with a broken heart. . . .

Siciliani caught the maestro backstage after the curtain calls.

"Tullio, you have brought us a goddess, I swear."

The maestro put two fingers over the artistic director's mouth. "You will bring the Furies down upon us with words like that. She is not a goddess, Francesco, but a girl with a great gift."

"We have to congratulate her—right now."

Serafin placed his hand on Siciliani's shoulder. "Didn't you yourself say that such a role is like running the marathon? We will leave her alone."

The maestro wouldn't let anyone near Maria's dressing room except for Battista.

Her eye shadow had run under the intense heat of the stage lamps. But she was much too exhausted to wipe off the black paint. She sat in front of the mirror and stared at the enigma of her own face.

"Maria, what's wrong?" asked the king of Verona.

"Titta, I have forgotten who I am. Where am I—right now?"

"In your dressing room at the Comunale."

"What Comunale?" she asked.

"In Florence," he said. "Should I bring you some lemonade?"

"Ah, Florence," she said.

She found a note on her dressing table where her wooden Madonna should have been. The precious piece of white paper did not even have an envelope. It sat there. Someone must have unlocked the door of her dressing room while she was singing and slipped it onto the table—and kidnapped her Madonna.

Maria was in a rage. "I will never be able to sing again. My little painting is gone."

"That's impossible," Battista muttered, his eyes scrolling around the room. "The door is always locked. And there should be a guard outside to protect all your valuables."

"But nothing else is missing, not my purse, not my money—just the Madonna. Some thief must have picked the lock. The door was half open when I returned this last time."

"It's a scandal, Maria. Thieves at the Comunale."

And he left to search for Siciliani.

As angry as she was, Maria unfolded the piece of fine white paper, which was drenched in perfume with the aroma of lilacs. It seemed to have a child's crisp handwriting.

Dear Maria,

Before I heard you sing Isolde at La Fenice, I was prepared to scratch your eyes out. But the sound of your voice ripped away all my resolve. It was like a wild animal who had come to play with us. And I, too, wanted to play. But I was saddened, Maria. It was as if I were witnessing a misfortune foretold.

I ought to know. It is my misfortune as well as yours. They will celebrate you, and then, on a hard night, they will eat you alive if you hit a wrong note, a diva who is not diva enough. Be kind to yourself, because in the end, that is the only kindness that counts.

Your new friend,
Alida Rampani

-13-

It was a small town in Tuscany, a town that may not even have had a name. But it did have a madhouse beyond its medieval walls—rather, a health spa for the rich with bars on the windows and no magic waters. But this spa did have a name: Albergo Angelina. And Titta drove her there from Florence in his white Alfa Romeo.

Maria had no trouble getting inside the albergo while Titta waited for her at a caffè in this Tuscan town. La Rampani occupied an entire floor. That's how pampered opera stars were, even in a madhouse. She did not intend to sing again, even though she could still reach the highest note of Bellini's most elaborate cadenzas. She was not insane. She'd simply detached herself from La Fenice and any other opera house in Italy or elsewhere.

With the renegade soprano were her "fireflies," her mischievous trolls, her devotees, who had surrounded La Rampani with the painted backdrops and the paraphernalia retrieved from the sets of half a dozen operas. She sat on a hand-carved wooden throne from Verdi's *Otello,* lifted from the prop room at La Fenice. She herself had played Desdemona several times. There were lions' heads carved into the armrests and legs of this magnificent chair. La Rampani occupied it wearing the unornamented white gown of "guests" at Albergo Angelina and a paper crown that her fireflies had created for their queen of queens. They'd sworn themselves to Alida and would never have deserted her for another soprano.

"Maria," the queen trilled from her throne. "Come. I give you permission to approach."

Maria snarled at her. "Bitch, you stole my Madonna. I will never be able to sing without it."

La Rampani stood up on her throne, clutching the lions on the armrests. "Steal? I never steal. I borrowed it so that I could seduce you into coming here."

"That is not what I would call seduction, Signorina Rampani. Which one of your termites broke into my dressing room?"

"I did," said a firefly in a blue neckerchief and a rumpled jacket that reached down to his knees.

Maria slapped him across the throne room. He slid hard and landed against the wall. The other trolls attacked her with screwdrivers and lock picks that they clutched like claws.

"Wait!" La Rampani shouted, and these trolls withdrew. She took the miniature Madonna out of her pocket and handed the painting back to Maria.

"How is that *stronzo* of yours? Your manager, Meneghini?"

Maria was bristling now. She wanted to hurl La Rampani off her throne.

"He is not a *stronzo*. Battista is my fiancé."

La Rampani peered down at Maria from the height of her throne. "Has he offered to marry you?"

"He will," Maria said. "He is entangled in family affairs."

"And when will he untangle himself?"

"Soon," Maria said, rubbing the rough surface of the little painting. But it couldn't seem to soothe her in this madhouse.

"Can't you see why I absconded, Maria? I was becoming the ghost of whatever parts I played."

Maria could not reason in this madhouse disguised as an inn. The Tuscan sunlight streamed through the bars on the windows and landed as stripes on La Rampani's skin and hospital gown.

"Signorina," Maria said, "if you are so allergic to queens, then why do you sit on a throne?"

"Because it soothes me to look at my subjects. Why don't you stay here instead of going back to that bricklayer?"

"Battista is not a bricklayer," Maria said. "He owns factories, signorina."

"Bricklayer," she said, and her fireflies repeated that word like a chorus in a production that was missing a musical score.

"Maria, you will not have a long career," the queen said. "You give too much. You have to learn to parcel your talents with each performance."

"I cannot parcel," Maria said. "I am not a spoon."

She went down to a lower floor, where other patients played checkers or gin rummy, and drank tea from cups that were chained to their chairs.

THREE

A Dangerous Diva

-1-

"Music, ice cream, and cake."

Maria was sitting at a caffè near the Roman Arena, nursing a butterscotch sundae with a long spoon and reading a short article about herself by the ferocious arts critic Laura Sordelo in *Oggi*, the most popular postwar Italian magazine. She did not interview Maria. But Laura had talked to Madame de Hidalgo about the six years she had spent with Maria in Athens. Hidalgo revealed Maria's three great passions. "Music, ice cream, and cake."

Those were the things that soothed Maria. "Callas had a chaotic childhood; her mother pushed her to sing in contests by the time she was eight. School ended for her at thirteen, when she arrived in Greece. It was music that saved her—music and ice cream."

"She is miraculous," Madame said, "because she concentrates on the notes. She's nearsighted and cannot see the conductor's baton. She has to follow her own internal beat. Her timbre was dark and heavy. And I had to teach her to lighten it, like the very best embroidery."

"And did you succeed?" Laura asked in the article.

"Sometimes," Madame said.

"And this is what we are left with," Laura wrote. "*La Perla nera*"—the Black Pearl.

That was the real subject of her article, which didn't even have a proper title in *Oggi*.

She wrote about this tempestuous diva with the desolate voice who had come from a foreign land "to devour us—eat us alive."

"She's invited to Verona, to Palermo, to Venice, to Florence, to Turin, to Rome, as if they were all satellites of La Scala," Laura wrote, "but when will the great Ghiringhelli invite her to Milan?"

Laura Sordelo had the power and the prestige to taunt Ghiringhelli, and Ghiringhelli, with his white lion's mane, had the power and the prestige to ignore her.

"Callas?" Ghiringhelli wrote in another magazine. "Who is this Callas? I never heard of such a musical monster."

And he could get away with this lie. He could also win any feud with a roving reporter. "We have no need of a mystical *Perla nera* in Milan. We have enough pearls of our own."

Maria had a second butterscotch sundae. She was scheduled to leave the next day for Argentina on a South American tour with Maestro Serafin and a troupe of Italian singers, starring tenor Mario Del Monaco, who had performed at La Scala, and would play Calaf, the mysterious prince in *Turandot* at the Teatro Colón. Mario was a handsome devil with a horde of followers, some of whom might even cross the ocean to hear him sing in Buenos Aires. Maria never got along with Mario. He didn't want a soprano with a far more mysterious voice to outmaneuver him in *Turandot.*

But Mario was not the real reason why Maria was in such a rebellious mood. She would not take a step until Titta married her. It was not entirely his fault. Because Maria was a member of the Greek Orthodox Church, the couple needed a special dispensation from the Vatican. The dispensation eventually arrived, but the Curia of Verona still stood in the way. Titta wanted to be married in his parish church, the Chiesa dei Filippini, the poorest in Verona.

Titta soon understood what this stalling was about. The Meneghinis had promised to repair the tiles on the roofs of every church in Verona if the final papers were not delivered. And so the king of Verona ran to the church chancellor, who lived on the Via Garibaldi. But the chancellor would not see him. It didn't seem to matter how hard Titta knocked or how hard he screamed. The chancellor still wouldn't come to the door. So Titta went to the vicar of San Tomaso with murder in his heart. He had all the documents signed and sealed within an hour.

These he flashed to Maria in his hand with all the flourish of a star tenor in his own private opera about the Meneghinis.

Maria clutched at the documents. "Darling, how did you convince the vicar?"

"I didn't. I stared at him. He signed. I left."

They walked to the Church of the Filippini, in a neighborhood of rotting mansions and villas, and handed the papers with their sacred seals to the parish priest, who'd been at the same parish since before the turn of the century and never missed a season at La Scala.

Don Octavio kissed Maria's hands. "He is a fool, that

emperor of Milan. He has his prima donnas, his lyrical wonders, but he does not have a soprano who can hug each note. You give a religious reading of every score. You have brought back bel canto, Signorina Callas."

"Meneghini Callas," Maria said.

Don Octavio could not conduct the service in the main sacristy, since Maria was not Catholic. But there was another sacristy, used as a storage room now, which was still consecrated. It had its own tiny altar. And that's where they were married, with two witnesses—friends of the king—after the altar had been cleared of junk. There were banners and canopies from another time and place, broken chairs covered in dust and spiderwebs, and an officer's uniform from an earlier war.

But there was no time at all for romance. After the consecration, everyone involved moved out of the sacristy and drank a glass of grappa.

The priest was crying. "You must break their hearts in Buenos Aires, Signorina Meneghini Callas."

"I will do my best," Maria said, brushing the priest's tears with her handkerchief.

The married couple grabbed Maria's luggage and left for Genoa; they managed to arrive a few minutes *after* midnight, when the *Argentina* was scheduled to depart, but the captain and his entire crew chose to wait for Maria.

She gave the king of Verona one final kiss before she climbed the gangway.

"Titta, wait for me. Don't run off with some other soprano."

-2-

The tour was troubling to Maria, particularly her time at the Teatro Colón. Nunco Rodriquez, the artistic director, and his cronies had no need for another diva. They had a diva of their own—Delia Rigal. She was tall and beautiful, with a voice that never wobbled. There was nothing wild or adventurous about her singing. The socialites of Buenos Aires, who purchased tickets for the entire opera season, adored her. Delia was the favorite prima donna at the Colón. And Nunco wanted her to play Turandot.

"I insist," he told Maestro Serafin.

The maestro's eyebrows moved about like live creatures. He'd been on an endless flight from Rome with La Rakowska. He'd invited Maria to come along and sit with him and his wife, but she was too frightened to fly.

Serafin still couldn't control his eyebrows; that's how much of a rage he was in.

"Señor Rodriguez, I'm sure Delia is a delight. But I already have my Turandot."

Nunco wasn't convinced. "*Your* Turandot is not known in Buenos Aires. I cannot sell tickets on the strength of her name. And Delia Rigal can pack the house—every socialite in Buenos Aires will come to hear her sing."

"Then it's a pity, señor," the maestro said. "We will have an empty house."

And he left the artistic director standing there in his own office under the dome.

There were repercussions. One of Delia's accomplices had raided the storage closet at the Colón and absconded with the costumes and elaborate headwear for the mythical

Chinese princess in *Turandot.* But La Rakowska had been to Buenos Aires before. And she found a tailor near the Colón who could outfit Maria as Turandot.

"This Delia," Maria said, "I should rip her hair out."

La Rakowska laughed. "It's not worth it. The audience will shun you for desecrating their darling. You already have a bad reputation in Buenos Aires. The opera fans call you the 'Tigress.' Someone has told them that you have fistfights with other members of the cast."

"It must be Mario," Maria said. "He always hogs the curtain."

"Never mind," La Rakowska said. "Be nice."

And they went to the grand salon at the Colón. Nunco was having a reception for the maestro and the singers he had brought with him to Buenos Aires. Half the socialites of the city were there. The women all wore dresses designed by couturiers who had come out of the workshop of Coco Chanel. Among them all was Delia Rigal, queen of the Colón, in a hat designed by Coco herself and long silk stockings that revealed her shapely legs. She had her own prince at the reception—Mario Del Monaco, the handsome Italian tenor whose aristocratic background fit in perfectly with the haut monde of Argentina and the New World.

They all flocked under the gilded chandeliers of the grand salon.

Maria felt soiled. She had to hide her bulky figure in a sacklike dress. She had none of the elegance of these socialites. She couldn't wear pumps in the grand salon, or she would have towered over all the guests. She looked scruffy in her flats.

A waiter offered her pink champagne. Her head began to swirl after one sip.

Delia wandered over to Maria with a calculated smile. She did not know a word of *Turandot.* She'd never sung the opera at the Colón or anywhere else. She'd plotted with Nunco Rodriquez. Delia hoped to poison Maria's appearances in Buenos Aires. She did not want any rivals at the Colón.

She clutched Maria's long, tapered fingers. "Forgive me for not welcoming you sooner, my dear."

Maria could feel the acid under Delia's velvety voice. But she couldn't shout at the Colón's favorite prima donna in front of all the socialites. Serafin would have banished her from the continent.

Mario swaggered in front of Maria in a pastel-colored suit from Milan. He kissed her on the cheek.

"*La Perla nera* has come to Buenos Aires. I will have to convince her of my love—onstage."

"I'm jealous," Delia said, clutching Mario's arm. "Maria, you'll have him all to yourself in *Turandot*."

"Well," Maria said, "I will lend him to you."

She left the grand salon without saying a word to the socialites or to the maestro and La Rakowska, or to Nunco Rodriguez and the other managers and directors of the Colón. Serafin was staying at the Plaza Hotel, where Caruso and Toscanini had stayed whenever they were in Buenos Aires and performed at the Colón. But Maria wasn't important enough to have royal rooms at the most royal hotel in town. She was booked at the Savoy, in a much smaller suite. It's where members of the chorus stayed.

From her balcony window, Buenos Aires had a strange, dreamlike aura, with its stretch of ghostly boulevards, which had earned it the pet name "Paris of the Pampas." Maria had never been to Paris. But she couldn't imagine boulevards without a living soul. There were more popular barrios at the very edge of Buenos Aires, she'd been told, where tango dancers—stringy little men with knives clenched in their teeth—fought like matadors over the heart of some voluptuous woman with ankles as thick as Maria's. That's what she dreamt while she perused the score of *Turandot.* She had steak for breakfast, lunch, and dinner at the Savoy, with *dulce de leche helado,* caramel ice cream, the closest flavor she could find to butterscotch.

She had steak before each rehearsal, unlike most other divas, who preferred to sing on an empty stomach. Steak and ice cream invigorated Maria, increased her breath control; she could sing entire passages on one long gulp of air. Her days were spent between the bare stage or the practice rooms at the Colón and the restaurant at the Savoy, where she sat alone at a corner table, sometimes devouring two beefsteaks and three dishes of caramel ice cream.

The maestro had little free time to devote to Maria. And the loneliness overwhelmed her. She would cry on transatlantic calls to Titta. "Darling, how I miss our little paradise—Verona. I am a misfit here. I do not dress like these South American aristocrats. I was an outcast from the moment I arrived."

She had a slight fever and an upset stomach from all the caramel ice cream. But not a single member of the cast came to visit. And La Rakowska was busy shopping on those forlorn boulevards.

Maria arrived at a dress rehearsal in rags. The maestro was furious. She wore a turban, rather than a mythical Chinese princess's headgear, and a bathrobe from the Savoy, decorated with ribbons.

Delia Rigal sat smiling in the audience with mischievous

delight at the spectacle of Maria in a bathrobe. She was surrounded by her coterie of followers. The maestro waved his baton at Maria with a bit of menace in front of the entire cast and all the socialites Nunco had invited to the dress rehearsal.

"Maria," the maestro asked in a wavering voice, "what is the meaning of this? We are performing *Turandot* tonight, not a clown show."

But Maria stood her ground. "Maestro, I'm not a couturier. My costume was stolen from the Colón's closet. And the seamstress I hired is working as fast as she can. But the embroidery is complicated. And she will not have it ready until the *prima*."

"Then we will proceed," Serafin said. And before he climbed into the conductor's pit, he whispered to Maria, "You've disappointed me. And I'm not quite sure I'll ever recover."

–3–

LOOKING LIKE A MOVIE STAR, Mario Del Monaco pranced through the first act of the *prima* in his royal tunic, as Calaf, the secret prince, declaring his wish to woo the ice princess despite the threat of his own imminent death should he fail to answer her three riddles. He was the perfect heroic suitor in his handsomeness and rich tenor's voice. He captured all the charm and mystery of Calaf and *owned* the first act, completely to himself. All the other figures seemed like pawns in his presence.

The audience waited and waited for Turandot. Her headpiece was braided with silver and gold and her kimono was embroidered with the finest thread. But it wasn't Maria's costume alone that stopped time at the Colón and kept the theater in a state of suspense. Maria wasn't wearing makeup except for the charcoal around her eyes. She entered in a blaze, her voice filled with a soft menace.

Suddenly, every other singer on the stage was invisible. Elegant and *manly* as he was, Mario couldn't compete with the demonic fury of Maria. She seemed to slice the air with her bitter melodies and her movements. The socialites of Buenos Aires had never had a mournful bird on their stage. Maria could have been singing a duet with the ghost of her dead canary Stephanakos. She herself had become a ghost, with violence in every gesture, a guttural harshness in her voice as the ice princess.

There was utter silence when the curtain fell after the final act. And then bedlam as cries from the Paraiso gallery arrived from under the dome, where a thousand patrons had to stand through the entire opera.

"Maria! Maria!"

She took her curtain calls with Mario, whom she had diminished with a single stroke of charcoal around her eyes. Calaf did not exist.

The maestro and La Rakowska had to break through the line of new devotees to get inside Maria's dressing room. Serafin had never visited her dressing room before.

"Maria, you must forgive me," the maestro said in a choking voice.

"Forgive?" Maria asked, wiping the charcoal from her eyes as she stared into her mirror. "Ah, I look human again. I was frightened by what I saw."

"You should be," La Rakowska said. "Maria, you were

a demon on that stage." Then she turned to her husband. "Now you must apologize."

"Maria, I shouldn't have scolded you. They used every trick against you . . . to guard the reputation of their diva. But you were possessed tonight. I swear, your voice came from another world."

"No, Maestro," Maria said. "It was the caramel ice cream. It works wonders."

She was summoned to see Nunco in his office near the upper tiers of the Colón, where all the fanatics had to move about in their poor man's paradise in order to watch Maria during *Turandot.* He handed her an envelope.

"I hope you're aware, Donna Maria," Nunco said with a smirk, "that you cannot take these pesos out of the country. It is forbidden by law. You must spend them in Argentina. We cannot have our currency devalued by foreign sopranos like you."

Maria was astonished. "I was never told. Is this how you have paid Maestro Serafin?"

"Of course not," Nunco said, rolling his eyes like a bad actor in his own troupe. "The maestro was sent a bank draft from Buenos Aires in the diplomatic pouch. Don't you have a manager?"

She couldn't blame Titta. How could he have known Argentina's monetary laws—involving diplomats?

She had played the Chinese princess over forty times, dug her heart into each performance, had used up the role. She could not enter Turandot's deep chill again and return from that darkness with her sanity intact.

She went with La Rakowska to a barrio called Palermo, which didn't have so many boulevards, and she bought a silver fox stole with her pesos from a fur shop near a meat factory. She didn't find any tango dancers in the street, and not one knife fight concerning the heart of a local beauty. She met only worn women with stooped backs, clutching leather shopping bags stuffed with vegetables. It reminded her of Athens during the war . . .

–4–

FROM HER BALCONY ON THE VIA SAN FERMO, Maria could see into the heart of the Roman Arena and watch the singers and dancers rehearse onstage, though their voices couldn't travel far enough to waft into her windows. It still amused her, because it was like watching a live puppet show, but these puppets had human limbs and strutted about at a furious pace.

Offers kept pouring in for Maria to sing *everywhere* except at La Scala.

Maria went down and sat at her favorite caffè and read Laura Sordelo in *Oggi* while spooning her second butterscotch sundae. The article wiped the taste of caramel from her mouth.

> *Will the lion of La Scala ever wake up? Or will Ghiringhelli guard his precious Tebaldi behind her own private curtain? She will never reach La Callas' high notes in this lifetime or another. Will he ever admit that the greatest soprano in all of Italy lives in Verona? Wake up, Antonio, wake up, before it is too late.*

Laura's remarks in *Oggi* had no effect on the lion of La Scala. But to her great surprise, Maria did get a telegram from Wally Toscanini, the maestro's daughter, a powerhouse in opera circles. The telegram was quite cryptic.

THE MAESTRO AWAITS YOU IN MILAN

It was dated September 22. Maria did have a suspicion of what it might be about—1951 would mark the fiftieth anniversary of Verdi's death, and La Scala hoped to celebrate that anniversary, with the help of Arturo Toscanini, in the town of Busseto, close to where Verdi had been born.

Toscanini had a godlike presence in Maria's life as a child. She listened to him on the radio every Saturday afternoon as he conducted the NBC Symphony of the Air. Toscanini had his own magic wand. He could slice into the deepest lines of any composer with his baton. Whatever he touched—Schubert, Brahms—had a range of emotion that no other conductor could summon from a musical score.

And so Maria and Titta had a rendezvous with the maestro and his daughter at Via Durini 20, the maestro's quarters in Milan. It resembled a fortress rather than a villa, with burnt sienna bricks and a steel door.

Wally had silver earrings and dark hair swept up in a bun. The maestro wore a dark suit and vest that must have come out of a medieval tailor shop. He was so thin that he couldn't stand straight. He wavered at a slight angle. Maria could see all the veins in his pale white skin. He was eighty-three years old, and could have been visiting Maria from another century. His mind was keen, but his voice was a monotone and had none of the music of his magic wand.

"Maria," he asked, "will you be my Lady Macbeth?"

As awed as she was by him, Maria answered shrewdly. "But Maestro, you have Tebaldi."

His tiny eyes flashed with anger. He was capable of the

worst tantrums. During rehearsals, he was known to rip a ringing telephone off the wall if it interfered with the thrust of his baton.

"I do not want a canary in a cage," he said in a much sharper tone. "What I want is a dangerous diva."

"But Ghiringhelli despises me," Maria said. "He will not let me near any project associated with La Scala."

"Ghiringhelli is an idiot," the maestro said. "Wally, am I right or not?"

His daughter smiled. "Papa, you will make us look like pagan warriors in front of La Callas and her husband."

"We are pagan warriors," the maestro said. And then he turned to Maria.

"Have you read Shakespeare's *Macbeth*?"

Maria felt embarrassed in front of the maestro and Wally. She was silent for a moment and then she seemed to stutter. "*Macbeth* was not in the c-c-curriculum at my public school in Washington Heights."

"*Perfecto*," the maestro said. "Shakespeare was a humanist. Verdi was not. His Lady Macbeth is a gangster, like Al Capone. . . . My spies have told me about your Norma and your Turandot. But how can I be sure that you have the devil in you? Come, you must audition for me. I have never once in my life conducted Verdi's *Macbeth*. It frightened me. I searched, but I could not find *my* Lady Macbeth, a soprano with enough venom, the venom that Verdi himself insisted upon. He wanted her to be ugly and evil, with the darkest voice that one could imagine."

He led Maria over to the piano, clutching her hand as if he were her suitor—or second husband. "Come. I will play and you will sing."

Maria was frantic. She had never studied Verdi's opera,

not a single note. She would have to sight-read on the spot. Toscanini opened the score of *Macbeth* as Maria hovered over him. He played with a relentless touch of the keyboard while Maria recited or sang every role—Banquo, Macbeth, Lady Macbeth, and Duncan, the Scottish king . . .

Titta watched his wife's eyes widen with a half-crazed alarm as she sang in a deliberate, sonorous voice, almost a death chant, urging Macbeth on to kill the king.

The maestro's long fingers suddenly leapt from the keyboard as he stopped in the middle of the first act. He hummed to himself for a moment. And then he seemed to pierce Maria with a half-mad look of his own.

"It's you, Maria, you I have been waiting for all these years. You will be my Lady Macbeth. I will speak to that fool Ghiringhelli and have him send you a letter of intent."

The maestro grew impulsive. Wally had never seen him move with such swiftness. He grabbed Maria and waltzed around the living room with her. Photos fell off the mantelpiece. Wally had to clutch antiques from the shelves before they crashed to the floor.

"Father," she said, "you must stop before you have a heart attack—I insist."

But the maestro didn't stop dancing. "Wally, can't you see how happy I am? Now I will conduct *Macbeth* before I die."

–5–

THE LION DID WRITE TO MARIA that October, declaring that he hoped to have her sing the role of Lady Macbeth under Toscanini's baton at Busseto. He talked of a meeting with Maria in Milan. Maria wrote him back. He didn't answer her letter, and the meeting never materialized. Maria phoned him at La Scala, but the lion couldn't be found. She called again. This time the lion came out of his inner sanctum to answer the call. He was quite congenial. He promised to prepare a letter that would confirm all the details.

"Ah, the maestro and Maria," he said. "That will be the spectacle of the century."

But the lion's letter never arrived. She couldn't get him on the phone again. Neither could Meneghini. But the lion couldn't avoid Wally, who was familiar with half the subscribers at La Scala. Lawyers were sucked into the maelstrom. Wally had collected all the financial support that Ghiringhelli would ever need for the performance. Still, the lion stalled. There were rumors that the maestro was ill. He wasn't ill. The lion had sabotaged the negotiations for his own perverse pleasure. Toscanini did not perform *Macbeth,* with or without Maria.

But things were no longer simple for this lion in his labyrinth at La Scala. Wally Toscanini was someone he had to reckon with. She had the power to have him plucked out of his labyrinth and tossed aside if she chose to do so. And she had already talked about Maria to Rudolf Bing, general manager of the Met. All Maria had to do was perform in Palermo or Florence—and wait for Ghiringhelli or Rudolf Bing . . .

It was eleven months and a myriad of engagements after her visit with the maestro and his daughter in Milan, and Maria was sitting at her favorite caffè with her long spoon, lapping up all the butterscotch she could find in her second sundae, when Titta sat down.

"Darling," she asked, "what are you doing here?"

"I had a phone call," he said. "Very bizarre. The caller revealed nothing to my secretary. Told her I should meet him at Maria's caffè. He was quite rude, it seems."

She smiled as Ghiringhelli arrived in a leather coat. He sat down without the simplest greeting and tossed a contract on the table.

"You will open the winter season," the lion said, "and be on call at La Scala for the entire *stagione.*"

"Where do I sign?" Maria asked.

Titta was in a panic. "Darling, what about all the little details? We don't even know what La Scala is willing to pay. And the dressing room you will have."

"Where do I sign?" Maria asked again.

The lion took out his Mont Blanc and handed it to Maria, who signed the contract with a flourish as the nib of the pen dug into the surface of the paper, creating a kind of canal. She capped the Mont Blanc and returned it to Ghiringhelli.

"I'll leave both you gentlemen. I'm sure you have a million things to discuss . . . Battista, darling, don't haggle too much. You'll get a sore throat."

And she departed with a naughty smile. She hadn't told Titta, but she knew every detail of the contract. It was Wally Toscanini who had confided in her on the phone and swore her to secrecy. Wally and La Scala shared the same lawyer. And it was Wally who had negotiated the most favorable terms for Maria. She would have her own maid at the theater to help her dress and undress and guard her wooden Madonna, also her own wigmaker, and she would never be asked to sing *Turandot* under any circumstances.

Ghiringhelli's own patrons had rebelled against him. They were lazy and spoiled on account of La Scala. They did not want to bother leaving Milan to hear and see this "dangerous diva" that Toscanini had wanted as his Lady Macbeth in a production that never took place because of Ghiringhelli's incompetence or one of his mysterious feuds.

As Maria pranced along the crooked streets of Verona, she wasn't dreaming of contracts or costumes, but of the taste of butterscotch on her lips.

-6-

THERE WAS NOTHING IN THE WORLD like the *loggionisti* at La Scala. They had captured the gallery and kept it to themselves, as conquerors. One could find *loggionisti*—wild bands of fanatics—in the upper galleries of opera houses everywhere in Italy, but none of them compared to these "gallery ghosts" in Milan. They were terrible snobs. None of them would ever have sat in the orchestra or in one of the box seats with ordinary opera lovers. True, a number of them couldn't afford the price. But some were as rich as Croesus. Others included a maimed general, car mechanics, college professors, scribes, a half-starved playwright, secretaries, pensioners, and pickpockets.

These *loggionisti* rarely went to other opera houses. Also, they seldom left Milan. And many were seeing La Callas for the first time. They loved their glorious nightingale, Renata, but they were growing restless. So they *allowed* Ghiringhelli to bring in a new soprano for this *stagione.* Still, their loyalty remained with Renata. And as curious as they were about La Callas, they would *serenade* her—sing her arias right on top of her if she dared miss a note, or they didn't find sufficient pleasure in her voice. They'd destroyed many a soprano with their serenades.

Sitting among them was Laura Sordelo of *Oggi*. She was a girl with a limp whom they had adopted. She'd caught polio as a child and still walked with a cane, had a metal brace on one leg. But everything she knew about opera had come from these *loggionisti* and *loggionisti* elsewhere. They recited the arcane language of opera among themselves, and Laura listened.

They chatted and hummed half the opera until the third bell rang. *I vespri siciliani* hadn't been performed at La Scala since 1908, but the *loggionisti* knew every whisper. The tension built in the auditorium as the audience heard the rustle of the curtains. The chandeliers had an odd hiss as the hall descended into darkness. Without a bit of reprieve, those in attendance were hurled back into the thirteenth century. They were in Palermo now, in the middle of the main piazza, which was occupied by foreign soldiers and their barracks, with bundles of armaments lying about—spears and shields, et cetera. The Kingdom of Sicily had fallen to the French. These soldiers bantered and caroused among themselves with cups of wine and an air of contempt.

The *loggionisti* were bored to death.

Suddenly, the Sicilian Duchess Elena entered the piazza, and the *loggionisti* livened to the movement of her arms and the defiant sway of her body—they could feel the violence within her without her having to utter a syllable of song. She was wearing stark black. The duchess was in mourning. Her brother Frederick of Austria had been executed by the French for high treason. And she walked among these enemy soldiers like a red-hot wraith.

Laura Sordelo could hear all the commotion coming from the gallery.

"Look at this *ragazza*," said Bernardo, a cobbler who constructed the finest shoes in Italy and was sought after by every fashion house in Milan. He was the leader of the *loggionisti*. "I love her. Watch the way she moves. She's surrounded by invaders, but her body is like a taut bow ready to deliver invisible arrows—with poisonous tips, mind you, poisonous tips."

"You're a dreamer, Bernardo," said Monica, an unemployed actress. "You always have to bring in metaphysics."

Bernardo scoffed at her. "What's so metaphysical about arrows and bows?"

Monica frowned. "They're invisible. And invisible arrows can't stick to your skin."

"Quiet," said the other *loggionisti*. "The *ragazza* is about to sing."

One of the drunken French soldiers, Roberto, menaced the duchess, commanded her to sing a song for his own amusement. But Roberto was too drunk to understand the real tone and tenor of her song, which was a rallying cry to rebellion.

The entire gallery gasped. They had never heard a *ragazza* with such a daring range, who could leap from contralto to way above high C without the least tremor, like a vocal acrobat, or a rocket that could sing while remaining still.

Stile fiorito, Bernardo mumbled to himself. La Callas could sing like the castrati, in the most flowery style, while still keeping to the score. This *ragazza* had brought bel canto back to La Scala. Tebaldi had no use for ornaments.

La Scala's nightingale sang in the purest velvet tone. But Callas was another creature. A much darker songbird.

The others had to hold Bernardo in his seat as he began to *serenade* Roberto and his fellow drunken French soldiers. He wasn't really criticizing them, sweeping them off the stage. He was merely insisting that no other singer could take flight the way Callas could . . .

The *loggionisti* wouldn't interfere with any diva's life, wouldn't wait outside her dressing room for her autograph, certainly not someone like Bernardo. He had a new cause—Maria Meneghini Callas. And he would choreograph in his mind every move she made in Verdi's opera, every gesture; he sketched the tiara she wore in the third act, at the very point the Sicilians rebelled, during vespers.

He could feel a tug at his arm and had to endure the perils of a whining voice in *his* gallery, a place that was sacrosanct, reserved for the *loggionisti* alone.

There was a second tug and the same whining voice.

"Bernardo, Anna needs a pair of shoes. I beg you. She'll murder me if I disappoint her again."

Bernardo stared at Anna Magnani's manager, Alfredo Longo, a pusillanimous nonentity.

"Didn't I tell you not to come here?"

"But you're never in your shop," Longo said.

"It's opera season. You could have sent me a wire."

Alfredo got down on his knees. "Is it my fault? She will wear no one else's shoes. 'Find the cobbler,' she said. 'I need a new fitting.'"

"Next week," Bernardo said. "Saturday morning at seven."

Alfredo was still down on his knees. "That's impossible, Maestro. Magnani doesn't rise before noon."

Bernardo was prepared to hammer him. "I'm a shoemaker, Alfredo. Toscanini is a maestro, not me. Magnani can come at noon. Now get the hell out of here."

Alfredo kissed Bernardo's hand. "*Mille grazie, padrone.*" And he removed himself from the gallery. That's when Bernardo saw the *ragazza* with the leg brace. He wasn't fooled by her pretense of anonymity. She was Laura Sordelo, who'd written pieces about La Callas before he'd ever heard of her and kept tossing darts at Ghiringhelli in print. That's why he tolerated this *ragazza* in the gallery.

The other *loggionisti* were gone. There was only Laura and himself in the wide arena of the gallery, its floor covered with candy wrappers and peanut shells. She had a quizzical look on her face.

"*Padrone,* I've never seen you so excited before. You love Tebaldi, but she never excited you—not like this."

"Signorina, put your notebook away, and then we can talk. I don't want to be quoted in that magazine of yours. I'm a shoemaker, not an opera critic."

Laura smiled. "A shoemaker with ten assistants and his own shop, who has half the women in Milan and Rome, including Anna Magnani, shivering for his shoes."

"It is happenstance, Donna Laura, a trick of fate. But I will tell you my own feelings about the diva. She is a comet who has wandered into our firmament and may soon wander away."

"But why, Bernardo, why would she ever wander?"

The cobber scrunched one eye. "Because there's always disaster following any diva. They grow old—too fast. Or they lose their wondrous breath control. Or *loggionisti* like us tire of them and search out some other goddess."

"Bernardo," Laura said, "you are a sinister man. To

talk about her destruction right after her debut in Ghiringhelli's house."

"It's not his house," Bernardo said. "But you're right. I am sinister."

And with remarkable rudeness, Bernardo left her sitting there and disappeared from the gallery.

–7–

WHILE REHEARSING *NORMA* FOR THE second half of her *stagione* at La Scala, Maria stayed with Titta at the Grand Hotel, within walking distance of the opera house. Verdi had lived at the same hotel whenever he was in Milan and had kept a suite there until the end of his life. In fact, he had died of a stroke during one of his sojourns at the Grand Hotel. The hotel had kept Verdi's residence, Suite 105, as a kind of museum and had given Maria her own private key, so that she could visit the suite where Verdi had supposedly finished *Otello.* The velvet drapes had a purplish color, the lamps were pink, but Maria couldn't be sure if the Grand Hotel had retouched the composer's suite for all the *turistas.* She liked to stand at his desk and rub her hand against the mahogany while Titta was attending to her contracts. And she would often wander across the halls outside Verdi's suite, wondering how he discovered his melodic lines. Other guests at the Grand Hotel seldom disturbed her, seldom asked the diva for her autograph. They must have imagined that she was preparing for a part . . .

She kept her eyeglasses on during rehearsals and wore a lumpish gray sweater and a simple brown skirt. She was very demanding and went through the entire opera each time in full voice. But her feet began to swell. Her ankles thickened more and more.

"I have lousy shoes," she said, but she didn't know where to shop in Milan. So she asked the manager at the Grand Hotel.

"Ah," he said, "we have the finest shoemaker in all of Italy just around the corner."

Maria smiled. "*Commendatore*, do you own shares in this shoemaker's shop?"

"No, Madame. But you will not be disappointed. You must visit his salon."

And he scribbled the address of the shoemaker on one of the hotel's cards.

Maria went around the corner in her shoddy shoes. She didn't find a shoemaker's shop, just a salon with a black curtain covering the window. She laughed to herself at the pair of words painted with consummate skill at a corner of the window: LADY MACBETH'S.

She went inside. A boy in a rumpled blue workman's smock stood behind a counter laden with women's shoes in every state of disrepair. Behind this boy was another black curtain, like the one in the window. On the side wall was a bulletin board with photos of La Callas, all of them ripped out of *Oggi*, *la Repubblica*, and *Corriere della Sera*. None were fashion shots. Not a single one was posed. They had been taken during rehearsals at various opera houses.

Maria hummed to herself and finally the boy looked up. He didn't recognize Maria as the woman on the wall.

"How can I help, signora?"

"I need a pair of shoes. My feet are killing me."

The boy leered at her. "But we are a custom shop,

signora. You cannot just walk in off the street. You must make an appointment to see the *padrone.*"

"But I do not have time for a special fitting," Maria said, wondering why the boy still didn't recognize her. "Can you please tell him that I was recommended by the manager of the Grand Hotel?"

The boy puffed out his chest. "Signora, that would make little difference to him. His biggest customers are actresses and queens."

"Then," Maria said, "can you please ask him if he would do a special favor for Madame Meneghini?"

The boy went behind the black curtain and returned in a minute with a leer on his face.

"I told you, signora. My *padrone* doesn't have the time."

Maria was furious. She stood there and began to sing "Casta Diva" as loud as she could. The light fixture above Maria's head began to rattle.

A very tall, thin man came out from behind the black curtain. He looked like Farinelli, the notorious male soprano of the eighteenth century. Women fainted when he sang. Men wore his one initial on their belt buckles. This Farinelli had the same rumpled blue smock as the boy behind the counter.

"It isn't fair," he said, "to sing like that in a poor cobbler's shop. I'm Bernardo Scarpia."

Maria felt much better now. "How fitting, to name yourself after one of the worst villains in all of Italian opera."

"Well, Madame Meneghini," Bernardo said. "We're all a little disguised. And please forgive my nephew. He hasn't met many opera stars."

Bernardo invited Maria behind the black curtain. His shop was all in a clutter, with strips of leather on the floor, with hammers, awls, a dozen shoemaker's benches, and a leather chair for his clients. He had half a dozen assistants hammering away at their benches as they shaped and built shoes with strips of leather; every shoe had a different design, a different color, a different pointed toe. But their hammering was unbearable. Each knock rang in Maria's head like a mortal blow.

"Quiet!" Bernardo shouted above the pounding of the hammers. "Go on your lunch break, all of you."

"But Don Bernardo," said one of the shoemakers, "we just came back from lunch."

Bernardo tossed an awl at the shoemaker, who had to duck, else he might have lost an ear.

"Well, go out again. We have a diva at Lady Macbeth's. And I don't want to be disturbed."

The shoemakers doffed their caps at Maria and walked through the same black curtain, while she sat down in the cracked leather chair and said, "If you work fast, Bernardo, I'll give you guest tickets—orchestra seats—for my opening of *Norma* at La Scala."

He had the hands of a violinist, not a cobbler. He took off her shoes and she barely felt his touch. "I never sit in the orchestra." He stared into her large liquid eyes. "I'm a member of the *loggionisti*."

Maria was stunned. "And I suppose you'll toss eggs at me one of these nights and hiss me off the stage."

His shoulders began to bob. Bernardo seemed to enjoy having Maria in his salon. "Only if you deserve it. We're your biggest fans. And if you grow lazy on us, Madame Meneghini, you will understand what the *loggionisti* are all about. But you didn't come to discuss opera."

"My feet are all swollen," she said with a look of despair. "And how can I rush across a stage on swollen feet?"

"I can't fix that," the cobbler said. "I'm not a doctor." But he caressed her feet with his long fingers. "You have as many bunions as there are barnacles on the Rock of Gibraltar."

He dug his hand into the leather cave of her shoddy left shoe. "It's much too tight. A foot has to breathe. And the leather that surrounds it has to be soft, Madame Meneghini."

She smiled at this impudent cobbler like the diva she'd become, and the diva she'd always been, even as a child listening to Toscanini on the radio.

"We're intimate now, Don Bernardo," she said. "You've touched my feet. You may call me Maria."

"Impossible," he said. "How could I judge your performance? The other *loggionisti* would declare me a traitor, unfit to sit among them, Madame Meneghini."

The cobbler never used a tape measure. He measured her feet with his hands, and then swathed them in strips of leather.

"Your shoes have no insoles. They cannot support your size and weight. They literally strangle your feet. They cannot absorb the shock of step after step after step."

"Don Bernardo," she asked, with an actress's ability to summon a look of terror, "how long will I have to wait?"

"I have many customers, madame. I will do the best I can."

Capriciously, Maria pecked him on the cheek and moved toward the black curtain. "Oh, I forgot. How much will your magical shoes cost?"

"That depends on the leather and the time it takes.

Don't worry. I'll bill you when the work is done. . . . Meanwhile, you can borrow these. They should fit."

And he slipped her feet into a pair of moccasins, as if she were a broad-shouldered Cinderella. Maria sighed deeply. It felt as if she were wearing velvet gloves on her big feet.

He tossed her other shoes into the bin.

"Bernardo," she whispered hoarsely, "you are divine, you know."

"Not at all, madame. I'm just a shoemaker who loves opera."

And with that she strutted through the curtain and out the store, and went back to the Grand Hotel. She rehearsed that night, then walked through the tunnel beneath the stage, and arrived at the domed roof of the gallery, with bats' wings silhouetted in the moonlight that shimmered through the metal ribs of the dome. She watched the flight of the bats for a moment and went to eat at Biffi Scala with all the opera buffs, and with Titta and Ghiringhelli at her table. She remembered all the tales that Madame Elvira had told about Biffi Scala, when Madame had reigned for one season as Rosina, and signed autograph after autograph.

Maria had to listen to Ghiringhelli's monologue as she drank a glass of Tuscan wine and stared at a plate of linguine with oysters while the autograph seekers stood in line.

Ghiringhelli interrupted his monologue to snarl at them. "Can't you see? The signorina is in the middle of a meal."

Maria ignored him and signed every autograph.

"You shouldn't spoil them, Maria," Ghiringhelli said, "or they will follow you right into the toilet."

Biffi Scala was the opera house's very own haunt—its bistro and caffè—and a waiter arrived with a napkin that had her initials sewn into it in silver thread. Maria wondered if Madame Elvira had also had her own private napkin at Biffi Scala.

"You know, Antonio," she said to the lion, who hadn't quite finished his monologue, "that little shit of yours, Mario Labroca, rejected my first audition, said my 'Casta Diva' was pure ventriloquism, that I had no right to sing it because I wasn't a mother and had not suffered enough. I'd like to tear out his heart—I will."

The lion laughed at her ferociousness. "I will warn him, darling." And he kissed her hand.

Maria had a second plate of linguine and sopped up the sauce with some Tuscan flat bread. "Antonio, one day I will rip your face off."

Titta pinched her under the table.

"Stop that," Maria said. "Let the lion fire me. Who cares? I will sing in the street, like La Gioconda."

Titta took her back to the Grand Hotel in Ghiringhelli's private limousine and put her to bed like a naughty child.

She woke to the sound of a telephone buzzing in her ear. It was deep into the afternoon.

"Madame Meneghini," said the concierge, "there is a package waiting for you at the front desk."

Maria went down to the desk in her bathrobe. The concierge handed her a shoe box with the words *LADY MACBETH'S* embossed in gold. Maria stood there, transfixed.

"Don't you want to open it, madame?" the concierge asked.

His obsequious voice broke the spell. Daintily, with

some caution, she opened the box and pulled out a pair of red shoes from a world of tissue paper—each shoe had a very long toe, like the prow of a pirate ship. Before Maria could protest, the concierge sat her down in one of the hotel's royal chairs, knelt on one knee, removed her moccasins, and helped her into her red shoes.

Maria stood up and prowled across the lobby in her Lady Macbeth's. She felt all afloat. Nothing pinched. Her feet didn't hurt for the first time since she could remember. She could have been riding on a magic carpet at the Grand Hotel.

She found a note inside the shoebox.

My Dear Madame Meneghini,

I hope my craftsmen and I have given you all that you desired.

There is no charge, madame. You have given me more delight than a cobbler like myself could ever deserve.

Humbly,
Bernardo Scarpia/Lady Macbeth's

Maria marched to Bernardo's salon in her red shoes.

"Where is Bernardo?" she sang, as if she were in the middle of an aria.

Bernardo's nephew, the boy behind the counter, said, "The *padrone* is not here today, signora."

"That's impossible," Maria said sotto voce. "I must thank him—for the shoes."

The boy leered at her, as usual. "The *padrone* is in Palermo."

"Why?"

"Ah," the boy said, suddenly empowered. "He gets into quarrels with the police from time to time. And he has to recuperate—in Palermo, where no one can find him."

"When will Bernardo be back?" she asked like a little girl.

"That depends," the boy said, "on the police—and the weather. The *padrone* likes it in Palermo."

Maria returned to the Grand Hotel with a humbled heart.

-8-

He was as tall as Maria, taller even, and moved with the litheness of a leopard, a leopard with black hair and blistering eyes. At the time he dressed in high-fashion colors and cuts of silk and cloth that made Titta look like a most provincial king. Luchino Visconti came from a long line of dukes on his father's side of the family. His mother was the heir to a pharmaceutical fortune. He grew up at a palazzo in Milan, where he had his own theater as a boy. It occupied an entire floor, and he managed to put on lavish productions of stories and novelettes that he wrote—with the sons and daughters of other dukes at his command as members of his cast and crew. His grandfather had his own family box—or *palchetto*—at La Scala, covered in deep red damask from Syria; and when the commune of Milan relinquished its support of La Scala, his grandfather took it upon himself and his fellow aristocrats to buy up all the boxes at the opera house, with their red velvet seats and private salons, where little galas could be held between acts of *Traviata* or *Otello.* These aristocrats seldom watched an entire opera.

They had a flute of pink champagne and often left in the middle of the second act.

Luchino had seen his first opera at seven and was a fanatic by the time he was ten. And when he saw Maria as Kundry—the wild woman in Wagner's *Parsifal*—he realized that he wanted to direct an opera, but only with Maria in it. He was forty-five and one of the most celebrated theater and film directors in Italy when he appeared in Maria's dressing room at the Rome Opera. His nobility was never in question. The ushers bowed and called him "Signor Conte."

Maria had never heard that title before. *Signor Conte.* Tied to rehearsals as she was, she had very little traffic with counts of any kind.

She had seen none of Visconti's films—Maria was addicted to Westerns all her life—but she was instantly drawn to him, to his intense wildness, as if he were a sorcerer in a silk coat.

"It would be the consummate pleasure of my life to direct you in *Traviata* one day, Madame Meneghini."

"Why?" she asked, almost belligerent, because without her glasses, she could see nothing more than the dramatic sweep of his face.

"Because," he said, "you are the greatest soprano Italy has ever had."

She stared into the blaze of his dark eyes. "And you, Signor Conte, are a flatterer. I am not even Italian."

"Yet here you are in Rome, Madame Meneghini."

And he handed her a single red rose. Its perfume was so intense, it nearly made her nostrils numb.

Visconti was rampant in Maria's dressing room, aware of the power of that rose. "I plucked it from my garden minutes before I left for the opera. I did not intend to offer it as a gift. But your Kundry diminished me."

"You talk in riddles, signor. And I am not so fond of riddlers."

"Madame, your voice was so resplendent, with so many colors and variations, I had an attack of vertigo."

Willful as she was, Maria put on her glasses, almost out of spite. But the man, she discovered, diminished *her*. His eyes did blaze with a hypnotic splendor—and charm. Still, she resisted him. She was not in the habit of planning future performances with perfect strangers, even celebrated strangers like Visconti.

She still had Kundry's wildness in her. She had worn a diaphanous gown in act 2 that revealed the ample contours of her body.

"Madman," she said. "Violetta is consumptive in your precious *Traviata*. Do I look consumptive to you?"

"No," he replied. "But you are still *my* Violetta."

Her voice had been ripped out of her after appearing on stage for almost five hours, and with whatever little she had left, she croaked, "You will have to forgive me, Signor Conte. I am having dinner with my husband."

The dark-eyed aristocrat seemed forlorn. "You mock me with that title, madame. I am Luca to my friends."

"But we are not friends," Maria said, as if they were both in the middle of a recitative. "At least not yet. And I do have to go."

Actually, she didn't have dinner at all. She was far too exhausted. She went back to her hotel, the Quirinale, with Titta, where she had antipasti and a pitcher of white wine brought up to their suite. She'd changed into her dressing gown, and one of her breasts must have slipped out. The waiter was impulsive—he tried to touch the diva's breast. Maria socked him so hard that he landed in the hallway, his white waistcoat covered in zucchini flowers and stracciatella from the antipasti tray.

The manager, Signor Gritto, arrived, while the waiter sat there, groggy-eyed, his jaw nearly broken.

"What is the meaning of this?" he asked, with a pompous tug of his mustache.

Titta was indignant. "Has the Quirinale become a bordello? This man of yours tried to rape my wife."

Signor Gritto stared at the *wounded* waiter. "Explain yourself, Tommaso."

The waiter began to sob. He clasped his hands and rocked in front of Maria. "Forgive me. Madame was so beautiful in her gown, I could not . . ."

"Tommaso," the manager said, "gather all your belongings and get out of the Quirinale."

"Please," Maria said, "don't fire him." She realized that the stranger's appearance in her dressing room at the theater had riled her. She shouldn't have hit poor Tommaso so hard.

"But his behavior is unacceptable," Signor Gritto said.

Maria stroked his arm with her tapered fingers; her breast was still uncovered. Visconti was a wizard. She'd never really left the stage. She was Kundry in her dressing room; she was Kundry right now. She'd bewitched that poor waiter, as she had bewitched the king and the knights of the Holy Grail in *Parsifal.*

"No," she said. "You mustn't fire the boy." She picked him up and swept the zucchini flowers off his waistcoat.

"Tommaso, be a darling and bring us up another plate of antipasti. I'm hungry as a wolf."

And Kundry collected her husband and returned to their suite.

-9-

It stuck with Maria, bothered her, as she pictured a starving, consumptive Violetta, who still weighed two hundred pounds. And she couldn't get rid of her aristocratic film director. Wherever she performed—Rome, Florence, Milan, Catania, Palermo, Genoa, Verona, Venice—that tall magician in the red scarf and silk coat was always in the audience, no matter how many times she played Medea, Norma, or Lady Macbeth. He didn't always visit her dressing room, but he was always there, leaving his signature red rose with one of the custodians.

Meanwhile, Laura Sordelo came out of hiding with her crutches and leg brace and agreed to interview Maria at Biffi Scala among all the cognoscenti and opera riffraff.

Maria had gone directly from her dressing room, with charcoal around her eyes. She saw a mouse in the tunnel under the stage. The mouse was shivering, and Maria fed it bits of chocolate from her pocket.

Laura had arrived with a notebook. Maria peered at her through her thick glasses.

"Signorina Sordelo, you were the first critic in Italy who ever took notice of me. But you yourself are not so visible. Sometimes I stand behind the curtain and peek at the audience in my glasses. I'm blind as a bat without them. But I have never seen you, signorina, not in *any* theater."

"That's not surprising, Madame Meneghini," Laura

said. "I always sit in the gallery with the *loggionisti.* I have learned from them."

Suddenly, Maria's mind sharpened. "Then you must know Bernardo—Bernardo Scarpia."

"Yes, of course," Laura said, with a slight air of triumph. "He sits in the king's seat, overlooking the entire theater. But he's abandoned his shoe salon and left for Sicily—I think the local police are after him. They're the thieves, I imagine, not Bernardo."

Maria was still perplexed. "But I sang in Palermo a few months ago. I climbed up to the gallery, and Bernardo wasn't there."

"Yes," said Laura, wincing at a sudden jolt of pain in her withered leg. "Bernardo is like a submarine. He has not resurfaced yet."

Maria revealed her red shoes with their pointy toes. "These are Bernardo's creations. They have done wonders for my legs. I can walk and walk without my ankles swelling. But their soles are worn."

Laura smiled. "Then visit a shoemaker, madame."

"I wouldn't dare," Maria said, almost alarmed. "No one but Bernardo can touch my feet . . . or my red shoes. But I don't want this mentioned in any article. It might scare Bernardo away."

"I told you," Laura said, a bit curt. "A submarine like Bernardo might never resurface again."

Maria smiled wickedly. "But you're also a submarine. Why did you suddenly decide to surface?"

Laura fumbled with her fork. "It's my editors. They insisted. Those fools, they said, 'Why is La Callas' timbre so dark?' That is not a question *I* would ever ask."

"Well, I will answer it," Maria said, her prominent

cheekbones bristling. "I had a lovely canary, Stephanakos—we did duets together. With him, I was Violetta." Maria paused for a moment to pat her lips with a napkin. "But had I been Medea, I would have frightened poor Stephanakos to death."

And then the diva took flight. "Enough about canaries. Who is this Visconti fellow? He says he wants to do *Traviata* with me. But why would I ever need him?"

Laura's eyes lit with fever. "He will create an ambience for you, an ambience that will surround you onstage."

"But Ghiringhelli doesn't like him," Maria insisted. "Says he's a Communist."

"Perhaps," Laura said. "A Communist with an eye for detail."

Maria grasped Laura's wrist with her shapely talons. "Don't utter a word to your editors, please. Swear on your life! But don't you think I'm too fat to play Violetta?"

"Madame, you're not fat at all. You carry your weight like a ballet dancer."

"Ah," Maria said, with the same wicked smile. "You're a flatterer, like Visconti."

Then the opera riffraff surrounded Maria, pestering her for autographs. Laura slipped away on her crutches. It troubled Maria to watch her drag that metal brace.

Still, she couldn't get out from under Visconti's spell. It must have been 1953. *Roman Holiday* was the cinematic hit of the season. She watched it several times at a movie house in Verona, enchanted by a new actress, an actress she'd never seen before—Audrey Hepburn, an ex–ballet dancer born in Belgium from a line of aristocrats. She plays the crown princess of some mysterious Middle European capital. Princess Ann is on a state visit to Rome, but she's trapped inside her embassy, with bodyguards galore. So she opts for a jailbreak and decides to have a Roman holiday, incognito.

All through the film, Maria muttered to herself, *Why can't I look like that? Why can't La Callas be another Audrey Hepburn?*

And Maria dreamt of herself as a tall, slim gamine with very high cheekbones. She was still living in Verona, above Titta's office. But his brothers were brutal with her, avoiding Maria on the stairs. The king of Verona wouldn't admonish his brothers. Maria tossed a slipper at him and one of his mother's precious plates.

"We're moving to Milan," Maria said. "That's final. I'm at La Scala now. And we won't have to live at the Grand Hotel, like Verdi. That hotel became his coffin in the end."

Titta found a villa for sale on the Via Michelangelo Buonarroti, with an enormous garden. That's when she realized that Titta didn't have his own private fortune. All his wealth was tied up in the family's holdings—its real estate and brick factories. The futuristic Alfa 2000 he bought came out of her earnings, not his. But he was able to grab up the villa, which happened to be near the opera house, by selling off some of the real estate he had hidden in his name. Still, there was so much bickering within the Meneghini family circle that it would take Maria months and months before she and Titta could move in.

She grew closer to Visconti. She would visit him at his palazzo on the Via Salaria whenever she was in Rome. An entire team of mastiffs followed him from room to room, with their great slobbering mouths. Colors vanished from his wardrobe. He dressed entirely in black, except for his cardigans, which came from Pozzi's, the one high-fashion shop in Milan that carried English clothing and accessories imported from Savile Row.

Visconti despised restaurants with their pomp and waste of food. So he gave dinner parties at his palazzo. Maria felt uncomfortable in her baggy dresses, while the women at the parties arrived in skirts, hats, and boots designed by Christian Dior; they were like silhouettes she couldn't escape from.

All she could counter with were her red shoes.

A crash diet wouldn't have meant much. She would have devoured whatever salami was left in the fridge as a midnight snack. So she kept nothing but steak tartar and raw vegetables in the house. She was determined to look like Audrey Hepburn's slightly older and heftier twin.

The doctors discovered a tapeworm in her gut from all the raw meat she had devoured. She swallowed every sort of medicine to rid herself of the tapeworm, but she'd barely sucked an inch off her waist. Her ankles had even thickened from standing so much, rehearsing so much, performing so much.

She hadn't moved into her villa on the Via Buonarroti yet, and while staying at the Grand Hotel for her latest *stagione* at La Scala, she discovered a shoe box from Lady Macbeth's outside the door of her suite. There was the same imbroglio of tissue paper and a brand-new pair of red shoes, with a note tucked inside the left shoe.

My Dearest Diva,

I did not miss your latest Medea, though I could not sit among my compatriots for fear of being recognized—and arrested. But as one critic declared: Your singing went beyond the notes, into a realm where myth and legend lie down together. I doubt that another soprano will attempt the same role in your lifetime or mine.

Your Devoted Servant, the Late Bernardo Scarpia (I'm still in hiding)

It didn't seem to matter how little she ate or how far she walked in her second pair of red shoes; her metabolism kept her close to two hundred pounds. The doctors she consulted in Milan couldn't console her.

"Maria, look how hard it was to rid your system of that tapeworm. You almost poisoned yourself with all those tonics."

And so she ended up with some Svengali, a medical doctor from Lausanne who'd lost his license and opened a clinic in Milan that served as a health spa. He advertised himself as Dr. Victor Dent. He wore a clinician's white coat and had a bad case of scoliosis, a curvature of the spine that couldn't be corrected. He must have been close to eighty, but he had a cherub's face, without a single line.

He did not mislead Maria. "It will be dangerous, Madame Meneghini."

"I'm used to danger," she said, though Titta was against the doctor's unorthodox treatment. She was fed doses of dry thyroid extract and exotic hormones that could burn off fat at an alarming rate and permanently meddle with her metabolism. Friends warned her that this colossal loss of weight would shrink her thorax and might very well harm her voice, as it would have less and less room to resound in her rib cage.

"I don't give a damn," said the diva. "I'll take that chance. I want to look like Audrey Hepburn."

Titta negotiated with artistic directors even while Maria

was deep inside the cocoon of Dr. Dent's clinic. She sang at one opera house after another and then disappeared for a few days. She would wander through the halls of the clinic in a white gown, like Lady Macbeth. She remembered the last time she had done the sleepwalking scene in Milan.

It soon became clear that she was driving Tebaldi out of La Scala. Even Ghiringhelli, Tebaldi's greatest fan, realized that audiences wanted this new diva with dark eyes and devilish vibrations in her voice. But a few of Tebaldi's diehards had brought their whistles to the opera, and they blew as hard as they could after the sleepwalking scene to disorient Maria and break her rhythm. But it backfired. Spectators rose up from their seats and applauded Maria for fifteen minutes, and as she stood there shivering with emotion and the intensity of the role, the madness she had feigned had suddenly become real and then disappeared as the clapping died down . . .

It felt more and more like a prison sentence, her time at the clinic. She had to swallow her own black bile. She vomited more than once.

"Signora," said Dr. Dent, rambling up to her with his crooked spine, "you could stop right here. You've already made significant progress."

"No!" she said. "No, no, no."

And she walked past the other ghosts in white gowns, who were much, much heavier than Maria. She plunged into the doctor's program like a mad diver. She gave no interviews, talked to no one but Titta.

Her voice had lost none of its vibrato and color variations, while she stuck to the regimen and dropped forty pounds—and then another forty—in thirteen months. She was a much different creature, less of the vixen who punched a waiter in the halls of the Grand Hotel, and more of a tall, svelte diva with startling dark eyes and a sensuous mouth. She dined on lettuce leaves for lunch and drank gulps of scented water. She still had enough strength to sing.

She'd become the rage of Italy. Every newspaper and magazine wanted an exclusive about the tempest over the diva's diet—and miraculous transformation. She awaited Laura Sordelo's call from *Oggi*. But Laura never called. So Maria rang her.

"Child," she said imperiously, "*everyone* is dying to interview me, except you."

There was a long silence before Laura spoke. "Madam Meneghini, you have come under the purview of the fashion editor. That is not my jurisdiction. I'm told you swallowed a tapeworm in a glass of champagne."

"It's a big lie, invented by the journalists themselves."

"But when will you do *Traviata* with Visconti?"

Maria shook the receiver in her hand. "I'm not a mind reader. It's up to the gods of Milan."

Ghiringhelli relented. He allowed "that Communist" to enter La Scala as Maria's stage director, a situation that was slightly baffling to Maria, since most celebrated conductors followed Toscanini's great example and wouldn't allow some stranger to interrupt the beat of their baton. And why did her Italian count have such a mania about *La Traviata*? What hold did this opera have on him? He was famous for his startling costumes and décor. He would shape this opera like a ballet master, choreograph every one of Maria's moves, no matter who wielded the baton. Violetta is a courtesan who has bewitched all of Paris. She is welcomed everywhere a courtesan is welcomed. She cavorts with noblemen. But she is still an outcast, a pariah who wears French perfume like other courtesans, rather than some aristocratic scent or eau de cologne.

It took Laura Sordelo to reveal the secret behind Visconti's desire to direct *Traviata,* with Maria as Violetta. Maria had to wait an hour to get through to Laura this time, and both were in Milan. But it was even worse than that, since all the operators considered themselves prima donnas and might leave you stranded with a dead connection while they did their nails.

Laura cursed them all and said, "It's simple, Maria. You remind Visconti of his mother, and there's no one on this earth he loved more than Donna Carla. You have her lovely arms and long black hair. You're both tall and beautiful."

"I have a big nose," Maria uttered in her own defense.

"*Basta!*" Laura said. "You're beautiful."

And Laura told her tales about Casa Visconti in Milan. It was the pinnacle of Milanese society in that Belle Epoque of peace at home and abroad prior to World War I. Donna Carla, with her catlike glide in her golden slippers and ambiguous smile under her mauve veil, and Don Giuseppe, with his tall, dashing military look and dominion over every cultural venue in Milan, were the handsomest and most desirable couple in creation. Luchino was his father's favorite. It was at the Viscontis' Wednesday gatherings that he first met Toscanini, who was the principal conductor at La Scala. When Toscanini took over as artistic director, he demanded that the lights be dimmed and that every opera be performed in the dark—all the chatter had to stop during a performance.

Il Maestro never missed a Wednesday gathering at the Viscontis' whenever he was in Milan. Was he captivated by

Donna Carla's magical scent? Luchino waited every night, after all the dancing stopped, for his mother to come to his room and read him a story, with pink champagne on her breath. Sometimes she had a coughing fit and couldn't finish the story she had started. Carla was consumptive. She and the children spent summers at Rapallo, on the Italian Riviera, while Don Giuseppe remained in Milan and had liaisons with both maids and menservants, and members of Milan's elite.

The marriage splintered. Luchino went to live with his mother at a much smaller house in Milan. Don Giuseppe had a palazzo built on the Via Salaria in Rome (Luchino would move into this palazzo after his father's death). His mother had become more and more ostracized because of her lovers and her defiance of Don Giuseppe. Milanese society had snubbed her and the exotic scent that she wore.

Luchino had made a solemn pledge that he would be the last one to kiss his mother while she was still alive. In 1939, she summoned him to her mountain retreat at Cortina. He could barely recognize her when he arrived. She was pale at fifty-nine, with sunken cheeks and wild, uncombed hair, while he remembered the voluptuous woman in the mauve veil. They kissed. She fondled his cheek with her swollen hand. She died in Luchino's arms, her eyes staring into some territory that did not include him.

"He never recovered," Laura said, "and that's why he's desperate to do *Traviata* with La Callas. He's like a doll maker, and you are the doll who will bring her back to life."

"But I'm still confused. Donna Carla was not a courtesan."

Laura seemed excited now. "Yes, she was—in Milanese society."

-10-

Luchino was breeding poodles now, and he offered Maria a prize black toy poodle, which she promptly named Toy. She went everywhere with that dog. A maid sat with Toy in an orchestra seat while she was rehearsing at La Scala. She went shopping with her poodle. It was Luchino who dressed her, who told her what to wear.

Maria and Battista had separate suites at the Villa Buonarroti. Titta was never around. He was always busy with Maria's affairs. La Tebaldi vanished. Rudolf Bing, the Met's new general manager, had swooped down and swiped her from La Scala. He wanted Maria, too. But Titta had demanded a phenomenal price for her services, and ironclad conditions concerning hotels and airplane tickets, as well as transportation for Toy. It was difficult to negotiate with him. The king of Verona didn't have any foreign languages in his quiver, and his Veronese dialect was hard to follow. Negotiations stalled and stalled.

Maria spent more and more time with Luchino. She often wore his clothes, dressed in black, while she borrowed one of his cardigans from Pozzi's. He was a nomad in Milan, moved from place to place in the middle of rehearsals. He brought Lila di Nobili with him to La Scala. She was the best costume and stage designer in Italy. Her sets gave the viewer a miraculous sense of depth, as if each person in the theater could float onto the stage and become part of the décor.

Visconti still had to prepare for *Traviata.*

He shifted the period of Verdi's opera from the 1850s to fin de siécle Paris, because, he said, the costumes of that era, with their tight bodices and bustles, would reveal the diva's particular beauty. But Maria remembered what Laura had told her. *I'm a mannequin. He's dressing me as his mother.*

Luchino wanted *Traviata* to recapture his mother's time, so that it would evoke his childhood at the Casa Visconti. Maria enjoyed this game of Donna Carla's ghostlike presence.

When he rehearsed, Luchino kicked everyone off the stage who wasn't connected to the production, and Lila and her assistants prepared all the sets. She had a chandelier painted for the party scene in act 1, surrounded by magnificent pieces of silk. And when this painted chandelier was lit, its aura illuminated the entire stage and summoned up the Belle Epoque with all its splendor and frivolous charm. Not even Maria was immune to the shimmering tableau Lila could bring to a set.

She fell in love with Luca.

The dangerous diva would purr in his presence. Still, if a handsome tenor appeared on the set, Maria would squint and say in front of the cast, "Luca, I can't see you, but I can smell you."

And he had to behave—during rehearsals.

Maria depended on him for everything. "Luca, where should I put my hand? How should I walk when Alfredo first arrives?"

Violetta's lover from the provinces was played by tenor Giuseppe di Stefano, who considered himself a much bigger star than a Greek soprano from Washington Heights. Dark, handsome, with "a golden voice" envied by other tenors, di Stefano was a favorite at La Scala. His many fans in the orchestra and box seats called him "Pippo." But the *loggionisti* didn't like him at all. They found Pippo lazy and arrogant. He performed when he was in the mood to perform. On other days he was flat, with his mind elsewhere, though his voice never betrayed him. They preferred Maria's wobbles, her lost notes, her voice wavering out of control, to the predictable evenness of this tenor's tone. And Pippo didn't care for all the attention Visconti was giving to Maria. He'd walk out of rehearsals, and Visconti himself would have to play Alfredo. Actually, Maria preferred Luchino; it was like a coda to their lovemaking in the midst of rehearsal.

He was rotten in bed.

His mind would drift, and Maria would have to catch him in the right mood. But it didn't seem to matter so much. She admired the absolute devotion he had to his craft. And she was drawn to his lithe, silent beauty. He was most beautiful to her when he was silent. Then she could feel his sad affliction. His mother remained more vital now that she was dead. He would stroke Maria's long black hair.

"You look like her, you know."

"But I'm not your mother, darling. I'm Maria."

And he would fall silent again. He didn't talk about money all the time, the way Titta did. Titta was also devoted to his mother. But it seemed cloying to Maria, as if Titta were enslaved by every word Mama Meneghini uttered. He was trapped in a fiefdom of family matters, while Luca was a dreamer. He dreamt as he rehearsed, imagined *Traviata* in his mind. He could summon up his own gods, while Titta had none. Battista clerked in Maria's behalf. She couldn't have had a career without Titta. But he couldn't help her with her art.

And Maria was hungry to learn. Luchino shaped Violetta, shaped her at every twist in a scene.

"No, Maria, Violetta can't afford to fall in love. Yes, she has lovers, like the baron. But she's isolated, alone. Falling in love with some boy from the provinces would weaken her. And yet . . ."

Luchino seized Maria's role, became Violetta. "Remember," he said, "I'm a courtesan who's dying of consumption."

Luchino crossed the stage in his loafers and black costume. He had a terrifying air about him. Not even Lila dared approach with questions about what to paint and where. He marched past Maria, as if he meant to ignore her, and suddenly stopped.

"Violetta gives herself to pleasure, because pleasure, she says, is the best remedy to her ills. And then this country boy comes along—Alfredo. He's loved her from afar, and destroys whatever devil-may-care attitude she has left." Then Luchino pointed to himself. "And *we* must feel this crisis in Violetta, this violent eruption of love."

"Violent?" Maria whispered.

"Yes! Violent!" Luchino shouted into the void of La Scala. "It erupts."

And he disappeared from the stage, a ghost dressed in black . . .

On the night of the *prima*, Maria insisted that Luchino stand in the wings with her until she made her first entrance.

"But I can't stay here forever, Maria."

"Luca," she said like a frantic child, "don't go!"

She could feel a darkness descend over him. He left her there as she listened to the overture and waited for her cue . . .

She wore a black velvet gown with long white fingerless gloves in act 1; while she herself seemed under control, her hands were like wild animals, revealing Violetta's confused state. Each courtesan had her own costume, her own mark, her own movement, different from Violetta's; it was as if they all had their private musical note. The audience worried about Violetta as she moved with abandon and just managed to skirt the orchestra pit. Alfredo's declaration of love was unsettling. He embraced her, and the audience could feel her sudden surrender—she herself was startled and overwhelmed. She realized for the first time that the Paris she'd been living in was nothing but a "crowded desert."

After the party, after all the noise and confusion, Violetta's quarters looked like a battlefield littered with debris, with the dead having departed to another room.

In the finale, the scene opened upon invaders in Violetta's bedroom—bloodsuckers. Workmen seized her belongings, plucked paintings from the wall to help pay debts that were piling up. She was an ex-courtesan dying of consumption, removed from the glamorous world of gentleman callers. One critic wrote that she sang with a "thread" of a voice that could still be heard in the galleries—that's how quiet the theater was, with everyone in the house caught in Violetta's grip.

Alfredo entered while Violetta was in bed. And here Pippo was as poignant as he had ever been, frightened of the rising specter who greeted him, yet still adoring Violetta. The audience was moved by his performance; it was without the least bit of mannerism. "Annina," Violetta said, like a penniless princess to her maid, "bring me my clothes." But Violetta didn't have the strength to put them on. Her cloak hung on her as if it belonged on a scarecrow. Her bonnet sat crooked on her head, the strings all askew. Her rigid fingers could no longer tie them.

And here Luchino took his greatest risk—with the audience, with Maria, and with his own reputation—as he choreographed Violetta's demise.

Any other director would have had her collapse or swoon and fall dead. But Luchino has her dying on her feet, with her enormous eyes open wide, staring past all the spectators into some private solace of her own.

Critics were brutal with Visconti. They called what he had done a desecration of Verdi and Violetta. But the audience at La Scala that night was riveted to Maria. Someone from the gallery shouted, "La Divina." Actually, it was Bernardo Scarpia, in disguise, dressed as a policeman from Palermo. He'd borrowed the uniform from his brother. He couldn't bear to miss Maria on her opening night. Perhaps he was thinking of Sarah Bernhardt—the Divine Sarah—or some other goddess. It didn't matter. Women in the boxes echoed his call. "La Divina! La Divina!"

Spectators insisted that Maria take a solo curtain call. They didn't want her to leave the stage—ever. Some would have remained in their seats half the night. There were roses strewn at her feet. Dozens of Maria's fans had come with bouquets. Maria couldn't keep from crying. Her own great joy was mingled with Violetta's sadness. The one rose she had counted on wasn't there.

Luchino was allergic to the least adulation. He fled once the opera was over. Maria knew where he had gone. He'd hide in Rome between performances of *Traviata*. And Maria had to catch him before he left. She returned to her dressing room to fetch Toy. Mama Meneghini was inside with Tullio and half a dozen minor impresarios who wanted Maria for other venues. None of her fans had arrived yet.

Mama Meneghini held a handkerchief to her eyes. "*Bambina,* I can't believe you're still alive. Violetta will remain with me for the rest of my life."

"Mama," Maria said, "I'll be right back." She knew that the Meneghinis were stealing from her, and that Titta was siphoning off some of her money to enlarge the family estate. She found her eyeglasses and raced across the tunnels in the same cloak she had worn in the death scene, and entered Biffi Scala through a side door. She looked slightly insane, her eyes lined with charcoal, her cheeks almost bloodless. She was still a corpse standing on her feet, with Toy in her arms.

She found Luchino at a table with several young tenors and boys from the corps de ballet. He'd been drinking white wine and smoking black cigarettes, his fingers stained and stinking of dark tobacco.

"La Callas," he said in a bitter tone, "you come to me like a trollop in a nightgown, wearing Violetta's charcoal eyes and clutching a toy poodle."

"Luca," she said, "the poodle was yours. And I couldn't change. I had to catch you before you left for Rome."

"Why?" he asked in front of his audience of young tenors and ballet dancers. "I gave you the gift of Violetta, and it is the only gift I have. We rehearsed. I held your hand."

She was sobbing now. "Put me in jail, darling. I wanted to say good-bye."

-11-

BING AWAITED HER. THE PRUSSIAN CORPORAL, as Titta called him—the Met's general manager was actually Austrian—could no longer plan a season without La Callas. She could have her suite at the Plaza and a first-class ticket on Pan Am, with a ticket for Toy, who would sit beside her in a travel kennel, but Battista would have to fly economy. Husbands weren't part of her contract.

Maria had a rage against the king of Verona. They had fistfights fairly often. He'd become a prize peddler, angling for a higher and higher price, when she cared more about costumes and rehearsal time. She made recordings now, and the royalties from the thirteen operas she had recorded so far were coming in at an almost alarming rate—for an opera singer. Bing publicized that La Callas would receive over a thousand dollars a performance, more than Tebaldi and any other diva had ever been paid at the Met. It wasn't done to applaud La Callas and flatter her, but to reveal her greed. The Prussian corporal wasn't really much different from Ghiringhelli. Both of them intensely disliked Maria and realized that they couldn't survive as impresarios without her talent—her imprint. She could fill La Scala or the Met. She sold out every performance. Devotees of La Divina camped outside the Met a week before tickets went on sale; they treasured Maria's recordings, but almost none of them had actually watched her perform.

La Tebaldi was her only rival.

Renata had become the Met's favorite soprano in her very first season. Opera buffs adored her as Desdemona, her debut role; half the women in the audience held handkerchiefs to their eyes, dazzled by the death scene. Bing didn't permit any of his performers the luxury of a solo curtain call. Renata stood in front of the curtain with the rest of the cast and refused to stand alone and take a bow, even as the audience clapped and howled, "Des-d-d-demona."

Now Maria had to conquer another opera house, after La Scala and La Fenice, and deal with Desdemona. Landing at Idlewild with Titta and Toy after a very long and bumpy flight, fatigued, with a dry, scratchy throat, Maria was besieged by a rowdy gang of reporters. One reporter, from *Newsweek*, kept tugging at Toy.

"Madame Meneghini, aren't you worried that you will have to sing in the same arena where La Tebaldi sings?"

"Arena?" Maria asked. "We're not prizefighters."

"But how would you compare yourself to her?"

And in a volcanic moment that she would later regret, Maria bit into the reporter. "There's nothing to talk about. It's like comparing champagne with cognac—no, Coca-Cola."

And her remark was reprinted everywhere.

Even Luchino was disappointed in her. He scribbled one sentence to Maria from Rome, on a piece of paper with tobacco crumbs. "Maria, preserve your cruelty when you're wearing the costume of Lady Macbeth."

Maria did receive a slap in the face, not from Bing or La Tebaldi, but from *Time* magazine. Two days before she was scheduled to open as Norma at the Met, Maria appeared on the cover of *Time*, looking luscious in a painting done in ruby red. But the cover story was damning in the worst way, sometimes praising Maria and ridiculing her in the same sentence. Entitled "The Prima Donna," it dubbed Callas the undisputed queen of opera while it also claimed that she feuded with other cast members, shoving them out of the way so that she could have solo curtain calls. An unidentified colleague of hers said that one day the entire cast of an opera would abandon her onstage and poor Maria would have to perform all alone.

But what Litsa said about Maria was even more damaging. She accused her younger daughter of having abandoned her, and of having written a letter declaring that if Litsa couldn't make enough money to live on, she could jump out the window or drown herself . . .

Six years earlier, Maria spent two months in Mexico City performing at the Palacio de Bellas Artes. Feeling a rush of nostalgia about her own childhood, she invited her mother to stay with her at the Hotel Prince. Litsa arrived with her blond hair coifed in a pompadour and her eyes painted blue, like Cleopatra. Mother and daughter went to banquets together; both were fêted, both were squired around in limousines. For Litsa, remembering the chubby little girl in Washington Heights and her own embattled life with George Callas, it must have felt like some kind of deliverance, her wildest dreams suddenly acted out. Her daughter was a diva and she herself was the momentary queen of Mexico City.

Maria bought her mother a mink coat and paid all her debts. She'd already been sending Litsa a stipend every month. But Litsa demanded more money, and wanted to move in with Maria and Titta.

Maria was petrified. She'd had enough of that blue-eyed Cleopatra. After she finished performing at the Palacio, she left Litsa enough money to remain at the Hotel Prince for another week and returned to Verona on the next flight. But the drama continued. Litsa kept dunning her for more and more money. That's when Maria, in a moment of pique, scribbled that she had to "scream" for her living, "scream" every day, and that if Litsa couldn't survive on what Maria was sending her, well, she had better jump in the river and drown.

Local columnists called Maria a monster, a virago, a witch. Television celebrities talked about her combativeness and the foul wind she brought with her to Manhattan. Their comments only increased ticket sales. Every performance was sold out. But Maria knew that audiences at the Met wouldn't welcome her with the same warmth they had reserved for Renata. There would be "hissing snakes" inside the opera house.

The *prima* was at the end of October. It was Indian summer, and Manhattan was in the middle of a heat wave. Worse, the antiquated cooling system at the Met was on the blink, and Maria would have to perform under a blaze of arc lights. She had a panic attack during the overture, and the house manager had to shove her onto the stage. Maria was terrified. The audience hardly helped. The clapping as she made her entrance had a bluntness that was like a knife blade in the neck.

It threw her off balance. She recovered as best she could and sailed through the first act on adrenaline alone. It wasn't Maria—it was Maria's mask. Her voice had fled somewhere into a forest of balconies and boxes.

The audience was mostly silent as the curtain descended upon act 1 like a funeral shroud. Maria raced half blind to her dressing room. She tossed out Titta and her maid, tossed out Toy. She sat alone at her dressing table with the little painting of the Madonna that she carried with her from performance to performance, no matter what country she was in. She didn't pray for some magical return of her mottled voice. She didn't think of *Norma* at all.

She noticed a spider in a crack in the wall—at the Met. She mimicked the spider's movements with her hand. The spider had its own rhythm, its own music, as if it were guided by Toscanini's baton. She hummed to herself. The spider disappeared.

She didn't need any warning bell.

She returned to the stage with a dagger in her hand. This was another Norma, from a much different and deadlier world. The audience trembled at the sight of that dagger, sensed her savagery. Maria heard the gasps but pretended not to hear. In this scene, Norma's two sons were asleep. She had come to murder them, and the audience could see that hint of murder in her huge dark eyes.

This was not opera. It was something else. Spectators had come to cry, to laugh, to be amused, not to hear the palpitation of their hearts. From this moment on, they couldn't take their eyes off Norma. She decided not to deliver the dagger blows, and the two boys awakened alive. But it felt like a lucky stroke. For the audience, Norma was still a murderess-in-waiting. Spectators would see that dagger in their sleep for many weeks to come, remember it for the rest of their lives. They would not permit Maria to leave the stage.

She shattered Bing's house rule and took a solo bow. It did not feel like much of a victory. She was far too nearsighted to observe a single face in the audience, but she could feel the depth of that cavern, like a dry wind. And the proscenium trembled as if she were caught in an earthquake—that's how long and loud people clapped.

She did not need her glasses now. She could summon

up the rusty gold and red of the boxes, the old ivory look of the proscenium, rubbed by human hands—polishers perhaps. The Met had its own *loggionisti* in the upper tiers, those who had to stand during the entire opera, who preferred their own legion to the velvet below and couldn't afford Bing's astronomical prices anyway. And they began to hum "Casta Diva" to Maria, Norma's hymn to the moon goddess, a deceitful hymn, a heartbreaking hymn, begging the Druids not to go to war, as she tried to protect her Roman lover.

These *loggionisti* did not want Maria to sing, only to watch her body sway while each of them hummed. And sway she did as she clasped her hands above her heart. Then they stopped. And Maria left the stage.

Four

Dumpy and Anna Bolena

-1-

She was a time bomb on two legs. No one dared defy this corpulent queen of high society. She was short and shapeless. But she never once disguised this fact with expensive gowns. She reveled in her shapelessness and preferred that her friends call her "Dumpy." And Dumpy she was. To her enemies, she was Elsa the Great. Elsa would have been enough. She was given a suite at the Waldorf Towers as an unpaid guest. It wasn't out of charity to Elsa. She was like a shark in sackcloth who pulled in other guests, such as Cole Porter, whom she called "Coley." She knew everyone she had to know and everyone else feared her. She had her own syndicated column in the *New York Post*, and both her endearments and her vitriol reached far and wide. That wouldn't have bothered Maria, until she realized how much Elsa Maxwell knew about opera and what a devoted fan she was.

"Callas leaves me cold," she declared in her column after Maria's *prima* at the Met. That would have been a call to war, until Maria discovered how perceptive Elsa was about *Norma*.

"Norma is a warrior—a high priestess—who had betrayed her tribe," Elsa declared. "And there is no other aria in Italian opera that's as heartrending as 'Casta Diva.' It serves both as a mask and a revelation. She appeals to a chaste moon goddess, while she herself has not been chaste. And as Callas reached the cabaletta—the final section of the aria—her voice sounded hollow, as if she were elsewhere. But Norma did come back to us in the second act . . ."

"Titta," Maria said after reading the column, "who is this bitch? I can't afford to have her as an enemy. She knows too much. I was nervous in that opening act. I was little Maria, the ragged girl from Washington Heights, and not La Callas. I failed. My voice *was* hollow. I was scared to death, Titta. Little Maria at the Met. It was the wooden Madonna in my dressing room that saved me. Callas sang the second act, not Maria. And Maxwell must have sensed that."

"She's a witch," Titta said.

"A perceptive witch—a witch we need to have on our side."

Maria had to wait. And then the opportunity arrived. It was a Greek charity gala at the Waldorf, where Elsa Maxwell was a guest. Maria wore a Balmain black gown that revealed her new exquisite slimness and the glory of her long arms and legs, while Elsa looked like a porcupine in a blue sack. Well into her seventies, she had an armada of varicose veins.

Catching sight of her, Maria introduced herself to the doyenne of café society.

Bowing like a little girl, Elsa delivered one of her shrewdest smiles. "Ah, Madame Callas, I'm mummified by your attention. I should think I'd be the last person in all of Manhattan you would ever wish to meet."

"You're wrong," Maria said, with her own wicked smile.

Elsa Maxwell remained suspicious. "Explain yourself, please."

"It's quite simple. You caught me when I wasn't at my best. And you pinpointed the cracks in my 'Casta Diva.' I'm only mortal, and you have been elected to the Legion of Honor."

"Trifles," Elsa said. "You can call me Dumpy. Everyone does."

She was blushing now. Maria had thrown society's sacred monster off her guard.

"Have you met my husband, Battista Meneghini?"

Elsa's eyes began to whirl in a very strange fashion the closer she moved to Maria. "Ah, the manager who asks for too much."

Titta's English was very poor, and Elsa's words keeled way over his head. Maria had to answer on his behalf. She was both his interpreter and his guide—in Manhattan.

"You must have been speaking to Mr. Bing. My husband calls him 'the Prussian corporal.'"

"But he's Austrian," Maxwell said.

"Trifles," Maria quipped.

The entire gala of Greek millionaires and their wives stared at this diva who had led her own assault on Manhattan and the chubby social doyenne who seemed on the verge of hysteria. It was obvious to everyone. The columnist had fallen in love with Maria at first sight and was confused about the colossal power of her emotions. She had been prepared to hate Maria. And suddenly, Elsa Maxwell could barely utter a word.

"I have to leave," she said, and retreated to her rooms above the ballroom.

And then the artillery began. A Tebaldi fan wrote a letter to *Time.* "This diva from Washington Heights says Tebaldi has no backbone. Well, she has one thing that Callas has not—a heart. I would never allow my own mother to become a beggar in the street." Maria didn't have to respond. Maxwell had changed alliances and was completely on her side. She chided Tebaldi's fan in her column for having attacked Maria. "Beggar? We have no beggars here. Madame Callas has a thriving new business. She sells hand-painted dolls of Maria performing in her various roles. I've seen the Norma doll. I bought one myself. But I can't talk enough about Maria and her amazing eyes. How hypnotic they are! Maria's eyes can be seen blazing out from the deepest balcony at the Met."

Maria invited her father to the opera. He sat with Elsa Maxwell in her own box. George Callas was alarmingly timid. His hair had turned gray. He didn't know the first thing about *Norma.* His eyes began to wander. He mumbled to himself.

They all went to the Russian Tea Room after Maria's performance. Maria still had charcoal around her eyes, and she sat at one of the red velvet banquettes with Elsa Maxwell, Titta, and George.

"Papa," she asked, "do you remember the Eskimo Pies we used to share, how I gobbled the chocolate skin—cheated you?"

But he had a blank stare, looking almost terrified.

"That—that was long ago," he said as he nibbled a blini, the fork shivering in his fist.

"Mr. Callas, aren't you proud of your daughter?" Elsa asked.

The fork spilled onto the tablecloth, as if George was a paralytic. It seemed obvious to Maria how uncomfortable he was at the Russian Tea Room, and how he must have dreaded sitting in Elsa Maxwell's box at the opera. He wasn't accustomed to metal tea holders and flaming dishes, even though he'd used a Bunsen burner most of his life.

Fame frightened him.

Reporters kept waiting outside his apartment house in Washington Heights. He had to dodge them if he wanted to shop at the local market for buttermilk. "Please," he said, "I know nothing about my daughter's career. She moved to Greece when she was a girl. And then she vanished again, into Italy. I've never been to La Scala. I know Greek folk songs. That's the extent of my musical knowledge."

And now men and women with puffy cheeks approached the banquette and asked for Maria's autograph. When they discovered that George was the diva's father, they wanted his autograph, too. He wasn't sure what to sign.

Elsa nudged him and asked, "Aren't you proud of your daughter?"

"Miss Maxwell," he said in a hoarse voice, "I lost her half a century ago."

The doyenne shook her head. "That's impossible. Your Maria isn't even thirty-five."

"Half a century ago," George Callas repeated, a tear in his eye.

Maria had ripped him out of his familiar little world. She had the waiter bring a phone to the banquette and she summoned Mr. Bing's private chauffeur. Then George shook hands with Titta and Elsa Maxwell, finished his blini, and accompanied his daughter to the Tea Room's revolving door, signing autographs at every other table.

Maria cradled him into the back of the limousine, as if her own father was a gigantic child. Both of them were crying now. She never felt more alone than in her father's presence.

"Papa," she said, "I'll visit you. I'll come uptown."

"Maria," he said, "you'll find nothing there. Don't you see? You've disappeared from your own past. I do remember the Eskimo Pies. You were not a diva then."

-2-

Elsa followed her everywhere. Maria couldn't go shopping, couldn't leave the hotel. The doyenne wrote her love letters. She talked of a beautiful life together with Maria. Battista wasn't even mentioned. Sometimes her letters were eight pages long. They rambled on and on. Elsa kept inviting Maria to lunch at the Waldorf, but Maria preferred to guard her handful of nickels at the Automat, where she could feast on a cup of coffee and a chicken potpie that came out of a slot in the wall. And she loved to shop at Woolworth rather than the monumental Fifth Avenue department stores. She could buy hairpins and sewing kits, and still have change from a ten-dollar bill. The fear of poverty had haunted her since childhood and felt like a hammer in her head.

"I don't want to die in the poorhouse," she would tell Titta in the middle of a meal. "Please don't let me die in there."

And nothing Titta said could reassure her. "But you have diamonds, my darling, that you could sell for a kingdom."

"I don't want a kingdom," Maria said, her dark eyes bulging out of their sockets. "I just don't want to die a penniless old hag."

So shopping at Woolworth and eating with nickels in her fist reassured her. She could spend as little as she liked. That was her kingdom.

But she couldn't escape Dumpy, not even at the Automat. Elsa appeared with her very own tray and a slice of apple pie in a deep dish.

"May I sit down with you, Maria?" she asked, suddenly in mortal fear of this diva who could lash out at anyone in the mirror of her eyes—anyone.

"Yes, Dumpy, of course you can."

"How thrilling. I've never been inside the Automat until now. It's magical—the girl in the booth. You give her a dollar, and she reaches into a well of coins and spits out nickels like a demonic adding machine. I will rhapsodize about it one day in my column."

Elsa must have been waiting for Maria outside the Met and followed her into the Automat.

Maria grew sick of love letters she was no longer willing to read. She felt like grabbing Elsa's shoulders and shaking the notion of romance out of her, but she worried about the postmortems she would discover in Elsa's columns. The attacks would start all over again.

"Darling," Elsa said in a trembling voice, "we could go on a cruise to Crete."

"But I'm leaving for a concert tomorrow in Dallas," Maria said, in the deadpan voice of a somnambulist.

"Why didn't you tell me?" Elsa asked, excited now. "I'd have booked my plane ticket by now."

The somnambulist stared into Elsa's eyes. "Dumpy, I'd prefer to go alone."

And she left Elsa at the table with her apple pie.

She flew to Dallas and stayed in the Presidential Suite at the Adolphus Hotel. She had three bathrooms and a television set built right into the footboard of her bed. The carpets swayed like a field of wheat under her slippers. Litsa broke into Maria's dream with her blue eyes and horrid mask of dark powder and rouge. She was a doll maker now, an entrepreneur, while Maria was impoverished, even with all her contracts.

Litsa cackled at her. "Maria, you can come and work for me. You'll paint all the dolls of yourself. But you'll have to work fast. I can't afford any slackers."

"Mother," Maria said in a child's voice, though she wasn't a child in the dream, "will you bring me Stephanakos? I'll work much faster if I can hear Stephanakos sing."

The cackling grew louder. "Dumbbell, Stephanakos is dead."

And Maria woke with the sound of tin inside her ears. She wasn't used to living in a palace. That's what the Presidential Suite seemed to her, with wheat fields in every room. She drank a glass of water from the pitcher near her bed. The bathroom she entered was as big as a battleship. She showered and had coffee and three strawberries in a bowl delivered to her suite. The berries tasted like blood. Maria rehearsed in front of a mirror ten feet high. Litsa's face appeared, and Maria couldn't reach her highest and lowest registers, no matter how hard she tried.

Darling, she told herself, *you'll be a disaster tonight.*

She arrived at the opera house in the Civic Opera Company's Cadillac, wearing a red silk gown with ruffled sleeves, and the audience arose and clapped as Maria appeared onstage. She had to quiet these opera addicts with a swan-like wave of her hand. She sang selections from *Macbeth* and *La Traviata* in the first half of the concert. And then she reappeared in a simple black gown that clung to her half-starved body like the velvet shirt of a condemned queen. The audience was startled by that curious gown, and again Maria had to calm all the opera addicts with a wave of her hand. She sang selections from Donizetti's *Anna Bolena*, a bel canto opera that had fallen out of favor because the role of Henry VIII's soon-to-be-beheaded second queen demanded the firepower of a dramatic soprano that couldn't be found in Italy or anywhere else until Callas arrived at La Scala.

As she sang, the stage suddenly darkened, and a spotlight swooped out of nowhere and landed on her face, forming a halo around her and her enormous eyes, capturing Anna Bolena in her isolation, revealing her frailty—and her strength. The audience had never encountered a queen before, a queen going to her death . . .

Maria hoped to rest on the return flight. She sat in first class, trying to relax before her connecting flight to Milan. And that's when Dumpy sat down in the seat right next to her.

Maria was appalled. "You weren't supposed to come to Dallas. You promised."

"I did not," Dumpy said. "How could I miss a preview of *Anna Bolena*? We've all been waiting for that opera to be revived."

"Where did you stay?" Maria asked.

"At your hotel—the Adolphus. And I sat in the orchestra at the Civic. In the very first row. And when they shone that light on your face, darling, I nearly dropped dead. You were a queen. You still are."

"Then the queen would like to be alone," Maria said. "Please ask the stewardess to find you another seat."

"You can't mean that," Elsa howled, with a hardness in her voice.

"I do," Maria said.

"There will be consequences."

Maria shut her eyes. "Dumpy, I don't give a damn."

–3–

SHE HADN'T EXPECTED TO WORK WITH HIM AGAIN. He'd told everyone how she had run after him, how she'd been jealous of all his male companions, how he had to accompany her to the very lip of the stage before every performance. He never mentioned the flowers he had sent her, the love notes he had written, the times they had spent together in Rome, how obsessed he was about dressing and undressing her, how he called her his Salome. He was selfish and spiteful, but Maria needed him. She couldn't have done *Anna Bolena* without Visconti and his stagecraft.

She did not call him Luca anymore.

Ghiringhelli was reluctant about rehiring him. "I don't care for his crowd of acolytes. They worship him. He brings a bad odor to La Scala."

"Then we'll have to forget about *Anna Bolena*."

"But why him? Do you hear what he says about you at Biffi Scala? That you were his tart."

"I'll have to learn to live with his insults."

Visconti noticed Maria's aloofness as they began to plan

their rehearsals for *Anna Bolena.* It excited him the more aloof she became. But he didn't try to win her back.

"Maria, do you know the story of Henry the Eighth and Anna Bolena?"

She mocked him now, his insolence, his defiance, the way he dressed all in black.

"What do I care about Henry the Eighth? Anna was a queen, wasn't she? I know how to be a queen."

And he didn't dare try to instruct her after that. It was a grueling role, a queen trapped in her own interior, who had to hit every single register the human voice would allow.

The sets were almost out of another world—only black, white, and gray, to capture the grimness of London and of the tower where Anna Bolena was being held. Henry VIII had tired of her, wanted another wife, and had to manufacture the charge of adultery against her. Jane Seymour, Henry's bride-to-be, wore red, and those who guarded Anna Bolena were draped in scarlet and yellow to clash against the gray that surrounded Anna everywhere.

Meanwhile, Anna herself wore dark blue and a blinding white bonnet, plus enormous jewels that matched the color of her eyes. Her appearance was complex. She was a vehicle, a weapon, and a victim. No one else, not Henry, not Jane, could match her dignity and strength. She knew how to play a queen, as she had told Visconti.

At the *prima,* Visconti accompanied Maria from her dressing room.

"*Cara,* should I escort you to the curtain?" he asked in a boyish voice.

"No, Luchino," she said like a queen. "You've lost that privilege."

And she whisked right past him.

She was Anna Bolena. She broke La Scala's record for curtain calls. The audience kept her in front of the curtain for twenty-four minutes, applauding Maria without a break.

That night, at Biffi Scala, Visconti told an interviewer, "Maria is a marvelous monstrosity. No one has her gifts. And whatever her faults, she's still La Divina—a gift from God."

FIVE

Enter Aristotle

-1-

> *I cannot thrive without your talent, Maria. I cannot exist. I would like to be at your side when you sing. Please don't shut me out. You will find that I am not an unfaithful companion.*
>
> *Yours, Elsa Maxwell*

Maria wasn't heartless. She had to relent. She took a chance and invited Elsa to stay with her on the Via Buonarroti when she was singing at La Scala. Elsa was also allowed into Maria's dressing room during performances. She rubbed Maria's back with a special balm, almost like a maid. And Elsa summoned Maria to a costume ball she was giving at the Waldorf during Maria's next sojourn in Manhattan. Battista chose not to attend.

Maria arrived at the ball as the female pharaoh Hatshepsut, wearing borrowed emeralds worth three million, and pursued by a pair of bodyguards from the jeweler Harry Winston; their eyes roved like red-hot rivets on the run, seeing *everyone* as a potential jewel thief. Maria wanted to shove them into a closet.

Elsa came as Catherine the Great. But it was Maria who stunned the other masqueraders at the ball with the exquisite bones of her face; she did have the eyes, nose, and mouth of a female pharaoh.

Another one of the masqueraders was the Greek shipping magnate Aristotle Onassis, wearing thick pink-tinted glasses. As myopic as Maria, he was meant to be Odysseus in a striped sailor's shirt. His wife, Tina, twenty-three years younger than Aristotle, was the heiress to a rival Greek shipping fortune. A petite blonde, she was captivating in a tall feathered hat.

Aristotle removed his tinted glasses as he approached the diva with the light-footed, vigorous dance of the ninth or tenth richest man on the planet. He didn't kiss her cheek like an ordinary cavalier. He shook her hand, and Maria immediately felt an electric spark. It disturbed her. She didn't need a *tombeur* like Aristotle Onassis in her life.

"Hello, Maria," he said, "I'm not so fond of opera singers."

"Neither am I."

Both of them laughed.

"It's my misfortune," he said. "All those arias sound like one long shriek and rattle my eardrums."

"Well," Maria said. "I found a perfect solution. You could bring earplugs to the opera. Should I find you some?"

It was like the beginning of a strange duel that Maria hadn't bargained for. He sent a bouquet of roses to her hotel, a simple bouquet, and a note with one word: *Ari.*

She wasn't flattered or amused. Maria had to reflect. She knew he was a hunter, and a real hunter like Onassis never gave up the hunt. She was performing *Norma* in Rome at the beginning of the year. And she had the premonition of something bad about to happen, as if she were the sorceress or embattled queen she so often played . . .

She attended few festivities during Christmas, since she had to study the score of her next opera and the next. It had rained for a week in Milan. There were icicles outside her windows on the Via Buonarroti. She caught a cold. Her doctor advised her not to leave for Rome.

"Impossible," Maria told him. "I have to rehearse with the entire cast. The *prima* is in less than seven days. The president will be there with his wife. And the entire program will be broadcast throughout all of Italy."

She arrived at the Hotel Quirinale wearing a silver fox stole and wrapped in scarves. She had a cough she couldn't contain, and the weather in Rome wasn't much better than the miasma she'd suffered through in Milan. She had to rehearse at the Teatro dell'Opera in her silver fox stole, rehearse in full voice as she always did, while the rest of the cast did not sing one note. It was her great virtue as a diva—and her downfall. Maria didn't know how to conserve her strength. Her "Casta Diva" echoed across the hollows of the theater like the saddest of chants.

She woke next morning without a voice. It was gone. La Callas had nothing but a hoarse whisper.

The Quirinale had to find a throat specialist on New Year's Day, a doctor in semiretirement who happened to be a fan of Maria's. He was eighty years old. He hummed arias while he looked into her throat. He bowed, and with a considerable tremor, he stood on one knee.

"You must not speak—not until twenty-four hours have elapsed, Your Highness."

Maria stared at her husband and whispered, "Titta, have they brought us a lunatic?"

The doctor stood up with the same tremor. "Forgive me," he said. "I have still not recovered from your *Anna Bolena* . . . Madame Meneghini, you have one of the worst cases of bronchitis I have ever encountered."

"But I have to sing *Norma* at the Teatro in two days," she managed to whisper.

"That would be a miracle," the doctor said, "even for La Divina."

He removed a syrup and a throat spray from his ornate medicine bag, which looked to Maria like a leather box where a hangman would keep his ropes in an opera she might perform one day.

"Alternate," the doctor said, pointing to the syrup and the spray. "Every two hours without fail. And you must inform the Teatro that you are in no condition to sing an opera as treacherous to the voice as *Norma*, that you are in no condition to sing any opera at all."

"But–I–have–never–canceled–a–performance–more–than–once–or–twice," Maria croaked.

"Queen Anna," the doctor said, "I am almost as bereft as you are. I have tickets to the *prima*. But you mustn't speak another word," and he left with his hangman's box.

She sat in bed, played with Toy, and even that was too much. She remained as still as a mummy, Toy beside her, just as still. When she woke, some of the hoarseness was gone. But she was in no condition to sing in *Norma*, as the doctor had decreed. She called Carlo Sampaoli, the artistic director at the Teatro, told him that he would have to find a new Norma for the *prima*.

Sampoli could hear the feebleness of her voice. He arrived

at the Quirinale after twenty minutes—in a rage. Shorter than Maria, he wore earmuffs and a coat with long cuffs.

"A substitute singer?" he asked, wagging his head belligerently. "It is a Maria Callas evening. President Gronchi will be there with his wife. We would have to refund every ticket. The Teatro dell'Opera will be ruined."

And he left Maria alone to deal with the implied threat of his recitative. Elsa Maxwell had arrived from the Riviera once she heard about Maria's plight. She swabbed the diva's throat, gave her honey and lemon from the Quirinale's own kitchen, sat vigil near her night table. Maria woke with a certain confusion.

"Dumpy, am I alive or dead?"

"Alive—I think."

"Good. Then we will go to the Teatro."

Elsa worried that La Divina had lost her reason. "It's the morning, Maria. You won't be called to the theater for another ten hours."

"But if we hide in my dressing room, no one will know where to find us."

And they marched like toy soldiers to the stage door. It was a desperate gamble. She would summon up whatever voice she had and hope it didn't kilter out of control. She'd brought her wooden Madonna. It was Dumpy who dressed her in a high priestess's white robes, Dumpy who swabbed her throat, Dumpy who fed her spoonfuls of syrup.

Maria looked magnificent in braided hair and a blue veil. The audience was in awe of her. Norma's high cheekbones heightened under the stage lights. She sang. But her breath gave out during "Casta Diva," and her voice sounded like someone shrieking underwater. Somehow, she managed to get through the first act, not as Norma, but as some battle-scarred stranger in Norma's robes.

She left the stage as members of the audience whistled and screamed. They mocked the diva and told her to return to Milan on a magic carpet.

She would have liked to lock the door of her dressing room and sit with her Madonna and Dumpy. But she couldn't rest. Sampaoli broke in with half a dozen assistants. He clasped his hands like a supplicant.

"Maria, you must go on."

"Are you deaf, Don Carlo? I cannot sing."

"It's of little importance," Sampaoli said. "You can mime your words. What matters is your presence onstage."

She sucked on a lozenge and said in a deep whisper, "If I wanted to be a mime, signor, I would have joined a puppet theater."

Sampaoli left her dressing room in a huff. He did not bother to go onstage. The audience had already waited an hour for the second act to begin. President Gronchi had left the theater with his wife, Carla, and a trove of bodyguards. The *loggionisti* had begun doing the second act on their own. They didn't have to wait for Norma and the Druids. Then, amid all the clamor, the crackle of the loudspeaker was heard. Act 2 had been canceled. No explanation was given, no mention of the collapse of Maria's voice.

Maria was able to escape the furor of the audience by taking a private passage that led directly to the Quirinale. But there was little consolation in that. Opera fanatics waited outside her windows all night, serenading her with obscenities until the police were called and dispersed these fanatics with their clubs.

All of Italy seemed aflame.

Parliament considered withdrawing the stipend from any theater in Italy where Maria was scheduled to perform. Elsa wanted to remain on the Via Buonarroti as a nurse. But she clung to the diva, clung so much that Maria could barely breathe. And she sent Dumpy back into exile on the Riviera.

Dumpy cried for twenty minutes before she left. "Can't you tell how devoted I am to you, my dear? We've become a threesome, me, you, and Toy."

She never mentioned Titta once.

"Dumpy, I am really grateful," Maria whispered. "I'll call the moment I need you again."

Maria's voice was back within a week, but the Teatro had canceled all her other engagements.

"Titta," Maria said, "would they have done that if I were one of their own? I'm a foreigner to them, and I'll always be a foreigner."

When Maria and Titta returned to Milan, they found the gate and the walls of their villa on the Via Buonarroti smeared with excrement. It chilled Maria to the bone—the hate that must have gone into that effort, the anger, and the expertise; there was a flourish to every stroke, as if these malicious Michelangelos meant to repaint Maria's abode with a barrel of shit.

Maria didn't even wander past the front gate.

Titta drove her and Toy to the tiny villa he had bought on Lake Garda, in the tiny town of Sirmione, where Maria could hide behind the convenient mask of Madame Meneghini. Toy sat on Maria's lap during the entire trip, comforting his mistress, while Titta fumed.

"They don't deserve a diva like you."

Maria stared out the window at a field of farm horses

with furry legs. "A diva in shackles, my darling. The audience owns me. Yes, I am Anna Bolena—sometimes. And they, King Henry all the time. I live by their whim."

–2–

Maria still had La Scala, but Ghiringhelli refused to visit her dressing room and acknowledge that she existed.

What did it matter? Maria had one more *Anna Bolena* to do at Ghiringhelli's palace. There were protesters waiting for her outside La Scala with baskets of rotten fruit and other ammunition, and Maria had to sneak into the stage entrance wearing dark glasses and a wig. Still, she rehearsed as fiercely as ever. Visconti was behind every move, like a magician dressed in black. For the *prima,* he had hired bodyguards to maintain decorum in the corridors, while policemen with machine pistols patrolled La Scala's main square. Such was the furor surrounding Maria.

Visconti was quite shrewd. He had Maria come out from behind the chorus to make her entrance. The audience still jeered at her, mocked her, wouldn't allow her to sing. Then it suddenly fell into utter silence, as if there was no Anna Bolena and Maria didn't exist at all. This silence persisted for the opening scenes. It was apparent how shaken Maria was, but she remained within the role. There was a queen in front of all the fanatics, no matter how much they denied her. And then, in the finale of act 1, as Anna was about to be arrested for adultery, she shoved the king's two guards aside with such violence, they nearly toppled into the orchestra. And like some untethered beast, she stood defiantly in front of the stage and shouted Anna's lines at the audience. "Judges—for Anna!"

Maria was attacking her own attackers. A defiant diva they might demolish, but they couldn't demolish a queen. As the curtain dropped at the end of act 1, the audience had suddenly switched sides with the same violence as Maria. People clapped and clapped, but Maria wouldn't appear.

So they serenaded her, "Anna, Anna Bolena," until Maria came forth from behind the curtain with a bristling rage. She stood there, wouldn't bow. She had become *their* queen.

She did not return to her dressing room at the end of act 2. She went directly to Lake Garda with Titta and Toy and her wooden Madonna. She was still wearing Anna's white bonnet.

She talked of retiring.

"Titta, I spill my blood on that stage every time, and what do I get as a reward? Shit on our walls and bile from the patrons at La Scala and from Ghiringhelli himself. I should be at the circus. 'Ladies and gentlemen, come and have a look at Maria Callas, the queen of pariahs.'"

Titta groaned. "Darling, you can't quit. You have so many commitments. And what about the recording sessions?"

"I'll sing in a studio, but I won't perform in front of a live audience. No more Callas."

"We'll lose our homes," Titta said.

Maria smiled. "Don't worry, darling. I'll become a street singer, like Gioconda. We won't starve."

But she did worry. Titta finagled a lot. He pocketed Maria's earnings, fed his own family on every single note she sang. So she'd arranged with the business managers at several opera houses to wire the fees from her performances into her own account. She didn't cancel her commitments. But somehow arguments arose.

She had running battles with Rudolf Bing. She had never revered him, like every other prima donna did. He was supercilious to all his singers and their managers. He was particularly rude to Titta, would snub him at galas and dinner parties, and Maria was just as rude to the Prussian corporal at the very same galas. He gave her a seamstress who was as myopic as Maria, and a wigmaker who was color-blind. He dimmed the lights in her dressing room, left her costumes in disrepair, and wouldn't let her have a decent set designer. He recognized the uniqueness of her gifts, the excitement she brought to the Met with every performance, and still some part of him wanted her to fail. That was Rudolf Bing. He couldn't bear the thought that a diva from Washington Heights was more popular than *his* opera house.

It had become a tradition to pay a prima donna in cash on opening night, after the first act, and to spite Maria and the extravagance of her fees, Bing arrived in her dressing room with a shopping bag from Saks stuffed with single dollar bills.

"Here, Maria," he said with a malicious smile, "here is your lucre. And if you're worried whether my accountant is correct, you can have Meneghini sit on his ass like a good manager and count every dollar bill."

The first bell had rung. Maria had to guard her vocal cords and get back to the whirlwind of *Tosca.* The Prussian corporal shouldn't have come into her dressing room to play his tricks. He could very well have been Scarpia, but this Scarpia wasn't in the score. She couldn't control her fury.

She clutched the shopping bag, heavy as it was with dollar bills, and hurled it at Bing.

Titta clutched his head. "Maria, look what you've done."

The shopping bag exploded as it struck Bing's chin, and Maria's dressing room rained dollar bills.

The bag had bloodied Bing's mouth, but he wasn't disturbed in the least. He spat a tiny clot of blood into his silken handkerchief, and said, "Maria, shall I ask the janitor to pick up your swag?"

"You can go to hell," she said, and, gathering her skirts, she kissed the Madonna on her dressing table, then marched right past Bing as the second bell rang.

He did offer her another contract. She fought with him over the operas she would or would not perform at the Met, and he finally fired her.

There was a photo of Maria in one of the tabloids, snarling at a photographer, and the caption read "Diva in a Nosedive at the Met."

She couldn't avoid reporters at the airport. Maria was front-page news no matter what she did, or where she went.

"Maria, Maria, will you ever return to the Met?"

But she wasn't Maria in front of the microphones; she was that operatic demon, La Callas.

"Of course," she said with an enigmatic smile. "Once Rudolf Bing is dead."

And she ran toward the gate, with Titta breathing heavily behind her, like a lost civilian on a battlefield.

She had Toy with her; Toy sat under her seat. The stewardesses wouldn't dare put her poodle in with the baggage. This time, Titta sat with La Callas in first class.

They didn't stop off on the Via Buonarroti in Milan. They went right to Lake Garda with Toy. She wouldn't be bothered there. It was at this exact moment, the moment she arrived, that Aristotle called on her private line. Onassis was either a wizard or a thief.

Titta took the call from the operator and cupped his hand over the receiver.

"Darling, what should I tell the Greek?"

"Tell him I'm in Venezuela," she said.

Titta stamped his foot while his hand was still cupped.

"Darling, he won't believe me."

Maria was furious. Acquiring a new mistress was like a war game to Aristotle. And Maria refused to volunteer.

"Tell him I'm in the tub. I have to soak for a few hours to rub off the filth of flying."

"But when should he call?"

"In a month," Maria said. "When my hair dries."

"But Maria," Titta whined. "You can't play games with a man like that. He could crush us with one finger."

"Let him try," Maria said. "Let him try."

Aristotle rang again and again, until Maria finally took the call.

"Maria, you're a naughty girl," he said in that melodic voice of his. "You keep avoiding me. I wanted to invite you and your husband on a cruise this summer on board my yacht. Sir Winston will be our guest of honor—and so will Maria Callas."

"Who is Sir Winston?" Maria asked.

Aristotle broke into a deep-throated laugh. "Churchill, of course."

Maria admired that man. He'd come to Athens during the civil war and revealed himself to an enormous throng of frightened, half-starved Greeks at Syntagma Square.

"Yes," she said, still suspicious of Aristotle. "I'm interested in meeting Sir Winston."

"Then I'm a happy sailor," he said. "You will enjoy the *Christina,* not because of the luxuries—I'm sure you can find them elsewhere—but because it is a world within a world. People have been known to get lost and never come out."

"Onassis," she said, "are you plotting to make me a prisoner on board your yacht?"

"Precisely."

–3–

HE DUBBED HIS YACHT THE *CHRISTINA* after his daughter, a stolid, moody girl now nine. As usual with Aristotle, there was a countermyth. Greta Garbo was a frequent guest aboard his yacht, and sometimes he would flatter the retired, reclusive star and declare that he had named the craft after her greatest film, *Queen Christina,* where she jaunts around dressed as a man. It was impossible to tell which tale was true . . .

The *Christina* dominated the harbor at Monte Carlo; it was the most commanding ship in all of Monaco. Monte Carlo itself sat on a cliff, with palaces of pale stone that shimmered in the sun and lent this portion of Monaco the illusion of a pink paradise sitting right on the Riviera.

Maria was glad she didn't live there. It would have been like being trapped inside a palace of postcards. Titta was morose. His mother was ill. He wanted to turn around and visit her in Zevio.

"Battista," the diva said. "We've just arrived. We can't disappear. We haven't even introduced ourselves."

They marched up the gangway and were met at the top by Tina Onassis in a diaphanous silk robe and Aristotle in the peasant clothes he loved to wear. His secretive eyes clung to Maria like magnets. She turned away. She wouldn't be his trophy guest on land or in the harbor at Monte Carlo. Beside them sat Sir Winston in an outsize deck chair. He had the biggest stomach Maria had ever seen on a man; it resembled an enormous pouch, camouflaging most of his head. Next to him was an outsize wheelchair. His two muscular bodyguards, Marley and Watts, would spend their days on the *Christina* lifting him from one chair to the other. Marley was a sergeant from Scotland Yard on special detail to the former prime minister. He had a pistol tucked under his belt. Marley took one scornful look at Battista and kept smirking at Maria, convinced that he would have a go at her before journey's end. His boldness angered Maria, who would have slapped his face or shoved him into the sea if Sir Winston hadn't been on board with his wife, Lady Clementine.

Sir Winston never traveled anywhere without his parakeet, Toby, who sat in a silver cage, a gift from the sister of his private secretary. The bird was Sir Winston's constant companion. His coat was dark green. He could whistle but couldn't sing. Yet he amazed Maria, because the bird could recite an entire sentence.

"I'm Toby, and I belong to the admiral."

"Stop showing off," Sir Winston muttered. "We have a new guest."

It was clear that he had never heard of La Callas. The intrigues of opera would have bored him. He preferred music hall melodies.

"Madame Meneghini," Sir Winston said, "you keep staring at poor Toby. Does my bird delight you?"

A shiver ran through Maria. Somehow this pompous bird reminded her of Stephanakos, her lost canary, and how much she missed singing duets with that bright yellow wonder of a male soprano.

"Forgive me, Sir Winston. I did not mean to stare. But I must kiss your hand." And she did. His hand felt rough against her lips.

"That's cheeky," said Sir Winston's bodyguard from Scotland Yard.

"Shut up," Sir Winston said, his eyes half closed, "and let the opera singer explain herself. I'm sure she had an excellent reason, Sergeant Marley."

"You see," Maria said, "I was in Athens during the civil war, when you arrived in your armored car. It ignited the population."

The old man with the babyish bald head was suddenly alert. "I remember that afternoon, indeed. I couldn't afford to have Greece fall to the Reds. All of Europe would have fallen."

Sir Winston's head began to droop. His bodyguards transferred him to the outsize wheelchair, trundled him as far as they could, then cradled him in their arms and carried him to Aristotle's lavish suite on the bridge deck.

Aristotle always sacrificed his own comfort for Sir Winston. The entire ship ran according to Sir Winston's clock. He rose promptly at nine, had his morning orange juice, then porridge twenty minutes later with a piece of toast, then a cigar and a jigger of brandy twenty minutes after that. He would read in bed—Herodotus perhaps or Marcus Aurelius—and write a letter or two until a quarter to twelve, when his valet dressed him and his bodyguards carried him to the lunch table, where he presided under a green canopy that covered the rear deck.

Aristotle had shaped his own history, but Sir Winston had shaped history itself. And Aristotle could never forget . . .

Sir Winston loved lobster bisque.

He ate portion after portion, with pastry the chef had prepared for him, a chocolate pie wedged with almond paste. He soiled two napkins at every meal. It was like a tornado, with a wind surrounding him, as he tore into a chicken leg. He allowed no one but the opera singer to pick at his plate. He'd become proprietary about Maria, though he still had no idea who she was. He'd adopted her, just as he'd adopted the parakeet.

He might cry in the middle of a meal when a particular memory struck him hard in the head.

"Lost lads."

Aristotle's other guests stared at him, bewildered by his heaving shoulders and the warp of his voice.

Lady Clementine had to explain. "He still has nightmares about Gallipoli."

She wiped his tears with her table napkin. "Darling, you must not revisit what cannot be revisited."

"Lost lads," he said again. Maria knew nothing about Gallipoli, and she knew even less about World War I.

"I was a fool," Churchill said. He'd been First Lord of the Admiralty, gripped with the desire to seize Constantinople from the Turks and restore it to the past grandeur of Byzantium.

The tears were gone. Sir Winston's eyes shone with the magnificent sweep of the Mediterranean as he summoned up past maneuvers.

"Constantinople—we couldn't take Constantinople without having Gallipoli within our grasp. I softened up the peninsula with a naval bombardment and asked for an amphibious landing, like some omniscient prince of warfare."

He stared at Toby with one eye.

"I was hardly a prince. The Turk sat behind his fortifications and laughed. We lost forty-five thousand lads in a wisp."

"But the battle raged for ten months," said Aristotle, who liked to serve as a buffer to Sir Winston's self-impalements, which came upon the great man like an attack of the gout.

"Sir Winston, it was your own admirals who failed you. Their bombardments were delayed and delayed. The Turks had time to regroup. You cannot be blamed for the slaughter. You could have had Constantinople within your grasp."

Churchill glared at him with his other eye.

"Constantinople," he spat. And suddenly, like a prima donna, he began to recite a poem that sounded like a song to Maria.

An aged man is but a paltry thing,
A tattered coat upon a stick, unless
Soul clap its hands and sing . . .
And therefore I have sailed the seas and come
To the holy city of Byzantium.

Agitated, the parakeet began to rock and rock in his cage. "I'm Toby, and I belong to the admiral."

Sir Winston tossed a chicken wing at the parakeet. "Stuff it, Tobe."

Lady Clementine signaled to the pair of bodyguards,

who removed Sir Winston from the lunch table and carried him to his quarters. The meal seemed diminished and forlorn without him. There was utter silence. Not even Aristotle could pick up the conversation as they all listened to the rub of the wheelchair on the deck.

There was a crisis. The old warrior couldn't lounge on the main deck this afternoon and have his constitutional nap, accompanied a little later with a furious game of poker, where he liked to cheat Aristotle and his own bodyguards out of a few copper coins. Sir Winston was incontinent. Onassis paid Marley and Watts to be his nurses as well as his bodyguards on board the *Christina*. They had to undress the old man and carry him into a tub with mosaic tiles and gold faucets shaped as dolphins. Onassis had hired a special maid on voyages with Sir Winston to wash and iron his garments and linen twice a day.

These baths and the maneuverings around them generally exhausted Churchill. But he recovered around five or six and his bodyguards dressed him in a dinner jacket and black tie and carried him to the main deck for the cocktail hour. He drank brandy instead and smoked a cigar with Aristotle.

"I do not care for poets," Aristotle muttered. "They are pests. I feed half the poets in Greece out of my own pocket. I prefer philosophers."

Churchill had a fever in his pale blue eyes. "I cannot name one philosopher who ever moved me to tears." Timid before Churchill's eloquence and his jowls and shiny bald head, Maria still intervened. "Sir Winston, isn't opera also poetry? I assure you. I have sung arias that would have made you cry."

"Madame Meneghini," he said with a viper's sting, "as

much as I admire your presence, I am unfortunately not familiar with that art."

He was silent during dinner in the main hall, while Christina and Alexander, Aristotle's eleven-year-old blue-eyed heir, ate with the crew in the sailors' mess and sang songs throughout the meal.

Aristotle and his guests retired to the screening room after dinner. This evening's fare was *That Hamilton Woman,* Churchill's favorite, starring Laurence Oliver as Admiral Lord Nelson with his mythic eye patch and missing arm in a folded sleeve and Vivien Leigh as Lady Hamilton. Olivier and Leigh were married now, but Maria had relished reading about the couple's earlier illicit romance in her favorite gossip column. She was bored by the film's battle scenes, but she loved Lady Hamilton, an ex-courtesan involved in an adulterous affair—with Admiral Nelson, an unhappily married man.

Sir Winston wept while he watched the Battle of Trafalgar, wept while Lord Nelson lay dying on his flagship, shot in the tailbone by a sharpshooter in the rigging of the French fleet. He'd watched the film over a hundred times and wept at every screening. Maria wept, too. But she didn't give a damn about flagships and cannonballs. She saw Lady Hamilton as another ex-courtesan, like Violetta. She could have been watching *Traviata,* with different sets and in a different milieu, or watching the possibility of her own future, as Lady Hamilton ended up a poor, broken woman in the back alleys of Paris, stripped of all her titles and elegant couture.

Sir Winston sat in silence at the end of the film. No one dared break into his reverie. Then he clapped, with a furious bump of his palms, clapped again and again.

Lady Clementine signaled to the bodyguards with the bat of an eye, and the pair of them carried Sir Winston up to his quarters. Titta was already seasick, and had retired to the stateroom Tina Onassis had given him and Maria. It was an honored spot, where Greta Garbo used to stay when she was on one of Aristotle's summer cruises.

Suddenly, Maria was all alone. The screening room was in the bowels of the *Christina.* Maria climbed up the three flights of a spiral staircase made of bronze and soon found herself on the rear upper deck.

Aristotle stood against the railing. He puffed on a cigar in deep contemplation. He hadn't seen Maria approach with her catlike steps. He was watching the last traces of Monte Carlo with its specks of shimmering light.

"You must love that man," Maria said very softly, as if she were talking to a shadow.

He turned to look at her. "I do. He was mocked after Gallipoli, stripped of his minister's rank—a naval man, like Lord Nelson, who wasn't allowed near his own nation's fleet. He painted; he wrote. He had no political future—until Hitler arrived. . . . Yes, he bumbles now; he falls asleep in the middle of a meal. An old man who shits in his pants. He was well into his sixties when the war began. And how nimble he was then."

Aristotle seemed radiant, despite his baggy trousers and big nose.

"Good night," he said, and touched Maria's hand.

–4–

They were sailing to Byzantium, as Sir Winston foretold, a Byzantium that was no longer there. They steamed down the boot of Italy, into the Tuscan archipelago, and stopped at tiny ports. That night, Maria stood under the green canopy of the rear deck. But there was no sign of Aristotle and the jubilant stink of his enormous cigar. Marley, the sergeant from Scotland Yard, appeared out of the shadows. He had a half-mad, brooding look. “Mind if I keep you company, love?”

Maria wasn’t talking to Sir Winston now. She didn’t have to craft her English. “I’m not your love, you piece of shit,” she said in the grating voice of a girl from Washington Heights.

“Well,” Marley said, “we’ll see about that.” And he reached out to fondle Maria. He was much too strong for her, this sergeant who could carry Sir Winston on his back. He grabbed Maria and dug his tongue into her mouth. It felt like a lizard covered in slime.

Maria bit his tongue.

He howled, and suddenly went flying across the deck as Aristotle appeared in his baggy pants.

Marley regained his balance and weaved in a crouch toward Aristotle. “I can have you arrested for assaulting a sergeant, you know. I’m from the Yard.”

“And I can have you killed,” Aristotle said. “We’re not flying under a British flag. And you’re not Nelson of the Nile. The only reason you’ll leave this boat alive is that you’re attached to Sir Winston. But if you ever go near madame again, I’ll rip out your heart. Am I clear?”

“Yes,” the Sergeant said, saluting Aristotle. “Abundantly, Mr. Onassis, sir.”

And he hobbled away from the deck.

Aristotle clasped Maria’s hand. They stood there in silence. She could feel his entire body ripple with anger.

Soon it became a ritual, those endless evenings under the

canopy. Sir Winston would command the day. But when dinner was over and they all left the screening room, Aristotle and Maria would meet on the upper deck. He never talked of love. He would embroider whatever tale Maria had to tell. She talked of Buenos Aires and the fur stole she had to buy because the impresario at the Teatro Colón tricked her and paid her in cash that couldn't leave the country.

And Aristotle told her how he had gone to Buenos Aires on a cattle boat when he was sixteen.

He didn't talk about the Turkish massacre of Greeks in the Anatolian town of Smyrna in 1922, or about his father, a wealthy tobacco merchant who was stripped of his home and his fortune by the Turks and somehow managed to avoid a firing squad even though a death sentence sat upon his head. All that history wouldn't have remained with Maria. But she loved how Aristotle had been a brothel boy in a high-class "hotel" right across from the Teatro Colón. The lords of Buenos Aires would leave the opera house in the middle of the first act, visit the courtesans across the road, and return to their children and wives in time to see the end of *Tosca*.

"I learned a great deal as a brothel boy."

"Ah," Maria said, "that's what I will call you now—my favorite brothel boy."

He was an insomniac who taught himself to thrive without sleep. And now he had someone to soften his insomnia.

Aristotle learned more from the clients at the Hotel Ariane than from the courtesans themselves. Stockbrokers gave him tips, and he invested his earnings with them. He became a master tactician within a year, and began investing for the girls as they grew rich enough to retire from the Ariane. He could have taken over the stewardship of the hotel, but

Aristotle chose not to. He bought up rusted tankers in the harbor, refurbished them, and had his own fleet before he was twenty-one . . .

Aristotle was a storyteller, and it didn't matter to Maria what he fabricated on the upper deck. His own tales consumed him, and both of them stayed longer and longer under the canopy, deeper into the night, lovers who had not established their boundaries yet and did not have to rely on the mechanics of making love to discover how involved they had become with each other in so short a time on the way to Byzantium.

Titta had kept her cloistered while he handled her business affairs, botching them up. Elsa Maxwell had brought this mistress of the libretto out of the wild and into a social swirl that tempted Maria more and more. Otherwise, she would not have made this voyage, would not have watched *That Hamilton Woman* with Sir Winston in his diapers, would not have inhabited the stateroom that once belonged to Greta Garbo. It had photos of her everywhere on the walls and a cigarette holder with her initials carved into the ivory mouthpiece.

On the fourth day of the cruise, Titta, still defeated by his motion sickness, wanted the *Christina* to dock somewhere in Sicily so that he and Maria could leave the ship and travel to Zevio, where the king of Verona could attend to his mother.

"Go," Maria said, "but you'll have to go alone."

Titta made a fist as if to strike her. But Maria didn't flinch. He'd defeated himself with that one motion.

"But she's dying," Titta said in a weepy tone.

"Your mother's been dying for the last two years.

Anyway, she doesn't like me. She says I married you for your money."

Titta's eyebrows rose in deep contemplation. "You must forgive her, darling. She was born into a much narrower world than ours."

Maria wasn't his darling any longer. Perhaps she had never been. He was a business manager from a small town who did not have the brilliance to deal with sharks like Ghiringhelli and Rudolf Bing. She cared about rehearsals and the shabby state of her costumes at the Met, and Titta was obsessed about spiraling fees that went into his account, not hers. She sang for pennies, it seemed.

There was spittle on his tongue.

"You're in love with that pirate with the long nose. I'm not blind."

She did not answer him.

He sulked in the stateroom, suffering from vertigo, as the *Christina* rocked toward Greece. Aristotle didn't pay much attention to Titta, but he was concerned about Sir Winston, and he had the chief engineer regulate the vibrations of his yacht so that it wouldn't disturb the afternoon naps of his most important guest.

That evening, Sir Winston told how he'd become a relic after the war, how quickly voters forgot that his broadcasts had led Londoners through the Blitz. He sat there at dinner in a silent rage, but livened after a lick of Armagnac and read a patch of poetry. He was looking at Lady Clementine and Maria as he recited words he must have memorized a long while ago.

Ah, love, let us be true

To one another! for the world, which seems

To lie before us like a land of dreams,
So various, so beautiful, so new
Hath really neither joy, nor love, nor light,
Nor certitude, nor peace, nor help from pain;
And we are here on a darkling plain . . .

Maria was a barbarian in matters of British poetry. But the words dug into her like a fist on fire. She, too, had lived on a darkling plain, devoting herself to whatever opera house had hired her, no matter if there were mice in her dressing room, or if she had to rush onstage with her wig in her eyes. It was all she ever knew.

Laura Sordelo had said there was "a perverse sexuality" to her singing, an "unveiling" she had never seen before. In an article entitled "Callas Without Her Clothes," Laura wrote:

> *The diva undresses for us at every performance, and we are too blind to notice. No other prima donna has given so much of herself, and La Callas, who reaches for the highest registers time after time, is hissed at if we ever catch her off-key.*

That night, under the green canopy, Maria talked to Aristotle for the first time about her career.

"Titta says I can't retire. But I am sick of impresarios who make all the rules, who tell me what I can and cannot sing and how much time I will have to rehearse. I will stay here with you. We will sail to Byzantium."

Aristotle appealed to her. "Maria, Byzantium does not exist. It is a Turkish town "

"Never mind. We will build our own fleet, like Lord

Nelson, and retake that town," Maria said with a certain fancy.

Aristotle winced, recalling the Greeks who had died in Smyrna.

The ship's captain arrived with a radiotelephone. "Sorry to interrupt you, sir. But the party said it was urgent."

Aristotle grabbed the telephone, excused himself, and wandered across the deck, whispering instructions once or twice. Then he tossed the telephone to the captain, thanking him, and returned to Maria. His face seemed pale in the moonlight.

"Aristo," Maria said, "are you in trouble? I'll squeeze whatever I can out of Battista. I'll have him sell the house in Milan."

Aristotle put his hand along her spine and caressed it with his fingers like a flute. Maria felt a sudden chill.

"Aristo, tell me. How much did you lose?'

"It doesn't matter. A conglomerate I was pursuing backed out of a deal. I will find a way to swallow them."

He seemed ragged in his sailor shirt, lost, alone, Odysseus marooned on his own yacht.

She kissed him on the mouth. "My brothel boy." He tasted of wine and salt.

–5–

THEY WALKED THE SHIP HAND IN HAND, in front of crew and guests alike. Lady Clementine was aghast. She wouldn't sit on the same side of the table with Maria during dinner. But as much as she badgered Sir Winston, he wouldn't budge in his loyalty to the *Christina*'s own Odysseus. He loved playing Cupid, and liked to pretend that he had inspired this shipboard romance. Titta sulked in his stateroom. Maria would return at six in the morning to shower and change her clothes.

"Darling, what are you doing with this Don Juan?"

She stood in front of the mirror with a coldness he had never encountered from Maria. He remembered the chubby girl with thick ankles and terrible eyesight who had first arrived in Verona and had depended on Titta for *everything.* He'd gone against his family's wishes and supported Maria for an entire year. He'd been her mentor, her lover, her king. He'd selected her wardrobe, every article. He'd waged war on impresarios to find her openings.

"You can have the house in Sirmione," she said.

He wasn't listening. He didn't hear a word. He'd married a sorceress in his own church. Her roles had consumed her, made her a madwoman. He'd have to get her off the *Christina,* kidnap her, bring Maria to her senses, get her away from this charlatan and his ship.

But the *Christina* sailed on.

Someone onboard must have spoken to the press. Speedboats appeared in the *Christina*'s wake, with a legion of photographers. Maria could no longer parade on deck. Aristotle had to hire a private army of speedboats to frighten the photographers away. It didn't always work. A new legion would appear, and then another.

Meanwhile, Aristotle stood on the bridge. "Who's the traitor here?"

Battista might have informed on his wife, but he would have been much too ashamed, Aristotle reasoned, like Hercule Poirot. Lady Clementine bristled, but she'd never have betrayed the trust of Sir Winston. Aristotle's wife had something to gain. Tina could have thrown a dart into Aristotle's most recent romance. But her father, Stavros Livanos, was not only her husband's partner and chief rival but was also far richer than Aristotle, and she wouldn't have wanted to sabotage any of her father's deals.

Aristotle didn't need help from Hercule Poirot. The ship's captain kept a log of every outgoing and incoming radio call. Sergeant Marley was the culprit. He'd been in touch with the *Daily Mirror*.

Sir Winston held court at the dinner table.

"Marley, how long have you been with me?"

"Fifteen years, on and off," the sergeant said.

"Have I ever abused you in any way?" Sir Winston asked.

"No, sir," Marley said, standing at attention.

"And how much did those Judases at the *Mirror* offer you?"

"A thousand quid."

"God's blood," Churchill said, "you betrayed us for a thousand quid? You're not a navy man. A navy man would never breathe a word about what happens on his boat. A navy man would guard the code of silence with his life. Do you know what will happen to you, Marley?"

Marley paused for a moment, measuring his words. "Punishment, sir? I will be reprimanded by my superiors."

Sir Winston couldn't hold back his spite or his spittle that flew into Marley's face.

"I know your superiors at the Yard. They will cast you away. And you won't receive a farthing. Marley, get out of my sight."

But Maria intervened. Marley was far more familiar to her than to anyone else on board, except Sir Winston himself. She'd encountered villains such as Marley in a dozen operas she'd performed, liars and cheats like Scarpia, who was also a policeman. And she had a certain affection for them. The opera house was more of a home than any home she'd ever had.

"Wait," Maria said. "Do you have any children?"

"Two, mum," Marley replied.

She scowled at him. And then she looked into the watery blue eyes of the old man. "Sir Winston, do me a kindness. I don't want this man to be punished. He will end in the poorhouse, and I know what it means to be poor."

"But Maria," Aristotle said. "We will not have another moment of peace on this cruise. Journalists will hound us at every port—because of this man."

"I know," Maria said, "I know. But I do not want any nightmares."

A speedboat took Marley to the nearest port.

The captain assigned another bodyguard to Sir Winston, a member of his crew. But the old man blubbered into his handkerchief. "I was fond of that lad. I spoiled him. He was like a son."

And he wouldn't ride in his wheelchair. He shuffled to his stateroom with his own two feet.

–6–

THE *CHRISTINA* COULDN'T DROP ANCHOR in Piraeus, the port attached to Athens. There would have been too many journalists waiting on the docks. So Aristotle stopped at a few other Greek ports and sailed on to Smyrna—now Izmir—a Greek enclave once upon a time where Aristotle was born. He could elude journalists in his hometown. Sir

Winston was adamant. He wouldn't be left behind with his parakeet. He wanted to accompany Aristotle on his sad, sentimental journey, and he did. He hobbled about with his cane, a bodyguard on either side to prevent him from landing in the rubble strewn along the narrow streets near the docks. Titta had also come along, walking a pace or two behind his wife.

Aristotle seemed to glide across the narrow streets in his slippers, recollecting the aroma of some delicacy he'd devoured as a boy; yet that aroma was mingled with flashes of blood in the water, his mind caught in the nightmare of Turkish horsemen slaughtering his own people with their scimitars, as they didn't want to spend their bullets on Greeks. Still, he bargained with the vendors on the dockside streets, talking mostly with his fingers as he removed a leather pouch from his pocket and dazzled them with a shower of silver coins; he returned with a fortune of baklava and other sweets for his fellow voyagers.

"Ah, I discovered the art of negotiation from such street merchants," he said as he bit into the baklava.

A police captain arrived in a battered van and stared at Sir Winston.

"Welcome to Izmir, my Lord."

"I'm a commoner," Sir Winston grunted, "and proud of it—knighted, but never a lord."

"Forgive me, Excellency," the captain said. "You have been my hero for so long."

Sir Winston knew how friendly Ankara had been to Adolf Hitler, but he still signed the captain's daybook and offered him a sweet.

The captain was enchanted. He sat next to Sir Winston as the police van rode up a crooked hill to Karatas, the former neighborhood of wealthy Greek merchants, who had once dominated the very top of the hill in stone houses with barricaded windows and a commanding view of the harbor below.

Aristotle had the police captain unlock his father's empty villa. All the furniture was gone, including the commodes and the ornate marble bathtubs, which had been torn right out of the tiles. There were little scars in the walls where paintings had been hung. The odor of urine and excrement was everywhere. His father's villa had become one gigantic chamber pot.

The captain told Aristotle that the villa had been used as a garrison for Turkish troops, then as a brothel that the clerics had shut down, then as an almshouse, until the gates were closed.

Maria followed Aristotle up an unsteady staircase to a landing where Aristotle's old room was located at the end of the hall.

The walls had gone yellow. There was nothing in the room but rat droppings and a book on the floor. It was an English primer that Aristotle had once used. Somehow this book had survived the various incarnations of the villa. Aristotle stood with his hand on the diva's shoulder. He was shivering.

"Maria," he said, "I had my best years right here in Karatas, and then came the Turkish riders. It still hurts, hurts like hell."

"Aristo," she answered, "we could have avoided Izmir and gone to another port. You might have been happier there."

"Yes," he said, "but a sailor must come home at least once in his life. . . . And the captain isn't correct. Father's villa didn't become a garrison. It was the headquarters of the Turkish high command. And I didn't have to beg and wander about while the city burned. The generals let me keep my own room. I did small favors for them—got the best tobacco and the best wine."

Maria was astonished. "But Aristo, they killed your people, slaughtered them with scimitars."

"Yes, darling, but I had to survive."

His wife decided to wage war, and told her children about their father's flirtations with La Callas. Christina and Alexander looked askance whenever they caught Aristotle and Maria holding hands. Tina invited the children to eat dinner with all the guests, so Aristotle and Maria had to sit apart, like captives at the dinner table.

Alexander was silent about his father's sudden turn of affections, but nine-year-old Christina was twice as bold as her brother.

"Papa," Christina said, "you must stay away from this soprano. She will eat you blind and feed your eyes to the sharks."

"Who says so?" Aristotle asked, timid in front of his child and proud of her pluck.

She looked him over from head to toe before she said, "The papers."

"But you never read the papers."

"Mama does," Christina said with exasperation. "And Papa, this is *my* ship. It was named after me. I make all the rules."

So he abided by Christina's rules, at least while she and Alexander were awake. But he felt a deeper longing late at night, while he was under the green canopy with Maria. Their bodies brushed with an electric spark. Still, he wouldn't undress Maria, not like some thief aboard his own vessel. So they fumbled about on the deck, as greedy children would, and lay there under a blanket until first light. His fingers wandered under her dress, like tiny periscopes made of flesh. It undid Maria, who had to catch her breath.

"Aristo, your daughter has made herself an empress."

"Yes," he said with a toothy smile. "She's quite a kid."

"I would strangle her if I didn't love you so much."

"Darling," he said, "shhh, I'm very superstitious."

"So am I."

She returned to her stateroom.

Titta was still awake. He sat in bed in his silk pajamas, watching her like a sentinel as she undressed and crawled into her matching pair of silk pajamas and scrunched in beside Titta, with her back toward him; Garbo's stateroom had a couch but no other bed.

He nudged her as her mind began to drift.

"You stink of him," Titta said.

He was silent for a few moments and then he snarled, "You're like an animal in heat."

She didn't answer, and as she drifted into sleep, he nudged her again. "A wild animal, just as you are onstage. But there you don't have Onassis' smell."

"Then you ought to be happy—good night."

"What night?" Titta said with a bitter laugh. "You spent the night with him."

But she was no longer listening.

-7-

And so they sailed to Byzantium, or whatever remnants remained in a city that skirted two continents and was a continent unto itself, with its very own waterway, the Golden Horn. Founded by a Greek colony long before the birth of Christ, Byzantium had been conquered and reconquered many times, renamed and rebuilt, until it ended up in the hands of the Ottoman Turks, who called it Istanbul. But for Greeks like Aristotle and Maria, it remained Constantinople, home of the Eastern Orthodox Church and its patriarch, Athenagoras, a daunting figure, who was seventy-three and six feet tall, with a white beard that nearly reached his kneecaps; he wore a black robe and a tall black headdress with a long black train. He sat behind a walled citadel in a Greek enclave of Istanbul known as Phanar, or the Lighthouse, with domed churches and rough-hewn wooden houses that overlooked the Golden Horn.

Aristotle proposed to visit Patriarch Athenagoras with Maria in that Greek ghost town of Phanar.

"I can't," Maria said, crossing herself. "It's haunted now."

Aristotle shook his head. "Think of all the mosaics you will miss—the most beautiful in the world."

"Then I will learn to live without mosaics."

The captain had dropped anchor on the Bosporus, a few miles from the Golden Horn. And Aristotle took a speedboat into the heart of Istanbul, with its mirage of minarets shimmering in the hot, bubbly water, with different colors, different designs. He thought about earlier trips to Phanar while he sat in the speedboat. The patriarch always welcomed him with a simple lunch of *gigantes*—gigantic baked beans—and a chopped salad of onions, garlic, and tomatoes with chunks of flat bread. And then Aristotle would walk the streets of Phanar, which always summoned up Smyrna's own Greek enclave, with its little nation of vendors, its fire-eaters who performed for crowds that would come together and evaporate, its sewing shops, where blind women could locate a particular button or needle with the rub of a hand. It was where Aristotle always felt at rest, not at the villa on the hill, where servants in blue smocks arrived with glasses of piping-hot tea and buns sprinkled with pistachio dust, and where Aristotle had to sit in a starched shirt with his great-aunts and recite what he had studied at school . . .

He returned to the *Christina* with Athenagoras in his black hood, which covered him like a cloak. The patriarch could have gone below to meet with Aristotle's guests in one of the air-conditioned salons. But he preferred to stay in the sun. He didn't seem to swelter under his black hood. So Aristotle summoned his entire roster of guests and crew. Lady Clementine wore her sun hat, while Sir Winston's bodyguards carried him from his stateroom to the upper deck and sat him in his usual chair. He took one look at the patriarch's black hood and long white beard and said, "God's blood—Byzantium."

Athenagoras blessed everyone on the *Christina*, but he was particularly curious about Sir Winston. He leaned over the statesman with his bejeweled pectoral cross and said, "No one alive, Sir Winston, will ever be able to thank you enough. I listened to every one of your speeches on the wireless in my sanctuary. We couldn't have survived without your eloquence. We would have been left without a church—homeless, Sir Winston, homeless in the wind. You breathed the dragon fire of poetry, and the Nazis had no answer, none."

"Your Holiness," Sir Winston said, "you're far too kind. I was one voice among many."

"Indeed," the patriarch said. "But history does not allow such luxuries. The many will never count as much as you."

Both of them drank brandy from Sir Winston's flask. Then, with brandy on his breath, the patriarch summoned Aristotle and Maria, asked them to kneel, and, placing one huge hand on each of their heads, he blessed them and chanted in a voice that echoed across the *Christina*, "Our two most illustrious Greeks. Maria Meneghini Callas, the most revered singer in all of opera, and Aristotle Socrates Onassis, the greatest mariner of modern times."

Titta was furious—it was like a consecration, a marriage ceremony, at the edge of Istanbul. The patriarch must have known that Maria was a married woman. And Aristotle's wife was on board. How much had Aristotle donated to the citadel in Phanar? Titta wanted to tug the patriarch's white beard and drag him across the deck. But he was powerless on this ship. Odysseus' own sailors would have restrained him and held him below. He watched Tina Onassis like a half-crazed hawk. He wondered why on earth she was smiling, and then he noticed how sinister her smile was.

"Don't worry," she said in a calm, dreamlike voice. "You will have your revenge."

"I don't want revenge," he said. "I want my wife."

Tina's smile deepened. "It's a little too late for that. Do you think this ceremony was for my husband's sake? It was for La Callas." Tina clutched Titta's hand. "But this time he went too far, flaunting Maria in front of my face, with our own children on the *Christina*. He's never done that before. He must be desperate."

"Or in love," Titta mumbled.

"Does it really matter? Nothing lasts with Ari. It never does."

Six

The Second Soprano

-1-

Aristotle despised opera and all its clatter and pomp, but his first real love had been an opera singer, a soprano like Maria. It was during his young manhood in Buenos Aires, when he was still a brothel boy attached to the Hotel Ariane, across from the Teatro Colón. It was at the very end of the soprano's South American tour. She called herself Consuela, Consuela Ramón. She must have been from Barcelona or one of the Spanish islands, and swore she wasn't a day older than thirty-five. She visited the brothel one afternoon with her entourage—her dresser, her wigmaker, and members of the corps de ballet at the Colón, where she monopolized every performance of *Carmen* with the fire of her art.

She was lustful and very tall. Aristotle had never met a woman remotely like her. She slept with every courtesan at the brothel, all in the same afternoon, like a sorceress with a scythe. And then she noticed Aristotle. He was wearing a striped suit, like the gangsters and tango dancers from the barrio of Palermo, near the Rio de la Plata, where the tango was born. These gangsters visited the brothel all the time and were the courtesans' favorite "guests," until this Spanish soprano came along.

She stared at Aristotle and started to laugh. "Are you the pimp of this establishment?"

"No, Madame Consuela. I keep the books."

She couldn't stop laughing. "I never saw a bookkeeper in a pin-striped suit."

She dragged the brothel boy up the stairs and into the domain of the courtesans and tossed them out of their dens. Then she occupied the largest room she could find, one that faced the Colón. She meant to have some fun with this boy. She interrogated Aristotle while she stripped him of his clothes.

"What is your name, child?"

"Aristotle Socrates Onassis, and I'm from Anatolia."

"Where the hell is that?" she recited in the lowest key she could.

"In Asia Minor, madame. My people called me Aristo, but I'm Ari now."

"Then I'll call you Aristo," she sang as she undressed in front of the brothel boy. She didn't tease Aristotle, the way the courtesans would, removing one article at a time. Consuela ripped off her clothes. She was full-breasted, with the milky skin of a goddess, though she had a bruise here and there, and a missing toe. She meant to amuse herself with the brothel boy. But the courtesans had taught him their own tricks and how to please every part of a woman's body. Consuela's orgasms were as loud as Carmen's cries at the Colón.

Everyone at the brothel shivered around her Junoesque frame; the floorboards creaked under her tread. She'd tired of the courtesans, but she couldn't seem to get enough of this boy. She had her tailor arrive the next afternoon and measure Aristotle from his neck down with a yellow tape attached to a retractable rod. He did not utter a single word.

Two days after that, a Rolls-Royce Silver Ghost parked in front of the brothel. A chauffeur in a crisp gray uniform with polished boots rang the bell. When Aristotle opened the door, the chauffeur handed him a large box and said, "This is for the Anatolian. Deliver it, please."

Aristotle thanked the chauffeur, went upstairs to his room with the box, and opened it. The box contained a velvet dinner jacket in midnight blue, a pair of matching trousers, three impeccably starched white shirts, an attachable velvet bow tie, a pair of suspenders made from alligator skin, knitted black socks, and a pair of Cordovans that fit him as well as Cinderella's slippers.

With these fineries came a note and a ticket to the Colón.

Tonight, Anatolia. Don't be late.

Come to my dressing room after the last act.

The racket of the opera rang in his ears. He grew numb from all the singing and chatter. Consuela was much taller than the rest of the troupe, and she dominated every moment, every scene. He was drawn to her wildness, to the violent sway of her body. This Carmen was never still—until she was stabbed to death by one of her suitors. The entire theater was forlorn until Carmen came back to life, appearing from behind the curtain.

The entire balcony stood and serenaded her. Aristotle thought he'd come to a madhouse. He'd never been to the opera, so it was the first time he'd encountered the full fury of a live performance and the splendor of velvet seats. Yes, there had been operatic moments at the Ariane, as two of the outlaws from Palermo fought over a girl, but never with knives and brass knuckles, or they would have been banned from the Ariane for life. It was a shove, a punch, or a tug, and the fight was over.

Aristotle went backstage in his dinner jacket and climbed upstairs to Consuela's dressing room. It was cluttered with admirers and colleagues, members of the cast. Her nostrils flared as she drank champagne, signed her autograph, and clutched the bouquets that her admirers brought. She did not notice Aristotle, not even with a nod. He had met several of her admirers, bankers and stockbrokers who were patrons of the brothel at the Hotel Ariane. They introduced him to their wives, women with painted eyes and silver fox stoles, who seemed to live in a constant daze. No wonder their husbands visited the Ariane.

Aristotle stood in the corner with a flute of champagne for half an hour while Consuela's admirers came and went. Then she yawned once and threw everyone out of the dressing room except Aristotle. She was still Carmen, wearing her costume, with all the makeup a prima donna had to wear. She wiped off the makeup with a wet rag, and said with a twist of her shoulders, "Hey, Anatolia, what are you waiting for? Help me undress."

And so he unclipped her costume and she wiggled into a skirt and blouse.

"Where are we going, Madame Consuela? To have dinner at the Savoy?"

She frowned at him, and he saw the wrinkles around

her eyes. "Don't *Madame* me. I've licked your juices, and you've licked mine. I want to see Palermo."

"But they are gangsters. They have knives, and I have none. I cannot protect you. If they dance with you, Consuela, I'm cooked. They'll steal you away."

She laughed with gusto, belched, and slapped her chest. "Anatolia, do I remind you of someone who can be stolen? Come."

She clutched his hand and led him out of the Colón. Consuela's Silver Ghost was waiting for her outside the stage entrance with her chauffeur, Abdul, who had traveled with her across three continents. The Silver Ghost sat in the hold of every ship they sailed on. Aristotle had never seen such a sedan, with its silver chassis, silver spokes, silver handles, and silver frames on the windshield.

Consuela sat in the rear with Aristotle, a bearskin rug on their laps.

"Abdul," she sang into a pipe with a mouthpiece, "take us to Palermo and don't bother us until we get there."

Then she pulled the blinds down over the glass plate that separated her and Aristotle from the front of the Silver Ghost.

"Anatolia," she muttered in a husky voice with some of the same fire she had onstage, "bite me to pieces."

She wiggled out of her blouse; she wasn't wearing a corset. Consuela never did.

"Bite me," Consuela whispered, "bite me until I bleed."

She turned away from Aristotle, held her arms over her head, and clutched the silver side rails above the rear windows, while he bit her neck and every portion of her back until it was covered with teeth marks. Consuela wailed with delight.

"Again," she shouted, "again, again."

Aristotle didn't draw blood, and he wasn't trying to. The pain that seemed to delight her aroused him, but she wouldn't let the brothel boy crawl under her skirt on the backseat of the Silver Ghost.

"Not here, Anatolia—not until I dance with those ruffians in Palermo."

"They never dance with strangers."

She smiled at him; she had one black tooth, which she covered whenever she sang in front of an audience. "We'll see."

The Silver Ghost stopped as silently as a huge cat. Abdul opened the rear door. "Palermo, señora."

They'd come to a barren hill near a shallow river, with a cantina at the top of the hill. A good deal of noise came from the cantina. It saddened Aristotle, who'd become a philosopher at the Ariane. He recognized the sound of all human folly. He wasn't frightened of what he would discover inside the cantina, though as a brothel boy he wasn't privileged to carry a pistol or a knife.

"I'm lazy," Consuela said. "Abdul, can't you drive us to the top of the hill?"

"There isn't a single road, señora, that leads to the top. And if I drive across this rocky terrain, we might puncture a tire and have to abandon the Silver Ghost. I doubt we will find a mechanic in Palermo who can fix your car."

"Abdul," she said, "you speak like a lawyer. I don't like it."

"You trained me, señora," Abdul said.

"Then I didn't train you well."

She left Abdul to guard her one possession, a car that cost almost as much as a battleship, and climbed to the top of the hill with Aristotle. They entered the cantina, which was made of wood and didn't even have a window. But Aristotle was surprised how luxurious the interior was. It had a zinc bar, with an enormous mirror above it, framed in gold. It also had a highly polished mahogany floor without a trace of sawdust or debris. The bartender wore a gaucho's black felt hat with a wide brim. But most of his male customers wore Borsalinos, like the gangsters who visited the brothel. Aristotle didn't recognize any of these men.

There were very few women at this cantina, and they didn't congregate with the men; they wore tight skirts and cloche hats like the latest Hollywood starlets, but they had mean faces with many scars. And Aristotle was worried that they might attack Consuela, who had captured the attention of the Borsalinos near the bar. The bartender served the two visitors a bitter white wine in shot glasses and wouldn't accept any pesos from Aristotle, who suddenly realized that this remote cantina must be a private club.

The Borsalinos didn't play checkers or cards, didn't hurl darts at the wall, while the women stood around and hummed to themselves. They were all waiting for someone. Then a thickset, hatless man arrived with an enormous satchel. He took an accordionlike instrument out of the satchel, an instrument with many buttons and a huge bellows. The bartender brought him a chair and he started to play, with this enormous instrument resting on his knees. Aristotle watched the bellows expand and contract like the chest of a primordial insect. No one danced. No one moved. And then these scarred women in the cloche hats summoned the men. They were the ones who chose a particular Borsalino. The partners swirled off each other's hips, their hands clutching, but with a wide space between their bodies—until their hips bumped.

Aristotle had seen the tango at nightclubs in Buenos Aires, but nothing like this, as if each step had a language and a ritual of its own. He wasn't blind to all the contradictions. The tango on this hill was aloof and passionate at the same time, as if its passion was born in the distance between the bodies, and the hunger it evoked.

Then Consuela broke into this precision on the polished floorboards. She seized the Borsalinos away from the women, one at a time, breaking up every couple, and the line of her body was much more precise. The Borsalinos lost their equilibrium. It was Consuela who held them in her grip. The women were furious. They took enormous hatpins out of their purses and menaced Consuela and Aristotle, lunging at their eyes.

"You must not humiliate us, you witch—you and your helper."

That's when Abdul arrived with a pair of pistols. He led Consuela and Aristotle out of the cantina. Consuela was laughing as she ran down the hill.

Aristotle brooded as they sped back to Buenos Aires in the Silver Ghost.

Finally he said, "Consuela, why did you sabotage their dance?"

"Because," she said. "I had to wake them from their dream."

Her strategies were beyond Aristotle's ability to comprehend. He stopped trying. He attended every performance of *Carmen* in his midnight blue. He went to parties with her at the homes of bankers who contributed to the Colón. He took her back to her suite at the Hotel Savoy in a drunken stupor and stayed the night. He was in love with this inscrutable woman who was probably twice his age. She lived her own form of poetry, reckless, even in her art.

"Anatolia, I will not sing tonight."

He was confused. "But isn't it very late to cancel a performance?"

She captured him in a curious glance. "Oh, I will sing. But I won't be there."

And Aristotle, who'd become a connoisseur of Consuela, could tell that she sang like a zombie that night—her mind in some other locale than the stage at the Colón. Yet the audience accepted these lapses, these sins. The prima donna was six feet tall. She was *their* Consuela, *their* Carmen, who towered over all her male protagonists.

And then she was gone.

She left without a note, without a word of good-bye. They'd made no plans. They rarely did. He went to her dressing room after her final performance of *Carmen*. There were no admirers, no bouquets. She'd checked out of the Savoy, fled with Abdul in her Silver Ghost. Had she left for Montevideo? He didn't inquire. He reeled around for a week, a brothel boy without an appetite.

Years later, when his fortune seemed to multiply without limits, he did inquire. She'd ended up at a home for the indigent in Bilbao, herself a silver ghost, suffering from emphysema. He had her transferred to a private clinic. He planned to visit Consuela, and he did. Bilbao frightened him at first. He'd never been to a town so big that was lost in another century. Even the boulevards looked medieval.

She didn't recognize him at first. She was very frail and stooped over. She'd lost her magnificent stature. She had cataracts, and all her teeth were black. She had a coughing fit and then recovered.

"Anatolia, is that you?"

"Yes, Consuela," he said with as much neutrality as he could manage, but he hadn't lost the sentimental attachment of a brothel boy in Buenos Aires to this singer out of his past. She was no longer beautiful, and she had abandoned him, but he hadn't come to Bilbao to seek revenge. Hardened as he was, after a millennium of business deals, he couldn't keep from crying.

He gave her a sip of water.

She squinted at him. "Anatolia, remind me. I can't remember your real name."

"Aristotle Socrates Onassis," he sang like a male soprano to this ghost in a white gown.

She cackled at him. "Then I'm a fool. You're famous. I could have married a millionaire."

"What happened to Abdul?"

"He was reckless," Consuela said. "Abdul was killed in a bar fight, trying to protect me. And here I am, unscathed."

Aristotle paid all her bills. She fell into a coma and died within a month. He had her remains shipped to a burial ground in Monaco that belonged to him and his portfolio of real estate. Aristotle was a superstitious creature. He fervently believed in ghosts. He might never have fallen in love with Maria without that first love, without Consuela. Maria was tall and reckless. And she had all the beauty and allure of a female pharaoh. But she'd lived underground all these years with Meneghini, that husband-manager of hers, who bungled every deal. Even Aristo, who understood so little about opera, could breathe in the sexual aroma of Maria's performances. It was as if the very perfume of her body was in every note she sang. No other soprano, except perhaps Consuela, provided so powerful an aphrodisiac. But with

Consuela it was pure seduction, and with Maria it was not. It was the enchantment and the power of a female pharaoh.

And after he brought Athenagoras onto the *Christina*, and after the patriarch blessed him and Maria, he knew how much his life would be rattled. He risked everything—his position in Monaco, his partnerships, his marriage, the devotion of his son and daughter. But that night he brought Maria to the stateroom he occupied while Sir Winston and Lady Clementine were on board. He undressed the diva and the first thing he did was bite her back. He wasn't using Maria as a mannequin. He was exposing a tender wound. He wasn't a mariner lost at sea, but Odysseus on a very different kind of voyage. The sharks would surround him soon enough. He'd have to end the tour and return to Monte Carlo.

Tina had mocked his prowess, called him an old man. But he held to Maria for half the night, their bodies trembling with the curious camaraderie of desire. It was as if he were back in Buenos Aires, at the Ariane, and she was a courtesan with one client—Aristo, the brothel boy, now fifty-three.

When he woke in the morning, Maria was not with him. He could hear shouting from her stateroom. He did not shower. He wanted to live with her aromas and dry spit a little while longer. He dressed in his sailor's clothes and climbed aloft in his bare feet. The yacht was already surrounded with a little mutiny of speedboats. These journalists and their camera crews had already paid off the Turkish police.

"Onassis, Onassis, will you sail away with the diva?"

He ignored their flashbulbs. It was seven in the morning and the heat was barely tolerable. He was startled when he saw Sir Winston in his deck chair without his bodyguards, nursing his flask of brandy.

"Couldn't sleep. . . . Here, have a sip."

Aristotle had a morning sip and returned the flask. "Sir Winston, how the devil did you get here?"

"Climbed down from the bloody bridge. But you're the one who has to be on guard. The knives, the knives. They'll cut you to pieces, these lads. They have no heart."

He stepped away from Sir Winston for a moment and had a member of the crew fetch a radiotelephone. He'd grown up speaking Turkish in his father's villa, and he was able to reach several ministers and Istanbul's chief of police at this early hour. A Turkish Coast Guard cutter arrived and disbanded all the speedboats.

"Well done," Sir Winston said, and shuffled back to his stateroom without the least bit of help.

He reappeared at lunch, sitting between Aristotle and Maria, much to Lady Clementine's dismay. He'd already suffered two strokes, and his fingers weren't always nimble. His doctor and his secretary, who were also on board, were banished to the far end of the table. He drank Dom Pérignon with Aristotle, finishing off a magnum between them.

"Maria," Sir Winston said, "I hear you've performed in an opera about King Henry and Anne Boleyn. Will you be kind enough to sing a bit of the opera for me? Poor Anne was one of my favorites. It would delight this old man if you could bring Britain's unluckiest queen back for a moment."

A hardened mask appeared on Maria's face, a mask that Consuela had sometimes worn whenever she was perturbed.

"Sir Winston," she said. "I am so sorry. I cannot sing on command. I must be in the mood."

Both Tina and Battista smiled at Maria's blunder. But

Sir Winston clasped Maria's hand and growled for another magnum of Dom Pérignon.

"I understand, my dear. I'm often asked to make a speech off the cuff, and I cannot."

That evening, Sir Winston had one of his uncontrollable fits. It would come upon him suddenly, without warning, as if he were doing battle with the wizards of old age, and these were his ruptured war cries. It had nothing to do with senility. He was as lucid as an alarm clock. But he would get violent as he ranted and raged. And his doctor was worried about Clementine. And so the captain called Aristotle from the bridge. And Aristotle arrived with Maria.

Lady Clementine was sobbing into a handkerchief. "He's a brute when he gets like this. Can't help himself."

Sir Winston was standing on his bed, wrapped in his own soiled linen. "Knives, I tell you. They always come at you with knives. God's blood, do you know what I will miss from the grave?"

"Lady Clementine?" ventured his doctor, who seldom took part in the actual cruise but followed Sir Winston everywhere.

"No, you imbecile. Not Clemy—Will."

"I'm confused," said the doctor.

"Will," repeated Sir Winston. "Will Shakespeare."

"Sir Winston," Maria said, "I cannot give you your beloved Will in the language you adore, but I can give you your favorite queen."

And without warming up in front of the mirror and testing whatever timbre she had left in the stateroom, she broke into *Anna Bolena* and sang the entire second act, including the roles of Anna and Henry VIII. Aristotle himself was hypnotized. Henry VIII was pompous, evil, and arrogant as Maria assumed the low registers of his voice, and Anna had the pride, the pluck, and the mournful resonance of a queen who was about to be beheaded.

Sir Winston was stunned into silence, seduced by Maria's ability to maneuver from role to role and by the resilience, the range, and rich vibrato of her voice.

He kissed her hand. The linen dropped around him like a rumpled flower and he stood naked.

"Dear child, be careful of the knives."

–2–

AND THERE WERE KNIVES, DOZENS OF THEM. Newspapers and magazines and television columnists called the *Christina*'s summer odyssey "the wrecking cruise." They blamed Aristotle and Maria for breaking up their own "idyllic" marriages. Yet the two marriage breakers quickly turned into the most talked-about couple of the year.

Odysseus and the Diva.

Tina divorced her Odysseus on the grounds of mental cruelty, never asked him for a cent, since she had her own fortune, and kept custody of her two children. That was a blow to Aristotle, who pleaded with her to maintain their marriage while he was cavorting with Maria. He didn't want to lose Christina or Alexander, his sole male heir. Tina mocked him, and with the help of Lady Clementine, she married a marquess and became a marchioness with a castle. The marriage didn't last.

She'd had a far better life on board the *Christina*. She'd been the sole queen in that principality of Aristo's yacht. The staff adored her. She could arrive with one of her current lovers. Aristo was confident enough to play the cuckold. He could control every one of her movements while she was on the yacht. It seemed to titillate him whenever Tina shared his bed. But she could barely arouse him after she gave birth to Alexander. He needed a streak of cruelty in all his sexual encounters. He could no longer find it with the mother of his first child. It grew worse after Christina was born. Tina had become his third child.

Still, despite all these difficulties, she fared much better as Aristo's wife. He never shouted at her, never belittled her. He took care of this child-wife, at least whenever he was around. He was on deck one day, with his bare chest and short pants, and gone the next, and she might not see him for months. But he called her every afternoon, with that delicate stutter of his. She'd left him twice before, but he always managed to win her back. He was the sailor, after all.

And then La Callas came along. Tina blinded herself, called it a flirtation. But it wasn't—it never was. She'd been distracted by the attention he paid to Sir Winston. And then she noticed the brilliance in his copper-colored eyes. That wayfarer of hers was in love. He was kinder to her than he should have been. And when he did take her to bed on the cruise, it was with a sudden passion that caught her by surprise. He hadn't made love to her in almost a year. He was dreaming of that damn soprano while he touched her with his sailor's hands.

So she left him. And he panicked. He cried on the phone. He didn't want to lose her and his children.

"Yes," he said, "I have a new mistress. But how does that change things?"

She had a laughing fit while he kept crying.

"Crocodile," she said. "You're in love with that bitch."

He was silent, and Tina hung up the phone.

Aristotle still had one more weapon in his arsenal. He called her father, Stavros Livanos, a shipping magnate every bit as powerful as Onassis, but without his flamboyance. Both had palatial Parisian apartments on the Avenue Foch, both had offices all over the world, but Livanos was seldom seen in public.

"Stavros," Aristotle said, "*Father*, our empire will crumble if we aren't careful. We have enemies. Can't you convince her to stay?"

"I will not," Livanos said in his own soft style. "My gallant son-in-law, you have attached yourself to a sorceress."

The sailor was entering a difficult sea. He had to be cautious. "Madame Meneghini is a soprano, Father, the greatest of her time."

"A sorceress," Livanos repeated in the same soft voice. "I have seen her perform. No human could sing with such pathos. I had nightmares after her Norma. And I will not even speak of Lady Macbeth. Any grown man should tremble after watching her Medea. Should I remind you, Aristotle? Medea is one of our own, a Greek myth. . . . Your singer is a sorceress."

"I will give her up," Aristotle blurted.

"Ari, you may lie to me at your own pleasure, but please don't lie to yourself."

–3–

She wanted to cancel her engagements, stop singing, end it all, the entire menagerie, that circus of preparations for every part—the costumes, the wigs, rehearsal after rehearsal, fights with the maestro and other members of the cast. End it all.

She'd devote herself to Aristotle. He called her his "yellow canary." He didn't want Maria to stop singing. It brought him prestige, to be the lover of such a fine canary, while he, Aristotle, was the sole guardian of her cage.

She hired an impresario, the best there was—Sandor Gorlinsky, born in Kiev, and based in London now. Theater managers shivered at the mention of his name and at the sight of his Siberian fur coat. He never bargained, didn't even worry about written contracts. The demand for Maria didn't wane, no matter what the price, even though she was feuding with Ghiringhelli and Rudolf Bing. Sandor could have ended that feud in a minute, but Maria wouldn't allow it. She preferred the recording studio now, where she could redo a lost note without a live audience hectoring her. Even the *loggionisti* were no longer entirely with La Callas. Rotten radishes dropped from the balcony like bombs.

She finished her recording session in London and returned home to the *Christina* for a Mediterranean cruise. She arrived on board with her maid, Bruna, and Toy. Only two years older than Maria, Bruna was her companion, her cook, her nurse, her fortune-teller, and sometimes her chauffeur and dancing partner.

Aristo introduced Maria as the ship's new *patronne*, but she was never as popular with the crew as Tina had been. Maria was too occupied with Aristo. People gawked at La Divina from the docks, while photographers followed her out to sea in their motorboats. Aristo gave her a room on the *Christina* with a Steinway, where she could practice her arpeggios and frills, and work on her librettos and scores. But she never practiced, never touched the keyboard, unless Aristo begged her to sing for one of his business partners.

She liked it best when he kept away from the dukes and duchesses and shipping magnates who had villas on one or another of the Greek islands. They had a languor in their eyes, like an endless, empty well. They ignored La Callas, who didn't have a family crest or a fortune. She was only a diva who appeared in opera houses, Ari's latest mistress. Their coldness to Maria angered the sailor, and he stopped visiting them in their hillside retreats. Instead, he went to the tavernas near the docks and drank ouzo with the fishermen, who had never heard of La Callas but kissed her anyway. He felt much more at home with the fishermen than with the nabobs on the hill. He would arrive bare-chested, engage in arm-wrestling matches, and dance on the tables whether he defeated the local champion or not. The fishermen knew about his fabulous wealth, but they would never let him pay for a meal.

It was these trips to the tavernas that she liked the best, and her time alone with Aristo.

He didn't invite her to live with him in his apartment on the Avenue Foch. He was worried about what would happen whenever Alexander and Christina came to visit. They couldn't abide *any* woman around Aristo other than their mother. And so he rented a much tinier apartment for her a few houses away on the Avenue Foch.

At night they went to Maxim's.

Aristotle had his own table reserved for him and his guests. He dined at Maxim's twice a day whenever he was in Paris. He didn't have lunch at the Grill, which was cluttered with tourists. He ate in the Omnibus, a streamlined corridor of banquettes that led into the Aquarium, as the *grande salle* was called. He never brought Maria to lunch. He met here with his partners and rivals, and sculpted one business deal after another—Odysseus rarely made a false move. The Omnibus had recently been remodeled. And workmen found gold coins, diamond rings, and ankle bracelets imbedded between the cushions and the banquette.

Aristo preferred Maria in black. And soon her entire wardrobe consisted of black dresses and skirts. He liked her in high heels, and soon she had to discard most of her sandals. He also preferred her with short hair. So she had her hair cut by Alexandre of Paris for Aristo's pleasure.

Her long nose seemed longer without a full shake of hair. But her big eyes were more startling, and her moist mouth more sensuous.

"Wonderful," he said, observing Maria as a gamine. "Now you don't look like a grandma."

"Good," she replied. "Grandpa Aristotle can take his *poule* to Maxim's."

Maria was a head taller than Aristo in her high heels, but he liked tall women.

He wouldn't allow Maria to wear eyeglasses whenever they were in public. "You're a canary, not a schoolteacher." She couldn't get accustomed to contact lenses, so she groped around in a perpetual fog to please her sailor. Still, she grappled with him.

"Odysseus, you're just as blind. And you go everywhere in your dark glasses."

"Yes," he said, "but I'm a businessman, not a diva."

She bit back. "Sometimes I think you are more of a diva than I am."

And off they went to Maxim's in Aristo's Rolls. He wore a velvet jacket and smoked the finest Cuban cigars. He plucked a pearl necklace from his pocket and slid it around Maria's neck with the nimbleness of a jewel thief. The pearls were from Cartier.

"You pirate," she said, without looking into a mirror, "how did you know that your spoils would match my dress?"

Aristo smiled. "A pirate's intuition," he said.

They arrived on the Rue Royale at a quarter past nine.

Runners in their pillbox hats surrounded Aristo and Maria. They escorted them into the Aquarium. There was only one empty table in the *grande salle*—Aristo's. The other diners kept staring at the diva. Aristotle was only a nabob with a long nose. He himself seated Maria. The rose-colored light from the many lamps and the mahogany beams and pillars surrounded Maria in a religious glow. La Divina had come to Maxim's. No one else seemed to matter. Not the latest movie stars, who seemed ordinary under the same light, not the concert pianists and couturiers, not the dethroned kings and queens from some European nation that had disappeared from the map, and not even a nabob like Aristotle, though it was his table.

Albert, Maxim's maître d', wouldn't allow any of the tourists from "Siberia"—those tables in the far corner of the Aquarium—to approach Maria and bother her about an autograph. Albert himself brought her the steak au poivre she preferred. Whenever Aristotle was away and she wanted to dine alone at Maxim's, he reserved the "red table" for her, the usual haunt of the Duke and Duchess of Windsor. As soon as it was time for her to pay for the meal, Albert would arrive with a Chaplinesque shrug and announce, "Please forgive us, Madame Callas, but we lost your bill and no one can find it."

Such was the sway that Maria had at Maxim's.

Aristo always kept an empty seat at his table. It was reserved for some lone wolf without a reservation. This evening's lone wolf was Pierre-Yves, a young couturier, who had come to Maxim's on a whim.

Born in Marrakesh, Pierre-Yves arrived in Paris at the age of seventeen, and began working for Balenciaga before he was twenty. He usually showed up at Maxim's with his own clique, but here he was at Aristo's table, almost a vagabond. Very tall and very slim, he wore thick eyeglasses and had to grope for a piece of bread. Seated next to Maria, he suddenly began to cry.

Maria gripped his hand. "What's wrong, Pierre-Yves?"

"I'm so happy," the couturier said.

"And since when does happiness make you cry?"

"But I always see you and hear you from such a distance at the opera, and if I hadn't shown up at Maxim's without a reservation, I wouldn't be sitting next to you now."

"Naughty boy," Maria said. "You could have visited me in my dressing room."

"Maria, I'm much too shy."

He removed a sketch pad and a stick of charcoal from his briefcase, and with several flicks of his hand, he sketched Maria in her pearls. He captured all her dignity and her power in a few strokes. Her dark eyes dominated the portrait. She could have been Norma or Anna Bolena sitting at Maxim's in modern dress.

"Flatterer," she said, passing the sketch around the table.

Aristo was intrigued. "My God," he said, "the boy has drawn the Belle Otero."

"Who's the Belle Otero?" asked a discarded duchess. "Was she a *poule?*"

"What *poule?*" Aristo declaimed in a mocking tone. "She was the empress of Maxim's."

And he revealed the story of the Belle Otero, as Albert, the maître d', had revealed it to him. Aristo reveled in the tale. He took his listeners back to the Belle Epoque, when courtesans who inhabited the Omnibus ruled the restaurant. They were known as the "plats du jour." And they were very particular about their clients. The most particular of all was the Belle Otero.

"Ari, what did she look like?" asked a former mistress of his, who happened to be a marchioness.

Aristotle paused, like the shrewd storyteller that he was. Then his copper eyes blazed.

"She looked a little like *my* Maria, I'm told, with a magnificent string of pearls around her long neck."

Her origins were obscure. Some said she was born in Spain. Others said Morocco. But she was an instant favorite once she arrived at Maxim's. The runners would have done anything for the Belle Otero, would have sacrificed their lives for her. She danced the fandango, leaping from tabletop to tabletop, upsetting the silverware, while Maxim's bankers and local lords dined with their mistresses or a courtesan they had just met. Her favorite client was Kaiser Wilhelm II, who called her his "little savage."

"Ari, did she die rich?" asked the same marchioness, fondling her own string of pearls.

Aristotle paused again. "No one knows," he said. "Otero's still alive. Albert gets an occasional postcard from her. She retired to Nice, where she probably gambled away whatever small fortune she had. I believe she's living in a charity ward. Albert and I contribute to her welfare."

"Ari," asked one of his banker friends at the table, "did you ever meet La Belle?"

"No," he said. "Otero was before my time. Anyway, can't you see? All the courtesans are gone."

Maria smoldered at the table. She wanted to rip the pearls from her throat and fling them at her Odysseus. She watched the nymphs on the murals behind her wandering about in various stages of undress, frolicking in diaphanous shawls and gowns. Maxim's Aquarium could have been a stage dressed for a scene out of *Traviata*. And Maria could end up like Violetta, or La Belle.

She was a courtesan without a tabletop to dance on.

She arose and rattled the silverware on Onassis' table.

"Darling," she said, "I have a migraine. Let's go."

"But we can't abandon all our guests," the sailor said.

"Then you can entertain them with your deep knowledge of other courtesans at Maxim's."

Maria fondled Pierre-Yves' shoulder and marched out of the Aquarium in her high heels. Aristo shrugged and followed behind her. She'd left the pearls near her steak au poivre, and Aristo had to run back and collect them like Maxim's own court jester.

–4–

SHE LEFT FOR ENGLAND THAT NOVEMBER to record *Tosca* at a London recording studio. She loved to shop at the local Woolworth near the studio, searching for hatpins and sewing kits and assorted bric-a-brac at bargain prices. But she went to Harrods to buy Christmas presents for Aristo's two children. She'd convinced herself that she could win them over.

She was staying at the Dorchester while she recorded *Tosca;* Aristo would ring her every evening at six, have roses sent to her room, and court her like a troubadour. Still, she couldn't fathom all this gallantry—so she went to Harrods, which was like a nineteenth-century castle in the middle of Knightsbridge. The clerks mobbed Maria. Some of them had seen her perform at Covent Garden; others had seen her photo in the *Daily Mail.* But she didn't know how to shop for a sullen ten-year-old and a twelve-year-old daredevil. And the diva who loved Woolworth, and could buy up half the world for a few copper coins, spent over five hundred pounds on cardigans and silk scarves for two spoiled brats, had the Christmas presents wrapped in Harrods' silken paper, and delivered to the Dorchester . . .

She spent Christmas on board the *Christina* with Aristo and his two children. He'd invited no other guests. He wanted Alexander and Christina to feel comfortable around Maria. But the children ate with the crew. And Aristo was reluctant to chastise them. Tina had custody, and he didn't want to lose whatever tiny hold he still had. Christina played with the captain's daughter, while Alexander piloted a speedboat with one of Aristo's sailors at his side. The children made fun of Maria, called her *Kolou*—"Big Ass"—behind her back.

Her gifts remained unopened in their elaborate Harrods wrapping paper.

Aristotle couldn't blind himself to the hurt look on Maria's face. He rocked her in his arms.

"Please don't hate them," he said. "They are my babies."

"I could never hate them," she said.

"Tina has poisoned them against you. And I am powerless. . . . But we will try again."

"Yes, darling, we will try again."

The sailor turned to Maria's career. He wanted her to sing at Epidaurus, the ancient Greek theater where the plays of Euripides, Sophocles, and Aeschylus had once been performed. No opera had ever been presented in the ruins at Epidaurus. The sailor believed in ghosts. He'd convinced himself that the spirit of Euripides would be at Epidaurus. She would perform her signature opera, *Norma,* twice in August. She would play a high priestess in Euripides' house.

Aristo was aware of the irony. No woman had ever performed Euripides in ancient Greece, or was even allowed into the theater at Epidaurus. Euripides' Medea was played by a man in a sorceress's mask. And Aristo relished the idea that Maria would be the first woman to conquer this ancient ruin and appear in an opera at Epidaurus.

But August was months away. And he'd invited Sir Winston on a cruise of the Mediterranean. Maria couldn't be *la patronne* of that trip, not even a guest. Lady Clementine disapproved of Maria's relations with Aristotle, called her "the divine slut," and kept up her alliance with Tina.

"But darling," Maria said, "didn't I sing for Sir Winston and bring him out of his mad fit?"

"Yes," Aristo said. "But Lady Clementine is adamant."

"Then toss her overboard. I'm the one who shares your bed."

Still, he sailed away without her. And Maria spent her evenings at Maxim's. She was toasted and adored but felt like a widow without Aristotle. Albert entertained her, though he often had two hundred other guests.

She was frightened of Epidaurus. She couldn't reach

her highest notes, even in the neutral atmosphere of a recording studio. She was burdened with her own fickle monster, the "Voice"; it could leap out of control without the tiniest warning. And it wouldn't have mattered how hard she trained.

But train she did. She arrived in Epidaurus near the end of July and immediately began to rehearse with Maestro Serafin.

"Tullio," she asked in a defeated tone, "will I fall flat here, now, in the cradle of the Greeks?"

"Maria," the maestro said, clasping her hands in his, "you will not fail in Sophocles' arena. If Sophocles won't protect you, I will."

A storm raged on the night of the *prima*, drenching the twenty thousand spectators who had come to see La Divina. The rain beat down on the limestone benches with a horrific smack and flooded the front rows of the orchestra. The performance had to be canceled. Superstitious as she was, Maria saw that pestilential rain as a sign that the ancient gods did not want a woman to perform in their arena.

Two nights after that uncommon August storm, she appeared on the proscenium in a dark gown with a very long train, an outfit that put the entire arena in her spell. She walked with the slow, deliberate grace of a Greek goddess. Maria hid her panic as well as she could. She hadn't sung before a live audience in almost a year. Maria's first notes wobbled, but she seized control, and her voice traveled across the expanse of that open arena like a lightning bolt.

This was a different Norma, much less harsh, but still a high priestess of the Druids, prepared to murder the two children of the Roman lover who had betrayed her. Her knife didn't wander. It had its own soft, musical sway. Her knife *almost* nourished the children, as if she were about to feed them porridge.

Maria believed in absolutes. She was a woman who had fallen in love. And the spectators could feel the warmth of that love and her fear of losing it in every one of her moves. Aristotle's own love wasn't absolute. He was Odysseus, after all, with cunning and deceit in every step he took. She must have known that he would never marry her, that she would be left out of voyages whenever Sir Winston was on board, that she would die alone. And the audience sensed her heartbreak, her hunger.

Norma leapt into the pyre, having betrayed her own people out of love for Pollione. The audience gasped. But La Divina couldn't be devoured, not by flames, not by thunderstorms, not by the treachery of her own voice. Some in the audience must have sensed that *this* high priestess had more to do with the ancient rites of Greek drama than with bel canto and Bellini's opera, that La Callas was a tragedienne who belonged with Sophocles and Euripides. And perhaps that is why a young girl in the audience crowned Maria with a laurel wreath after her performance, as Euripides himself might have been crowned, or one of his anonymous actors, with an arsenal of male and female masks, while Maria remained unmasked.

–5–

PRINCE RAINIER AND PRINCESS GRACE often dined with Aristo and Maria at Maxim's. Something seemed very wrong with Grace. Her smile was fictitious. She had vacant blue eyes, and she drank a lot of whiskey and wine. She could barely string together two sentences that made sense. Rainier had to snap his fingers at Albert to get him to retrieve the princess's wineglass. She drank just as much whenever she and Rainier had dinner on board the *Christina* in the harbor at Monte Carlo, where Maria was the hostess and Aristotle's consort. But Maria was never invited to the prince's palace above the great winding stone wall of Monaco, where the hot wind caressed everyone's eyelids.

She turned bitter. "Why am I never included on a single dinner invitation?"

Aristo didn't have much of an answer. "You know Prince Rainier. He's such a snob."

"Why don't you tear up his invitation and toss it in his face?"

"He's my partner," Aristo said. "I'll lose my slot in the harbor if I misbehave."

Maria tossed her head back. "Misbehave? That's very gallant of you, isn't it, darling?"

But Aristo still lost his slot.

Rainier used his privilege as a prince to create new shares in the company he owned with Aristo in order to buy him out. Aristo had to sell his real estate holdings in Monaco for less than half their value or lose everything. He moved his offices and his yacht away from Monte Carlo. He could have fought back, but the scandal would have hurt his other companies and made him vulnerable on every side.

So Odysseus sailed the seas, sometimes with Maria. He bought her a plush apartment with a host of balconies at 36 Avenue Georges Mandel, in the sixteenth arrondissement, on a street flanked with chestnut trees. He kept his own apartment on the Avenue Foch. She began to realize that he had other mistresses, one in particular, Princess Lee

Radziwill, the younger sister of America's First Lady, Jacqueline Kennedy. It enraged Maria, and frightened her, the idea of losing her sailor to a princess, while she was a half-blind vagabond from Washington Heights.

Lee was a tall, angular beauty married to Poland's "Pauper Prince," Stanisław Radziwill, or "Stash," who lost his title when he moved to England after the war. Lee and Stash often went to Maxim's on their trips to Paris and sat at Ari's table. Maria should have been suspicious when Aristo made a bumbler like Stash head of Olympia, the Greek national airline he now owned.

And then she discovered a love note to Lee and a pearl necklace wedged inside one of Aristo's cigar boxes.

Maria stared at the note for an hour and then took a bunch of sleeping pills, but Bruna found her lying half dazed on the bathroom floor of her new apartment. She called Maria's doctor, and until the doctor came, she waltzed Maria from room to room, made her drink half a gallon of hot coffee, put an ice pack on her forehead, scolded her, sang to her, and wept with her. The doctor took her pulse and ordered her to stay in bed.

The sailor called her a dozen times. "Bring your princess," she said. "We'll all have tea." And she hung up on him. He arrived with a single rose.

"I'll give her up," he said.

"Liar."

She wanted to strangle him, but he was sly with Maria. He'd come to her with a sad demeanor. So she suckled the sadness out of her sailor on the priceless Persian rug, while Bruna blushed and ran into the kitchen like a maid in exile.

-6-

NOW THAT HE HAD LOST ACCESS TO MONACO and its magnificent harbor, Aristotle wanted to buy Ithaca, the fabled kingdom of the first Odysseus, but the island had 58,000 inhabitants, and Aristotle couldn't evict them all. So he bought an abandoned island ten miles from Ithaca, in the Ionian Sea. It was called Skorpios, since it was shaped like a scorpion. And it pleased Aristotle to have an island with its own killer sting.

No one really understood him. Whatever he had, this Odysseus wanted more. He was in love with a canary, but that very love seemed to anger him. She mothered him as he had never been mothered, yet he had a need to run from Maria and then return to the island of her flesh. Their lovemaking was tempestuous and quiet at the very same moment. Their bodies seemed to fit, as if the wanderer had found his own lost soul. She didn't have his fears that the fullness of their love might devour him. She'd been a queen and a high priestess, a singer like Tosca and a courtesan, had become the characters she had portrayed, so that life with Battista had been a respite from her other selves. But now she had such stage fright that she couldn't approach the curtain without Bruna beside her. Bruna was also in her dressing room; Bruna removed all the paint after every performance. Bruna—and Toy—accompanied her on every trip. It was harder and harder for her to gather the courage to sing. She wanted to stay home with Aristo—but her Odysseus didn't have a home except for his yacht.

And now he had Skorpios.

Aristotle's Ithaca didn't have a well, so he had to

transport potable water from other islands. Maria loved to watch as he stood bare-chested in the sun and planted trees with the workmen he had hired. Barren as it was, the island didn't have a single beach, so he also had to import tons of sand and create a beach of his own. He reveled in the sand like a little boy. This new, sudden happiness was infectious. He would make love to Maria on *his* sand dunes after the workmen were gone.

The island had no inhabitants other than a family of wild boar. Maria fell in love with the piglets—the baby boar—that leapt among the rocks. And she had the mad idea to domesticate one of these piglets, turn it magically into a pet and bring it on board the *Christina* to play with Toy.

"Robber," Aristo said. "Have you any idea what that piglet's mother would do to us?"

But she still brought a baby bottle with warm milk onto the island during their next trip. And when a piglet suddenly appeared on the beach that Aristo and the workmen had built, Maria scooped it up into her arms and fed the piglet with the bottle's rubber nipple. The piglet took such deep sucks that the sound seemed to rocket across the island.

Aristo hadn't taken a pistol or a flare gun from the *Christina*'s miniature armory. All he had was one of the workmen's spare shovels. He dreaded what would happen next. The piglet's mother came charging out of the rocks with a warlike glint in her gray eyes.

"Maria," Aristotle whispered, "stand still."

He stuck two fingers into his mouth and began to whistle. The mother boar stopped in her tracks. Her face didn't seem any less ferocious. The tread of her hooves had left clouds of sand dust.

"Darling," Aristotle said in that same deadpan whisper, "put the baby down—and the bottle."

Maria put the piglet and the baby bottle down in the sand. The mother boar approached with widening nostrils and her enormous flat head. She destroyed the rubber nipple with one rip of her teeth, grabbed the piglet by the scruff of its neck, and ran off into the rocks.

"Maria, was the adventure worth it? My warden will have to kill that mother pig, or we won't be able to invite any guests onto the island. She's too dangerous now."

"You and your rules," she said, throwing the milk bottle at him. But they still made love in the sand.

Maria tried to find some order in Aristotle's scattered life—his sudden disappearances and reappearances that were just as sudden. It wasn't all business. She knew that now, but she still longed to be with her Odysseus. Maria sang when she had to sing, with Bruna accompanying her to the curtain. A tiredness had settled in and a crippling fear whenever she had to stand in front of an audience in one of her wigs, which were as copious as an ancient Greek actor's masks. Yet theater managers peppered Sandor Gorlinsky with more and more invitations for La Divina. Milan couldn't go through another season without La Callas on its card. Bing wanted her back at the Met. But Maria preferred to wander about with Aristo, far from any opera house.

And then fate smacked La Divina right between the eyes. It was Princess Lee again—rather, her sister. Jacqueline had given birth to a baby boy, Patrick, six weeks early. The boy had trouble breathing and died after two days. Jackie fell into a deep depression and locked herself inside the presidential residence on Pennsylvania Avenue. Lee told Aristotle about Jackie's dark mood during one of their trysts, and so Aristotle, with his Greek gallantry, offered to put his yacht at Jackie's disposal—a Mediterranean cruise would give her time to deal with her grief. The president considered Onassis a pirate and warned his wife not to go.

Jackie defied Jack.

She flew to Athens in October and boarded the *Christina,* with Lee and Stash acting as chaperones. Of course, Aristo couldn't invite his concubine on a cruise with the First Lady. Maria had to endure her exile on the Avenue Georges Mandel. But there was no way to avoid the repercussions of that cruise. It was on Maria's television every morning and night, as if Odysseus had abducted the grieving mother—and wife—from the president of the United States.

Paparazzi pursued the First Lady from port to port. Pictures of her in a white bikini appeared on magazine covers. Meanwhile, Aristo, with his tinted glasses and sunburned beak, soon had one of the most recognizable faces in the world.

He was photographed hand in hand with Jackie in his native town of Smyrna, leading her through the marketplaces, feeding her baklava and Turkish delight. The White House wasn't unaware of all the havoc caused by this Mediterranean cruise. Jack called the *Christina* and told his wife to end this odyssey, but she said the odyssey wasn't over yet in that wondrous lisp of hers. She still had lots to learn about Anatolia.

And Aristotle still called Maria every evening at six.

"Promise me you won't bring her to *our* island," she said, a rippling anger in her voice.

"I promise," he said. "Skorpios isn't on the itinerary."

But he didn't tell Maria about the necklace he gave to Jackie on the last day of the voyage.

"A memento," he said to the First Lady, "nothing more."

She smiled and had him clip on the necklace with his powerful hands.

Lee was furious. She told Jack about the necklace. He shrugged. "My wife loves beautiful things."

A month later, Jack was dead in Dallas.

And in that moment, a metamorphosis occurred, as the First Lady was transformed into the Widow, with a halo around her. The Widow was revered wherever she went.

Lee invited Aristo to the funeral, and he stayed overnight at the White House, where "the pirate" met the entire Kennedy clan and also managed to clutch the Widow's hand.

Back in Paris a week later, he reserved a portion of the Aquarium to administer—with the help of Albert—Maria's fortieth birthday party. Meantime, the managers of Covent Garden had been chasing Maria for a whole year to do *Tosca* at the Royal Opera House in London. Maria stalled until Franco Zeffirelli agreed to direct the production. She had worked with Zeffirelli before. And she knew that Floria Tosca wouldn't be a superficial songbird, but a diva with great depth and a talent for mischief, and that the costumes and the décor would have Zeffirelli's own sense of flair.

That December, a little after her birthday, Maria dreamt that she was about to have a baby. It wasn't an idle dream. She wanted a baby at any cost. Titta had once told Maria that they couldn't afford to have a child—she would lose a year of performances, and a diva could be forgotten in a year, cast aside. But this would be Aristo's child. And she longed to retire. Still, she was reluctant to tell him.

Finally, she told the sailor while they were on the deck of the *Christina*, staring at his island—Skorpios—and drinking Dom Pérignon. She knew how touchy he was on the subject of another possible male heir.

"Darling," she said, "we can have our own child."

He didn't comfort her. "You're over forty, Maria, and a married woman."

For an instant, she considered whacking him over the head with the champagne bottle. But she loved the sailor more than she loved her own life . . .

He cajoled her with diamonds and a cluster of bouquets. Didn't they have an ideal life? He was fifty-seven years old, would be the "grandfather" to his own child. His competitors would mock him. Maria capitulated. She was more depressed than she'd ever been.

Maria had to leave for London in two weeks. She wouldn't sit at the piano, or even glance at the score and the libretto of *Tosca,* though she knew both by heart. She lay in the dark. She didn't even have Toy to comfort her—Maria's poodle had suffered a heart attack. Toy had wagged his tail, whimpered once, and died in Maria's arms.

Bruna had the curtains drawn. "Madame, you must get out of bed. Your ankles will swell, and you will not be able to sit on an airplane."

It was Bruna who was guardian of the purse. Maria never paid her a salary. Bruna simply took whatever she needed for herself out of the purse. She had her own suite of rooms on the same floor as Maria. She shopped for both of them, cleaned for both of them, and never hid her feelings.

"Madame Maria, you cannot pull *Tosca* out of a magician's hat. London will never forgive a lazy performance."

Maria put one hand on her hip and raised her head in a kind of haughty, lighthearted gesture.

"Am I Floria Tosca now?"

"Yes, madame."

They flew to London and stayed in Aristo's suite at Claridge's. Maria missed her dog. She would have to darken her eyes in the dressing room without Toy digging into her lap.

Zeffirelli had lured the celebrated baritone Tito Gobbi to perform opposite Maria as Baron Scarpia. He knew the fireworks that would fly between both singers. Gobbi was as gifted an actor as Maria, while the Scarpias she'd had in the past were commonplace. That's why she'd never enjoyed playing Floria Tosca—and that opera had fallen out of whatever little repertoire she had left.

The sailor sent roses to her dressing room. But her mind drifted. During a dress rehearsal she wandered too close to a lit candle and her wig caught on fire. She continued her aria with a plume of smoke trailing behind her. Zeffirelli's assistants had to follow her around the stage with wet rags until the fire was smothered and the plume of smoke disappeared. While all this happened, Maria didn't miss a note.

Gobbi was also aware of her poor eyesight. And in their scenes together, he led her away from the prompter's pit with a subtle touch of his hand.

Maria was petrified during the night of the *prima*. She didn't have Toy in her dressing room, her little baby who had died of old age. She had a touch of bronchitis, but she refused to cancel the performance. Zeffirelli and Bruna walked her to the wings, her nails digging into Zeffirelli's hand.

"Franco, what if I fail?"

He kissed her cheek. "Well then, Maria, we will fail together. What could be more comforting that that?"

The audience was mesmerized the moment Tosca appeared on stage, as powerful and tempestuous as Maria herself. People had never seen a Tosca so sensual and full of jealousy. Gobbi himself was amazed. And Zeffirelli didn't want her performance to be buried at Covent Garden. He wanted to capture this version of *Tosca* on the big screen, with Tito Gobbi as Scarpia. Zeffirelli himself would direct the film.

She'd had offers to do *Tosca* on Italian public television, but Visconti had warned her against it. "You will look like a gray ghost, Maria, and everything around you will seem flat. No matter how elaborate each set is designed, it will have no depth at all—none. I beg you to keep away from television. It is a vast grave."

And so she shunned television and agreed to Zeffirelli's offer. He was a novice in films, like her. But she cherished his enthusiasm and his mastery of detail. And he knew how to have a set designed that would provide Maria with the depth she needed, so she wouldn't be a figure on a cardboard stage. The film would be shot at Shepperton Studios in Surrey. Contracts were prepared.

And then Aristo stepped in.

He flew Zeffirelli to Athens on Olympic Airways and had him board the *Christina* at the harbor in Piraeus. Then they sailed to Skorpios with Maria. Aristo didn't mention the *Tosca* contract once. He talked of the gardens and tobacco fields he would bring to Skorpios, elements out of his childhood on Smyrna; even more than that. Odysseus would re-create the kingdom of Ithaca on this other island. Skorpios already had a stucco house and a primitive chapel left there by a previous inhabitant, a wanderer like Aristotle.

"It will be *our* paradise, Franco. You will be one of the

chosen few . . . Perhaps we will shoot a scene from *Tosca* right on the island."

"That would be my pleasure," Zeffirelli said. "But it will be expensive. We'd have to bring the cameras and relocate the entire crew."

Aristo laughed in a diabolic manner. "I will pay all the expenses. It will not be a burden on the budget of the film."

When Maria tried to interrupt, he snapped at her. "You know nothing. You're a canary."

Her eyes flared, but she didn't answer him. She left the table and went to her room.

The sailor squinted at Zeffirelli. "Franco, your budget makes no sense. Maria will need two hundred and fifty thousand as a minimum and twenty-five percent of the gross."

"But that's impossible," Zeffirelli said. "I would have to work for free."

"Fine," the sailor said. "Then I will finance the film."

Zeffirelli felt as if he were talking to a cunning child, bent on destroying the film project.

He excused himself and went to visit Maria. She was lying in bed, her body turned away from him. She didn't want to look at the one man who had given *Tosca* back to her—as a gift.

"Maria," he said softly, "we will never have another chance—*Tosca* on film."

The diva whispered like a little girl. "Franco, I'll never go against Aristo's wishes. He's the only man who has ever made love to me, really made love. I can't lose him. I can't."

-7-

MARIA RETURNED TO THE MET AFTER AN EXILE of seven years. It was *Tosca* again. She didn't have Franco Zeffirelli or any of his sets. But she did have Tito Gobbi. And Tito was enough. The Met was moving to Lincoln Center. And Maria would be the last diva in the old palace on Thirty-ninth Street. All her performances had been sold out. Bing pretended to be ecstatic. But his mind had already moved uptown.

Maria cursed herself for allowing Sandor Gorlinsky to lure her back to Manhattan, the land of her lost childhood. Litsa had pushed her into contests before she was nine, the radio prodigy who won a Bulova watch.

The dressing room at the old Met was as shoddy as ever. The sets were shoddy. And she was frightened of the audience. Bruna had to grip both her hands as they marched to the wings—it was like a death march. But when she appeared onstage, the audience clapped and shouted, "Callas, Callas," for five minutes, as the orchestra grew silent. Her arrival had halted the movement of the opera. And for a very long moment there was no Tosca, no dust of a dying opera house, no mice gnawing at the scenery, no lover in a church, no police chief, only Maria Callas . . .

Her voice had wobbled more than once. It was Tito Gobbi who saved her, and their miraculous "duel" in Baron Scarpia's office. Each of their movements was nuanced, like a ritualized dance. Tosca needed to save her lover, Cavaradossi, and Scarpia wouldn't release him unless Tosca gave herself to him. The audience could sense his carnality, his evil, his lust. As police chief, he was the lord and master of

Rome. Tosca and the baron bit at one another with a ferocious eloquence, a violent pas de deux.

Maria didn't realize that the Widow had been in the audience until she appeared with Bing at a small reception for benefactors and members of the cast. The Widow was wearing a white satin Dior gown that clung to her sleek figure. She had brown eyes as big as Maria's.

It was Bing who brought her over, that slick, maneuvering snake. "Jackie, didn't I tell you that no one can sing *Tosca* like Maria Callas? She haunts the role, makes it impossible for anyone to follow her."

"Rudy, quiet," the Widow said. "You have a habit of killing people with your compliments." She shooed him away and shook Maria's hand. "Madame Callas, thank you. It was the only *Tosca* of yours I've ever seen. And I won't embarrass you, but it was the most thrilling time I've ever had at the opera."

Then she turned to Tito Gobbi, who stood alone in the corner, unrecognized.

"Signor Gobbi," she said, "I've never been so frightened by Scarpia as I was tonight. You made that monster into a bloodcurdling poet."

That cruise on board the *Christina* was nothing, a bagatelle. Now Maria knew she really had a rival.

–8–

Her blood pressure was low. Her ankles swelled. She began to have dizzy spells. She gasped and clutched her throat during the fifth and last performance of *Norma* at the Paris Opéra and swooned in front of the audience. The diva sank to the deck of the stage like a dead woman. The entire production fell out of time, into some other dimension, where singers didn't have to sing. The curtain dropped soundlessly, like a sail on a windless sea. The house manager appeared from behind the curtain. His face seemed bulbous, raw, and red.

"*Mesdames et messieurs*," he shouted, as if he were delivering a recitative torn from the opera itself, "*je regette. Madame Callas ne peut continuer.*"

She lay there with her hands curled like opening flowers. She could have been in a coma. Finally, the stagehands arrived with a makeshift stretcher and carried the diva back to her dressing room, where she regained consciousness and drank a few sips of water from the cup in Bruna's hand. Bruna was almost as pale as her mistress. The house physician wanted to order an ambulance. Then her physician arrived. He was very stern with the diva.

"I warned you not to sing. Your blood count was low. Madame Callas, you didn't have the breath to carry an entire opera on your back."

She wouldn't ride in an ambulance no matter what the two physicians said. And she wouldn't get back onto the stretcher. Bruna clutched her arm and walked Maria out of the Paris Opéra, step by step. Both her fans and her deniers besieged Callas at the stage door. A brawl broke out. Bruna led Maria to her limousine.

She was driven through the brick and stone arch of the American Hospital in Neuilly. Her hemogoblin was indeed very low, and the doctors there administered a blood transfusion. She was given a private room, far from the other patients at the hospital. Odysseus had the room decorated with wildflowers before Maria was wheeled in. He'd returned from a trip to Greece and sat at her bedside. He paid all the hospital bills.

"Darling, we'll run off to Skorpios and remain there. You can sing to the wild boar. That audience will never betray you."

"I thought you had to shoot the mother boar," Maria said.

Odysseus looked into Maria's big brown eyes. "I didn't have the heart."

He stayed with her until midnight, but Maria wasn't left alone. The doctors allowed Bruna to sleep in a chair next to the window. And in the morning, Bruna scrubbed her with a washcloth, sang songs to her, and played a furious game of checkers, allowing Maria to move checkers mysteriously across the board.

Maria was scheduled to sing four performances of *Tosca* at Covent Garden. The fourth performance was meant to be a gala in honor of Queen Elizabeth and the Queen Mother. Maria delayed and delayed. Her blood pressure was alarmingly low. She told the house manager at Covent Garden that her doctor had forbidden her to fly. The first three performances were given to another soprano. Then Maria suddenly showed up at the Savoy. She sang the fourth *Tosca* in front of Queen Elizabeth and the Queen Mother. She could have been in a trance during all three acts, as if *another* Maria Callas had showed up with Bruna, a demon who dared not approach a high C, a demon devoid of breath control.

The opera lovers at Covent Garden were polite with the diva. The *loggionisti* in the upper tiers remained silent. Maria had an audience with the queen. "How darling of you to sing for Mum and myself," the queen said, wearing a simple blue gown with a diamond broach pinned to her breast, while Maria curtsied in Tosca's costume and Tosca's paint.

"It was my great pleasure, Ma'am."

Bruna had given her a shawl to wear. She had to keep herself from shivering. She no longer had the stamina or the concentration to perform *Tosca* again, and *Tosca* was the least punishing opera in her repertoire—all she had to do was stab Scarpia and leap off a parapet.

–9–

ODYSSEUS HAD PROMISED HER A SUMMER on Skorpios. Meanwhile, Sandor Gorlinsky kept dangling contracts from opera houses in Lisbon, Dallas, and Rio. She refused them all. She sang in recording studios, but she could hear the sound of metal in her voice, and she wouldn't release the recordings, no matter how hard Sandor and the record producers pleaded with her.

Silent Maria.

But the summer she had dreamt of, without a single engagement, turned sour very soon. Odysseus' mind was elsewhere. He seemed like a lost son without the old warrior—Sir Winston had died in bed at ninety, after another stroke. Odysseus couldn't stop mourning. His melancholy grew, and he kept snapping at Maria. Unrelenting sadness had made him quite cruel. He attacked her in front of guests on Skorpios.

"My dear, you're nothing but a whistler who has lost her whistle."

However much Maria loved her pirate, she didn't

remain silent. "And you, dearest, are nothing but a sailor in short pants."

They had a fistfight, and Zeffirelli, who was on the island that week, broke it up. He couldn't bear seeing myopic Maria stumble about with tears in her eyes. He left Skorpios after two days.

Aristo was much kinder to Maria after Zeffirelli was gone. Perhaps *part* of his anger was a performance, Aristo's way of being operatic with others as an audience. He made love to Maria on board the *Christina,* his body clamped to hers. Afterward, they stood naked on the upper deck, drinking Dom Pérignon in the moonlight. Aristo looked like some gnarled warrior-god. And Maria was a deity with swollen ankles and a slim waist.

"You miss him," she said.

"Maria, I couldn't ignore his pain. Treated like some circus clown who had to wear diapers. Everywhere he went, he had to give the victory sign. People forgot how vigorous he was during the war. And he wasn't young, wasn't young at all. . . . He loved to hear you sing."

"Darling, I sang for him *once,* when he was having a mad fit."

"But you cured him," Aristo said, "and he never forgot."

They danced across the deck, with the island looming in front of them like a rival monster. And then Aristo disappeared. He left a note beside their rumpled bed.

Business beckons. I'll be back.

Maria panicked, being all alone with the crew, beside that strange Garden of Eden Aristo had built on Skorpios, with its manor house, its medley of sheep, its exotic flowers—it still seemed like a barren island. The wild pigs were gone.

And then Sandor Gorlinsky called. "Maria, darling . . ."

"Stop," she said. "Where am I wanted this time?"

"Palermo."

Maria mused to herself. She loved the isolation of Sicily, removed from the bureaucratic nightmare of the mainland; she loved Palermo and its palm trees; she loved the Grand Hotel, with the glaring yellow light of its entrance; she loved the suite at the hotel where Wagner vanished from the world and labored over *Parsifal* and its last act; she remembered the little tunnels at the back of each elevator car, where coffins could be placed for the crime lords of Palermo, who all had suites at the Grand and intended to die somewhere within the grounds of their favorite hotel; and she loved the Teatro Massimo, with its twin bronze lions that guarded the grandiose stairway, its slightly tilted stage, and its seven golden tiers of boxes that seemed to rise to Palermo's very own paradise.

"Don't tempt me, Sandor."

"Twenty–thousand–dollars," he said with all the drama of this impresario of impresarios.

"And what will I have to do, darling? Live with the mafiosi at the Grand for three months, sing *Norma* a dozen times, and undress the maestro and every male member of his orchestra?"

"Don't be crude, Maria. One performance."

"That's insane. The Teatro Massimo doesn't have that kind of cash. And I don't have the breath to perform an entire opera, not even once."

"But that's the beauty of it," Sandor said. "You can sing as little as you like."

Maria was even more suspicious. "Who's crazy enough to shell out twenty grand for a parade of arpeggios?"

"You have a patron—in Palermo."

"I have patrons everywhere," Maria said, "but however much they love me, none of them loves me that much."

"Well, this one does."

"Who is he?" Maria asked. "What's his name?"

"It's Palermo, darling, and in Palermo no one uses names—ah, but he did mention Baron Scarpia once in our negotiations."

Maria laughed—it was the lord of the *loggionisti*, Bernardo Scarpia, the cobbler who looked like the notorious male soprano Farinelli, and had a shoe salon in Milan, Lady Macbeth's; he supplied Maria with magnificent handcrafted red shoes until he ran off to Palermo with the police right on his tail. She should have guessed that Bernardo was behind this mad adventure.

"I accept."

She and Bruna took a late flight out of Athens that week. A limousine was waiting for them when they landed in Palermo. The dry heat seemed to rise off the pavement and burn through Maria's sandals. The chauffeur offered them both a thermos of lemonade. "Compliments of the Grand Hotel, Madame Callas."

They rode across rude streets lined with broken lintels and palazzi that had lost their balconies; Maria had never seen so much filth in the streets, so much uncollected garbage. And suddenly, among the crooked pavements, the Grand Hotel loomed with its crisp yellow lights. A bellhop collected their baggage. La Divina had arrived with her "train"—her one companion and traveling partner. They didn't even have to check in; this was Palermo, which had its customs and unwritten rules.

They were shown to their suite. The furniture was

all hand-carved and made of cherrywood. The armoires reached the high ceilings and must have come from some lost Norman palace. The city had had many conquerors, had been invaded many times, had gone through several bloodbaths—it was defined by its defeats. And yet it seemed to flower amid all the blood. It had a street life—a local festivity—that couldn't be found in any other European quarter . . .

Maria and Bruna had arrived near midnight and the dining room was closed. They had sandwiches and a fruit salad—Macedonia—waiting for them in their suite. Bruna was starving, and she gobbled her sandwich, but Maria was far too nervous. She couldn't find a note from the Teatro, or from the cobbler. There were no instructions—none. She picked at the diced peach in Bruna's salad bowl with the miniature fork the hotel had provided. It was a habit of hers—to hunt for food in someone else's bowl.

They skipped breakfast and walked the crooked streets of the conquered town. The crime lords owned Palermo, in spite of all the prosecutors and the police. Maria and Bruna stumbled upon a puppet theater in a piazza behind a bus depot. The puppets were as tall as Maria and had limbs that bent like hers. They were propelled by strings attached to the puppet master's hands. He stood on a platform behind the stage, most of him hidden by a ragged silk curtain, but his hands were visible, and they moved faster than Maria's eyes could catch, so his fingers remained in a constant flurry.

It was a tale of seduction that troubled Maria, because the characters in this puppet opera hovered a bit too close to the plot of *Tosca;* there was an all-powerful police chief with a mustache and a celebrated soprano whose lover was being held in custody by the chief. Mustacchio will return the lover in one piece if Julietta will give herself to this rogue. Of course, it's played out in comic fashion. While Mustacchio gropes, Julietta whacks him with a stick. They grapple in a convoluted dance, flying across the stage.

The audience howled with laughter.

"Mustacchio, fight harder, fight!"

"Julietta, no mercy!"

Julietta loses her wig in the heat of battle and remains a bald soprano for the rest of the fight. She drives Mustacchio onto the splintered edge of the stage and drags off her lover, another doll, but one with dead limbs, because it isn't attached to any strings.

Maria went backstage and returned with an enormous parcel tied with puppet strings. Bruna didn't ask her any questions. But she found her way back to the hotel. Neither of them had any lunch. Maria bathed. Bruna combed her hair. Maria put on a black dress. The front desk called. A limousine from the Teatro Massimo was waiting for them.

Maria came downstairs with her companion and the parcel from the puppet master.

They rode to the Massimo in the limousine.

The maestro and his orchestra were waiting for Maria. The maestro was Polish, and she had never sung under his baton. She listened to the sound of his violins. She was satisfied. Maria didn't rehearse once. She gave him instructions and went to her dressing room. She'd sung at the Massimo before, several times, and was familiar with the treacherous tilt of the stage. Maria was also familiar with the acoustics, with the danger zones where her voice would sound hollow and where it would resonate.

She'd talked to no one, not the prompter, not the

manager, not the stagehands. She waited for the first bell to ring. She walked out of the dressing room with Bruna, hand in hand, five minutes before curtain time. She didn't have any stage fright at this mysterious séance.

She could hear the constant hum of the audience. She plucked out her glasses and peaked through the curtain. The house was packed except for the two front rows of the orchestra, which seemed stark with their empty seats. The curtain rose with a rough, irregular ripple. She removed her glasses and stepped out onto the stage. The audience stirred and gasped at Maria. She stood in her bare feet, dressed in the costume of a puppet—a rag doll—with a red wig and white paint; she revealed nothing but her nostrils, her enormous eyes, and her mouth.

A small army of men appeared in mourners' black apparel, marched down the orchestra aisle, and waited for their *padrone*—it was the cobbler, dressed in evening clothes, with a silk bow tie and black shoes he must have crafted himself. He sat in the center of the front row, and his lieutenants surrounded him until the two front rows were nearly full.

The cobbler did not give her a single sign of recognition, but Maria was performing for him, and not for the sinister lords and ladies of Palermo in the opera house's golden tiers. She played Floria Tosca as a rag doll, a puppet who could sing. Her puppet master was in the front row. She mimed each moment of the entire scene in Baron Scarpia's rooms in a stuttering ballet as she sang to an invisible Scarpia, jostling around him with a puppet's staccato moves, as if the cobbler held all the strings.

She sang "Vissi d'Arte," as a puppet might, in a staggered melody.

I–lived–for–art, I–lived–for–love.

She stabbed an invisible Scarpia in staggering strokes.

Those in the audience couldn't take their eyes off this puppet soprano.

The scene ended. There was utter silence. And then a shouting cadence came from every corner of the Teatro Massimo.

"Ancora! Ancora!"

The puppet soprano stared at her master in the front row. He had a wolfish grin. He nodded. Myopic Maria pointed in the direction of the Polish maestro in his pit. The music accompanied her moves. The scene with Scarpia began all over again. And it was uncanny how this maestro, who had never met Maria, could adapt his orchestra to her own musicality.

The puppet stabbed the invisible Scarpia with an invisible knife, and the audience could almost feel the force of that blade.

It was Maria Callas. The audience could not let her go. She curtsied in her clown's costume until the cobbler stood up and left with his array of bodyguards . . .

Maria returned to her dressing room, where Bruna helped her remove the puppet's long sleeves and legs, the wig, and the white paint.

"Madame Maria," Bruna said, "I am exhausted. I cannot imagine how you absorbed every single one of the puppet's tricks."

"Bruna, did I have a choice? I arrived at the Teatro without a program or a plan. I had to scratch out a performance on my own."

"And if we hadn't gone to the puppet theater this morning, madame?"

"Well," Maria said. "I would have been tossed out of Palermo on my ass—with you."

A limousine was there at the stage entrance. But the driver didn't take the two women back to the hotel. He delivered them to a trattoria along a dark street. Several of the cobbler's men stood outside the little restaurant with their hands in their pockets. "Welcome, La Divina," one of them said as Maria entered the restaurant with Bruna. It was almost as dark inside. There were only five tables and a tiny bar. The owner of the restaurant, who looked like Mustacchio, sat Bruna at a table with the cobbler's lieutenants, while Maria was shown to the cobbler's private table in the rear.

He was sitting in his undershirt. "Forgive me," he said, "but I hate opera clothes."

"Well, Baron Scarpia," she said, "should I strip down to my underpants?"

He laughed and revealed his jagged teeth. "You are perfect, Madame Callas, the way you are."

"I'm your Maria. You paid me to perform. And you could have commissioned your own opera with that kind of cash."

"I did," he said. "I did. You appeared onstage, Maria, with *Tosca* as a puppet show."

"But it was purely an accident. Bruna and I were walking near a bus depot and . . ."

"There are no accidents in Palermo, I assure you. It was intervention, divine or not. What would you like to eat?"

"Whatever you're eating, Baron," she said. Maria was having a glorious time.

A waiter with a pistol inside his belt brought them a jug of Sicilian white wine, a dozen pieces of flat bread covered with crushed tomatoes and olives, and two enormous salad bowls filled with chopped vegetables and slivers of octopus.

Maria ate with gusto for the first time in weeks. "Baron, what is this salad called?"

"It doesn't have a name," the cobbler said. "The owner prepares it for me."

"Then I'll call it *insalata Scarpia* in honor of you. But why did you bribe me to come to Palermo? All you had to do was ask, Bernardo."

He turned sad for a moment and sat with a fork clenched in his fist. "It wasn't a bribe. We're in Sicily. And nothing is done direct. You would have been in danger from my enemies. And so I had one of my counselors tempt you out of retirement—that way, the offer did not come from me. But I had assurances."

"From whom?" Maria asked, puzzled by all the secrecy.

"The grand council," the cobbler said. "It's hard to explain. But there's much less killing if we all meet. And I had assurances that you would not be harmed. After all, they wanted to hear you sing. And I, Maria, missed you the most. But I'm a prisoner on this island, even if I have hundreds of soldiers."

"Then I'm glad," Maria said, caressing his knuckles with her hand. "I'm glad I played Floria Tosca as a puppet—for you, Bernardo, for you."

He ate in silence for a moment. Then he brushed a sliver of octopus from his mouth with the trattoria's enormous napkin. "But you reinvent everything you touch, Maria. And I'm not making it up. The maestro at the Met said the same thing."

Maria grew a bit alarmed. "What maestro? Rudolf Bing? He hates my guts."

The cobbler studied his wineglass and took a sip. "I read it somewhere in a magazine. He said you've ruined opera for him. He shudders to have another soprano in your place. You always give the definitive performance. He cannot dream of Violetta or Tosca or Norma without dreaming of you."

"He loves to lie," Maria said with a wild look.

One of the cobbler's lieutenants approached the table and whispered in his ear. The cobbler stood up. "He doesn't hate you, Maria. He fears you, because whatever he produces will never be equal to the way you imagine a role. But I must go now. It seems I've overstayed my welcome in this part of Palermo."

"Bernardo," Maria asked in the petulant voice of a diva, "will we ever meet once more in my lifetime?"

"I do not think so. Whatever the council grants, it does not grant again."

He kissed her on the mouth, like a devotee rather than a lover. And he was gone with all his men.

–10–

IT WAS NEVER THE SAME AFTER PALERMO, as if she'd confronted her own wildness in that dark town, and she and Aristo had become part of a puppet theater that couldn't really define the limits of its tale. He saw Maria less and less. He never made excuses. Their longing and lovemaking didn't seem to suffer. But their trips to Skorpios grew shorter, and she was no longer the *patronne* on board the *Christina,* but an exalted guest.

And then she heard the news about her Baron Scarpia.

Bruna pointed her to the current issue of *Paris Match.* It was an exclusive. The Sicilian cobbler, Bernardo Scarpia, who had designed footwear for Anna Magnani, Sophia Loren, and Maria Callas, had been stabbed to death in one of the rear hallways at the Palermo opera, during the last act of Verdi's *Otello.* No killer, Maria realized, could have gotten near her Baron Scarpia unless Scarpia was betrayed by his own men.

She didn't know how to commemorate the cobbler. She wondered if Bernardo had had a suite at the Grand Hotel like the other crime lords of Sicily. She wanted flowers put on his grave. She had Bruna telephone the manager at the Grand Hotel. He was very brusque with Maria when she got on the line.

"I am sorry, Madame Callas, but I do not have any recollection of a Bernardo Scarpia. He was never registered here."

Bernardo Scarpia must have been the alias of an alias. That's how he was known among the *loggionisti.* Maria didn't ask Bruna to continue the search. She could not mourn some anonymous crime lord, only the cobbler who had crafted her shoes. She and Bruna lit a candle for Bernardo, and wore prayer shawls at their own private ceremony on the Avenue Georges Mandel.

Now she had to reconsider her life as Aristo's concubine. She was still a married woman, under Italian law. But the Greeks did not recognize her marriage in Verona, as the ceremony had been conducted outside her faith—she'd married Titta in a Roman Catholic church. So the diva renounced her American citizenship and became a Greek citizen. All of a sudden, Maria was free to marry again. But Odysseus' mind wasn't on marrying Maria.

She was the last to learn that Aristo had been courting the Widow. It was complicated and secretive, as it usually was with Onassis. People expected Jackie to find another king like Jack, another Camelot, and not a short Greek shipbuilder with a big nose. But they weren't aware of Odysseus' seductive power. Still, he had to be on his guard.

Paparazzi followed her everywhere.

She was now the prisoner of the people's own desires. They had written a scenario for her, a movie script she was meant to follow. But Jackie was far too perverse to bend to their will. She'd become the mystery guest on the *Christina*, a cruise where Maria wasn't allowed to remain on board.

Maria tossed her wineglass at Aristo. They had a fistfight in front of the crew.

Banishment was her reward. Maria had a royal fit and promised never to see Onassis again, but he'd woo her back with a long phone call. He'd take her to Maxim's, dance the fox-trot with her, and disappear again.

He was plotting a novel kind of business deal: marriage to the queen of America and entrance into the realm of the Kennedy clan. But Robert Kennedy was running for president, and if word ever got out that the Widow intended to marry a shifty Greek tycoon, it might cost him the election. So Odysseus had to meet the Widow on the sly. He used the rear entrance to her Fifth Avenue duplex, and went up the service elevator. And then, in June 1968, moments after Bobby had secured the California nomination, he was shot by a half-crazed Palestinian gunman. He fell into a coma and never recovered. During his funeral in Manhattan Jackie seemed remote, unmoored. She rode the funeral train that took Bobby's casket from New York to Washington. It was packed with eleven hundred guests, who cavorted like members of an Irish wake, while Jackie sat in a private car, welcoming one visitor at a time, as if she were Bobby's widow, too. She was in her own dream state, forlorn, uprooted, and for a moment thought she was still the First Lady.

"Where's Jack? Tell the president I have to see him immediately, or there will be consequences."

When she awoke from her dream state, Jackie realized that she could no longer live in America. "They're killing Kennedys," she said, and feared that she and her children would be targeted next. And so negotiations began for her marriage to Onassis. It wasn't clear whether she proposed to him or he proposed to her. It really didn't matter. They were to be married at the chapel on Skorpios a few months after Bobby's death.

The phone rang in Maria's flat well past midnight on the day before the marriage. Bruna had to rouse her mistress, who'd become addicted to sleeping pills.

Maria wore her nighttime mask. "Go away, Bruna, go away."

"It's him, madame, the sailor."

"Tell him to dance with the mama boar on his island," Maria said, still drugged from the pills.

"He's crying."

Maria grabbed the phone away from Bruna.

"Sailor, what's wrong?"

"Darling, come to Athens. Take the morning flight. We'll have lunch at the Grande Bretagne. Once she hears about it, she'll break—"

Maria hung up the phone.

Paparazzi hovered like jackals near Maria's apartment house. Some even climbed the chestnut tree outside her windows. Bruna had to close all the curtains and drapes until nothing of her mistress could be seen. La Divina was quickly becoming the martyr and the ghost of Avenue Georges Mandel.

On the morning of the marriage, television cameras and entire crews invaded Skorpios to catch a glimpse of the bride and groom. Images of them catapulted onto front pages and magazine covers worldwide. There seemed to be no other event that could compare with this modern version of "Beauty and the Beast"—the vivacious president's widow and the short gnomelike Greek shipping magnate.

Maria still kept photos of Aristo in every room of her spacious apartment, still strolled among them like a sleepwalker in pajamas, but she had all the television sets turned off, and all the newspapers and magazines that arrived on her doormat remained unread. Letters of condolence cluttered her mailbox; she had Bruna stuff them into the trash bin. Visconti called.

"Maria, you're much better off without him. We'll do a film together. I'll find the right script."

She listened without listening. "Yes, Luca. . . . No, Luca, I promise. Ciao."

When Zeffirelli called, Maria was a bit more alert. Franco had never abandoned or betrayed her. He didn't talk about past, present, or future projects, didn't even talk about Onassis and *his* betrayal of her. He serenaded Maria, sang her favorite arias from the operas they had done together, pretended to sing in Maria's own voice, faltering here and there, missing a note on purpose.

He made her laugh, and she hadn't laughed in a long time.

"*Cara*," he said, "come have lunch with me. You can pick the time and place."

"Franco, I'm not ready to leave my fortress. But when I am, you will be the first on my list."

Sandor besieged her with offers; she had a certain notoriety now that she was the jilted mistress in an international melodrama, somehow attached to Onassis' new wife by an invisible piece of string. It was opera à la carte. Those who had criticized the Widow soon relented and began calling her "Jackie O." She was as popular as she had ever been, perhaps even more so, because the Widow's adorers pitied her for having married the gnome. And now impresarios wanted Maria at any price. She could select whatever repertoire she wished. She could lecture; she could do somersaults and stand on her head. Bruna had to intercept every call, even from Sandor.

"I am so sorry, Monsieur Gorlinsky, but madame is indisposed. She asks that you try her again—next month."

The paparazzi stopped climbing the chestnut trees outside Maria's balcony; they had moved on to other matters. Maria could have left her fortress without being badgered. But she had little desire to venture out, to have lunch or dinner at Maxim's.

"Bruna, they'll look at me with pity, or worse, with contempt. We'll stay here."

"But your ankles will swell, madame."

"Then I'll walk from room to room every other hour."

But she didn't walk. She lay abed, like an invalid. She took sedatives day and night. She dreamt even while she was awake. And in her dreams, Aristo made love to her with a savage tenderness that was his mark on Maria, biting her, caressing her, like her private piano tuner, who had mapped every portion of her body, every limb.

The days passed. She took more pills. Bruna had to bathe her. Madame might doze off in the tub and drown. And then, one morning, Maria lost Aristotle's aroma, lost the remembrance of his touch, as if she had some rare aphasia of the limbs, and she was cut off from Aristo. She panicked. The doctor gave her vitamin D shots.

"Bruna, I'd put her in a clinic. But she's Maria Callas. And I might end up with a lawsuit. But make her walk. Her legs are all swollen, and the circulation is so poor. It's being on the boards that saved her from an embolism."

And so Bruna walked her mistress from room to room, even when she was half asleep. And Maria heard some strangely familiar sound arise out of her dreams. Her body jolted upright. Bruna went to the window, drew back the curtains, undid the bolts, and the two of them stepped out onto the balcony.

Aristo was in the street, serenading Maria like a Greek troubadour, whistling a tune with his knuckles in his mouth, as if he were his own harmonica. He looked like a vagabond in his rumpled denim shirt.

"Ah," Maria said, "the sailor is here." She felt a rage build in her. She stepped back inside the apartment. "Bolt the window, Bruna. His canary has fled. Her heart does not beat for him."

He called from the bistro at the corner. Maria ordered Bruna not to pick up the phone.

"But that is cruel, Madame Maria. And you were never cruel to the sailor."

"Then I will learn," Maria said.

Her sleep was chaotic that night. Maria was all twisted

up in her sheets, mummified. The mama boar appeared in her dreams. The boar was not protecting her piglets. She had the Widow's silky voice, her musical lisp.

"Maria, Skorpios is mine."

Maria bolted out of her dream and rescued herself from her own entangled sheets. She could hear the sailor whistling to her from under the chestnut tree. She peered at the clock on her night table. It was ten past three in the morning. She didn't have to summon Bruna. Her maid stood outside the bedroom door in a blue nightgown.

"Bruna," the diva said in a voice that was both resilient and resigned, "let the sailor in before he wakes the entire building."

"Yes, madame," Bruna said with a hidden smile.

"And tell him to be quiet on the stairs."

SEVEN

La Divina

-1-

Onassis looked at the female pharaoh in her pajamas and quaked with desire. Bruna prepared an omelette with greens and roasted potatoes at five in the morning.

"Sailor," Maria said, "doesn't she ever feed you, that wife of yours?" Then she clapped her supple, serpentlike hand over his mouth. "Never mind. I don't want to hear about your domestic relations."

But he told her anyway. It seems the sailor had met his match. Jackie O was as much a wanderer as he was. Her shopping sprees were notorious. She spent 300,000 dollars at a clip on the best of Balenciaga and Yves Saint Laurent, and never wore a single one of the items. She sold them back to a certain buyer, who then resold them as dresses and pantsuits from the private collection of Jackie O.

"Shame on you," Maria said. "She's much better at business than Aristotle Onassis."

But Bruna was perplexed. "Monsieur Aristo, couldn't your accountants put a stop to this sort of speculation?"

"My hands are tied," the sailor said. "It would cause a scandal if word ever got out."

"What about *our* island?" Maria wanted to know.

Odysseus shook his head. "She's fired all my gardeners and hired her own. She wants to redo all the flower beds."

Bruna watched these two lovers who hadn't made love in what seemed like half a century. Their hands would touch whenever Aristo slid past his former companion. The paleness had gone out of Maria. Her skin glowed in the early-morning light. Bruna had opened all the shutters and pulled back the drapes.

"You cannot blame your wife," Maria said.

"I know," Aristotle replied. "She still grieves. I'm aware. I can see the great distance in her eyes. But the Kennedy clan will never accept me. I am a wealthy juggler with a fleet of oil ships. I might have gone to Cambridge if the Turks hadn't set fire to my native town."

"Cambridge, ha!" Maria said. "Your schooling stopped, just like mine. You will never have their *smoothness*, and neither will I. We are primitives, Aristo, tigers who like to gnaw. That is our art."

The sailor had to leave. Jackie O was waiting for him on the Avenue Foch. He kissed Maria as they stood in the doorway, almost like strangers who had kissed for the first time.

That elusive glimmer of magic—the carved-out moments of Maria's happiness—left with the sailor. She went back into the bedroom like a somnambulist in one of her own operas.

"I miss him," Maria said. "I miss him so much."

-2-

The diva wasn't left without a dog. Onassis had given her two other miniature—toy—poodles, Pixie and Djedda, both females. Maria rarely left her apartment without them. The diva was still in demand. Sandor kept sending her proposals, and had to include a clause in these contracts that Pixie and Djedda would fly wherever Maria flew. Sandor kept enticing her. She could sing less demanding roles.

Sandor darling, she scribbled on one of the contracts, *I'm not a goose. If I can't sing Norma, I'll sing nothing at all.*

Suddenly, the bad boy of cinema came along: Pier Paulo Pasolini, a slim little man with sunken cheeks who frequented male prostitutes, she had been told. He published erotic novels and poems that had sent him hurling through the courts. He had a violent sense of politics. He wanted to rip through Italian society, to shove the entire bourgeoisie in front of a firing squad. And he was dying to do a film with Maria. He plagued her on the telephone, but she had Bruna to shield her from Pasolini.

"Monsieur, I told you, Madame Callas is indisposed. . . . No, she does not have a moment to spare."

Finally, after the twentieth call, Maria took the phone.

"*Madonna,*" she said, "what the hell do you want? I'm a member of the bourgeoisie. Shall I volunteer myself for your firing squad, Maestro Pasolini?"

She was startled by his soft, almost childish voice. He didn't sound like a gangster, or a provocateur.

"You must not listen to the journalists. They distort; they lie. Anyway, you're an artist, Madame Callas, the greatest of our time."

"Maestro," she said, "you cannot win with flattery. Tell me what it is you want."

"To sit with you and talk about a film project," Pasolini said in the same seductive voice.

"Then you have confused me with another Callas," Maria said with a feigned touch of hauteur. She was beginning to enjoy this conversation, considering how lonely she was, a diva with two dogs. "I am not a film actress, Maestro."

"Ah, but I do not want a film actress. I want the Callas who hypnotized audiences everywhere as Violetta and Lady Macbeth."

The diva grew dizzy for a moment.

"To play what?" she asked, all her modesty gone.

"Medea."

–3–

HE WAS A PIXIE OF A MAN.

He had such small hands and feet. But his doll-like look was disrupted by the dark, burning eyes of a brigand. Maria had invited him to Avenue Georges Mandel. They sat in her kitchen, having coffee and a lemon cake that Bruna herself had prepared.

His manners were impeccable for a brigand. He scooped up every crumb.

"Maestro, you could get Sophia Loren—why me?"

He rubbed his tiny hands together with a nervous thrust. "Sophia is much too modern. She never had a primitive soul. Can you imagine Sophia playing a sorceress who presides over human sacrifice? She would be laughable. But *you* could be a goddess—a queen—a sorcerer—a witch. Everything, Maria, and nothing."

Maria took a sip of coffee and stared at this maniac of a director. "Maestro, between everything and nothing is an enormous hole. I might fall in and never be found."

"Exactly," the maestro said. "That is my Medea."

They settled on the terms. Pier Paulo did not want Cherubini's "modern" Medea, or Euripides' ancient one; he wanted to go back much further into primitive times, where Medea could be crafty, ruthless, sensual, and barbaric, a loving mother who still sets fire to her two sons, as only Callas could play her. Pier Paulo had a limited budget and couldn't spare much of a salary for his star. Maria didn't have Onassis to sabotage her plans, and she accepted Pasolini's offer. All her expenses would be paid, and Bruna, Pixie, and Djedda could accompany her wherever they filmed. Pasolini wanted to recapture the mythic kingdom of Colchis, a region supposedly south of the Caucasus, at the eastern edge of the Black Sea, where Medea presided as the daughter of a king and granddaughter of the sun god Helios. There was no such kingdom on the current map. And he hoped to find *his* Colchis in Cappadocia, a rocky region in central Anatolia. So he went to Turkey with his cameras, his cast, and his crew. With Maria and her dogs, they got on a plane to Ankara, then rode in a rented fleet of buses to the mountainous terrain of Cappadocia, with its treacherous sand dunes and deep red clay, where even the wiliest of men were known to "drown" in the sand and disappear.

The sun was relentless, and Pasolini was obliged to film in over 110 degrees. Parts of his equipment melted and couldn't be replaced. Yet he shot whatever had to be shot. Maria's dogs nearly died of thirst. Pasolini had to bus in precious water and food from a hundred miles away. Sand flew out of the faucets at the hotel where they all slept.

Bruna even bathed in this Cappadocian sand. "Madame Maria, the sand is a miracle. It can absorb sweat and dust."

As a pagan goddess and queen, Maria had to wear a heavy headdress, a long braided gown, and enormous ropes of jewels that weighed over fifteen pounds. She had to run along the dunes and hills of clay in one particular scene, with the cameras tracking her as she ran and ran, and she fainted in the midst of filming under that murderous sun. Pasolini caressed Maria's forehead with a wet cloth, and when her eyes opened, she whispered in a wavering voice, "Maestro, please forgive me. It's my low blood pressure. I've wasted valuable time."

He stared at Maria with a fixed regard of wonderment. "You are Medea, you really are. You have her magic and her wildness."

He had a coterie of lovers around him—hotel clerks and bus drivers—but he fell in love with Maria. He crafted poems for her while they were in the dunes. He danced with her, played with her dogs. He talked of running away with Maria, abandoning production.

"Maestro," she said, "I'll spank you if you repeat such foolishness."

She was happy now, after all the idleness on the Avenue Georges Mandel, where she never woke before noon. She was the first one on the set in Cappadocia, at six in the morning. She listened to Italian soap operas on her transistor radio between shots. And she was the only one who dared argue with Pasolini.

"Maestro, you shoot so many close-ups of me. Your film will have no movement."

He smiled at Maria. "Every other star begs for close-ups, and you want to hide."

He tore up the script and had his characters improvise. Dialogue would not bring him back to pagan times. Every gesture had to be part of a primitive dance . . .

They flew out of Ankara, continued filming in remote areas of Italy, and ended up in the vast Roman studios of Cinecittà. Bruna had read somewhere that director Federico Fellini lived deep within this film city and never stepped outside its walls.

"That's ridiculous," Maria said. "I've met Federico in my dressing room at La Scala, met him many times. You were with me, Bruna."

"No, Madame. That was his double. Fellini has a phobia. He cannot leave Cinecittà."

Maria didn't believe a word of Bruna's—Fellini cloistered in Cinecittà, as a prisoner of his own art.

"Ah, then I will congratulate Federico's double the next time I see him."

Pasolini finished shooting in late August; Maria and the maestro looked at the rushes in Rome. La Divina could not recognize herself. Perhaps the maestro had discovered another Callas, far more primitive than Maria.

"Paulo, is it true that Fellini lives inside Cinecittà and never leaves?"

"That is my impression," the maestro said. "It is a crisis of faith. He trusts only his actors, his props, and his crew. The rest has no meaning. The rest is not real."

"But I have seen him at La Scala," Maria said.

"Yes, I can imagine him giving up his sanctuary for

Maria Callas. But it is a private matter, between him and his demons."

And the maestro walked out of the screening room.

–4–

Medea HAD ITS GALA AT THE PARIS OPÉRA in January. Every seat was sold out a month in advance. The First Lady of France was present. Madame Pompidou arrived in a hat made of peacock feathers and reigned over the first tier of boxes with her bodyguards. Onassis also reserved a box of his own. But his wife had suddenly appeared on the Avenue Foch, and he had to cancel his reservation at the last moment; Jackie O would have loved to attend the gala and sit with Madame Pompidou. She was curious about what Pasolini had done with Medea, but people would have gazed at her all night and compared her with that Medea on the screen, with La Callas. So she summoned Onassis to the Avenue Foch like a general dealing with a bad little boy. He was obliged to leave instructions for the chief usher to hand Maria a note.

> *Darling Medea, so disappointed I'll miss your debut on the big screen.*

He'd called Maria every day while she was in Cappadocia. He whistled outside her window after she returned to France. She still wouldn't sleep with him. Her anger only increased his ardor . . .

Maria entered the auditorium in a red dress, with the same ropes of jewelry she'd worn on the set. The spectators broke into a clamor of raw adulation at the first sight of her. Her long absence from the opera house had only added to her legend. The diva had become a demigoddess in a red dress. She did not want to sit in a box with Madame Pompidou, did not want to be introduced by Pasolini or anyone else. She stood near the front row for ten minutes and the pandemonium still didn't subside. So she raised her hand. Every eye was on La Divina. The clamor lowered a little. Maria still had to shout.

"Doucement, s'il vous plait."

Maria claimed her seat in the front row. She could wear her glasses in the dark and not be overwhelmed by the whirling figures on the screen. Her heart thumped like a crazy mandolin. She was counting on a new career. Perhaps she could move inside Cinecittà, like Federico, and wander as she wished from film to film. The chandeliers sizzled for a moment and then the auditorium went as dark as a bat cave.

Maria landed in *Medea.*

It was a world of clay and sand—Colchis, where Medea was far more mysterious than her father the king. The redness of the landscape dominated the screen—red, red everywhere, except for a few isolated spots of green, bits of shrubbery emerging from cracks in the clay. The sand dunes were deep brown, like dried blood. A boy was being sacrificed to the gods of Colchis. He wore a wreath on his head. He had a demented smile. A holy man hacked him to pieces with a hatchet. The tribesmen drank his blood from wooden bowls. Medea stood in the background as the high priestess of this sacrifice. Then came the first close-up of her, in profile. The outline of her face was almost numbing, as her beauty bled right onto the screen.

The audience was stunned by the carnage, by the ghoulish delight in drinking human blood. It wasn't opera, where even the worst horror could be redeemed by the softness of song. Pasolini had taken his audience back to a prehistoric period, where ritual ruled in a land of long silences.

Spectators could not involve themselves with the carnage they saw on the screen. This Medea had no melodies, no chants to reveal her pain. But it was Maria who suffered the most by what she saw. She could not hide from the ruins of her own irrational love, could not abandon the sailor who had abandoned her—and stood beneath her window like a lost boy.

The critics adored *Medea* and its depiction of a time when ritual ruled and every rock was red with blood, but *Medea* played to empty houses and vanished so abruptly that everything about the film seemed like an apparition, a ghost that went away.

Maria's new career was another apparition.

Yet Pasolini wasn't dissatisfied. He had espresso and Bruna's lemon cake at the apartment on Avenue Georges Mandel. *Medea* was a citadel, he said, against the bourgeoisie.

Maria wanted to pinch the maestro until he screamed. "But darling, it's the bourgeoisie who buy the tickets and saw our masterpiece at the Opéra. They didn't like it at all."

"Because it did not reflect their own desires," the maestro said. "They do not have adventure in their blood."

"Blood, blood," Maria said. "Maestro, we needed more romance."

–5–

SHE'D GONE BACK TO GETTING UP AT NOON. She might even have gotten up later if Odysseus hadn't been so ardent in his pursuit of her. He seemed less concerned about the secrecy of his maneuvers with Maria. He always whistled before he came upstairs. She hadn't seen her sailor in a week. He didn't arrive in a rumpled shirt. He'd come to Maria in a dinner jacket. Maria was perplexed. Bruna always prepared a light supper for them with a dish of black olives and a decanter of red wine.

"Wear a black dress," he barked.

"Why?" she asked, prepared to hurl a shoe at him.

"Hurry," he said.

She didn't like surprises. If she had to live in the shadows, she preferred to spend her time with the sailor at home, where she wouldn't be frowned upon as the discarded mistress of the world's most celebrated shipping magnate, who was proud of his disheveled appearance.

She wore a black dress and the last pair of red shoes she had from the late Bernardo Scarpia. The sailor removed a string of pearls from his pocket and clasped it around her neck—pearls, always pearls. She shuddered at these expensive gifts now that he had a new wife.

"Where are we going?" she asked, more and more perturbed. But he wouldn't answer.

"Can Bruna come with us?"

"No," he said. "Not tonight."

She wanted to slap his face. But she put on her mink stole, hugged Bruna, and kissed her two dogs good-bye. She got into the lift with Aristo. His limousine was waiting for them outside Maria's apartment house. The driver looked like one of the Sicilian gangsters Maria had seen in Palermo. He wore a red silk neckerchief that matched the color of Maria's shoes. He appraised Maria like some scout with an insatiable lust.

"Stop that, Enrique," the sailor said, "or I'll pull out your tongue with a pair of pliers."

"Yes, boss," the driver said with a satyr's embarrassed smile.

Maria realized in an instant that this Enrique drove many of Aristo's women around, mistresses like Maria, clandestine or not. And he must have felt a kind of propriety about them perhaps. Maria climbed into the backseat. Her mind wandered. The limo stopped at Maxim's.

Maria wouldn't get out of the car. "Aristo," she said, "I won't be paraded in front of all those people. I'm not a poodle—and I'm certainly not your wife."

The sailor had to plead. "But they all love you, Maria. Maxim's is not the same without you."

"And whose fault is that?" Maria shouted, prepared to strangle him with his own pearls.

The sailor shrugged, went inside on his own, and returned with Albert, the maître d', surrounded by runners in their red uniforms.

It was Albert who reached into the limo and clasped Maria's hand. "Madame Callas, I cannot tell you the pleasure it gives me to have you once again chez Maxim's. We all missed you so much. Many of our patrons could not be consoled."

Albert was a master at flattery. But it didn't seem to matter. Maria still got out of the car. The runners darted around Maria as Albert escorted her and the sailor through the Omnibus with its polished banquettes and into the Aquarium, where all the chatter stopped. Diners applauded La Divina, as if she'd come to them after the last curtain call. Maria acknowledged the applause with a smile that lulled her out of her loneliness.

She missed this red room.

Albert took her mink stole and sat her at Aristo's table, next to Pierre-Yves, who had become the most famous couturier in Paris, with his own fashion house. All his models were androgynous—women dressed as flirtatious boys, as scamps. He could not have dealt with the ripeness of Maria. But he still adored her art. He knew she had lost her wind and would never get it back. But he heard the diva's voice in his head whenever he designed a jacket or a pantsuit for one of his gamines. He took out his sketchbook and did an outline of La Callas as Anna Bolena.

"Maria, you will always be my queen, no matter where you are."

"Pierrot, please," she said, and tore up the sketch. She didn't want to be reminded of who she had once been.

Maria was on familiar ground inside the Aquarium. Brigitte Bardot sat at the next table in her bare feet. Liz Taylor arrived in a silvery turban. Maria could only catch a blurred capsule of them with her weak eyes.

Everyone at her table talked about *Medea.* Maria was convinced that none of Aristo's Greek partners and their wives had seen the film.

Albert had prepared a party for Maria. He directed a performance on the Aquarium's little stage. He had models from Pierre-Yves' fashion house parade around in costumes from the Belle Epoque, with long flowery hats and waspish waists, and toss clusters of wisteria at the tables.

"*Mesdames et messieurs,* close your eyes and let me take you back to another time, when Maxim's was filled with coquettes like these, when bankers and industrial barons fought for the right to have a coquette at their table."

"And accompany them upstairs to one of Maxim's

palatial private rooms," said an industrial baron at Bardot's table.

Albert wagged his finger at the baron and had the coquettes climb down from the stage in their stylish boots and hurl whatever wisteria they had left into the air. The tycoons at the tables poured them glasses of champagne.

The sailor wasn't amused. Perhaps these coquettes reminded him a little too much of his own "coquetry" in regard to Maria. He summoned Albert and whispered in his ear. The coquettes vanished from the Aquarium, and Maxim's stage turned into a bandstand with a five-piece band. The sailor invited Maria to dance.

They were a curious couple.

Maria had to stoop to dance with the sailor, and they looked like a centaur with two heads. No one else was out on the dance floor. Maria could sense his moodiness in the awkward glide of his feet.

"I am lost without you, Maria. I had hoped Maxim's would lure you back into my orbit. I'm a schemer, I admit. But I have only defeated myself."

"My wily Odysseus," Maria said. "You have a wife and a bunch of children, two of them your own . . . and I have a pair of dogs."

"We could run away."

Maria laughed. "The paparazzi would be inside our underpants wherever we went."

She could see the sadness whirl around his copper-colored eyes. He had deceived her, abandoned her, but she loved his hapless chivalry, this sailor in short pants who'd come to Maxim's disguised in a dinner jacket.

She had a runner fetch her mink stole. She took Aristo by the hand and left Maxim's without waving good-bye.

They returned to her flat. She fed him hot milk and didn't send him away. This grizzled man was as much her child as Pixie or Djedda. She undressed Aristo, kissed him with an aching hunger as he lay there with his catalog of little scars from the battles he'd had as a schoolboy in Smyrna. He'd never been so passive with Maria as she pinned him to the bed and left bite marks on his back.

"Let her see for herself," she said with all the vengeance of a diva. "Let that wife of yours know that La Callas has marked you with tattoos."

"Shhh," Odysseus said.

–6–

It was Maria who had remained the child.

Jackie O was a strategist with an iron will. She appeared in *Paris Match* one week later, sitting with Aristotle at Maxim's. They dined there every night at Onassis' table. She had recaptured her terrain. There were parties at Onassis' flat on the Avenue Foch, excursions to Skorpios, cruises on the *Christina.* And then this panorama of appearances stopped as abruptly as it had begun and Jackie returned to Manhattan. She was less of an exile than she liked to think. Her marriage to Onassis soon became a series of exotic moments in a busy schedule. They quarreled in public. He belittled her, and she belittled him. She had dreamt of moving with her children to the Continent. But her real life was in Manhattan.

Meanwhile, the sailor had multiple dwellings on multiple continents but considered the *Christina*—or the island of Skorpios—as his home.

He began whistling under Maria's window again.

She stood behind the drapes with her glasses on and watched him whistle his heart out. His face turned red, and she began to worry. So she sent Bruna downstairs with a cup of water. He looked so ragged and distraught that she signaled from the window for Bruna to bring him upstairs. She wanted to murder the sailor and make love to him—both at the same time. Her ragged boy didn't carry a centime in his rumpled pants. She had to stuff his pockets with cash so he would have taxi fare. God knows where his driver was—lost in traffic, the diva supposed.

She fed Aristo, had Bruna buy him sweaters and socks. Sometimes he'd march into Maxim's without a shirt, and Albert had to outfit him, as if a scarecrow had come through the revolving doors. Yet the sailor owned an airline, ran a fleet of tankers, and met opposing parties in boardrooms without having to prepare a single note.

Maria pitied him and hated him and would have gladly set his feet on fire. She was Medea in the making.

Bruna was appalled. "Madame, you wouldn't harm him. You love that man, and you always will."

He slept at Maria's, since he didn't feel at home on the Avenue Foch now that it was packed with his wife's gatherings of Yves Saint-Laurent and Balenciaga, like a storage bin. So Maria had a vagabond in her bed. She was tied to this monster of a man, to his aromas, to the little bumps on his hands. Their lovemaking had gone topsy-turvy. She was the aggressor now. And the vagabond with stubble on his face had become her victim, who welcomed her roughness, the scratches she delivered—more tokens he would have to hide from his wife.

It mattered less that he was often gone for weeks,

sometimes a month. She'd been invited to teach a series of master classes at Juilliard for nascent opera singers. It would mean several months in Manhattan. But she'd developed glaucoma and had to take special eyedrops every two hours. The ophthalmologist at the American Hospital had warned her. "Caution, Madame Callas. You must keep this prescription with you wherever you happen to be. You do not want to end up like the blind beggar woman in *La Gioconda*."

"Ah, you know your opera," La Divina said with a wan smile. "I have never played Gioconda's blind mother."

"But you will go blind if you neglect these drops."

She had begun to see halos around the chandeliers at Avenue Georges Mandel and to bump into shelves as she lost part of her peripheral vision. Bruna administered the medicated eyedrops every two hours. And then Maria had to leave for New York . . .

She was given a suite at the Plaza that overlooked the park. She would have to audition three hundred students and winnow that number down to twenty-five. The first thing she did was call her old teacher, Madame de Hidalgo, who had formed Maria in Athens, honed whatever gifts such an awkward Greek American girl had, and revealed to her the magic of bel canto. Madame left Greece after the war, wandered awhile, then taught at the conservatory in Ankara, and later went to Milan, where she lived on a small pension.

Every time Maria noticed a slight spillage in her accounts with Sandor Gorlinsky, he would say, "Ah, Maria darling, I knew you would want to contribute to Madame de Hidalgo's welfare fund, and it simply slipped your mind."

Maria seemed alarmed. "But you must not tell her the source of that income. She is very proud and will send back whatever you give her."

"Of course," the impresario said. "I have arranged things with her landlord. Hidalgo will never know."

And now Maria had Hidalgo on the line.

"Madame, I am scared to death. I have never taught a class. How will I ever choose twenty-five among such a large crop? I feel like a mad lady stuck in a cucumber patch."

Madame de Hidalgo laughed. "Remember that first time, Maria? How clumsy you were in your sandals, like a wrinkled potato in a smock, with thick eyeglasses. I would have gladly sent you home. And then I listened—I heard you sing. And I felt a knife in my heart with your first notes. I turned away from you and cried, with wonder and joy and complete exhaustion. You were a volcano, Maria."

"I was not."

"You erupted right in front of me, and I wasn't prepared. So you must not make quick judgments. You must listen with a third ear."

Maria frowned. "Thank you, Madame, but I have had enough trouble holding on to the two I have."

Hidalgo was silent for a moment. She seemed very serious. "You could not have become a virtuoso without that third ear."

La Divina felt frustrated. "But where is it, Madame?"

"It has no visible shape. But it does exist, almost like an antenna. And that third ear will help you decide which students to keep and those you will have to discard."

–7–

MARIA HAD A FEW DISTANT FRIENDS from her days at the Met, but she preferred to dine alone in her suite at the Plaza while she listened to the howling of the wind and watched the trees bend all along the panorama of Central Park. The utter isolation seemed to calm Maria.

She sent for Bruna and Pixie and Djedda, flew them across the Atlantic at her own expense. And she took Bruna with her to Juilliard as her assistant commandant with a German tape recorder. Faculty and students stared at Maria with their mouths agape. They had seldom been that close to a goddess from La Scala and the Met. They could have reached out and touched her, but none of them dared. The entire school was in a frenzy over Maria's visit.

She was escorted to the audition room by a member of the faculty, who couldn't stop chattering. The accompanist sat at the piano. Maria tested the keys. The sound seemed harsh and jarred Maria's nerves. She had to wait while the piano was removed and a second Steinway was wheeled in.

She tested the keys again.

The room began to fill with faculty members. And then a cavalcade of students arrived. Maria had a sudden tremor as she recalled her own audition at the Athens Conservatory, how she'd sat on a bench with applicants who were so smartly dressed, with buckles on their shoes and ribbons surrounding their perfect complexions, while she looked like a servant girl with thick ankles and a plague of pimples. The applicants at Juilliard seemed so much more confident than a row of Greek boys and girls on a hard bench. They'd come in corduroys and blue jeans, with music sheets that they handed to the accompanist, set pieces from *Carmen*, *Traviata*, *Norma*, *Macbeth*, *Don Giovanni* . . .

Maria had their names on a list. She introduced herself to each student, interviewed them for a moment, trying to put them at ease. But they must have sensed her wild devotion to the craft, and it made them nervous to be in the presence of La Callas. So she stopped the interviews and had them sing; she listened while Bruna recorded the sounds. She didn't strike anyone off the list. She wanted to listen again in her suite.

She couldn't audition more than nine students on that one afternoon. That's all her concentration allowed. She wouldn't accept interviews from music critics concerning her own career or how she intended to conduct her master classes. Maria didn't have a clue. She wouldn't have lunch or dinner with faculty members. She wouldn't appear on television, though Juilliard would have liked her to publicize the classes. She was a teacher now, not a prima donna on vacation from her art. Maria was concerned about the vibrato and vocal cords of her students rather than the reputation of a music school in Manhattan.

She returned to the Plaza, listened to the tapes again and again, trying to discover that third ear Madame de Hidalgo had talked about. Maria didn't have Madame's gift. But as she listened, a depth of talent was suddenly revealed, a touch of emotion in a musical line. And she checked a name on the list.

It took Maria over a month to complete audition after audition. She didn't put up the names of the students in her master class on the dean's bulletin board until a day before the classes began. She let her hair grow. Her peripheral vision improved, and she stopped seeing halos around chandeliers. Bruna still administered the eyedrops. Maria could wear her horn-rimmed glasses without Aristo harassing her. And that's how she went to her first master class, in a long black dress, high heels, and a silver pendant she had worn in *Medea*.

She looked like a widow in that black dress, or an aristocratic schoolmarm, her auburn hair swept into a knot that reached well below her neck. She was startled when she appeared onstage at Juilliard's main auditorium, where she was meant to conduct the master classes. The auditorium was packed with people.

She had forgotten for a moment that she was La Divina, and not that little girl in Greece. The audience had risen like a bolt when they caught sight of Maria and applauded with such vehemence—shouting, "La Divina, La Divina"—that she was confused and lost her bearings.

Maria was adrift. She recovered and raised her left hand, as if she were a maestro signaling to her very own orchestra.

Most of the rumbling stopped.

"Please," Maria said. "I am here to conduct a class."

Then she looked about her and her heart squeezed with a terrible tightness. She had to struggle to catch her breath. She noticed Franco Zeffirelli in the audience with Odysseus' new wife. Jackie O was in a white autumn dress and a blue Hermès scarf. Maria was filled with a sudden rage. What was the Widow doing here at Juilliard, watching Maria train young baritones and sopranos? Had she come to mock Maria? To taunt a vanquished rival? Perhaps Maria had never been a rival at all. Just a nuisance in the Widow's way.

But Maria's anger restored her equilibrium. She looked ferocious in her long black dress. The stage was barren except for Maria's chair, a tiny table, and a microphone on a stand. The first three students were disappointing; the best of the best, she had chosen them herself. They must have been terrified by that sea of faces in the audience. Their voices didn't project, even with a microphone in front of them. They seemed to stutter as they sang.

Maria sat with her feet wide apart, like a Cossack general. She clapped her hands with each student's swallowed note. "Legato, legato," she said. "Sing with an open throat. I do not want to feel a chipping at the notes. The sound must be liquid . . . like oil. Study every note, please. The soul of an opera is born into that one single note."

She began to accompany her own students as she sat in her chair. Maria's voice reverberated across the auditorium like a continuum of soft rifle shots.

This Cossack general wasn't stern with her students. But she didn't coddle them.

One student stood at the microphone and said, "I can't trill."

"That's bad news," Maria told her. "My dear, you're like an acrobat with one leg. Whatever talent you have, you'll still fall off the wire."

She had to stop in the middle of the class, withdraw to the wings, where Bruna was waiting with the eyedrops.

"Am I too harsh?" Maria asked. "I do not want to be harsh."

"Madame, perhaps you are not harsh enough. Some of them need a good scolding."

"No, no," Maria said. "I am a teacher, not a shrew."

She returned to her table.

She had to pluck some confidence out of her students, help them discover a pure vibrato, and she wasn't sure how. She had a sudden brainstorm. She stood up and stole the microphone, hid it behind her desk.

The next student climbed onto the stage and said in a timid voice, "Madame, how will I be heard—without a microphone?"

"Simple! By singing with an open throat," Maria said.

The student soprano had decided upon *Rigoletto,* one of the most violent of Verdi's operas. Rigoletto is a vitriolic hunchbacked court jester who belongs to the duke of Mantua. He helps the duke seduce the wives of his own courtiers. The hunchback has a vulnerability, however: his beautiful daughter Gilda, whom he has hidden away. But Gilda has met the duke at church and has fallen in love with him. She sings this love to her father in "Caro nome."

The student soprano sang Gilda's aria in full voice, as Maria beat every note on her table with a ballpoint pen; but *this* daughter of Rigoletto did not reveal the least emotion. Maria kicked at the table, stood up, and said, "My God, you're not a zombie. Be like an animal. Gilda is a passionate girl, and you must convey her palpitating emotion even before you sing. The very act of breathing is an emotion."

The next student, a young Swiss baritone, sang selections from *Pagliacci,* but he seemed to avoid as many encounters with high notes as he could. Maria didn't bother to hide her own disenchantment. "I don't care if you crack on the top note. Caruso cracked many times."

Then she returned to her table. "It's time to stop. I'm an ogre, I really am. That's enough for today."

The students stood in front of their seats and started to clap and cheer—"Brava, brava"; then their own monitor, the Swiss baritone, handed Maria a bouquet of purple roses.

"None of us can thank you enough, Madame Callas. To take the time out of your busy schedule and devote it to us—that is a gift we will treasure all our lives."

La Divina held the purple flowers close to her heart. These students didn't realize the solitude that the master classes had replaced. They were the ones who had bestowed the gift upon her, and had thrust her out of her loneliness. She would never march through *Norma* again at the Met. All Maria could do was sing idle pieces at a student parade . . .

She had to greet visitors as she left the stage. And there she was, Jacqueline Onassis in her Hermès scarf, with that divide of Aristo between them, and she pretending in her breathy, hyperbolic voice that the divide didn't exist, as she was the conqueror and Maria was only an icon with the ragged remains of a voice.

And while Mrs. Onassis stood there, the paparazzi flashed away at her and Maria. Jackie O got rid of them with a swipe of her hand.

"I learned so much, Madame Callas. How a voice is sculpted, almost out of clay. No one else could have taught this class with your conviction, with your magnificent ear."

My third ear, Maria mused.

Jackie clasped her hands. Her fingers were as tapered as Maria's. "I wish I could attend every class." She pretended to pout. "I have other obligations, I fear. But I will command my secretary to sit in my seat and take prodigious notes. I wish I had your discipline, your talent. Your art is a mystery, Madame Callas. And yet you are willing to dive into it, note by note, and share that mystery with your students."

"I am only following the score, doing my best to reveal what the composer wanted."

"But I do not have the courage to dive that far down into the deep," Jackie said, and left with all the paparazzi.

-8-

The master classes exploded into myth.

Juilliard was frantic. Tickets to each performance were impossible to find. Pictures of Maria behind her little desk appeared in papers and magazines across the globe, yet she still declined to give a single interview. It didn't seem to matter. The legend grew. Little by little, she sang more and more at each class. And her students revealed more emotion as they worked on their technique. She did mold them from clay, as Jackie had said. She had to offer her autograph wherever she went, even in the breakfast room at the Plaza.

And then one afternoon, she saw a woman in a tattered coat limping along outside the Plaza with a cane and a leg brace. It was Laura Sordelo, once *Oggi*'s star roving reporter. She was now the lone editor of an opera magazine, a pamphlet that she herself produced. The circulation was fewer than five hundred printed copies. But it was exactly the kind of magazine that Maria preferred. She wouldn't have to talk about her diet, her dogs, and the pendant she "borrowed" from Pasolini's prop closet.

She invited Laura up to her suite at the Plaza. The waiter brought them a platter of club sandwiches and a Caesar salad. Laura must have been starving. She tore into the sandwiches while Maria nibbled on her salad and Bruna fed the dogs.

"Madame, I am sad," Laura said after her second club sandwich. "To watch La Callas participate in a sing-along at Juilliard."

Maria felt stung.

Ungrateful girl. I feed you and you devour me.

"It was not a sing-along, Laura. It was a master class."

"And will you discover another Callas at Juilliard?" Laura asked with the same mischievous smile.

"That's not the point. These students have their own gifts, their own talent. And I . . ."

Maria looked at the leg brace, at Laura's shrunken left calf.

"Laura, I'm too frightened to appear *alone* on a stage. All the confidence I ever had is gone. And so for a moment or two I can be the hunchback's daughter."

"And have Rigoletto murder you by mistake in a maddened fit? Madame, I *love* the master classes. I have learned so much—about you. How each performance of every opera you sang was unique, so unlike another. That is what I will remember and what I will write about."

She kissed Maria and limped away with a sandwich in her fist. And the very next morning, Maria and Bruna left for Paris with the dogs. There were a dozen roses waiting for Maria outside her massive wooden front door on Avenue Georges Mandel. These roses were from Giuseppe di Stefano, who had once been her chaotic partner in song. He'd walk out of a performance if she took a single curtain call without him. She'd had fistfights with Pippo in public, shouting matches at Biffi Scala.

Having a wife and three children in Milan didn't stop Pippo from seducing every young soprano he could find at whatever opera house he happened to be in. Pippo was always on the prowl. Still, most critics agreed that the best recording ever made of *Traviata* featured Pippo and Maria Callas. His articulation was perfect. Pippo never missed a note. But he had fallen on hard times. His eldest daughter, Lucia, was dying of cancer, and the cost of her treatments was prodigious.

So he left a bouquet outside Maria's door. He was two years older than La Divina. He'd abused his voice. He lost his sweetness of tone and all he had left was a loud falsetto. Pippo was still on the prowl, but in a different way. Maria felt sorry for the tenor and invited him to lunch at Avenue Georges Mandel. He was half an inch shorter than Maria, a handsome man with a sturdy build.

Pippo was in a hurry after all these years. Bruna could see the desperation in his eyes.

She'd prepared a chopped salad and a cheese platter with salted crackers, but Pippo began talking business after his first bite. He wanted to go on a world concert tour with Maria.

"Pippo," she said, "hold your horses. I haven't sung in years."

"But I've seen articles everywhere about your master classes," Pippo said with a sliver of Camembert on his lower lip. "All the critics agree. There was electricity in the auditorium every time you corrected a student with an aria of your own."

Maria was adamant. "As a teacher, yes. I wasn't performing, no matter what the critics say."

He persisted throughout the lunch. "It would do wonders for both of us, Maria."

She was terrified. She would have to work for months, spend a year perhaps retraining her voice. And Pippo couldn't go on tour without Maria. No one would have him. He would be an accessory, an ornament, at every recital, no matter how many duets they sang together. He was utterly deflated by the end of the meal. Maria wouldn't budge.

Still, she was hungry for companionship, even if she fought with Pippo half the time. It was better than watching Westerns on television day after day. She had no interests, no pursuits, other than opera. She was a diva without a cause, without a vocation. So she smiled at this handsome Sicilian tenor.

"Don't be so gloomy, Pippo. It depresses me. Come back later—go!"

–9–

SHE HAD ARISTO TO THINK ABOUT and his heir, Alexander, who often rebelled against his father and came to Maria for advice. He had mocked her when they first met, called her "Big Ass," but now that his father had married the Widow, he would show up at Avenue Georges Mandel and rant against Aristo while Bruna fed him a full meal.

"I'm twenty-four, Auntie Maria, and Father keeps me on an allowance."

"He's old-fashioned," Maria said. "That's his way of caring about you."

"Shackling me, you mean."

Alexander loved fast cars, fast boats, and fast planes. He had a license to fly small aircraft, but he could never become a commercial pilot, since he had such poor eyesight, like his father. Aristo had given him his own toy, Olympic Aviation, an air taxi service, but still wouldn't pay him a salary. Alexander had a monthly allotment instead. So he was always feuding with his father, and Maria was caught in the middle.

"Give him time," Maria said. "He's frightened of what might happen. He has no other heir but you."

The sailor was proud of his son's accomplishments as a pilot.

Alexander had rescued heart attack victims on several Greek islands in the Ionian Sea and flown them to Athens in one of Olympic Aviation's fleet of hydroplanes. He celebrated Maria's forty-ninth birthday by arriving at her door a month late with a bottle of Dom Pérignon. He'd come from the Athens airport in his pilot's cap. He took off his thick glasses, kissed Maria between the eyes, and said, "I'm so sorry I made fun of you, Auntie, the first time we met. Can you ever forgive me?"

"There's nothing to forgive, Alexander. You thought I was stealing your father away."

They drank the champagne from crystal cups. The boy pilot was practically blind without his glasses, as blind as Maria.

"You were almost my stepmother," he said after his third sip.

"Yes, almost," Maria said, hiding her bitterness as best she could.

They danced from room to room, the blind leading the blind, while the boy pilot hummed some ridiculous tune he had picked up at a cabaret in Monte Carlo.

He was dead within a month.

It was a freak accident at the Athens airport. Alexander was training a new pilot aboard his father's Piaggio, the very craft on which he had learned to fly. A third pilot was also in the cockpit. The Piaggio was airborne for fifteen seconds. It suddenly veered to the right, struck the ground, spun over and over again like an insane acrobat, and stopped. The two other pilots were plucked out of the plane. Alexander was covered in blood. His right temple had been smashed in, and he could only be identified by the monogram on his blood-soaked handkerchief.

He was rushed to the nearest hospital. Aristo had a neurosurgeon flown in from Boston. A blood clot was removed from Alexander's brain. But he never regained consciousness and was put inside an oxygen tent with a life-support machine. Onassis swayed like a drunken sailor as he watched his son suck in air inside the tent with the help of that machine.

Much of this Maria learned from his daughter, Christina, and from Aristo himself, who was almost incoherent on the phone. Aristo waited until Christina arrived at the hospital and said good-bye to a brother whose head was wrapped in gauze and whom she couldn't even recognize, and then Aristo had the life support switched off.

Why should he keep suffering? the sailor had asked himself.

But he couldn't seem to part with Alexander. He wanted to have him frozen, kept in storage forever, or until some surgeon in the far future could reconstruct his brain. "This is madness," Christina said, and made all the arrangements that had to be made. The funeral was held on Skorpios, and Alexander was buried beside the little chapel that belonged to Aristo's island, while the sailor himself stood like a frozen man until the boy was in the ground, and then he disappeared to a hidden corner of the island.

Maria wasn't invited to the burial.

She had to suffer Alexander's death in secret, all alone. But she had her own ceremony at Georges Mandel. Alexander had left his pilot's cap with her. And she wore it while she and Bruna knelt in front of her little wooden Madonna and prayed that Alexander's soul would have a safe voyage through purgatory.

At first, the sailor was like a battery charged with lightning bolts, convinced as he was that Alexander's death was no accident, that the Piaggio had been tinkered with, sabotaged. And he blamed all his enemies, some real, some imagined. His fortune had hemorrhaged; he couldn't find enough fuel for his tankers, and Olympic Airways was losing passengers to other airlines. He still offered a million dollars to anyone who could provide information about the plane crash.

Jackie consoled him as long as she could and then returned to Manhattan to be near her children and the Kennedy clan. And so he wandered across Skorpios like a gardener who had forgotten how to garden, or else he sailed along Sicily and the coast of Greece, hiding in his stateroom like a lone pirate who had lost some of his prestige.

He no longer whistled when he stood under Maria's window.

He climbed the spiral staircase to Maria's third-floor apartment, and both Maria and Bruna were startled how diminished he had become. His back was stooped. He could barely keep his eyes open. That sweeping step of his was gone. He was a man without a melody.

The first thing the diva did was comb his hair. Bruna shaved him and then Maria kissed her sailor. He saw the pilot's cap on Maria's mantel and started to cry.

"Maria," he said like a schoolboy, "may I have the cap?"

"Of course, darling. I saved it for you."

He clutched the cap and stroked it, as if its contours held a piece of silk.

Maria couldn't mollify the madness in his eyes.

"They killed my boy. I will find them wherever they are and break their bones with my bare hands."

His clothes were rumpled. So Maria undressed her sailor and led him into the tub, and while she scrubbed him and sang the Greek lullabies he had heard as a little boy in Smyrna, Bruna washed and dried and ironed whatever he had worn on his way to Georges Mandel. Maria did not want to imagine what might have been as she wrapped the sailor in a bath towel. But the lullabies reminded her of her own mother. These were the songs that Litsa had once sung to her. And it disheartened Maria. The only connections she still had with Litsa were the checks that Sandor cut every month and the Bulova watch Maria had won.

Maria dressed Aristo, who looked like an aging doll that could barely open its eyes. Yet the touch of his skin still aroused Maria, still excited her.

"Darling," he said, "let's go to Maxim's. Albert wouldn't dare touch my table. And we'll invite Bruna." He tried to attach his cuff links, but Maria had to help him. "Bruna, have you ever been to Maxim's?"

"No, Monsieur Aristo."

"See," the sailor said. "It will be a special occasion. The magazines will have a field day. *La Callas and her maid storm Maxim's with Onassis.*"

"Not tonight, darling," Maria said. She didn't want to be outmaneuvered by the Widow again. It's Jackie who would storm Maxim's and give interview after interview.

"Bruna will prepare whatever you like." And she turned to her companion-maid with a magisterial look. "Tell Monsieur Aristo that you're not disappointed about Maxim's."

"But I am disappointed, Madame Maria. I would like to sit and stare at Alain Delon. . . ."

"Another time," the sailor said. "There will always be another time."

He had a business appointment that afternoon near the Arc de Triomphe. The lift was broken and Maria wouldn't let him climb down the stairs all by himself. His eyes were still half closed. She held his hand as they went down the carpeted steps. He had the pilot's cap in his pocket. He nearly tripped once or twice.

"Darling," Aristo said, "I'll be back tonight."

He never came.

Aristo went on a cruise to the Antilles with his wife. Then he retreated to Skorpios and would wander the island with a mongrel dog and a bottle of ouzo in his pocket. He named his mongrel Argus, after the dog in the *Odyssey* who waited to die until Odysseus came home to Ithaca to kill the suitors who had plagued Penelope, his wife. But Argus couldn't protect a man with half-closed eyes. Members of the *Christina*'s crew had to keep Aristo from stumbling. He had built a tomb for Alexander near the chapel on the island, and rather than return to the *Christina* at night, he would sleep on a knoll beside the tomb. Crew members covered him in a blanket and often slept beside him and the dog.

Sometimes he would call Maria in the middle of the night on his radiotelephone. He'd been drinking ouzo, and he made every sort of promise. He would divorce the Widow and sweep Maria away to Skorpios. It was one more epic tale by this teller of tales. He was king of his own Ithaca, with a mongrel dog as his guide and faithful crew members of the *Christina* to feed him and cover him in blankets.

–10–

Pippo went on pestering Maria.

He'd gone to London at his own expense and plotted the different venues of their world tour with *her* agent, Sandor

Gorlinsky, who still wore a mink coat in the midst of a heat wave. Sandor didn't push, but Pippo did.

It was a perilous idea. Pippo had lost every credential he'd ever had as an opera star, except his perennial habit of seducing young dancers and singers. And Maria would have to sing with this wrecked tenor and without a maestro and a full orchestra. They would have nothing more than an accompanist at the piano, while an orchestra might have revealed whatever colors Maria had left in her voice. But not even Sandor, with all his silk and savviness as a negotiator, could have had any concert hall cover the expense of a full orchestra for a solo performance, despite having La Divina as the star attraction.

Maria traveled as lightly as she could. She left Bruna behind to care for Pixie and Djedda. She was worth ten times whatever Pippo was paid, but she shared all her revenue with him, or he would have snapped at her and sabotaged each performance. Even in his ruined state, Pippo had a certain charm. He did not have the sailor's magical touch, but he knew how to entice Maria. And she didn't have to be alone in a Berlin hotel. He was no more faithful to Maria than he was to his wife, but she didn't really mind his indulgences. It kept him from falling apart. The audiences cheered Maria, not the tenor she was with. Sometimes he would refuse to perform. And Maria had to appear onstage alone.

It was a disaster from beginning to end. She hadn't performed in front of an audience in years, except for the singing she did at the master classes. And in trying to conserve her voice for a "pilgrimage" that would take her and Pippo to three continents, she avoided the calamity of high notes whenever she could, and her ability to express her feelings often froze. Pippo was as flamboyant as ever. But it was like watching a wounded soprano with an animated doll. Despite this, the tour was a financial success. Audiences loved Maria in Hamburg, Frankfurt, Munich, Madrid, and everywhere else she sang. They wouldn't let La Divina leave the stage. And they often delivered Pippo's role during a difficult duet, while Pippo himself became a specter and often hid behind the curtain in the middle of a performance, his face fueled with anger and frustration.

The critics were not very kind. One Londoner described Maria's performance with Pippo as "a train wreck in slow motion." Another critic said Pippo sounded like "a rampant player piano," and called Maria "a shadow who sometimes sang."

"Emotion," Maria had informed her students at Julliard. "There must be emotion in every gesture. You have to move and sing like an animal in hunger and pain."

That animal instinct was gone, frightened out of Maria. The tigress had turned into a cub.

By the time she finished the tour, she suffered from low blood pressure and a ruptured hernia that had to be repaired. Her glaucoma had worsened, since she had no one to help her administer the medicated eyedrops. And she often forgot to administer the drops herself.

Bruna cried when she saw the state Maria was in.

"I should never have left you alone, Madame Maria. Pixie is a skeleton and Djedda won't move from your pillow. And I'm not sure you have survived any better than your poodles. Look at you."

Maria seemed confused and cautious about every move she made. Doctors came and went. Maria was given vitamin shots in her buttocks. Bruna fed her pasta primavera in bed, petrified as she stared into Maria's blank, expressionless face.

The diva's eyes roamed across the room, as if some essential part of her had gone out of her body and couldn't be found.

"Shall I call an ambulance, madame?"

Suddenly, Maria smiled, but it was a waxen smile, and Bruna was alarmed. Then Maria smiled again, signaling that she'd come back to her own little world at Georges Mandel. She lay with Pixie on her lap.

"Bruna," she said, "I'm fine."

It was the sailor who deteriorated after Alexander's death. He was diagnosed with myasthenia gravis. He couldn't keep his eyes open unless his drooping eyelids were taped to his eyebrows. He lost fifty pounds in two months. His back was stooped over. He was a skeleton with gray hair who had to take cortisone shots to keep the myasthenia gravis under control. He stopped taking the shots despite what his doctors had warned. He had no will to look after any of his holdings. Olympia Airways fell out of his grasp. It didn't have enough equity to keep its planes in the sky. He collapsed in Athens after a meeting with the Olympia board, suffered from severe abdominal pains.

Aristo flew to Paris.

He stopped at Maria's on his way to the American Hospital to have his gallbladder removed. His driver, Enrique, had to ride upstairs with him in the lift.

The sailor barely had the strength to walk. He seemed cavalier about the operation. His face was so pale that Maria could see the cobwebs under his eyes. Bruna fed him his favorite—lemon cake—and a cup of chamomile.

"Maria," he said in a barely audible voice, "have you recovered from that world tour?"

"Darling," she said, doing her best not to cry in front of

Enrique and the sailor, "you were right. I'm a whistler who has lost her whistle."

Aristo smiled. He looked radiant for a moment. "You're still . . . my favorite canary."

It terrified her to see his eyes taped open like that. It was clear to Maria that the sailor had lost his desire to live. But he still had an appetite.

Bruna cut him another slice of lemon cake. She had to feed his driver, too. Enrique smirked with every bite.

"We have to leave, mum. We shouldn't have come here in the first place. He was due at the hospital an hour ago. The doctors want him prepped. But the boss insisted. He's a stubborn one. 'Have to see my canary,' he says. 'Have to say good-bye.'"

Maria pleaded with the brute. "Can't you keep him here a little longer? I'll pay you, pay you whatever you want."

"Can't, mum," he said, with a triumphant glare. "The boss's missus might get very angry. She doesn't know about this little diversion in the route, this little detour."

"But couldn't I follow you to the hospital?" Maria begged.

"Sorry, mum. You're not on the list."

"List? What list?" Maria asked, wishing she could tear the tape from the sailor's eyes.

The driver was cocksure. "Mrs. O was very specific, mum. It might be a hot item, having you visit him at the hospital. Could appear in all the scandal sheets. Nothing personal, mum. Mrs. O adores you and your singing. Said so herself. Gave her the willies to watch you onstage. Utterly operatic, she says. The way you inhabit a character's interior landscape—in her own words, mum."

Enrique grasped the sailor by the arm. "Off we go, boss."

Aristo had a menacing look in his taped eyes. "I haven't finished my chamomile."

"Then have your last sip, boss."

The sailor tossed the chamomile in his cup at Enrique. "I keep that hospital afloat. The doctors can wait for me."

He started to shiver. He seemed so frail that Maria took him in her arms.

"I'm—a—fool," he said in a slow, meandering voice. "Only a fool would foul his own nest."

He slid out of Maria's grasp, kissed Bruna's hand, as if he were greeting a princess.

"You must protect Maria. She has a weakness . . . for wanderers like me, who can settle nowhere but in a hospital bed." Then he turned to Maria with those monstrous taped eyes. "Darling . . ."

Enrique removed the display handkerchief from his breast pocket with a dramatic flair and patted his face. Maria wanted to rip Enrique's eyes out with her fingernails, but she couldn't keep the sailor in her salon. He was en route to the American Hospital. Enrique gathered up the bag of bones and led him to the door.

"Ta-ta, mum," the driver said. "Can't keep the surgeon waiting."

"Will someone call us?" Maria asked in a dolorous voice.

"That depends," Enrique muttered with a cryptic smile. He held all the power. He was suddenly the maestro of an opera that was being performed for the first time, an opera without a single song. "I'll have to ask Mrs. O."

He left with the sailor, a wealthy beggar with a shuffling gait.

Maria could hear the grinding of the cables in the hollow above the lift.

She parted the curtains, unlocked the window, stood on the balcony, waited until Aristo appeared with Enrique, and watched them drive off.

Maria leaned over the balcony rail until she could no longer catch sight of the Rolls. Then she screamed like a wounded animal. Bruna had to lure her back from the balcony.

-11-

He landed in a coma, drifting in and out of consciousness.

The surgeon had removed his gallbladder and considered the operation a success. It didn't seem to matter to this maestro whether the sailor would survive or not. No one called from the hospital; no one got in touch with Maria. Whatever she discovered was from the newspapers and the TV. When she called the hospital, she was told that she couldn't see the patient in room 207 of the Eisenhower Wing. Maria wasn't on the list. She couldn't even get inside the gate without a visitor's pass.

But Bruna had her own network. A maid at another building on Avenue Georges Mandel had a daughter who was a nurse at the American Hospital, and happened to be in charge of the same corridor the sailor was on. This nurse, named Alma, was a devoted fan of La Divina's and was willing to risk her own career; Alma loved the intrigue of uniting Maria with Onassis at the hospital where she worked.

On a windy March afternoon, Maria arrived in a red cloak at the hospital's rear entrance, which also served as a passageway that led to the morgue. She knocked once. Alma was waiting. She was a handsome girl with red hair who had lived in London.

"Ah, Madame Callas, I saw you in *Traviata.* And when you died standing on your feet in the third act, I wept for days."

"But you must have been a child," Maria said.

Alma plucked at her nurse's cap. "Madame, I've been going to the opera since I was seven."

She took Maria on a serpentine route that brought them to her own corridor on the Eisenhower Wing. No one interfered with a nurse in a billowing blue cape. She stopped outside the sailor's room.

"The coast is clear, madame," Alma said, enjoying her part in the intrigue. "I can allow you two minutes with monsieur. Otherwise, it might be fatal. The hospital has its own police."

"Thank you, Alma," Maria said, clasping the nurse's hand.

She entered the room without her glasses to please the sailor, who was attached to a whole congress of tubes. He couldn't have spoken. He had a tube stuck in his throat. It hadn't cost him his dignity. He was a voyager on his last voyage.

He seemed younger now. All the grayness was gone. The diva didn't know what to do. She couldn't kiss him, or she might have upset all the tubes. So she hummed a tune.

He opened one eye. His canary had come.

"Darling," she sang, as if she were Floria Tosca calling her lover Cavaradossi from the wings. But Cavaradossi wasn't at the American Hospital with a tube in his throat.

"Darling," she sang again.

Aristo's fingers curled, then flattened.

"Madame," Alma whispered, "you must leave. The doctors are coming with their residents."

And the two conspirators escaped without being noticed. Maria didn't want to cry in front of this nurse. She put her glasses back on, but she could barely see in front of her. She was struck with blindness at the American Hospital. Alma had to lead the diva to the rear door.

Bruna was outside with Maria's blue Mercedes. She thanked Alma and tried to hand her an envelope stuffed with cash. Alma looked with horror at the envelope. Her red hair blazed in the sun.

"Please," Alma said. "It was my gift to Madame Callas. Don't soil it now."

Bruna pocketed the envelope. She seemed bruised. "Forgive us, Alma."

"There's nothing to forgive."

Alma pecked Maria and Bruna on the cheek and scooted inside the door.

Bruna drove back to Georges Mandel.

Maria was silent in the lift.

She was silent in the vast expanse of her flat, with Pixie and Djedda at her feet.

Bruna administered the magic eyedrops and most of Maria's sight was restored. She drank some chicken broth that Bruna had prepared, drank it from a bowl, like a farmer's wife in the countryside. Maria wandered across the flat and retired to her bedroom with the dogs. She lay down with Pixie and Djedda beside her. She didn't fall into a dream. She could conjure up whatever memories she wished, the curator of her own past.

She tried and tried, but nothing happened. She lay on a mountain of pillows with her two dogs.

Maria found herself caught in a whiplash, thrust back into the eighth grade. Her kneesocks sagged. They'd lost their elasticity, and no matter how far she bent over and tugged at the socks, she couldn't keep them up near her knees.

She was onstage in the auditorium. The other girls didn't have sagging socks. And they didn't wear thick glasses that obscured their features and robbed them of their robustness.

Maria peered out into the audience. She saw German soldiers in the first row, and wondered what they were doing in Washington Heights. She saw Bernardo Scarpia in a red scarf. He sat with the *loggionisti*, who didn't have a balcony of their own in this school's primitive auditorium. She noticed Sandor in his perennial mink coat, sniffing the stale air as he scouted for talent. Had he come to sign the *new* Deanna Durbin? The young sensation from Canada was fifteen. She'd just appeared in her biggest hit, *One Hundred Men and a Girl*, about Patsy Cardwell, whose father is a trombone player who can't find work. Patsy puts together an orchestra of one hundred unemployed musicians and manages to get Maestro Leopold Stokowski to lead them on a world tour. And not only that, she performs the "Drinking Song" from the party scene in *Traviata* for an audience full of socialites.

Every girl in America who had dreams of becoming a Hollywood soprano went to see *One Hundred Men and a Girl* five or six times. They began to dress like Deanna Durbin, talk like Deanna Durbin. And except for Maria in her thick glasses and sagging socks, the other contestants onstage at P.S. 189 had Deanna's smile.

They sang first, imitating Deanna as much as they could. One or two added a tap dance routine. Another did a somersault. They caterwauled like felines in heat once they reached a high note. They tripped over their roulades and made a stuttering sound. None of them could render the least hint of the party scene in *Traviata,* nor approach the playful innocence of Deanna Durbin and the pluck of Violetta, who didn't give a damn about the vicissitudes of falling in love.

The school ensemble couldn't compete with the "one hundred men" in Deanna's film. Its piano was badly out of tune. Its tuba sounded like a steamboat whistle. Its oboist had a toothache. Its string section seemed to hack away on rotten saws. It hindered the Deanna Durbin doubles, only added to the cacophony of these wailing cats.

The mothers and fathers and siblings in the audience clapped at the caterwauls, while the eighth-grade sopranos bowed like prima donnas and disappeared into the wings.

It was Maria's turn. She hitched up her socks and stood on one leg. She stared deep into the barrenness of the stage and dismissed the student orchestra with its bent instruments and broken strings.

And then she froze.

She saw a blue-eyed blonde behind her wearing stilettos and a beaded gown. Her own mother had come backstage, rather than sit with German corporals and the *loggionisti.* A man in a braided officer's cap stood with his arm around Litsa's waist. Maria recognized the monocle and kid gloves of Air Marshal Speidel, military governor of Athens until he was whisked away for the unforgivable act of loving Bellini more than Berlin. Why was Speidel here? Was he the commandant of Washington Heights? Litsa looked at Maria with such savage sullenness, as if she meant to annihilate her in a single glance. Maria had to move out of her mother's sight lines, or remain stranded there forever. She hopped on one leg.

Her glasses had begun to fog under the school's stage lights. She whirled about once. And unlike the Deanna Durbin doubles, who sang in an utter void, Maria, with her sagging socks, captured in her mind's eye Violetta's drawing room on the barren stage, with all its nobles and bankers and courtesans; she managed to create an ambience as she strutted about the stage, holding up an imaginary gown with one hand and greeting an imaginary nobleman with the other, until the audience followed her every gliding step, transfixed by a girl in thick glasses who had imposed herself upon the auditorium. And only then did she sing "Libiamo," welcoming the audience to enter Violetta's drawing room and share some of her gaiety, with a sad quiver in her voice.

This was no Deanna Durbin. It was Maria Callas in sagging socks, with her dark timbre that revealed the despair beneath Violetta's lightness of tone.

Maria won the contest, of course.

The principal should have awarded her a Bulova, but Speidel shoved him aside.

"To Fräulein Maria," he said, "who was *wunderbar* as Violetta."

Speidel strapped the watch—with its golden dials and silver crown—on her wrist.

But no one in the audience clapped. The faces of the fathers and mothers were marked with venom. The *loggionisti* tossed stale cabbage heads at Maria. She'd become a renegade in a wrinkled dress. The stage began to rock, and Maria lost her balance. Her Bulova fell off and the crystal shattered. The watch was worthless now.

She began to wail.

She felt a hand caress her hair. Bruna was on the bed

with her. Maria must have frightened the dogs with her screams. Pixie and Djedda hid under the pillows.

"Madame Maria, you had a bad dream."

"I wasn't dreaming," Maria said. "I lost my Bulova. It broke."

"The watch you won as a child, madame?"

Maria nodded.

Bruna arose from the bed, went through Maria's closets, and returned with a velvet case.

The Bulova sat inside its sarcophagus like a mystery made of silver and gold.

"Shall I wind the watch for you, madame?"

Maria shuddered. "No, no. It's much too precious."

The dogs came out from under the pillows. Bruna put the Bulova back in its proper closet. The diva heard *Traviata* in her head. For a moment she was Violetta, whirling about in her drawing room. She realized that La Callas herself had become a sarcophagus. Even if she never sang again, she was entombed in every role she had ever played. Watching Westerns didn't help. She would always be Violetta, whirling about in one room and dying in another.

Bellevue Literary Press is devoted to publishing literary fiction and nonfiction at the intersection of the arts and sciences because we believe that science and the humanities are natural companions for understanding the human experience. We feature exceptional literature that explores the nature of consciousness, embodiment, and the underpinnings of the social contract. With each book we publish, our goal is to foster a rich, interdisciplinary dialogue that will forge new tools for thinking and engaging with the world.

To support our press and its mission, and for our full catalogue of published titles, please visit us at blpress.org.

Bellevue Literary Press
New York